NORSE MYTHOLOGY™

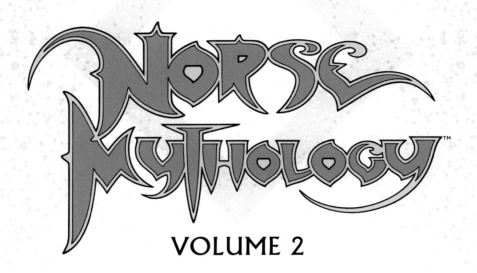

VOLUME 2

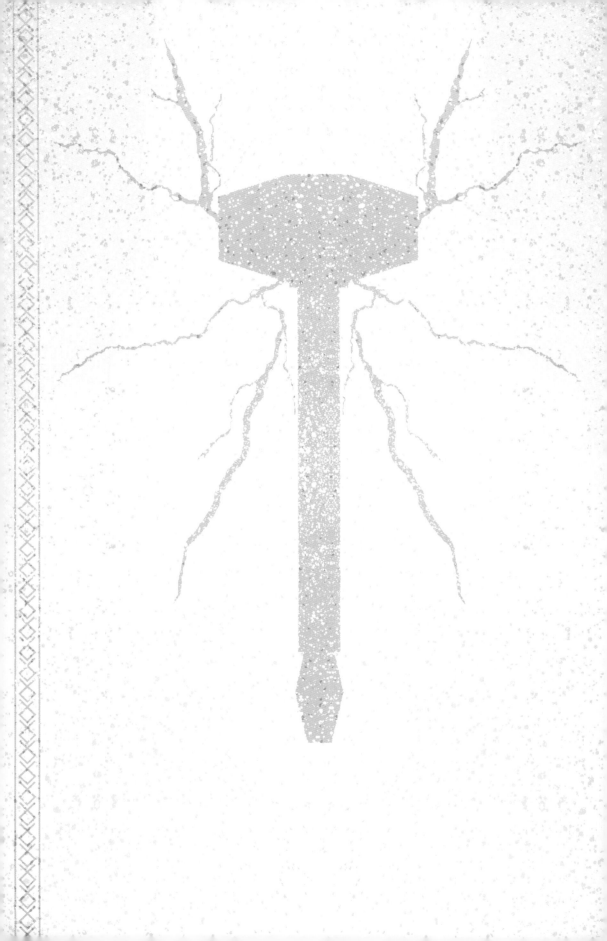

Story and Words by **NEIL GAIMAN**

Script and Layouts by **P. CRAIG RUSSELL**

Letters by **GALEN SHOWMAN**

NORSE MYTHOLOGY™

VOLUME 2

DARK HORSE BOOKS™

Publisher
MIKE RICHARDSON

Editor
DANIEL CHABON

Assistant Editors
CHUCK HOWITT and **KONNER KNUDSEN**

Designer
KEITH WOOD

Digital Art Technicians
ANN GRAY and **JOSIE CHRISTENSEN**

Special Thanks to
CAT MIHOS, MERRILEE HEIFETZ, and
SARAH-KATE FENELON

———————◇✖◇———————

 Facebook.com/DarkHorseComics
 Twitter.com/DarkHorseComics

Advertising Sales: ads@darkhorse.com
To find a comics shop in your area,
visit comicshoplocator.com.

NORSE MYTHOLOGY VOLUME 2
Neil Gaiman's Norse Mythology™ © 2017, 2021, 2022
Neil Gaiman. Illustrations of the cover and standard
covers © P. Craig Russell. Dark Horse Books® and the
Dark Horse logo are trademarks of Dark Horse Comics
LLC, registered in various categories and countries.

This volume collects issues #1 through #6 of the second arc
of the Dark Horse comic-book series *Norse Mythology*.

Published by
Dark Horse Books
A division of Dark Horse Comics LLC
10956 SE Main Street
Milwaukie, OR 97222

DarkHorse.com

First hardcover edition: April 2022

Ebook ISBN 978-1-50672-218-4
Hardcover ISBN 978-1-50672-217-7

10 8 6 4 2 1 3 5 7 9
Printed in China

Neil Hankerson
Executive Vice President

Tom Weddle
Chief Financial Officer

Dale LaFountain
Chief Information Officer

Tim Wiesch
Vice President of Licensing

Matt Parkinson
Vice President of Marketing

Vanessa Todd-Holmes
Vice President of Production and Scheduling

Mark Bernardi
Vice President of Book Tradeand Digital Sales

Randy Lahrman
Vice President of Product Development

Ken Lizzi
General Counsel

Dave Marshall
Editor in Chief

Davey Estrada
Editorial Director

Chris Warner
Senior Books Editor

Cary Grazzini
Director of Specialty Projects

Lia Ribacchi
Art Director

Matt Dryer
Director of Digital Art and Prepress

Michael Gombos
Senior Director of Licensed Publications

Kari Yadro
Director of Custom Programs

Kari Torson
Director of International Licensing

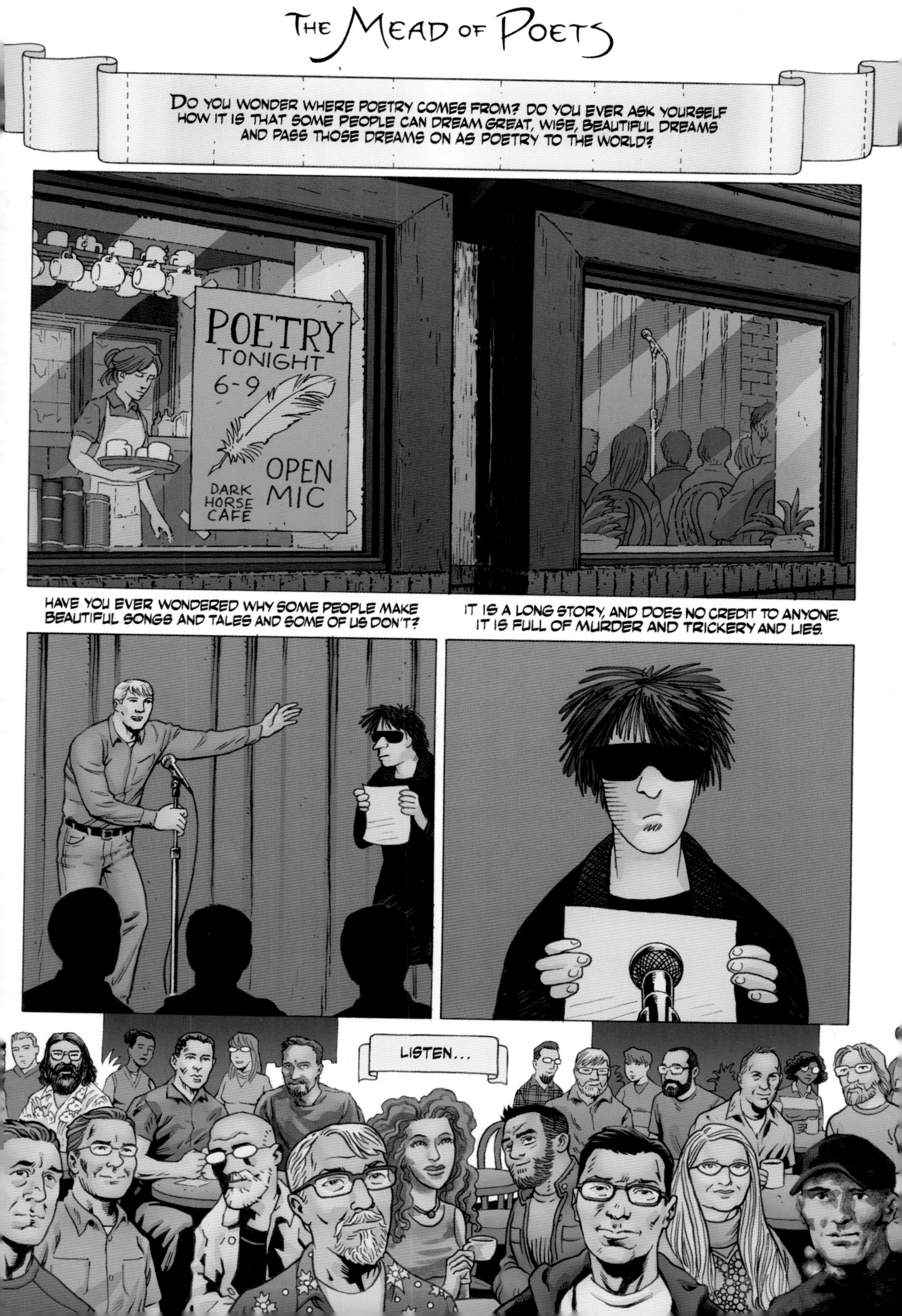
THE MEAD OF POETS
DO YOU WONDER WHERE POETRY COMES FROM? DO YOU EVER ASK YOURSELF HOW IT IS THAT SOME PEOPLE CAN DREAM GREAT, WISE, BEAUTIFUL DREAMS AND PASS THOSE DREAMS ON AS POETRY TO THE WORLD?
POETRY TONIGHT 6-9
OPEN MIC
DARK HORSE CAFE
HAVE YOU EVER WONDERED WHY SOME PEOPLE MAKE BEAUTIFUL SONGS AND TALES AND SOME OF US DON'T?
IT IS A LONG STORY, AND DOES NO CREDIT TO ANYONE. IT IS FULL OF MURDER AND TRICKERY AND LIES.
LISTEN...

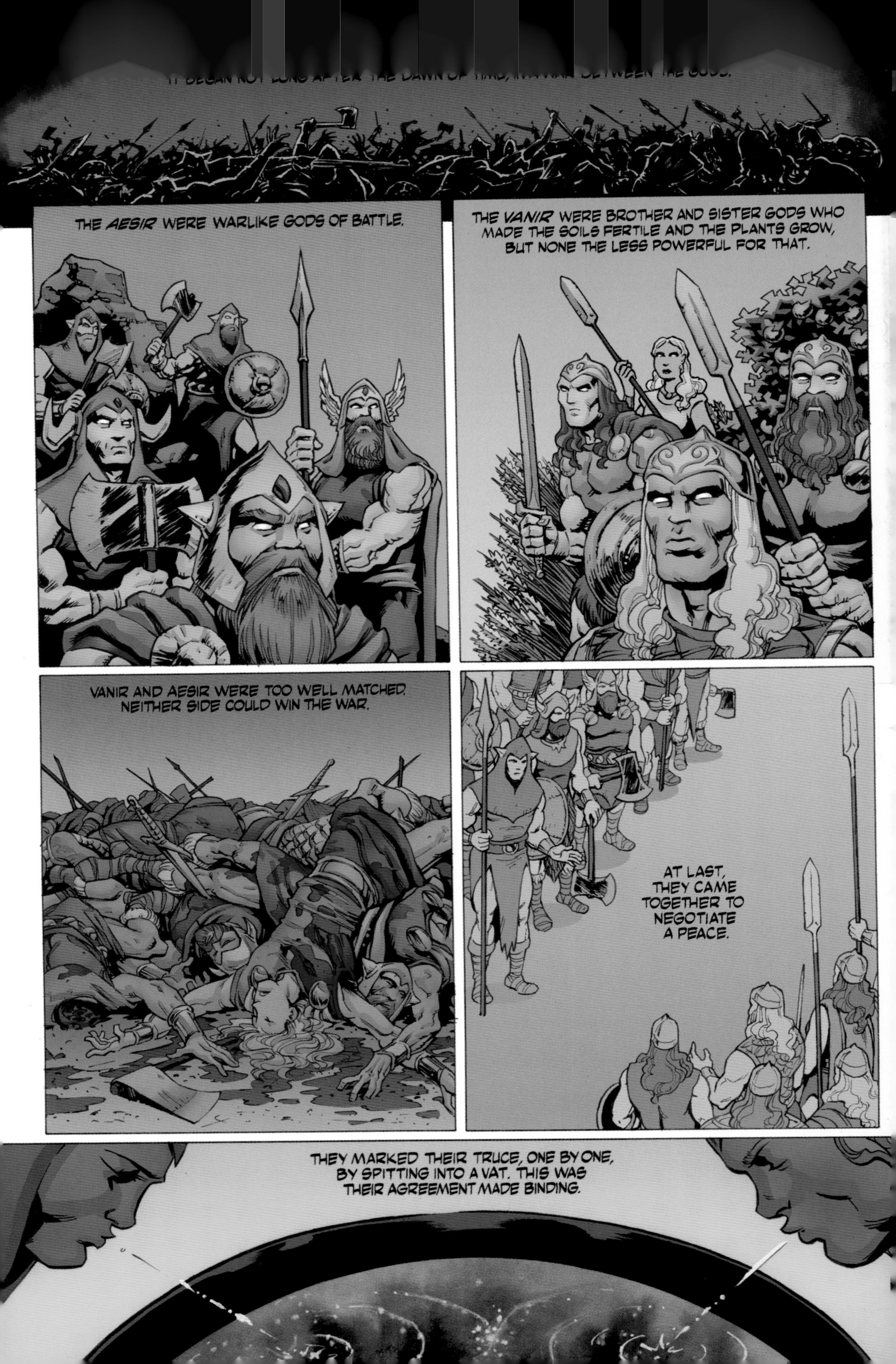

IT BEGAN NOT LONG AFTER THE DAWN OF TIME, IN A WAR BETWEEN THE GODS.
THE AESIR WERE WARLIKE GODS OF BATTLE.
THE VANIR WERE BROTHER AND SISTER GODS WHO MADE THE SOILS FERTILE AND THE PLANTS GROW, BUT NONE THE LESS POWERFUL FOR THAT.
VANIR AND AESIR WERE TOO WELL MATCHED. NEITHER SIDE COULD WIN THE WAR.
AT LAST, THEY CAME TOGETHER TO NEGOTIATE A PEACE.
THEY MARKED THEIR TRUCE, ONE BY ONE, BY SPITTING INTO A VAT. THIS WAS THEIR AGREEMENT MADE BINDING.

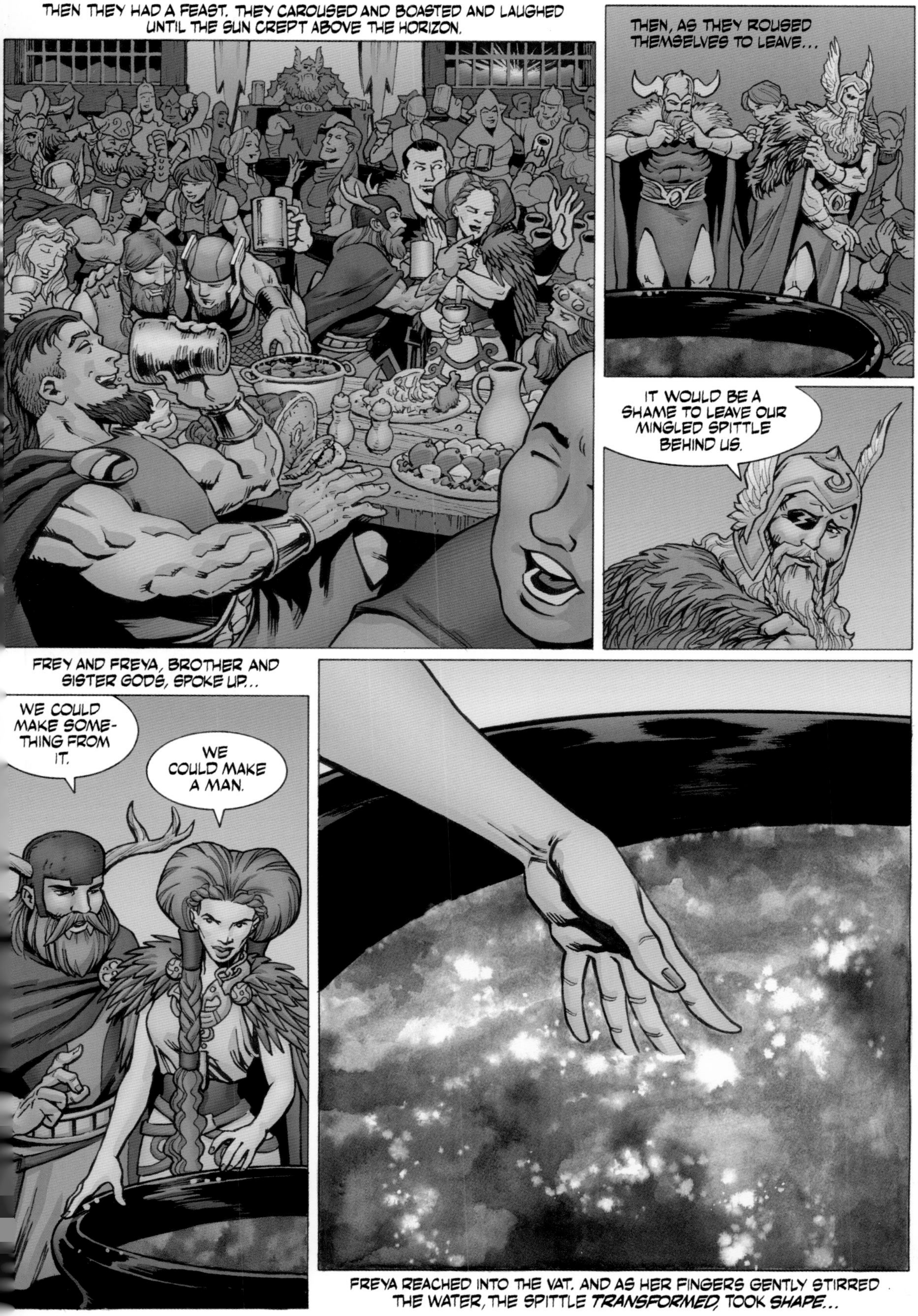
THEN THEY HAD A FEAST. THEY CAROUSED AND BOASTED AND LAUGHED UNTIL THE SUN CREPT ABOVE THE HORIZON.
THEN, AS THEY ROUSED THEMSELVES TO LEAVE...
IT WOULD BE A SHAME TO LEAVE OUR MINGLED SPITTLE BEHIND US.
FREY AND FREYA, BROTHER AND SISTER GODS, SPOKE UP...
WE COULD MAKE SOME-THING FROM IT.
WE COULD MAKE A MAN.
FREYA REACHED INTO THE VAT. AND AS HER FINGERS GENTLY STIRRED THE WATER, THE SPITTLE *TRANSFORMED*, TOOK *SHAPE*...

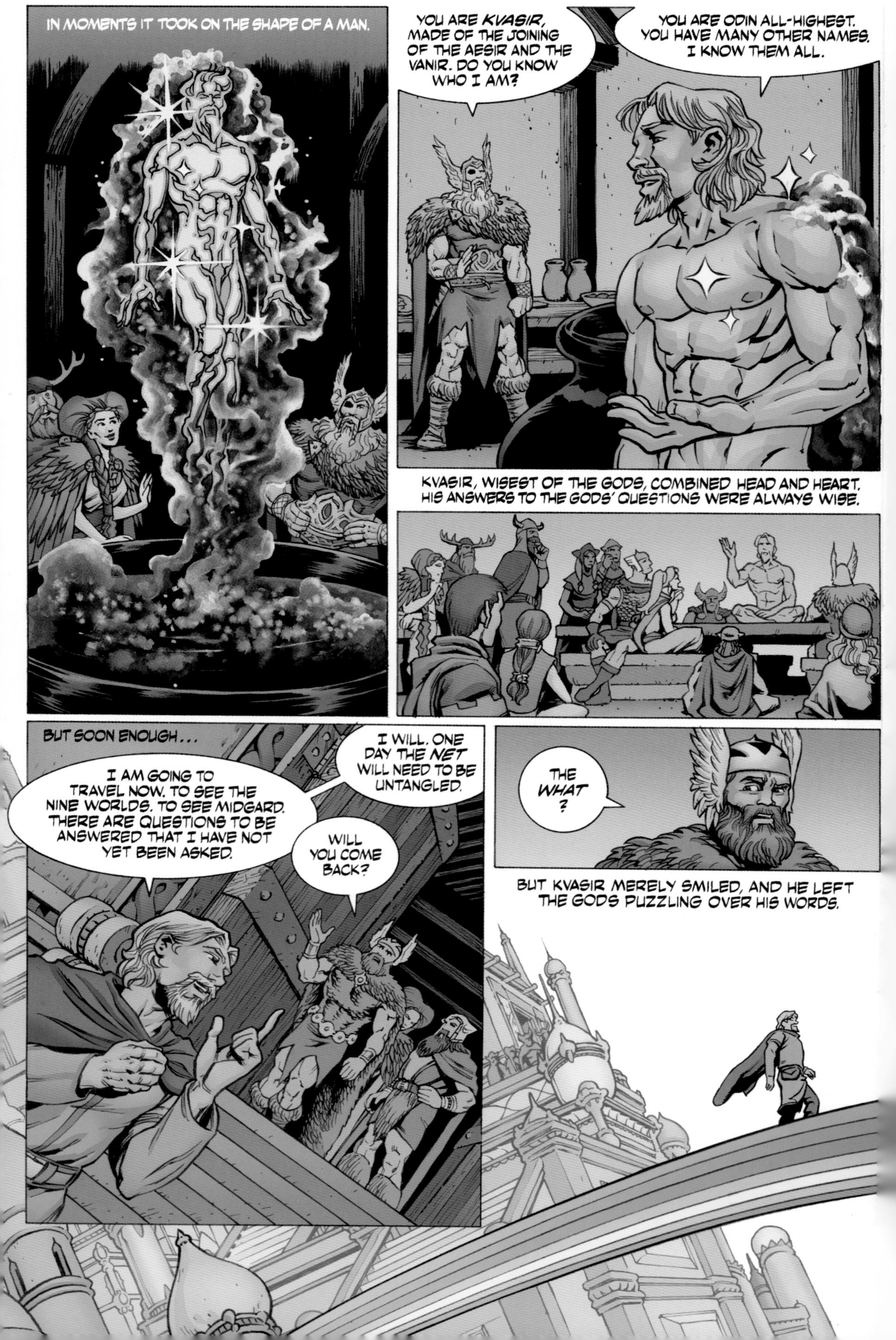
IN MOMENTS IT TOOK ON THE SHAPE OF A MAN.
YOU ARE *KVASIR*, MADE OF THE JOINING OF THE AESIR AND THE VANIR. DO YOU KNOW WHO I AM?
YOU ARE ODIN ALL-HIGHEST. YOU HAVE MANY OTHER NAMES. I KNOW THEM ALL.
KVASIR, WISEST OF THE GODS, COMBINED HEAD AND HEART. HIS ANSWERS TO THE GODS' QUESTIONS WERE ALWAYS WISE.
BUT SOON ENOUGH . . .
I AM GOING TO TRAVEL NOW. TO SEE THE NINE WORLDS. TO SEE MIDGARD. THERE ARE QUESTIONS TO BE ANSWERED THAT I HAVE NOT YET BEEN ASKED.
WILL YOU COME BACK?
I WILL. ONE DAY THE *NET* WILL NEED TO BE UNTANGLED.
THE *WHAT*?
BUT KVASIR MERELY SMILED, AND HE LEFT THE GODS PUZZLING OVER HIS WORDS.

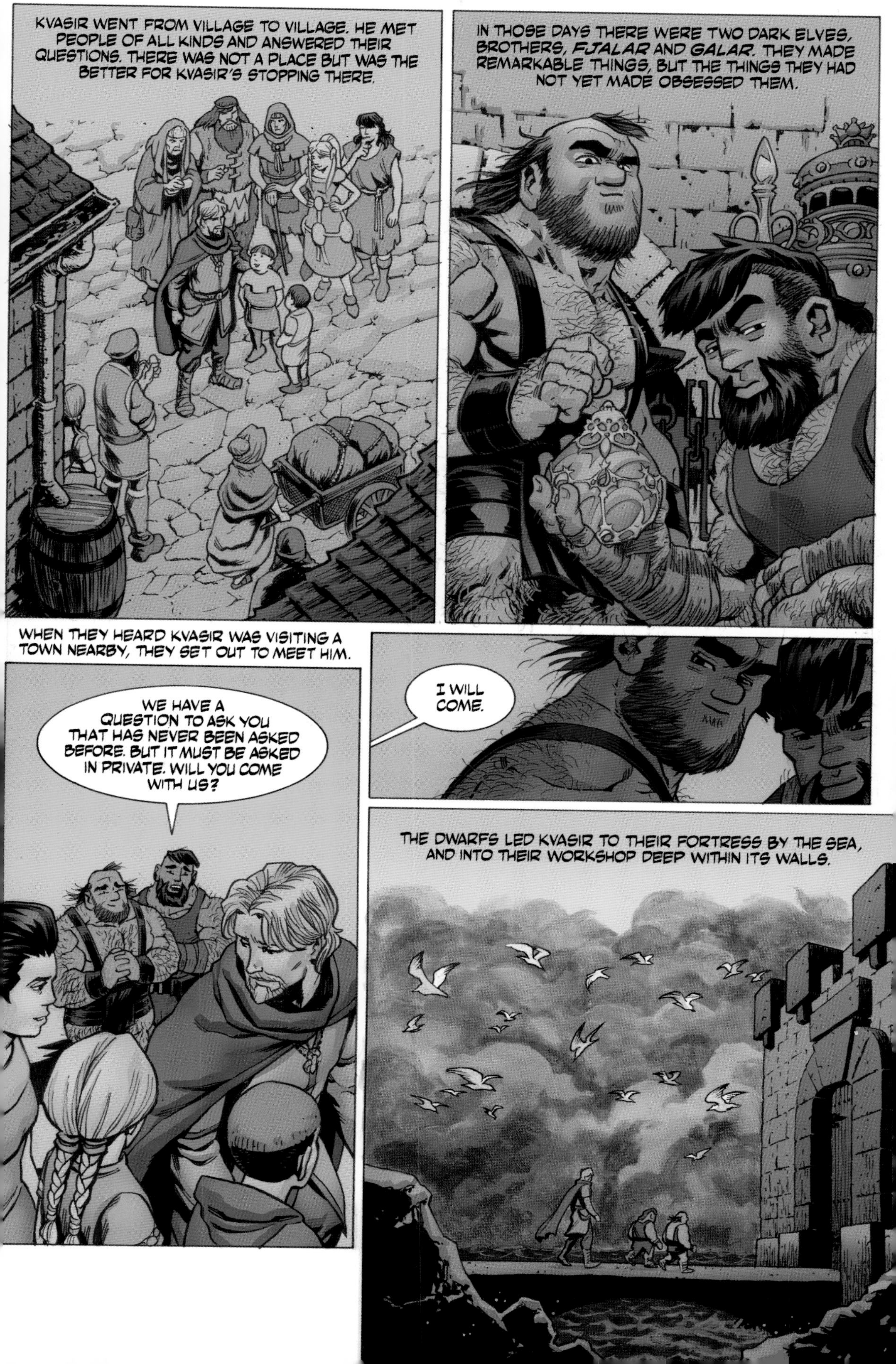
KVASIR WENT FROM VILLAGE TO VILLAGE. HE MET PEOPLE OF ALL KINDS AND ANSWERED THEIR QUESTIONS. THERE WAS NOT A PLACE BUT WAS THE BETTER FOR KVASIR'S STOPPING THERE.
IN THOSE DAYS THERE WERE TWO DARK ELVES, BROTHERS, FJALAR AND GALAR. THEY MADE REMARKABLE THINGS, BUT THE THINGS THEY HAD NOT YET MADE OBSESSED THEM.
WHEN THEY HEARD KVASIR WAS VISITING A TOWN NEARBY, THEY SET OUT TO MEET HIM.
WE HAVE A QUESTION TO ASK YOU THAT HAS NEVER BEEN ASKED BEFORE. BUT IT MUST BE ASKED IN PRIVATE. WILL YOU COME WITH US?
I WILL COME.
THE DWARFS LED KVASIR TO THEIR FORTRESS BY THE SEA, AND INTO THEIR WORKSHOP DEEP WITHIN ITS WALLS.

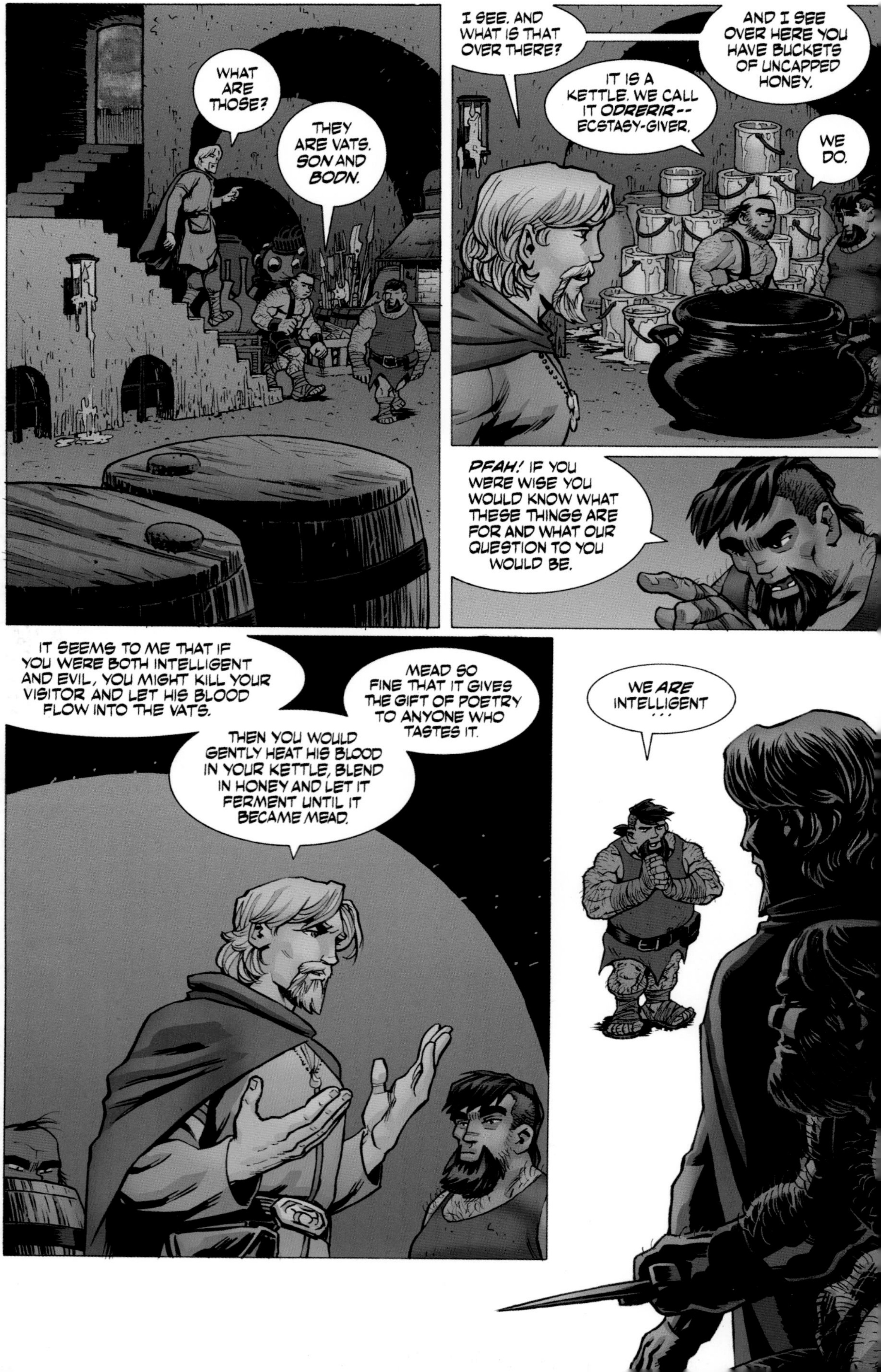
WHAT ARE THOSE?
THEY ARE VATS. SON AND BODN.
I SEE. AND WHAT IS THAT OVER THERE?
IT IS A KETTLE. WE CALL IT ODRERIR-- ECSTASY-GIVER.
AND I SEE OVER HERE YOU HAVE BUCKETS OF UNCAPPED HONEY.
WE DO.
PFAH! IF YOU WERE WISE YOU WOULD KNOW WHAT THESE THINGS ARE FOR AND WHAT OUR QUESTION TO YOU WOULD BE.
IT SEEMS TO ME THAT IF YOU WERE BOTH INTELLIGENT AND EVIL, YOU MIGHT KILL YOUR VISITOR AND LET HIS BLOOD FLOW INTO THE VATS.
THEN YOU WOULD GENTLY HEAT HIS BLOOD IN YOUR KETTLE, BLEND IN HONEY AND LET IT FERMENT UNTIL IT BECAME MEAD.
MEAD SO FINE THAT IT GIVES THE GIFT OF POETRY TO ANYONE WHO TASTES IT.
WE ARE INTELLIGENT . . .

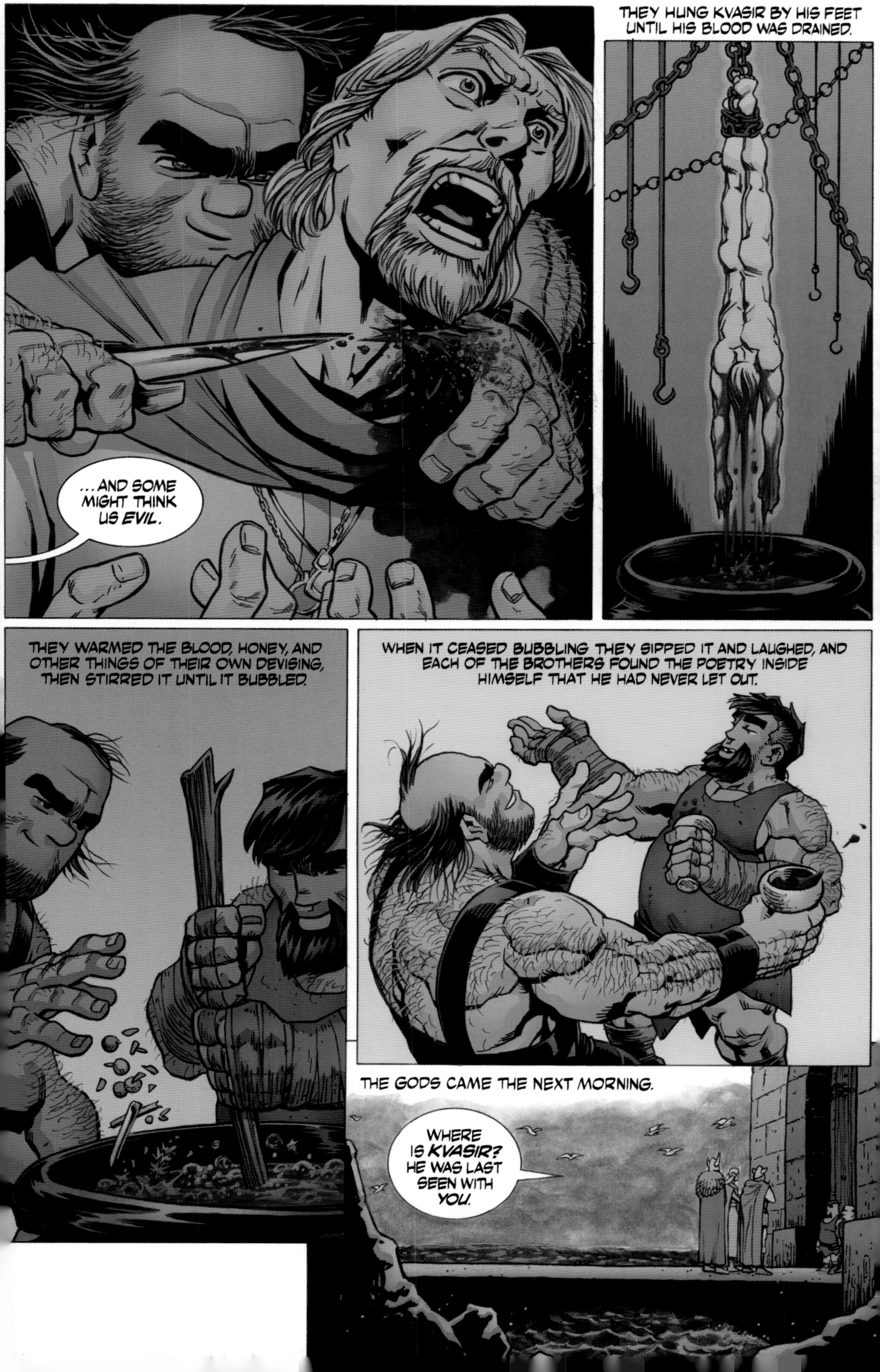
...AND SOME MIGHT THINK US EVIL.
THEY HUNG KVASIR BY HIS FEET UNTIL HIS BLOOD WAS DRAINED.
THEY WARMED THE BLOOD, HONEY, AND OTHER THINGS OF THEIR OWN DEVISING, THEN STIRRED IT UNTIL IT BUBBLED.
WHEN IT CEASED BUBBLING THEY SIPPED IT AND LAUGHED, AND EACH OF THE BROTHERS FOUND THE POETRY INSIDE HIMSELF THAT HE HAD NEVER LET OUT.
THE GODS CAME THE NEXT MORNING.
WHERE IS KVASIR? HE WAS LAST SEEN WITH YOU.

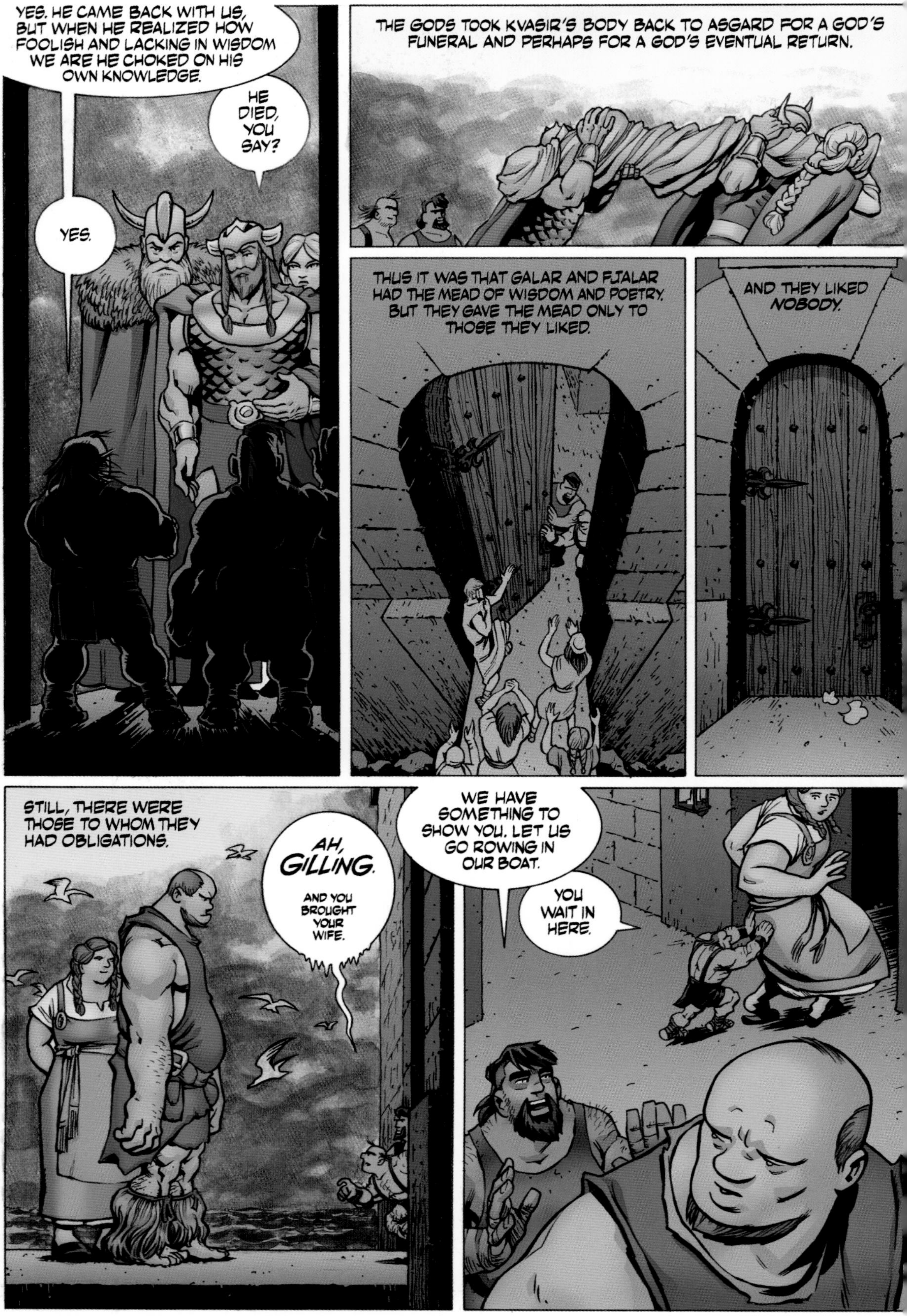
YES. HE CAME BACK WITH US, BUT WHEN HE REALIZED HOW FOOLISH AND LACKING IN WISDOM WE ARE HE CHOKED ON HIS OWN KNOWLEDGE.
HE DIED, YOU SAY?
YES.
THE GODS TOOK KVASIR'S BODY BACK TO ASGARD FOR A GOD'S FUNERAL AND PERHAPS FOR A GOD'S EVENTUAL RETURN.
THUS IT WAS THAT GALAR AND FJALAR HAD THE MEAD OF WISDOM AND POETRY. BUT THEY GAVE THE MEAD ONLY TO THOSE THEY LIKED.
AND THEY LIKED *NOBODY.*
STILL, THERE WERE THOSE TO WHOM THEY HAD OBLIGATIONS.
AH, GILLING.
AND YOU BROUGHT YOUR WIFE.
WE HAVE SOMETHING TO SHOW YOU. LET US GO ROWING IN OUR BOAT.
YOU WAIT IN HERE.

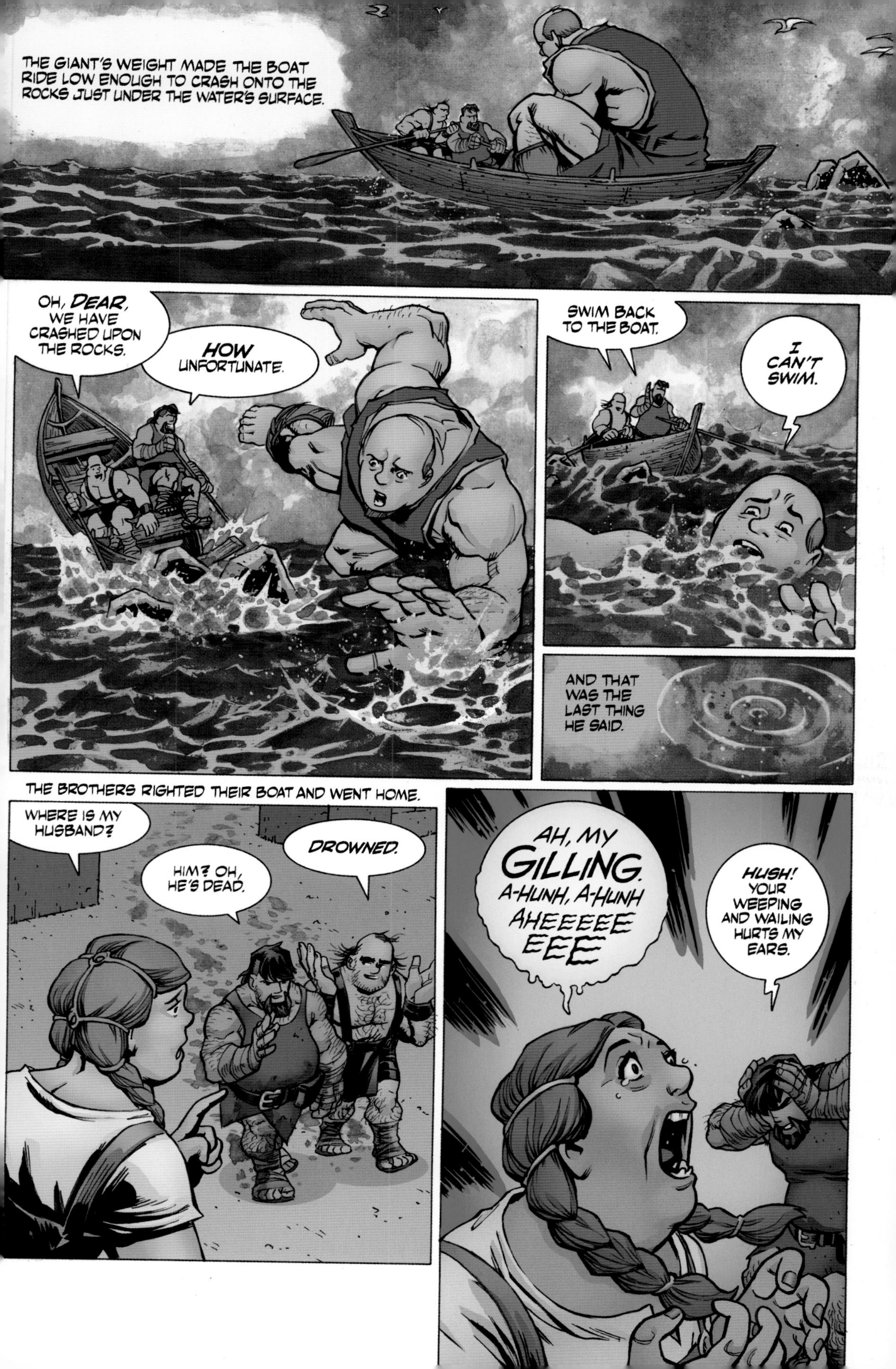
THE GIANT'S WEIGHT MADE THE BOAT RIDE LOW ENOUGH TO CRASH ONTO THE ROCKS JUST UNDER THE WATER'S SURFACE.
OH, DEAR, WE HAVE CRASHED UPON THE ROCKS.
HOW UNFORTUNATE.
SWIM BACK TO THE BOAT.
I CAN'T SWIM.
AND THAT WAS THE LAST THING HE SAID.
THE BROTHERS RIGHTED THEIR BOAT AND WENT HOME.
WHERE IS MY HUSBAND?
HIM? OH, HE'S DEAD.
DROWNED.
AH, MY GILLING. A-HUNH, A-HUNH AHEEEEEE EEE
HUSH! YOUR WEEPING AND WAILING HURTS MY EARS.

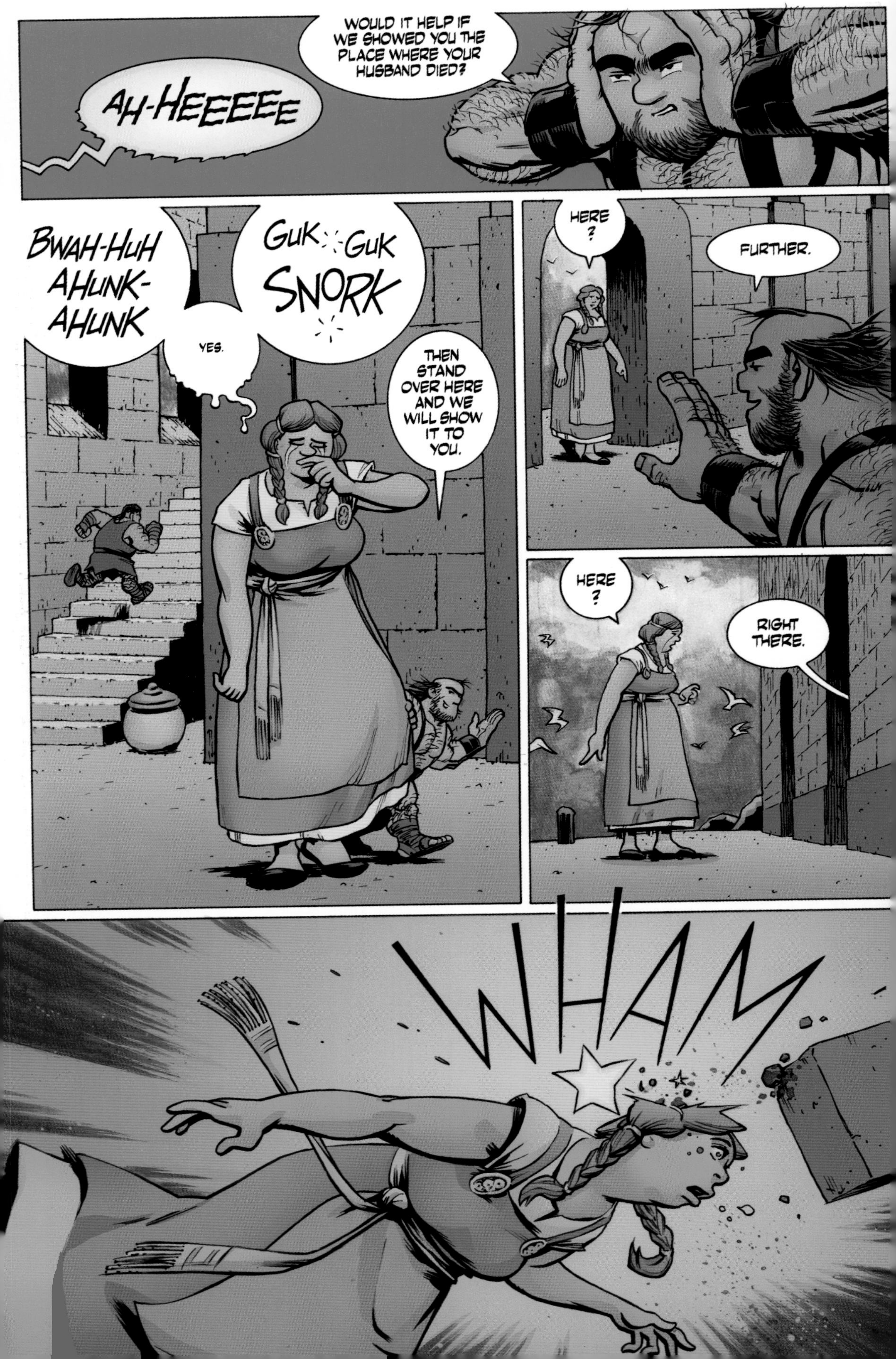
WOULD IT HELP IF WE SHOWED YOU THE PLACE WHERE YOUR HUSBAND DIED?
AH-HEEEEEE
BWAH-HUH AHUNK-AHUNK
YES.
GUK GUK SNORK
THEN STAND OVER HERE AND WE WILL SHOW IT TO YOU.
HERE?
FURTHER.
HERE?
RIGHT THERE.
WHAM

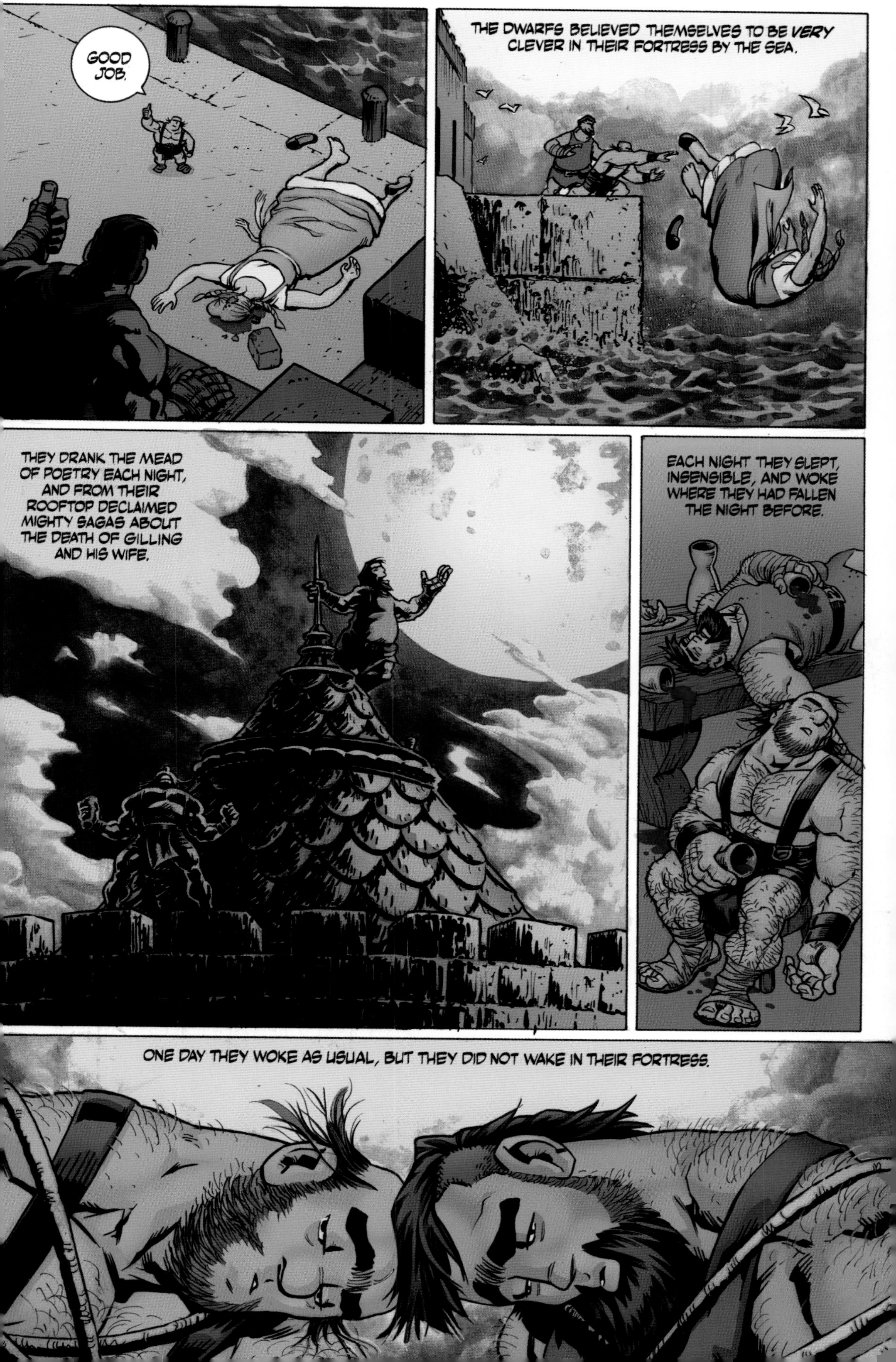
GOOD JOB.
THE DWARFS BELIEVED THEMSELVES TO BE *VERY* CLEVER IN THEIR FORTRESS BY THE SEA.
THEY DRANK THE MEAD OF POETRY EACH NIGHT, AND FROM THEIR ROOFTOP DECLAIMED MIGHTY SAGAS ABOUT THE DEATH OF GILLING AND HIS WIFE.
EACH NIGHT THEY SLEPT, INSENSIBLE, AND WOKE WHERE THEY HAD FALLEN THE NIGHT BEFORE.
ONE DAY THEY WOKE AS USUAL, BUT THEY DID NOT WAKE IN THEIR FORTRESS.

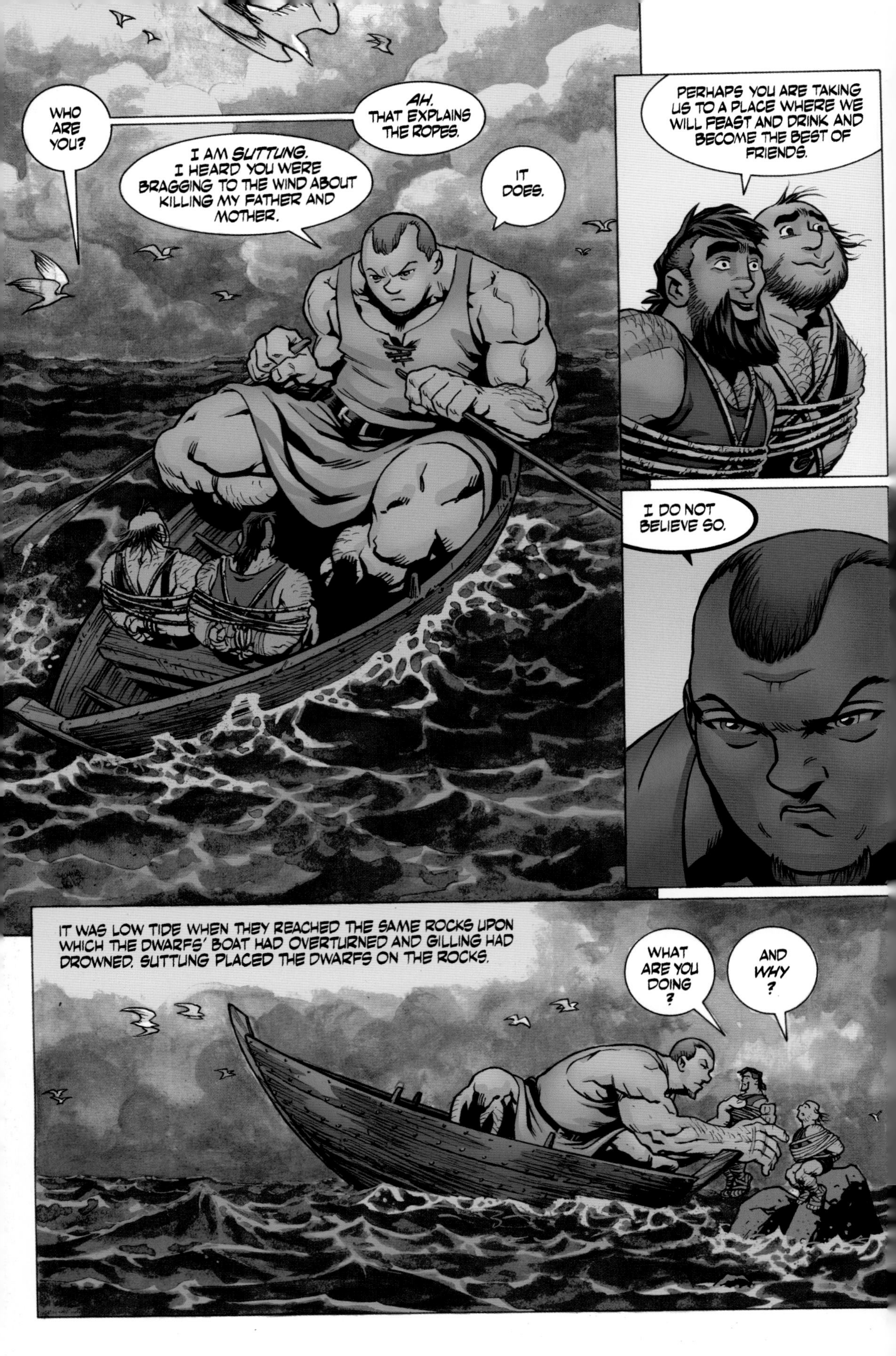
WHO ARE YOU?
I AM *SUTTUNG.* I HEARD YOU WERE BRAGGING TO THE WIND ABOUT KILLING MY FATHER AND MOTHER.
AH. THAT EXPLAINS THE ROPES.
IT DOES.
PERHAPS YOU ARE TAKING US TO A PLACE WHERE WE WILL FEAST AND DRINK AND BECOME THE BEST OF FRIENDS.
I DO NOT BELIEVE SO.
IT WAS LOW TIDE WHEN THEY REACHED THE SAME ROCKS UPON WHICH THE DWARFS' BOAT HAD OVERTURNED AND GILLING HAD DROWNED. SUTTUNG PLACED THE DWARFS ON THE ROCKS.
WHAT ARE YOU DOING ?
AND *WHY* ?

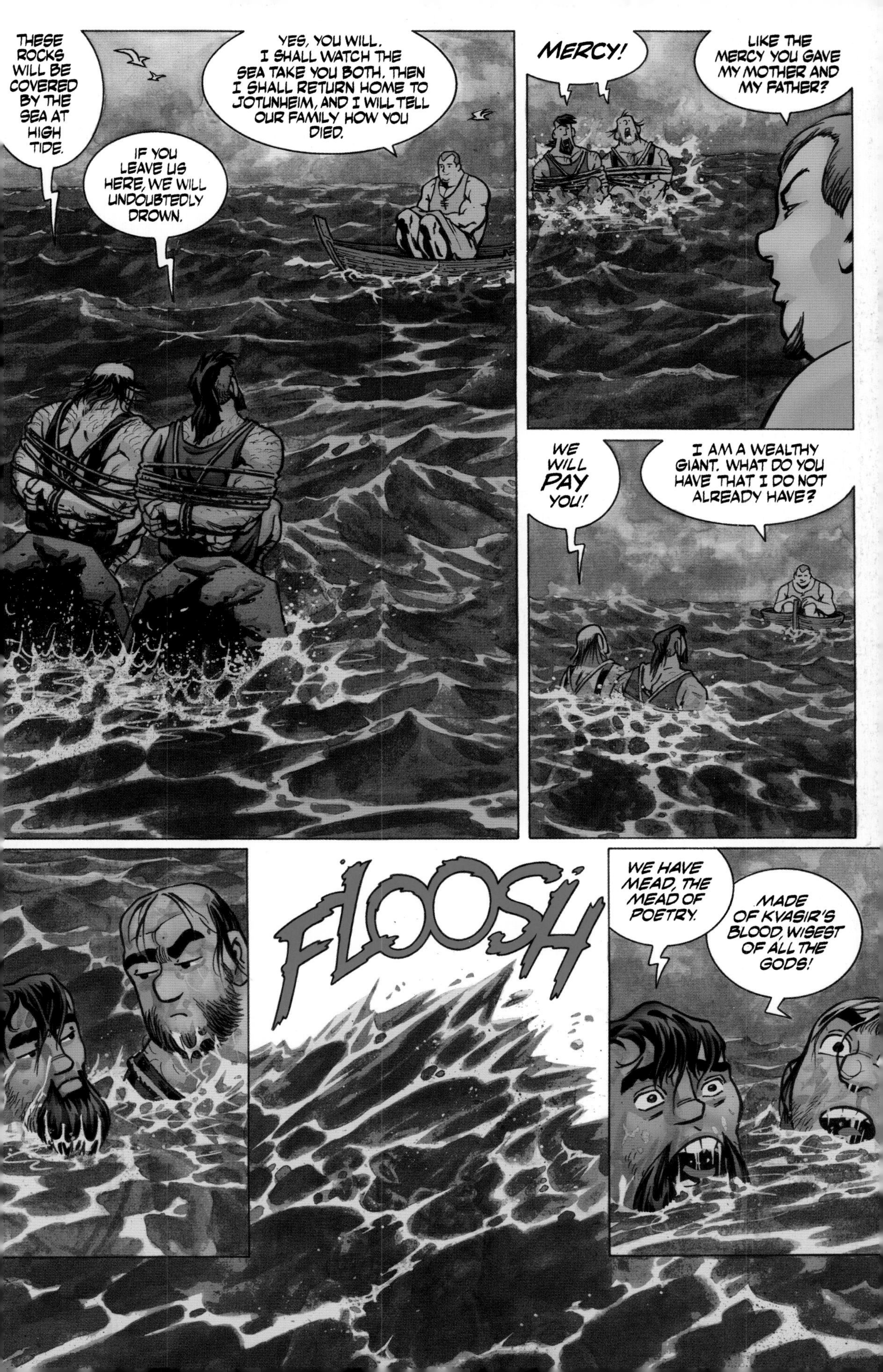
THESE ROCKS WILL BE COVERED BY THE SEA AT HIGH TIDE.
IF YOU LEAVE US HERE, WE WILL UNDOUBTEDLY DROWN.
YES, YOU WILL. I SHALL WATCH THE SEA TAKE YOU BOTH. THEN I SHALL RETURN HOME TO JOTUNHEIM, AND I WILL TELL OUR FAMILY HOW YOU DIED.
MERCY!
LIKE THE MERCY YOU GAVE MY MOTHER AND MY FATHER?
WE WILL PAY YOU!
I AM A WEALTHY GIANT. WHAT DO YOU HAVE THAT I DO NOT ALREADY HAVE?
FLOOSH
WE HAVE MEAD, THE MEAD OF POETRY.
MADE OF KVASIR'S BLOOD, WISEST OF ALL THE GODS!

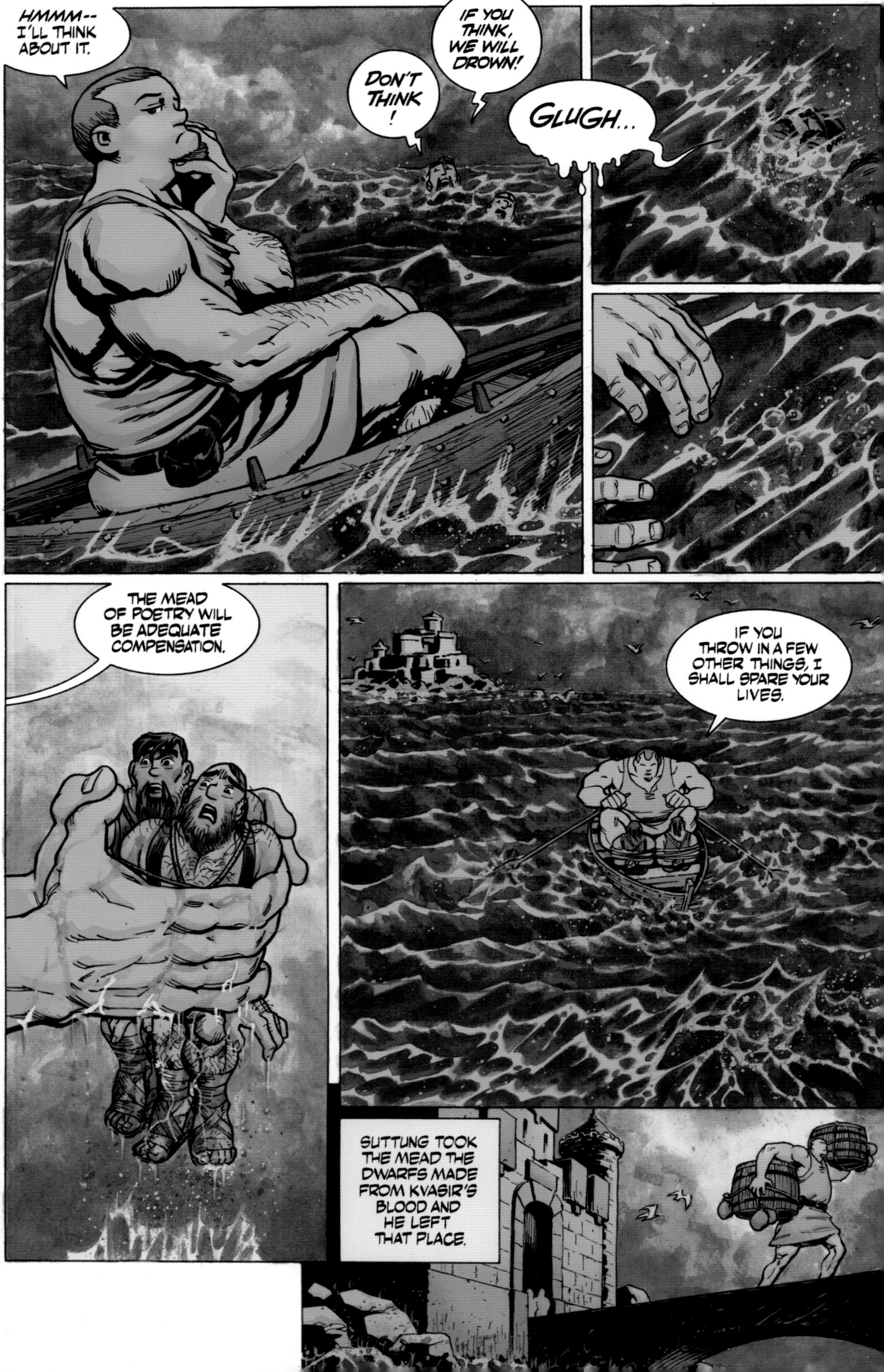
HMMM-- I'LL THINK ABOUT IT.
IF YOU THINK, WE WILL DROWN!
DON'T THINK!
GLUGH...
THE MEAD OF POETRY WILL BE ADEQUATE COMPENSATION.
IF YOU THROW IN A FEW OTHER THINGS, I SHALL SPARE YOUR LIVES.
SUTTUNG TOOK THE MEAD THE DWARFS MADE FROM KVASIR'S BLOOD AND HE LEFT THAT PLACE.

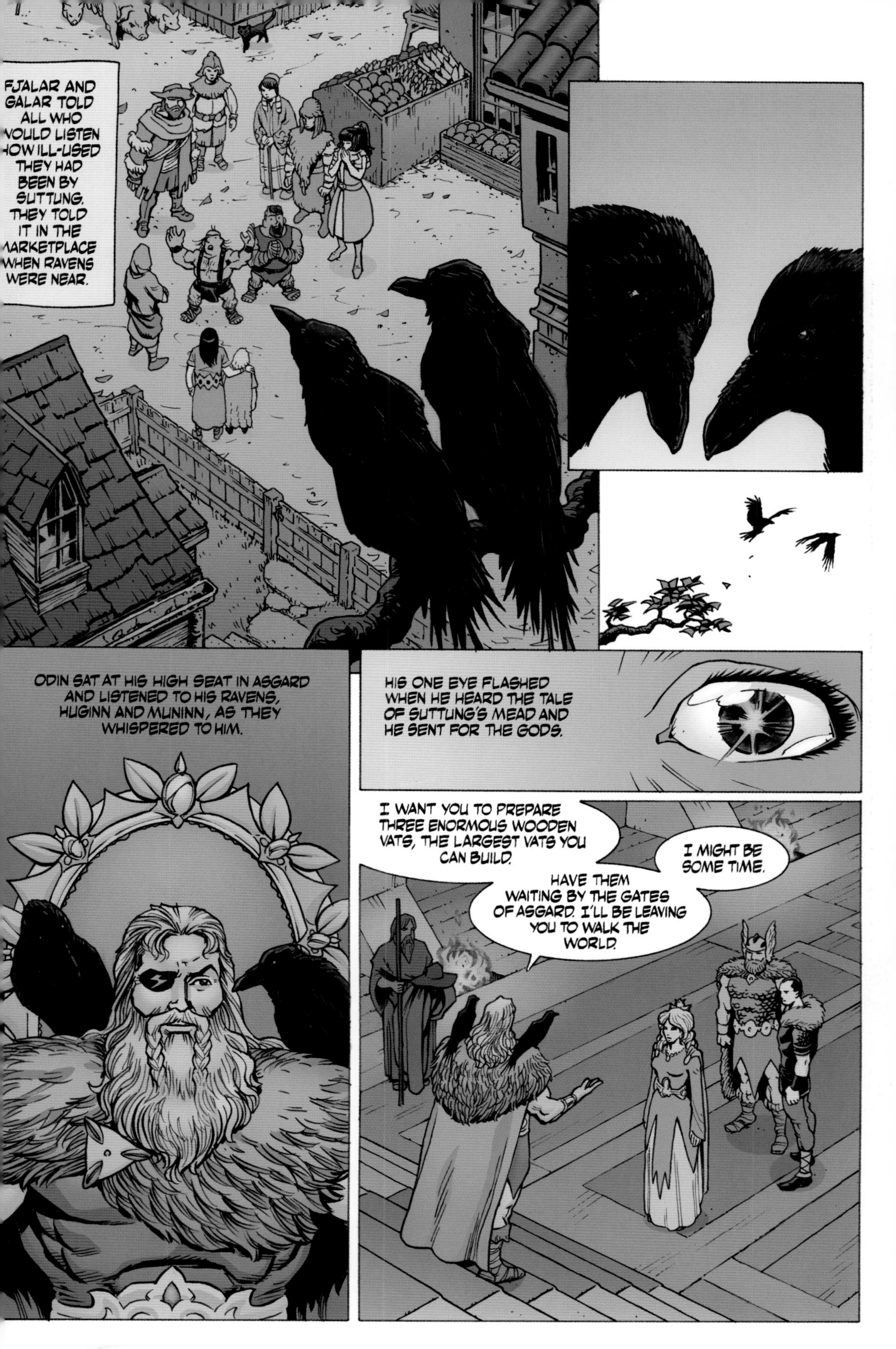
FJALAR AND GALAR TOLD ALL WHO WOULD LISTEN HOW ILL-USED THEY HAD BEEN BY SUTTUNG. THEY TOLD IT IN THE MARKETPLACE WHEN RAVENS WERE NEAR.
ODIN SAT AT HIS HIGH SEAT IN ASGARD AND LISTENED TO HIS RAVENS, HUGINN AND MUNINN, AS THEY WHISPERED TO HIM.
HIS ONE EYE FLASHED WHEN HE HEARD THE TALE OF SUTTUNG'S MEAD AND HE SENT FOR THE GODS.
I WANT YOU TO PREPARE THREE ENORMOUS WOODEN VATS, THE LARGEST VATS YOU CAN BUILD.
HAVE THEM WAITING BY THE GATES OF ASGARD. I'LL BE LEAVING YOU TO WALK THE WORLD.
I MIGHT BE SOME TIME.

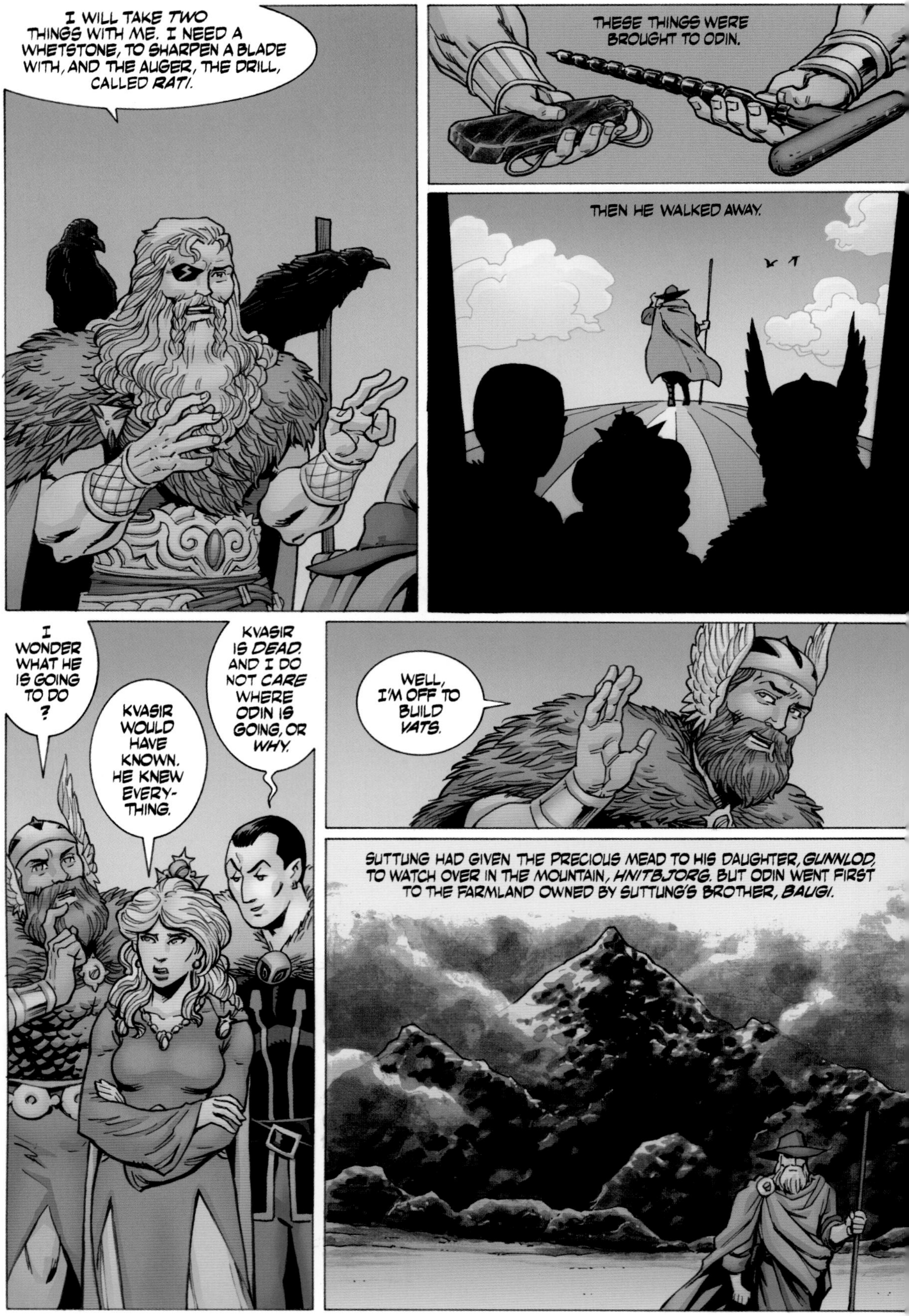
I WILL TAKE *TWO* THINGS WITH ME. I NEED A WHETSTONE, TO SHARPEN A BLADE WITH, AND THE AUGER, THE DRILL, CALLED *RATI*.
THESE THINGS WERE BROUGHT TO ODIN.
THEN HE WALKED AWAY.
I WONDER WHAT HE IS GOING TO DO?
KVASIR WOULD HAVE KNOWN. HE KNEW EVERY-THING.
KVASIR IS *DEAD*. AND I DO NOT *CARE* WHERE ODIN IS GOING, OR *WHY*.
WELL, I'M OFF TO BUILD *VATS*.
SUTTUNG HAD GIVEN THE PRECIOUS MEAD TO HIS DAUGHTER, *GUNNLOD*, TO WATCH OVER IN THE MOUNTAIN, *HNITBJORG*. BUT ODIN WENT FIRST TO THE FARMLAND OWNED BY SUTTUNG'S BROTHER, *BAUGI*.

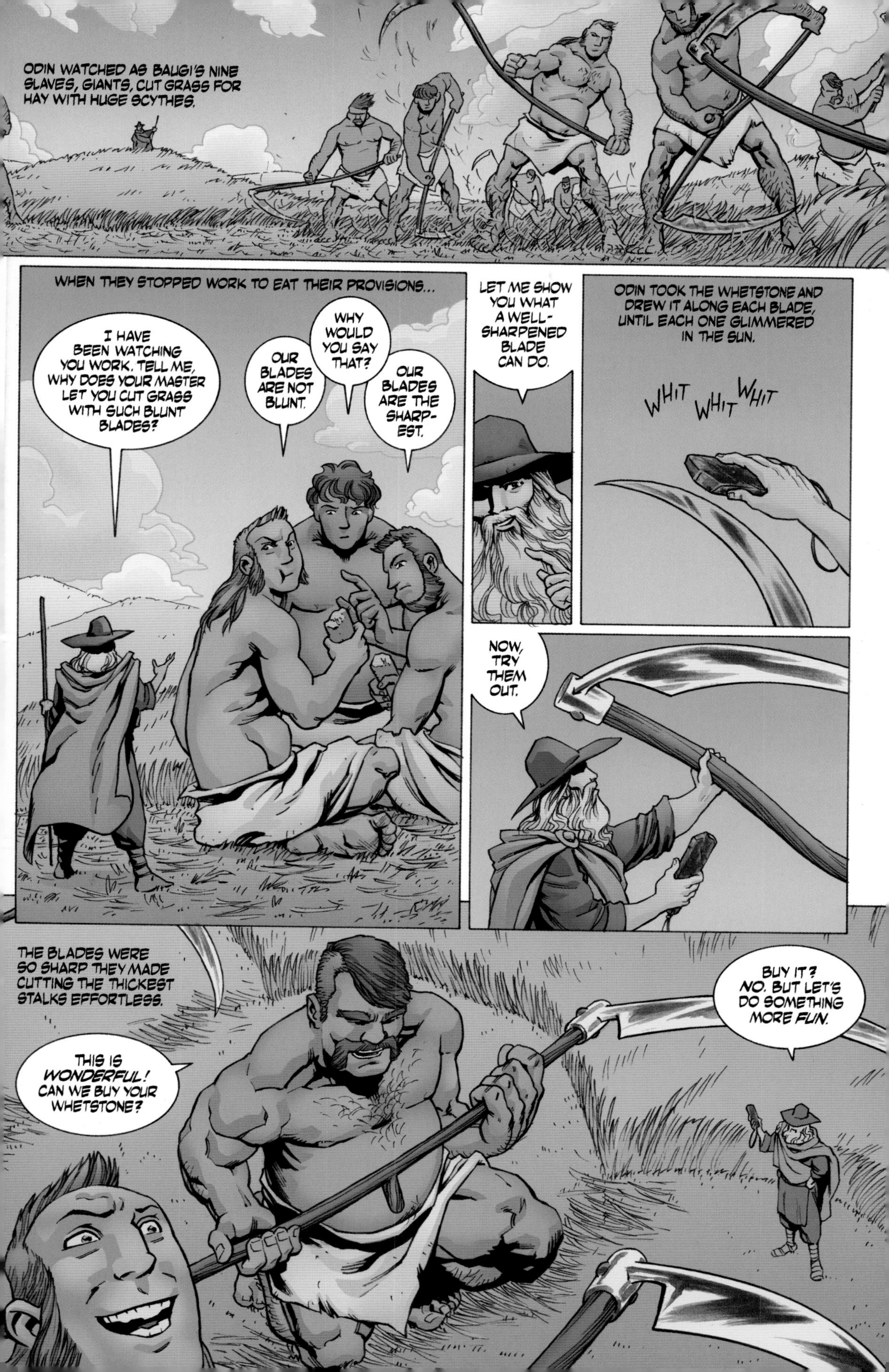
ODIN WATCHED AS BAUGI'S NINE SLAVES, GIANTS, CUT GRASS FOR HAY WITH HUGE SCYTHES.
WHEN THEY STOPPED WORK TO EAT THEIR PROVISIONS...
I HAVE BEEN WATCHING YOU WORK. TELL ME, WHY DOES YOUR MASTER LET YOU CUT GRASS WITH SUCH BLUNT BLADES?
OUR BLADES ARE NOT BLUNT.
WHY WOULD YOU SAY THAT?
OUR BLADES ARE THE SHARP-EST.
LET ME SHOW YOU WHAT A WELL-SHARPENED BLADE CAN DO.
ODIN TOOK THE WHETSTONE AND DREW IT ALONG EACH BLADE, UNTIL EACH ONE GLIMMERED IN THE SUN.
WHIT WHIT WHIT
NOW, TRY THEM OUT.
THE BLADES WERE SO SHARP THEY MADE CUTTING THE THICKEST STALKS EFFORTLESS.
THIS IS *WONDERFUL!* CAN WE BUY YOUR WHETSTONE?
BUY IT? *NO.* BUT LET'S DO SOMETHING MORE *FUN.*

ALL OF YOU, STAND IN A CIRCLE HOLDING YOUR SCYTHES.

CLOSER...

WE CAN STAND NO CLOSER. FOR THE SCYTHES ARE VERY SHARP.

YOU ARE WISE. NOW, WHO CATCHES THE WHETSTONE SHALL HAVE IT!

AND SO SAYING...

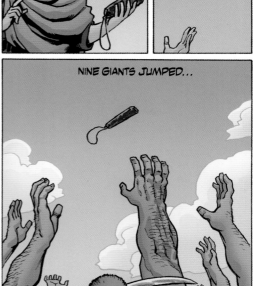

NINE GIANTS JUMPED...

NINE BLADES GLINTED IN THE SUN.

THERE WAS A SPRAY AND A SPURT OF CRIMSON IN THE SUNLIGHT...

...AND THE BODIES OF THE SLAVES FELL TO THE FRESHLY CUT GRASS, EACH WITH HIS THROAT CUT BY HIS FELLOW'S BLADE.

ODIN RETRIEVED THE WHETSTONE AND WALKED TO BAUGI'S HALL.

I AM CALLED *BOLVERKR* AND I NEED LODGING FOR THE NIGHT.

A *DISMAL* NAME. IT MEANS "WORKER OF TERRIBLE THINGS."

ONLY TO MY ENEMIES.

WELL, THEN, COME IN. LODGING IS YOURS FOR THE NIGHT. BUT YOU COME TO ME ON A DARK DAY. YESTERDAY I WAS A RICH MAN, BUT TONIGHT ALL MY SERVANTS ARE DEAD. THEY SLEW EACH OTHER. I DO NOT KNOW WHY.

A DARK DAY INDEED. CAN YOU NOT GET OTHER WORKMEN?

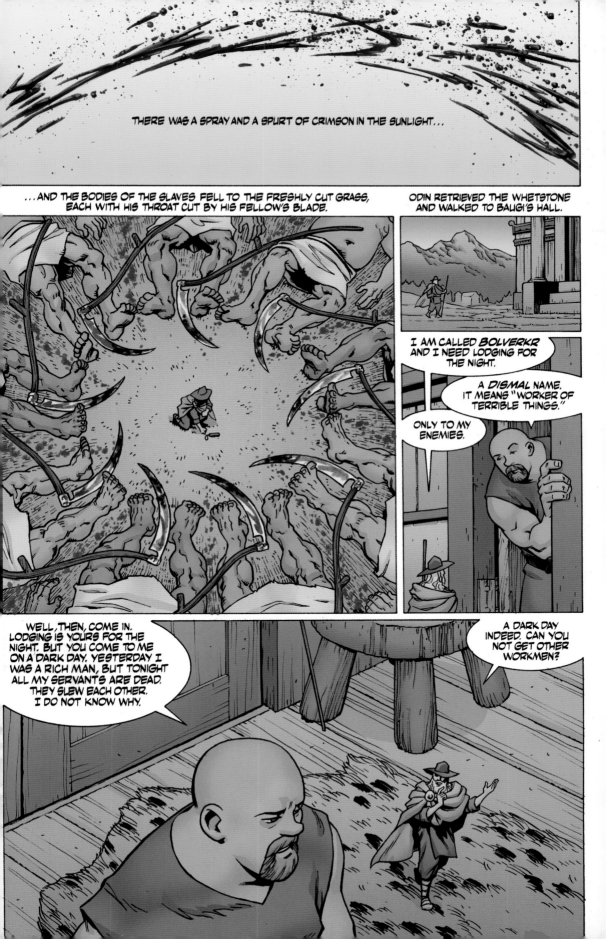

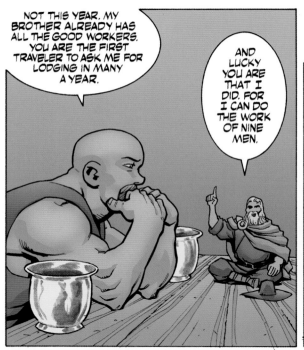

NOT THIS YEAR. MY BROTHER ALREADY HAS ALL THE GOOD WORKERS. YOU ARE THE FIRST TRAVELER TO ASK ME FOR LODGING IN MANY A YEAR.

AND LUCKY YOU ARE THAT I DID. FOR I CAN DO THE WORK OF NINE MEN.

YOU ARE NOT A GIANT. HOW COULD YOU DO THE WORK OF *ONE*, LET ALONE *NINE*?

IF I CANNOT DO THE WORK OF NINE MEN, THEN YOU NEED NOT PAY ME. BUT IF I DO...

YES?

I HAVE HEARD TALES OF SUTTUNG'S EXTRAORDINARY MEAD. I WOULD LIKE TO TASTE IT. THEY SAY IT BESTOWS THE GIFT OF *POETRY*.

BUT...BUT IT IS NOT MINE TO GIVE. IT IS *SUTTUNG'S*.

A *PITY*. GOOD LUCK WITH YOUR HARVEST.

WAIT!

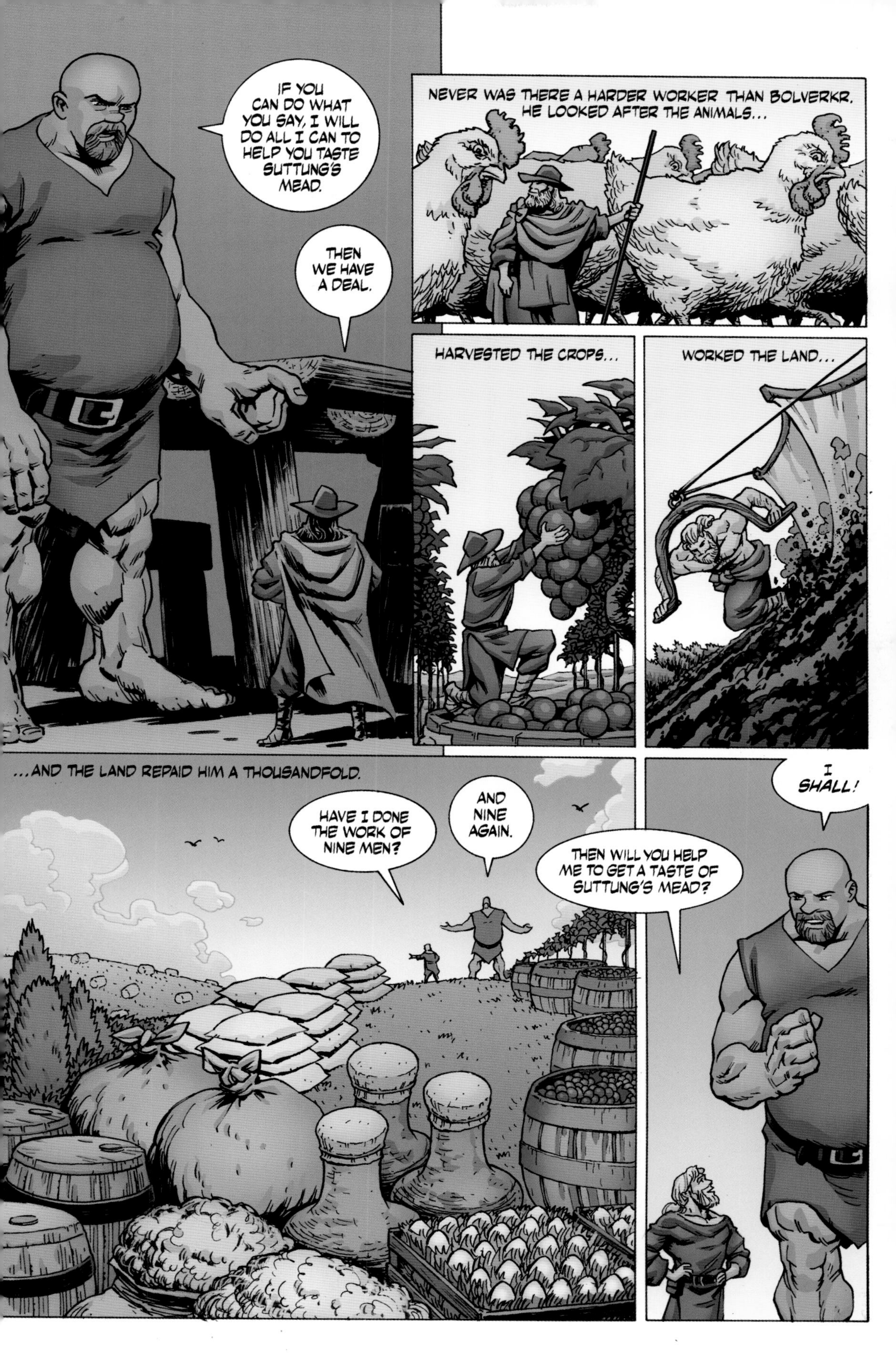
IF YOU CAN DO WHAT YOU SAY, I WILL DO ALL I CAN TO HELP YOU TASTE SUTTUNG'S MEAD.
THEN WE HAVE A DEAL.
NEVER WAS THERE A HARDER WORKER THAN BOLVERKR. HE LOOKED AFTER THE ANIMALS...
HARVESTED THE CROPS...
WORKED THE LAND...
...AND THE LAND REPAID HIM A THOUSANDFOLD.
HAVE I DONE THE WORK OF NINE MEN?
AND NINE AGAIN.
THEN WILL YOU HELP ME TO GET A TASTE OF SUTTUNG'S MEAD?
I SHALL!

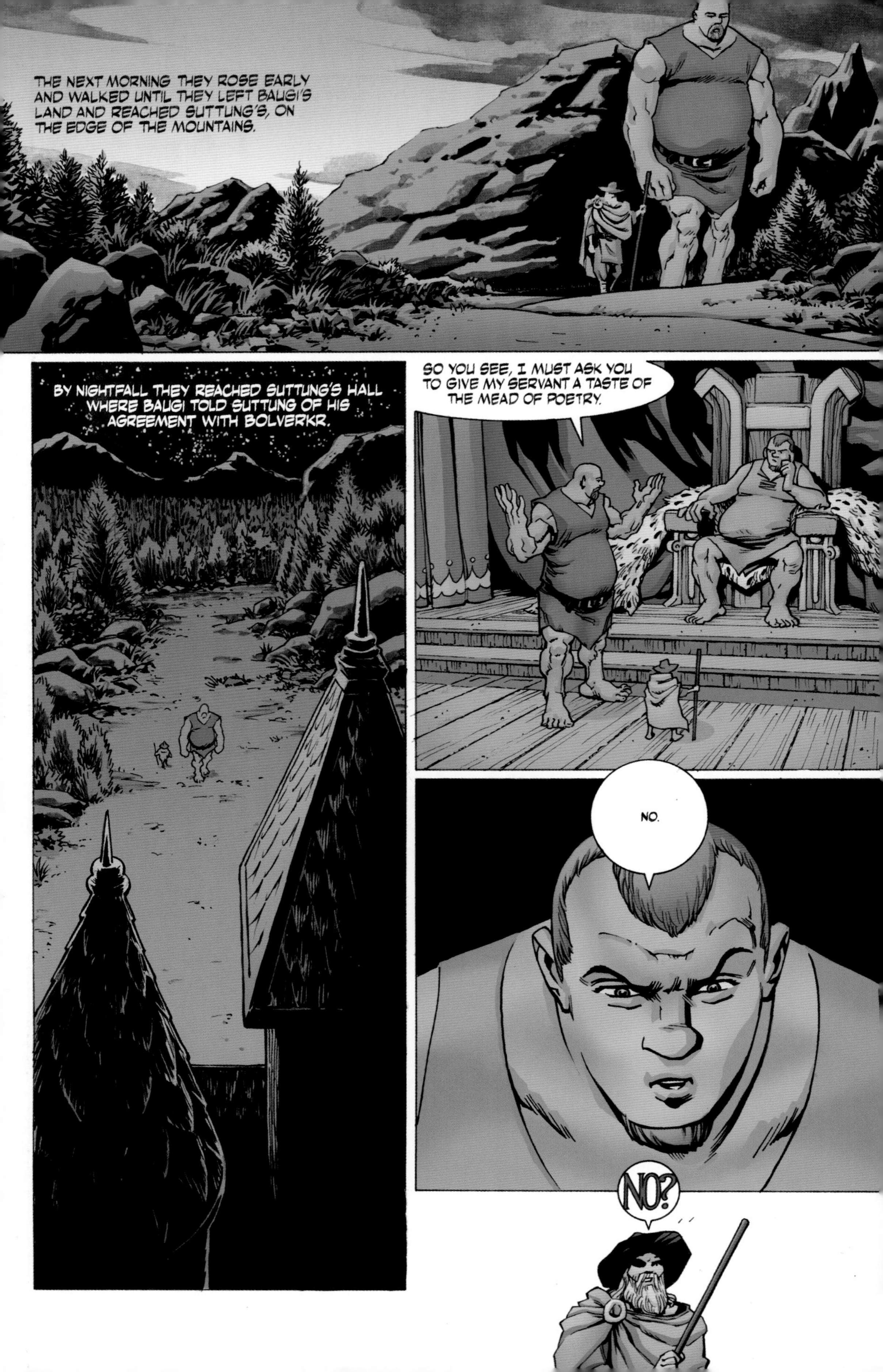
THE NEXT MORNING THEY ROSE EARLY AND WALKED UNTIL THEY LEFT BAUGI'S LAND AND REACHED SUTTUNG'S, ON THE EDGE OF THE MOUNTAINS.
BY NIGHTFALL THEY REACHED SUTTUNG'S HALL WHERE BAUGI TOLD SUTTUNG OF HIS AGREEMENT WITH BOLVERKR.
SO YOU SEE, I MUST ASK YOU TO GIVE MY SERVANT A TASTE OF THE MEAD OF POETRY.
NO.
NO?

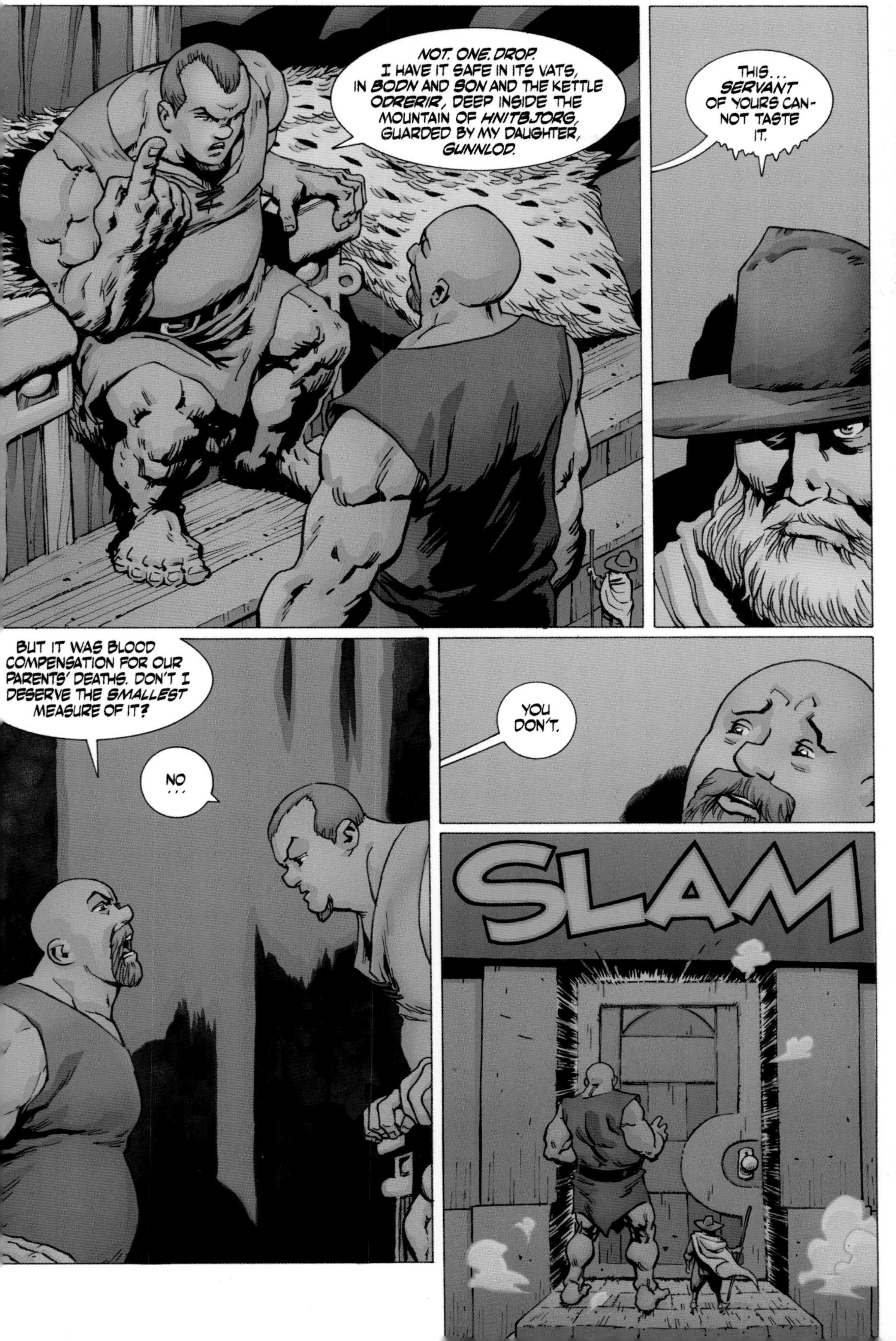
NOT. ONE. DROP. I HAVE IT SAFE IN ITS VATS, IN BODN AND SON AND THE KETTLE ODRERIR, DEEP INSIDE THE MOUNTAIN OF HNITBJORG, GUARDED BY MY DAUGHTER, GUNNLOD.
THIS... SERVANT OF YOURS CAN-NOT TASTE IT.
BUT IT WAS BLOOD COMPENSATION FOR OUR PARENTS' DEATHS. DON'T I DESERVE THE SMALLEST MEASURE OF IT?
NO...
YOU DON'T.
SLAM

I'M SORRY ABOUT THAT. I DID NOT THINK MY BROTHER WOULD BE SO *UNREASONABLE.*

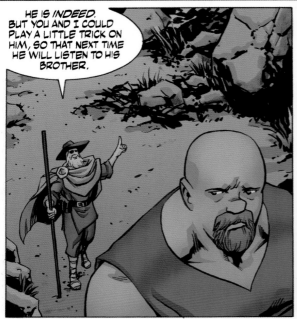

HE IS *INDEED.* BUT YOU AND I COULD PLAY A LITTLE TRICK ON HIM, SO THAT NEXT TIME HE WILL LISTEN TO HIS BROTHER.

WE COULD DO THAT.

WHAT ARE WE GOING TO DO?

"FIRST WE WILL CLIMB HNITBJORG, THE BEATING MOUNTAIN."

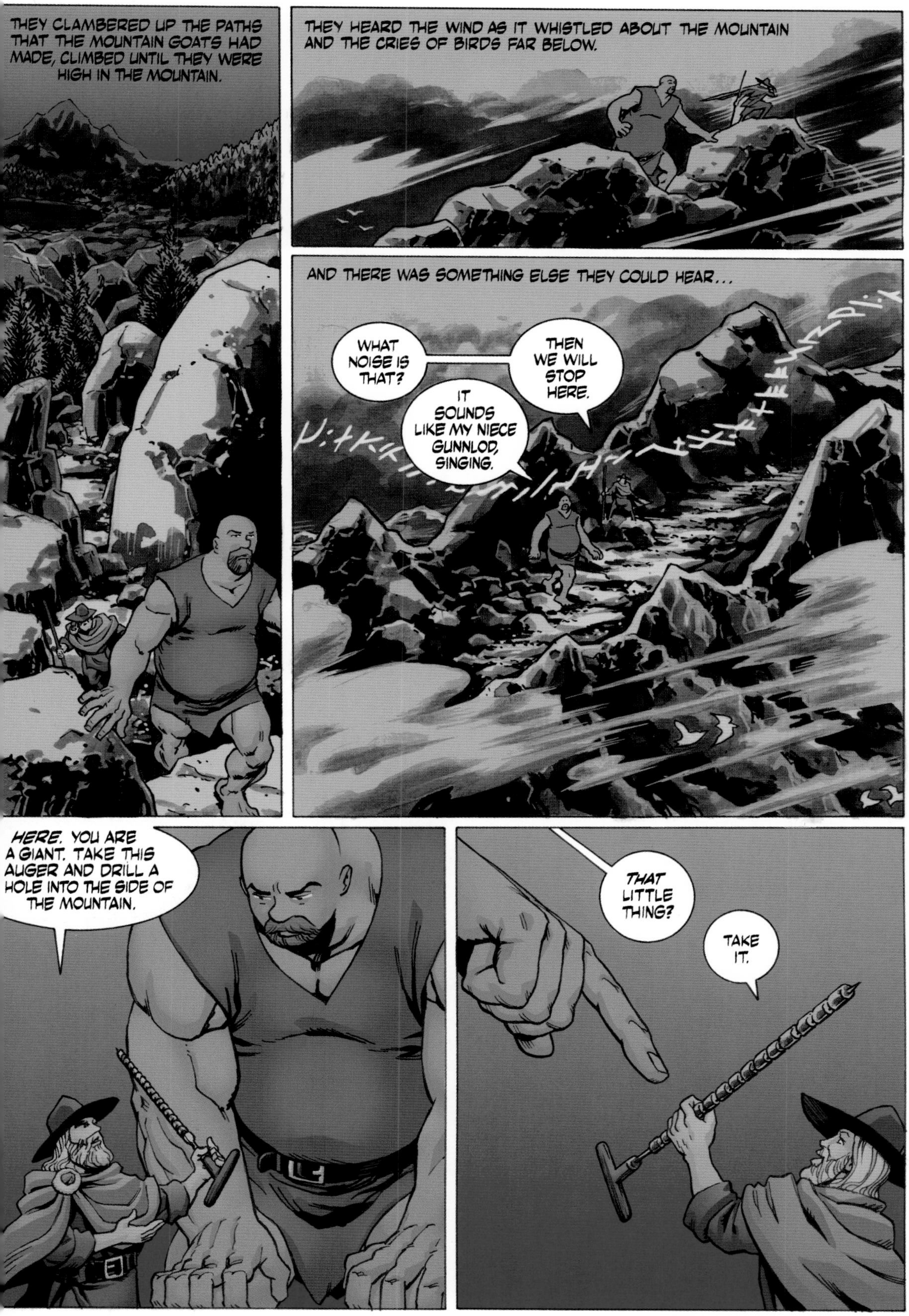
THEY CLAMBERED UP THE PATHS THAT THE MOUNTAIN GOATS HAD MADE, CLIMBED UNTIL THEY WERE HIGH IN THE MOUNTAIN.
THEY HEARD THE WIND AS IT WHISTLED ABOUT THE MOUNTAIN AND THE CRIES OF BIRDS FAR BELOW.
AND THERE WAS SOMETHING ELSE THEY COULD HEAR...
WHAT NOISE IS THAT?
IT SOUNDS LIKE MY NIECE GUNNLOD, SINGING.
THEN WE WILL STOP HERE.
HERE. YOU ARE A GIANT. TAKE THIS AUGER AND DRILL A HOLE INTO THE SIDE OF THE MOUNTAIN.
THAT LITTLE THING?
TAKE IT.

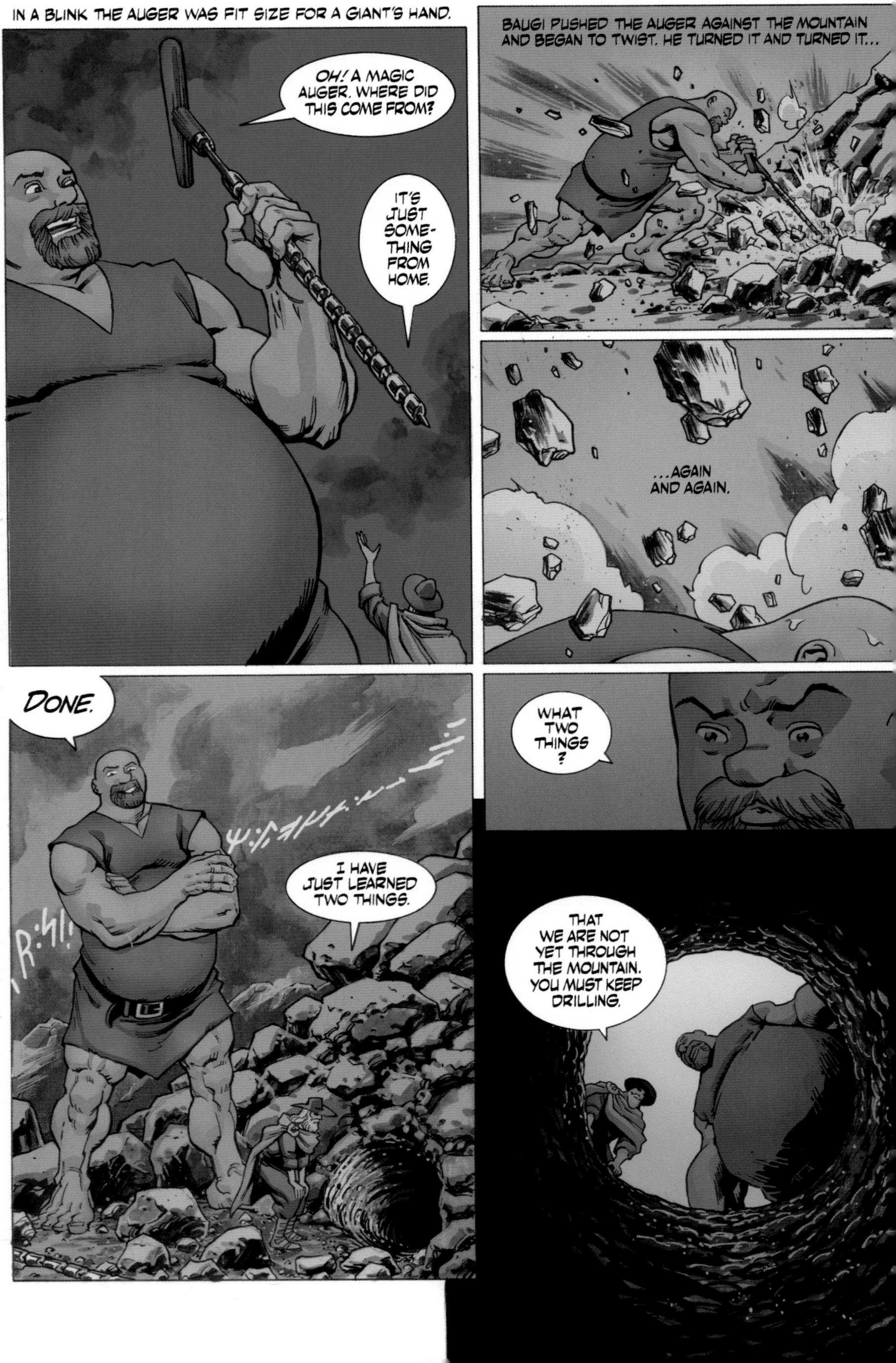
IN A BLINK THE AUGER WAS FIT SIZE FOR A GIANT'S HAND.
OH! A MAGIC AUGER. WHERE DID THIS COME FROM?
IT'S JUST SOME-THING FROM HOME.
BAUGI PUSHED THE AUGER AGAINST THE MOUNTAIN AND BEGAN TO TWIST. HE TURNED IT AND TURNED IT...
...AGAIN AND AGAIN.
DONE.
I HAVE JUST LEARNED TWO THINGS.
WHAT TWO THINGS?
THAT WE ARE NOT YET THROUGH THE MOUNTAIN. YOU MUST KEEP DRILLING.

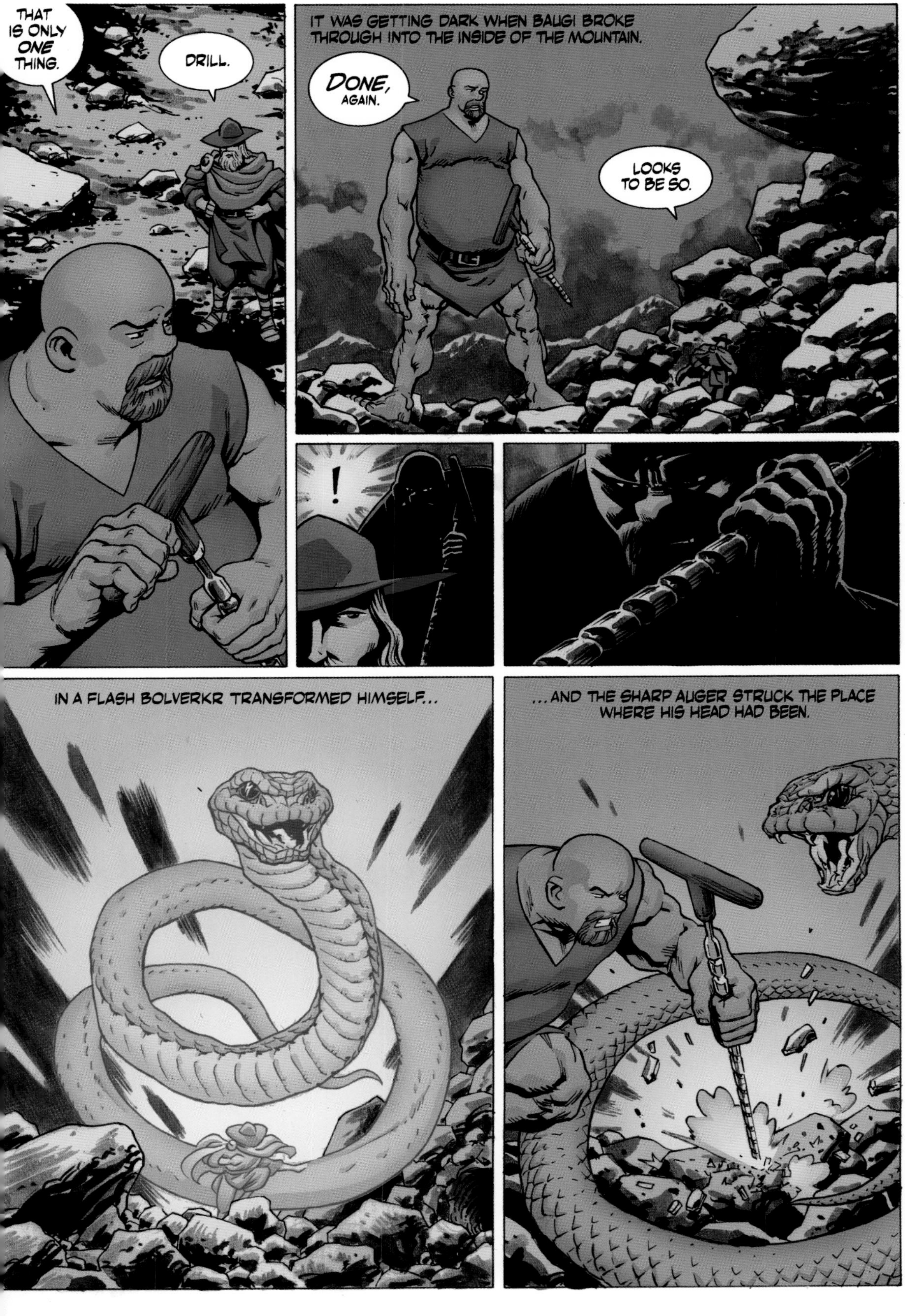
THAT IS ONLY ONE THING.
DRILL.
IT WAS GETTING DARK WHEN BAUGI BROKE THROUGH INTO THE INSIDE OF THE MOUNTAIN.
DONE, AGAIN.
LOOKS TO BE SO.
!
IN A FLASH BOLVERKR TRANSFORMED HIMSELF...
...AND THE SHARP AUGER STRUCK THE PLACE WHERE HIS HEAD HAD BEEN.

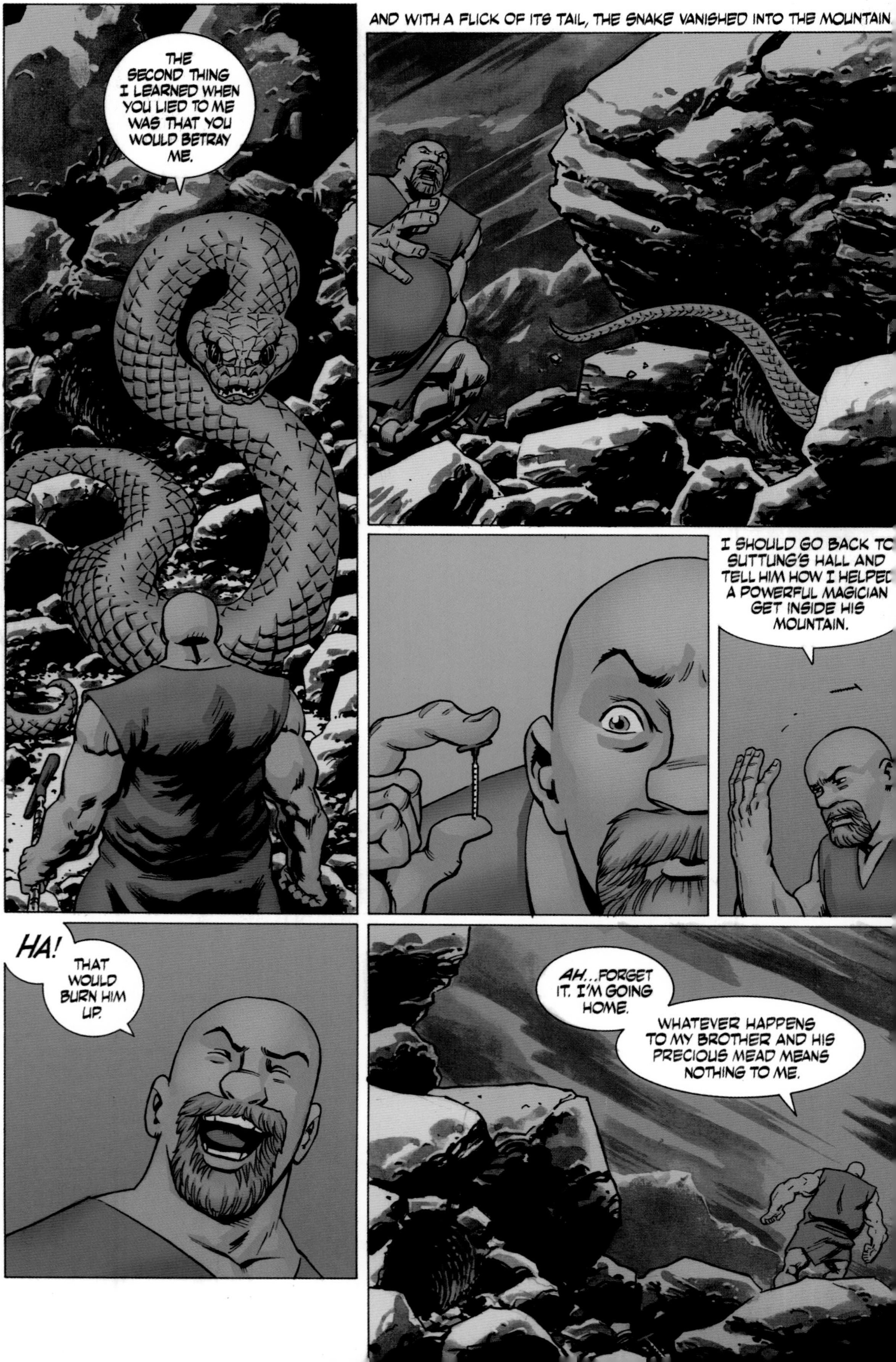
THE SECOND THING I LEARNED WHEN YOU LIED TO ME WAS THAT YOU WOULD BETRAY ME.
AND WITH A FLICK OF ITS TAIL, THE SNAKE VANISHED INTO THE MOUNTAIN.
I SHOULD GO BACK TO SUTTUNG'S HALL AND TELL HIM HOW I HELPED A POWERFUL MAGICIAN GET INSIDE HIS MOUNTAIN.
HA! THAT WOULD BURN HIM UP.
AH...FORGET IT. I'M GOING HOME.
WHATEVER HAPPENS TO MY BROTHER AND HIS PRECIOUS MEAD MEANS NOTHING TO ME.

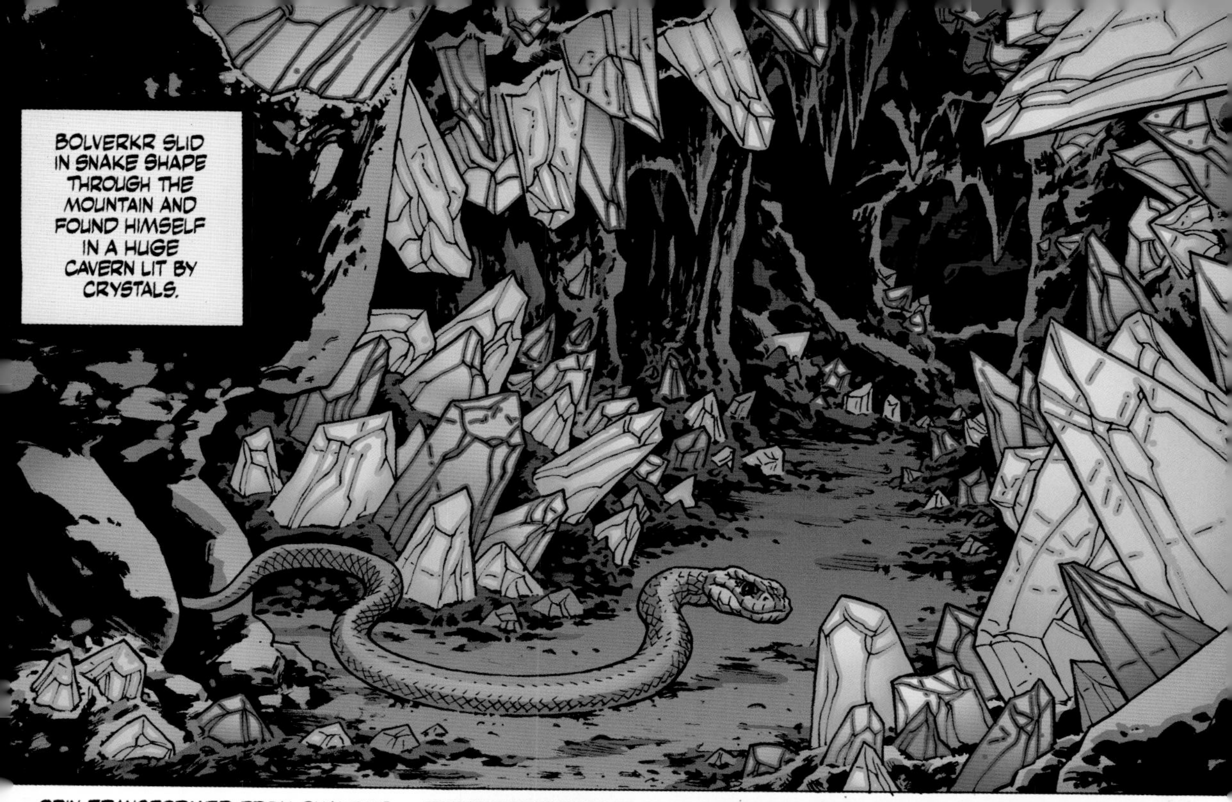
BOLVERKR SLID IN SNAKE SHAPE THROUGH THE MOUNTAIN AND FOUND HIMSELF IN A HUGE CAVERN LIT BY CRYSTALS.

ODIN TRANSFORMED FROM SNAKE TO MAN, GIANT-SIZED AND WELL-FORMED.

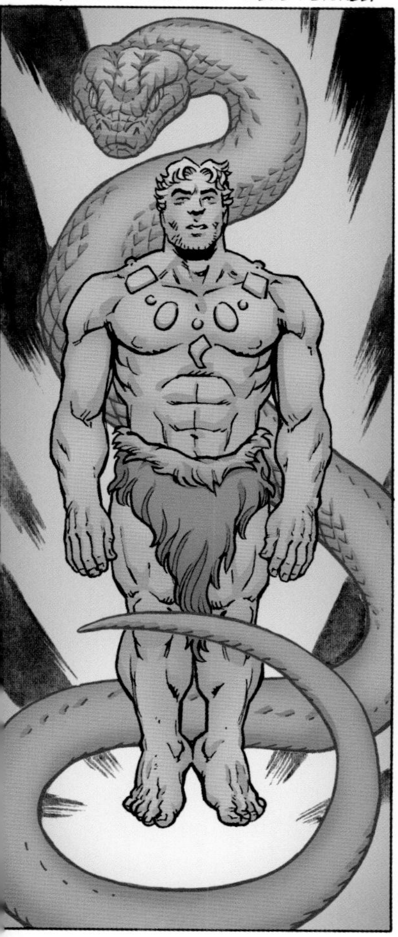

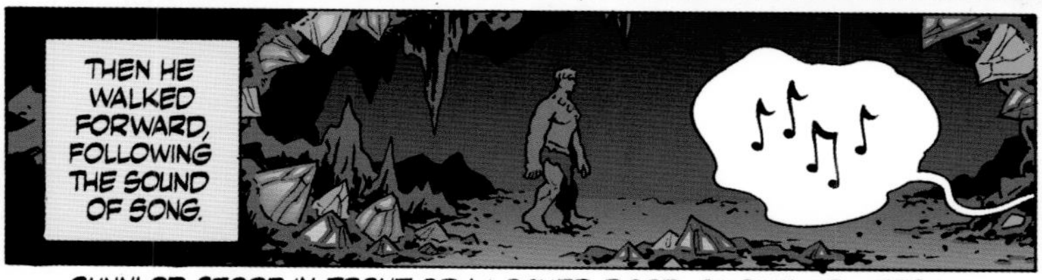
THEN HE WALKED FORWARD, FOLLOWING THE SOUND OF SONG.
♪♫♪

GUNNLOD STOOD IN FRONT OF A LOCKED DOOR, SINGING TO HERSELF.

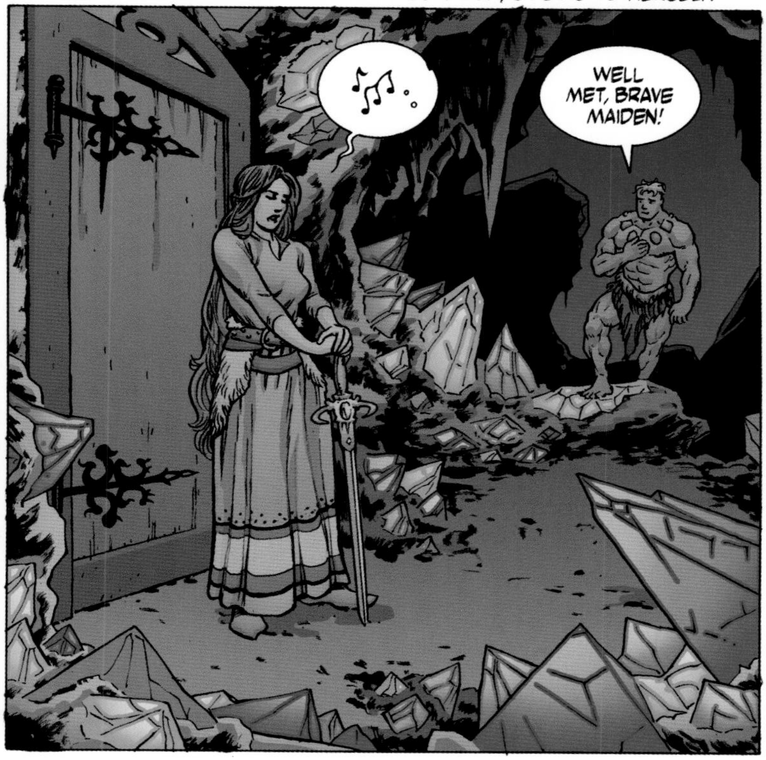
♪♫
WELL MET, BRAVE MAIDEN!

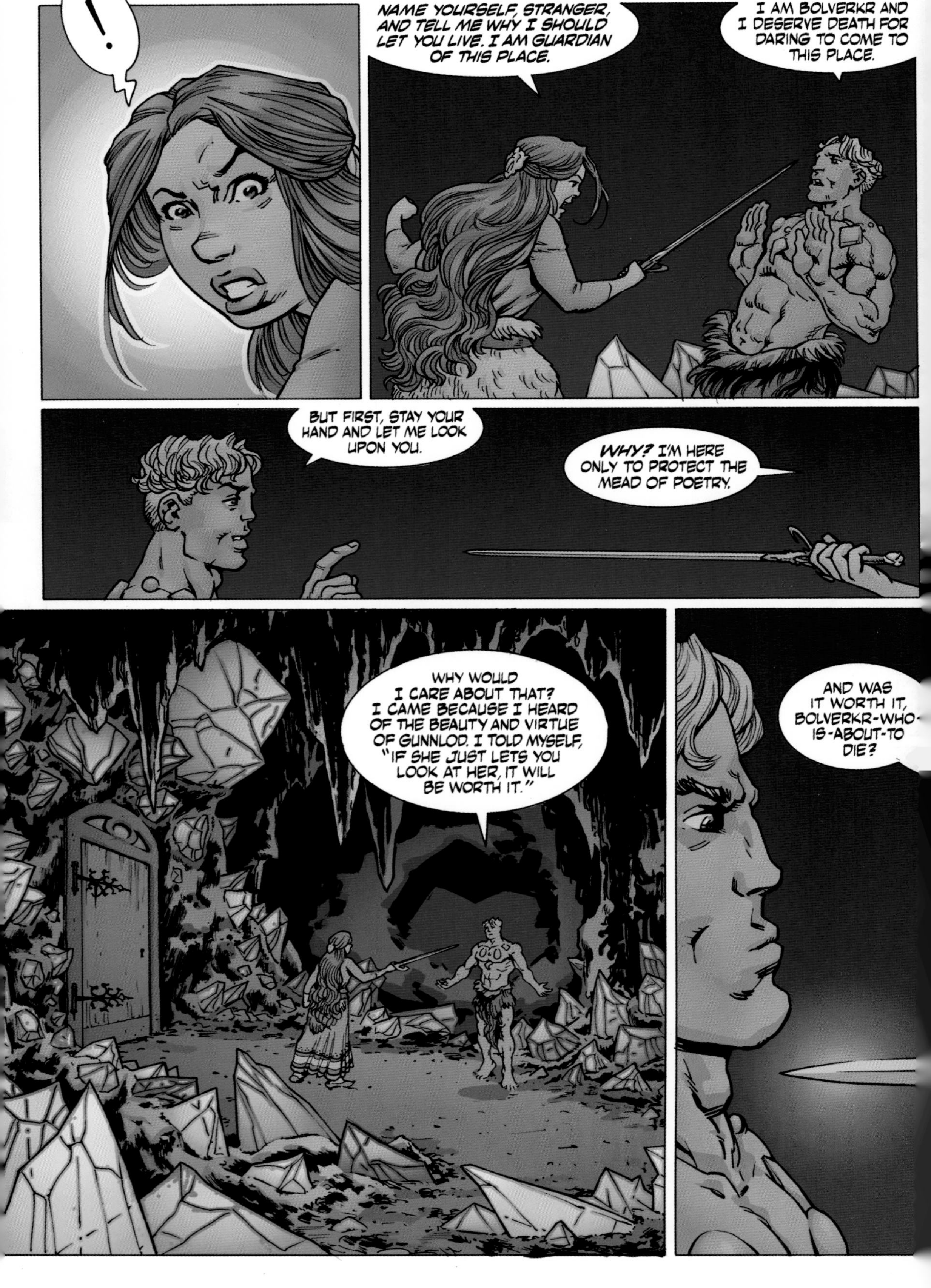
!
NAME YOURSELF, STRANGER, AND TELL ME WHY I SHOULD LET YOU LIVE. I AM GUARDIAN OF THIS PLACE.
I AM BOLVERKR AND I DESERVE DEATH FOR DARING TO COME TO THIS PLACE.
BUT FIRST, STAY YOUR HAND AND LET ME LOOK UPON YOU.
WHY? I'M HERE ONLY TO PROTECT THE MEAD OF POETRY.
WHY WOULD I CARE ABOUT THAT? I CAME BECAUSE I HEARD OF THE BEAUTY AND VIRTUE OF GUNNLOD. I TOLD MYSELF, "IF SHE JUST LETS YOU LOOK AT HER, IT WILL BE WORTH IT."
AND WAS IT WORTH IT, BOLVERKR-WHO-IS-ABOUT-TO DIE?

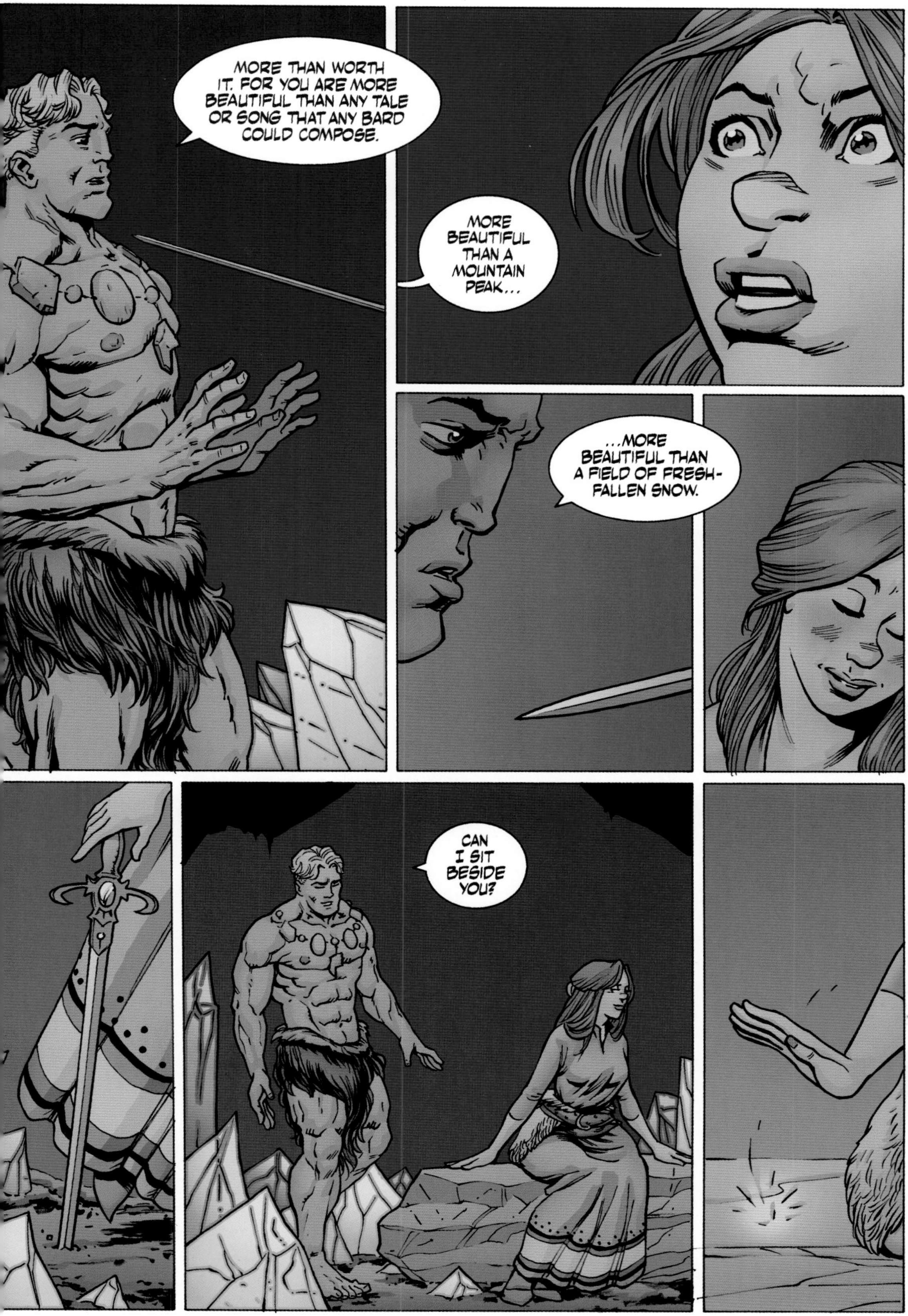
MORE THAN WORTH IT. FOR YOU ARE MORE BEAUTIFUL THAN ANY TALE OR SONG THAT ANY BARD COULD COMPOSE.
MORE BEAUTIFUL THAN A MOUNTAIN PEAK...
...MORE BEAUTIFUL THAN A FIELD OF FRESH-FALLEN SNOW.
CAN I SIT BESIDE YOU?

SHE HAD FOOD THERE IN THE MOUNTAIN, AND DRINK. AND AFTER THEY ATE...

I WISH I COULD TASTE ONE SIP OF THE MEAD FROM THE VAT CALLED SON. THEN I COULD MAKE A TRUE SONG ABOUT YOUR EYES.

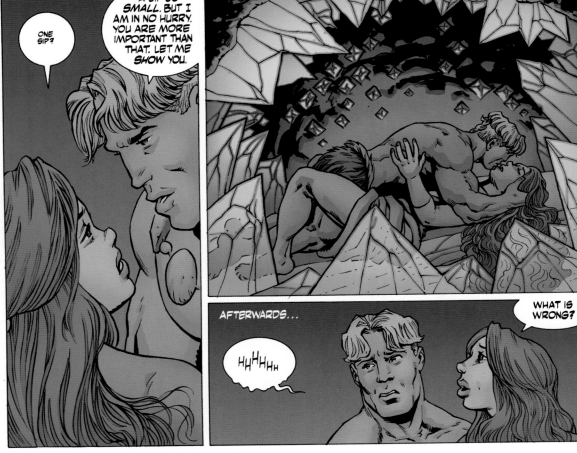

ONE SIP?

A SIP SO SMALL. BUT I AM IN NO HURRY. YOU ARE MORE IMPORTANT THAN THAT. LET ME SHOW YOU.

AFTERWARDS...

HHHHHH

WHAT IS WRONG?

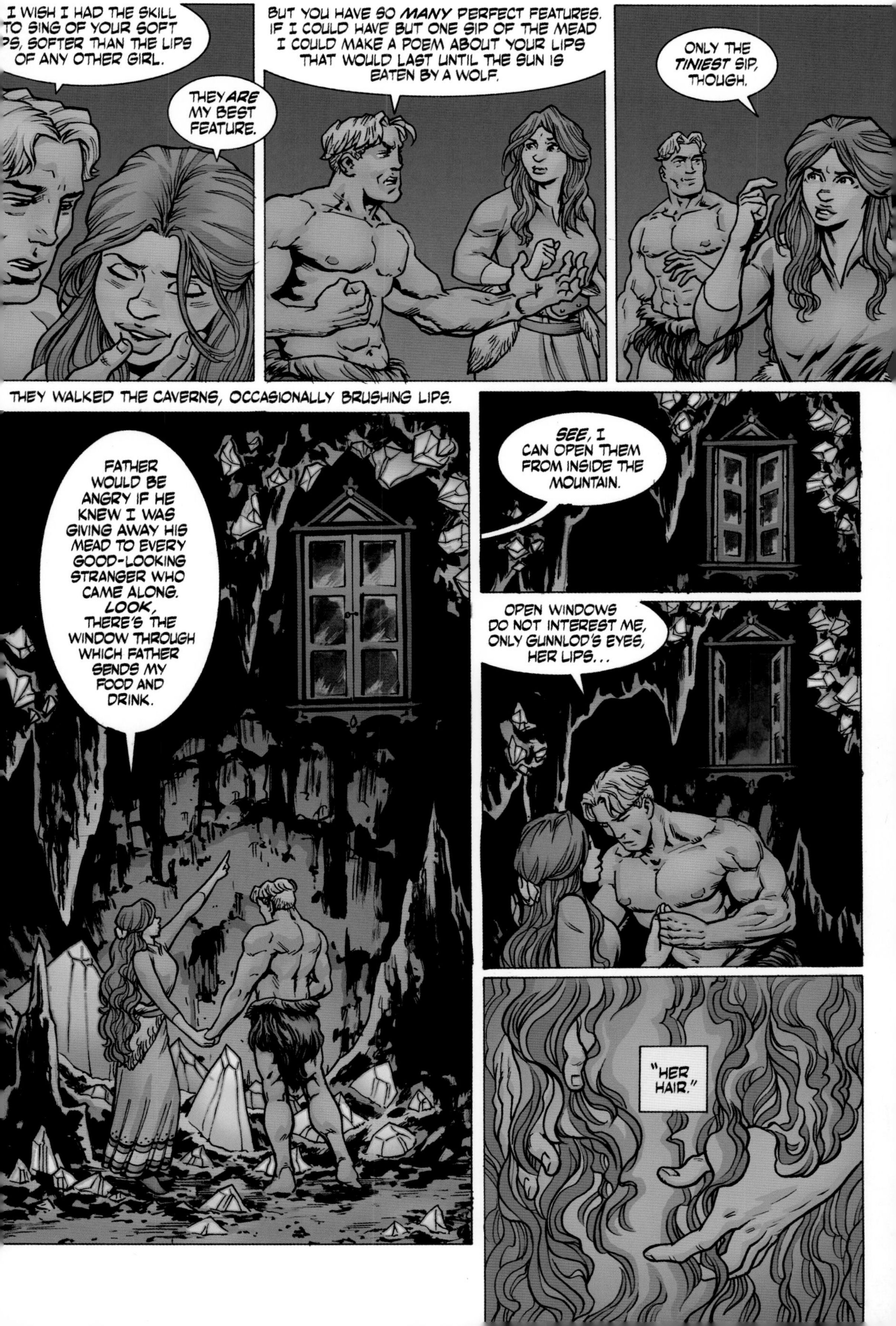
I WISH I HAD THE SKILL TO SING OF YOUR SOFT LIPS, SOFTER THAN THE LIPS OF ANY OTHER GIRL.
THEY ARE MY BEST FEATURE.
BUT YOU HAVE SO MANY PERFECT FEATURES. IF I COULD HAVE BUT ONE SIP OF THE MEAD I COULD MAKE A POEM ABOUT YOUR LIPS THAT WOULD LAST UNTIL THE SUN IS EATEN BY A WOLF.
ONLY THE TINIEST SIP, THOUGH.
THEY WALKED THE CAVERNS, OCCASIONALLY BRUSHING LIPS.
FATHER WOULD BE ANGRY IF HE KNEW I WAS GIVING AWAY HIS MEAD TO EVERY GOOD-LOOKING STRANGER WHO CAME ALONG. LOOK, THERE'S THE WINDOW THROUGH WHICH FATHER SENDS MY FOOD AND DRINK.
SEE, I CAN OPEN THEM FROM INSIDE THE MOUNTAIN.
OPEN WINDOWS DO NOT INTEREST ME, ONLY GUNNLOD'S EYES, HER LIPS...
"HER HAIR."

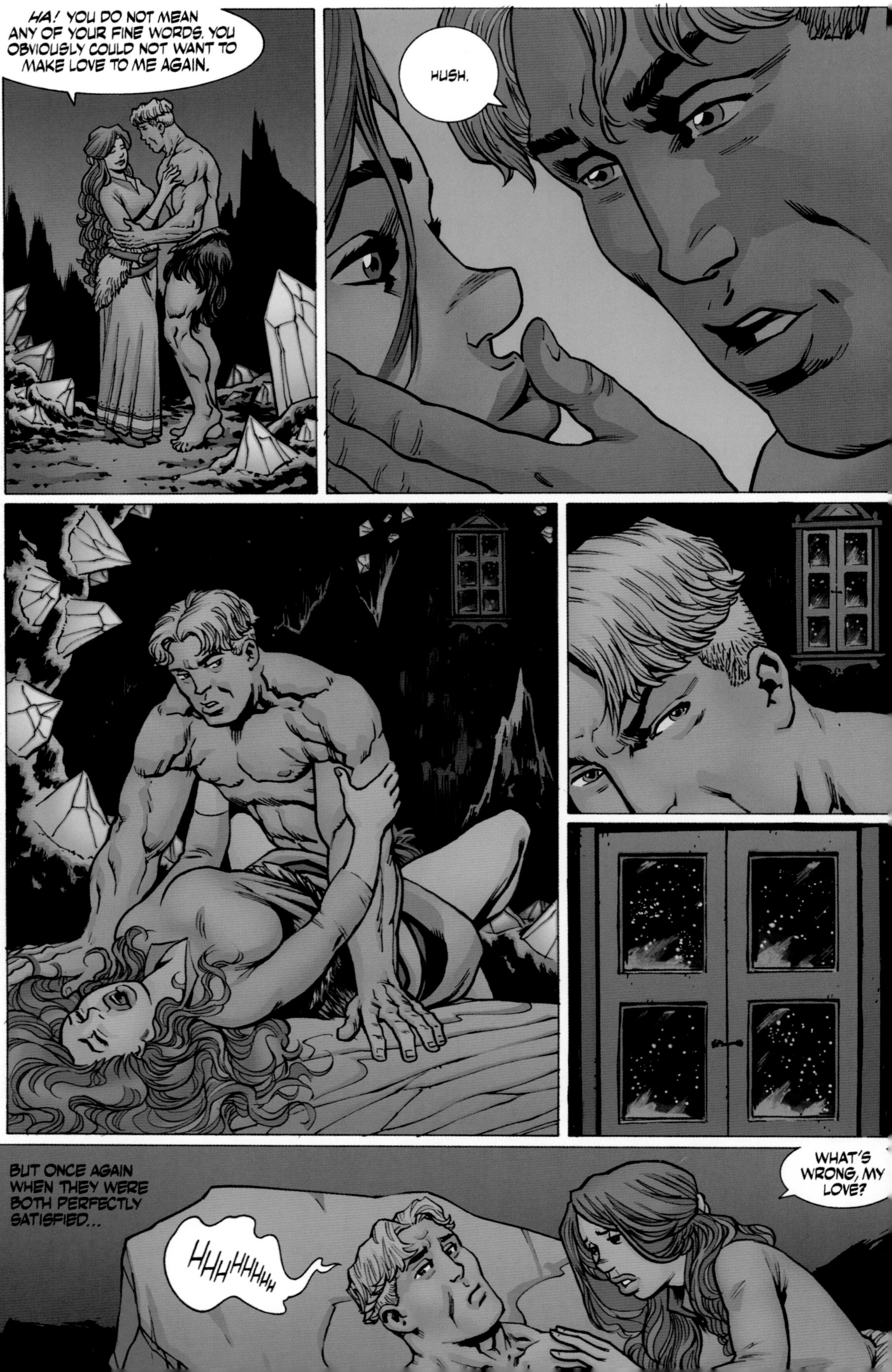
HA! YOU DO NOT MEAN ANY OF YOUR FINE WORDS. YOU OBVIOUSLY COULD NOT WANT TO MAKE LOVE TO ME AGAIN.
HUSH.
BUT ONCE AGAIN WHEN THEY WERE BOTH PERFECTLY SATISFIED...
HHHHHHHH
WHAT'S WRONG, MY LOVE?

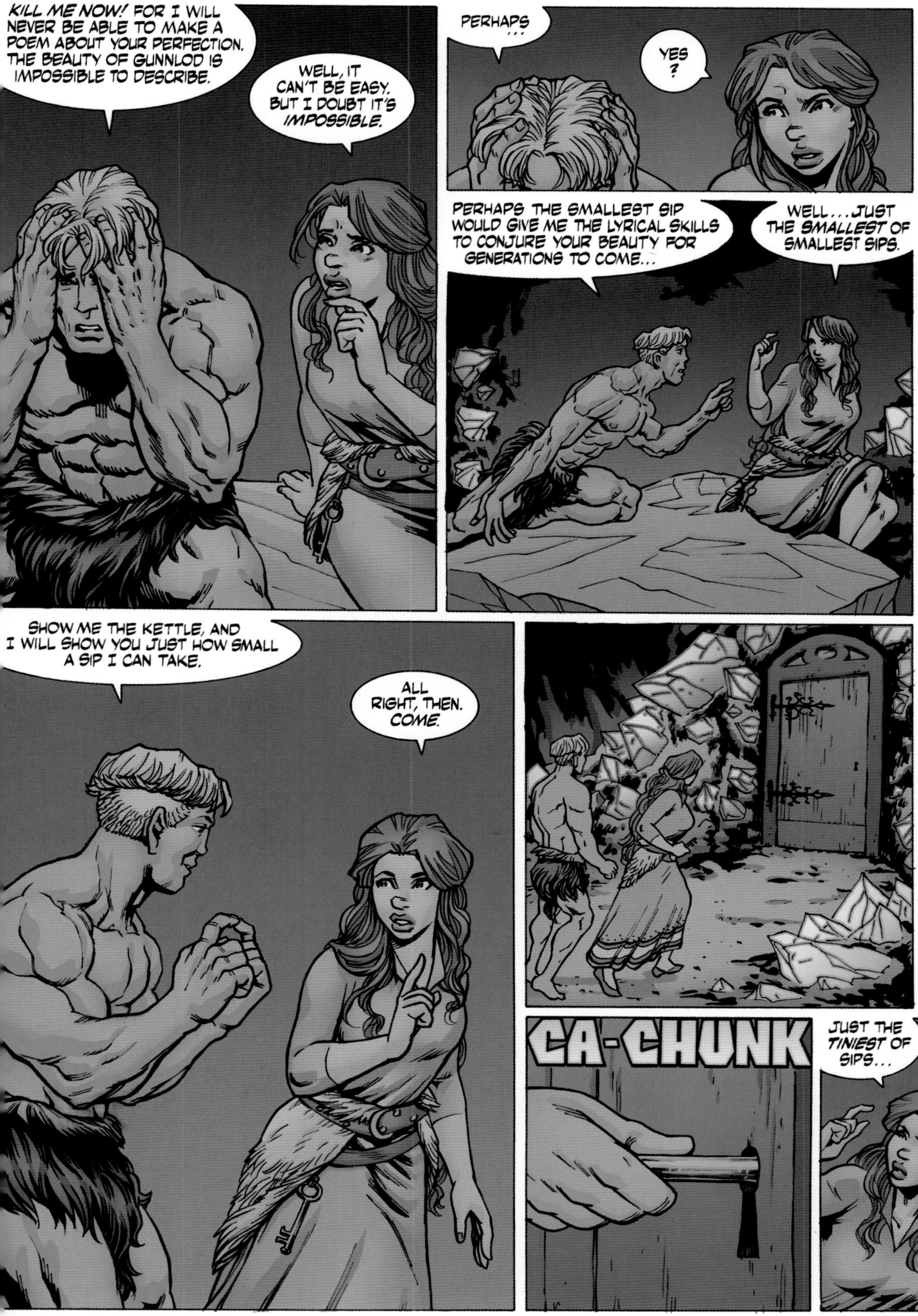
KILL ME NOW! FOR I WILL NEVER BE ABLE TO MAKE A POEM ABOUT YOUR PERFECTION. THE BEAUTY OF GUNNLOD IS IMPOSSIBLE TO DESCRIBE.
WELL, IT CAN'T BE EASY. BUT I DOUBT IT'S IMPOSSIBLE.
PERHAPS . . .
YES ?
PERHAPS THE SMALLEST SIP WOULD GIVE ME THE LYRICAL SKILLS TO CONJURE YOUR BEAUTY FOR GENERATIONS TO COME...
WELL... JUST THE SMALLEST OF SMALLEST SIPS.
SHOW ME THE KETTLE, AND I WILL SHOW YOU JUST HOW SMALL A SIP I CAN TAKE.
ALL RIGHT, THEN. COME.
CA-CHUNK
JUST THE TINIEST OF SIPS...

THE SMELL OF THE MEAD OF POETRY WAS HEADY ON THE AIR AS ODIN APPROACHED THE TWO VATS AND THE KETTLE.

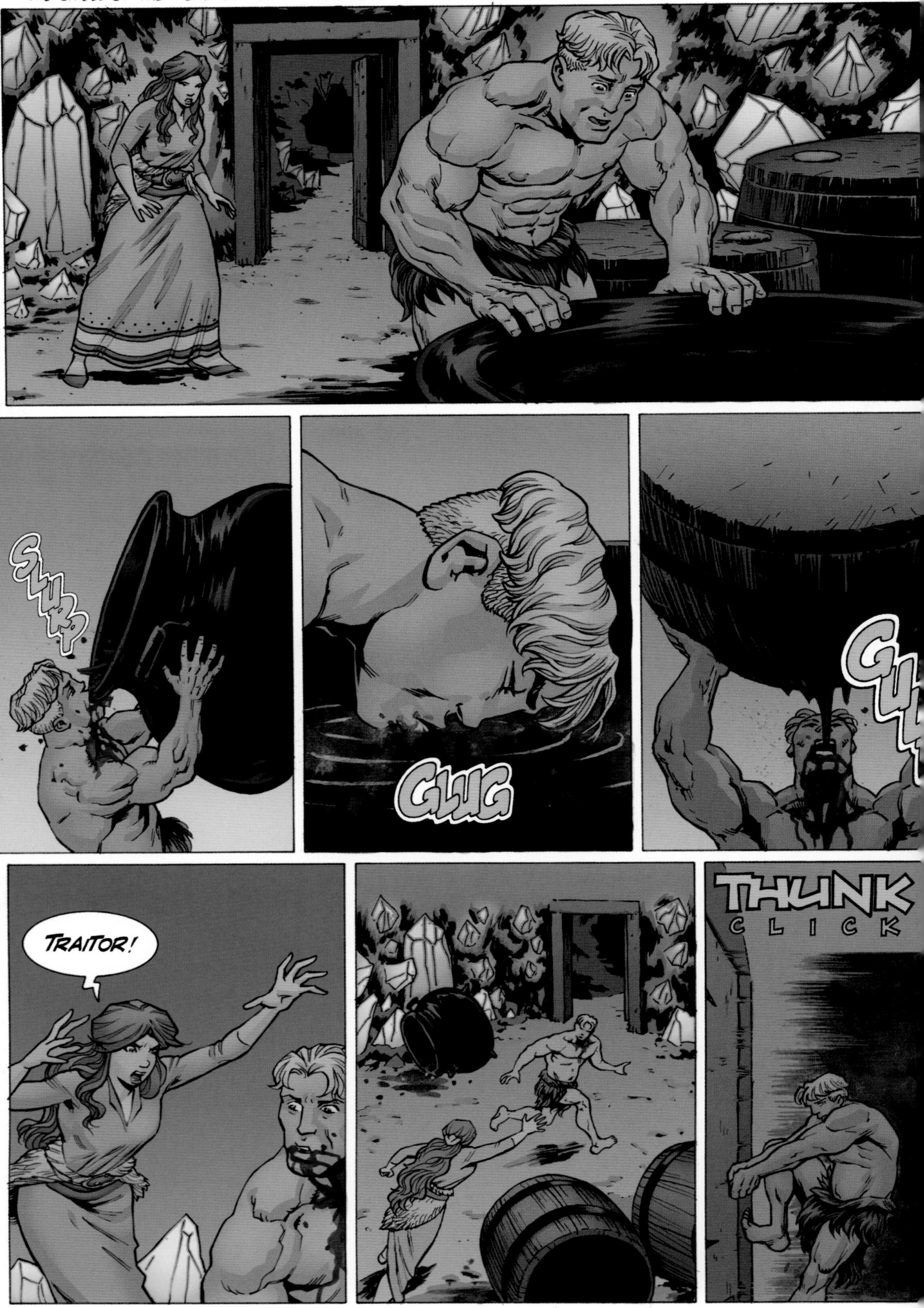
SLURP
GLUG
TRAITOR!
THUNK
CLICK

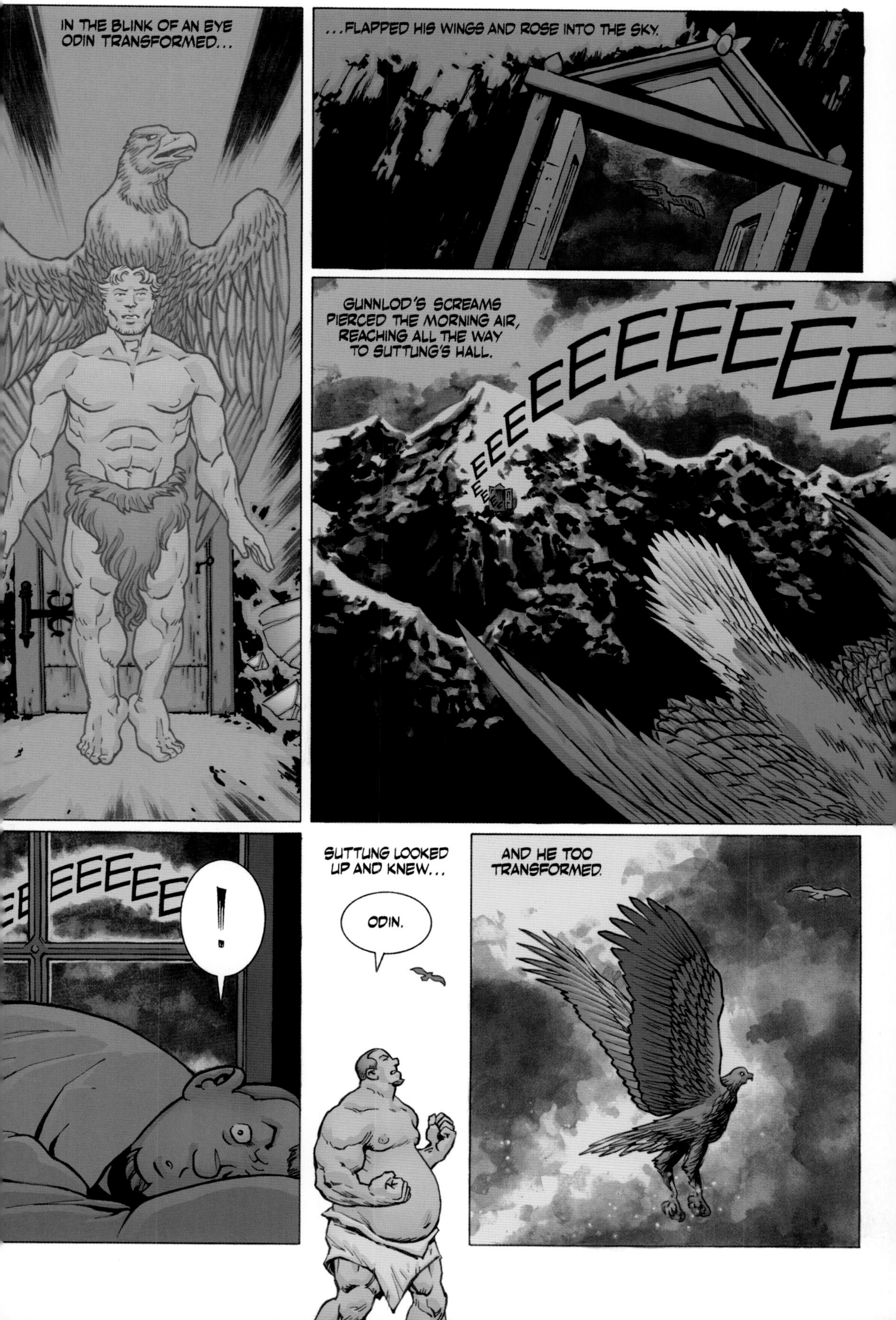
IN THE BLINK OF AN EYE ODIN TRANSFORMED...
...FLAPPED HIS WINGS AND ROSE INTO THE SKY.
GUNNLOD'S SCREAMS PIERCED THE MORNING AIR, REACHING ALL THE WAY TO SUTTUNG'S HALL.
EEEEEEEEEEEEEEEE
EEEEEEEE
!
SUTTUNG LOOKED UP AND KNEW...
ODIN.
AND HE TOO TRANSFORMED.

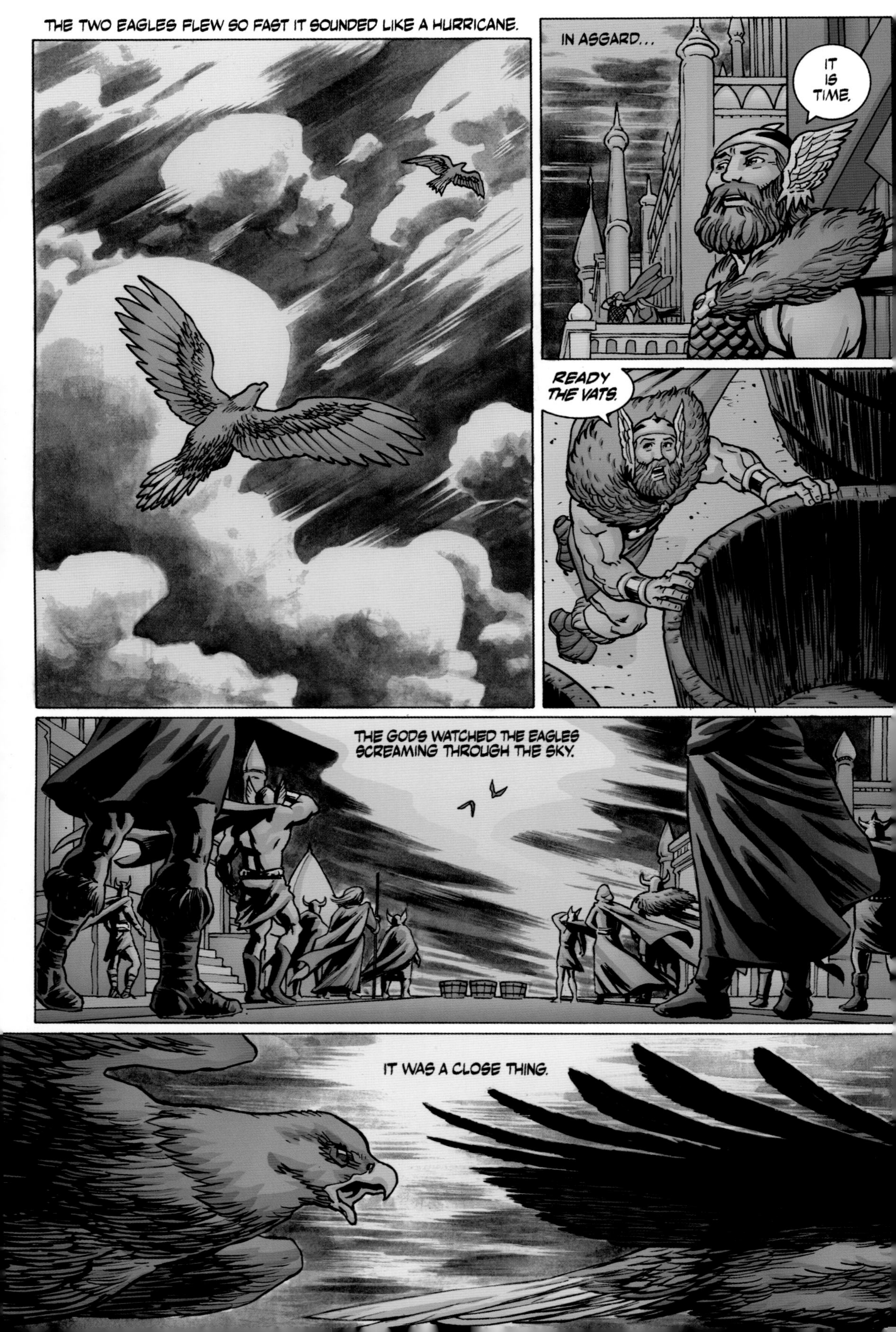
THE TWO EAGLES FLEW SO FAST IT SOUNDED LIKE A HURRICANE.
IN ASGARD...
IT IS TIME.
READY THE VATS.
THE GODS WATCHED THE EAGLES SCREAMING THROUGH THE SKY.
IT WAS A CLOSE THING.

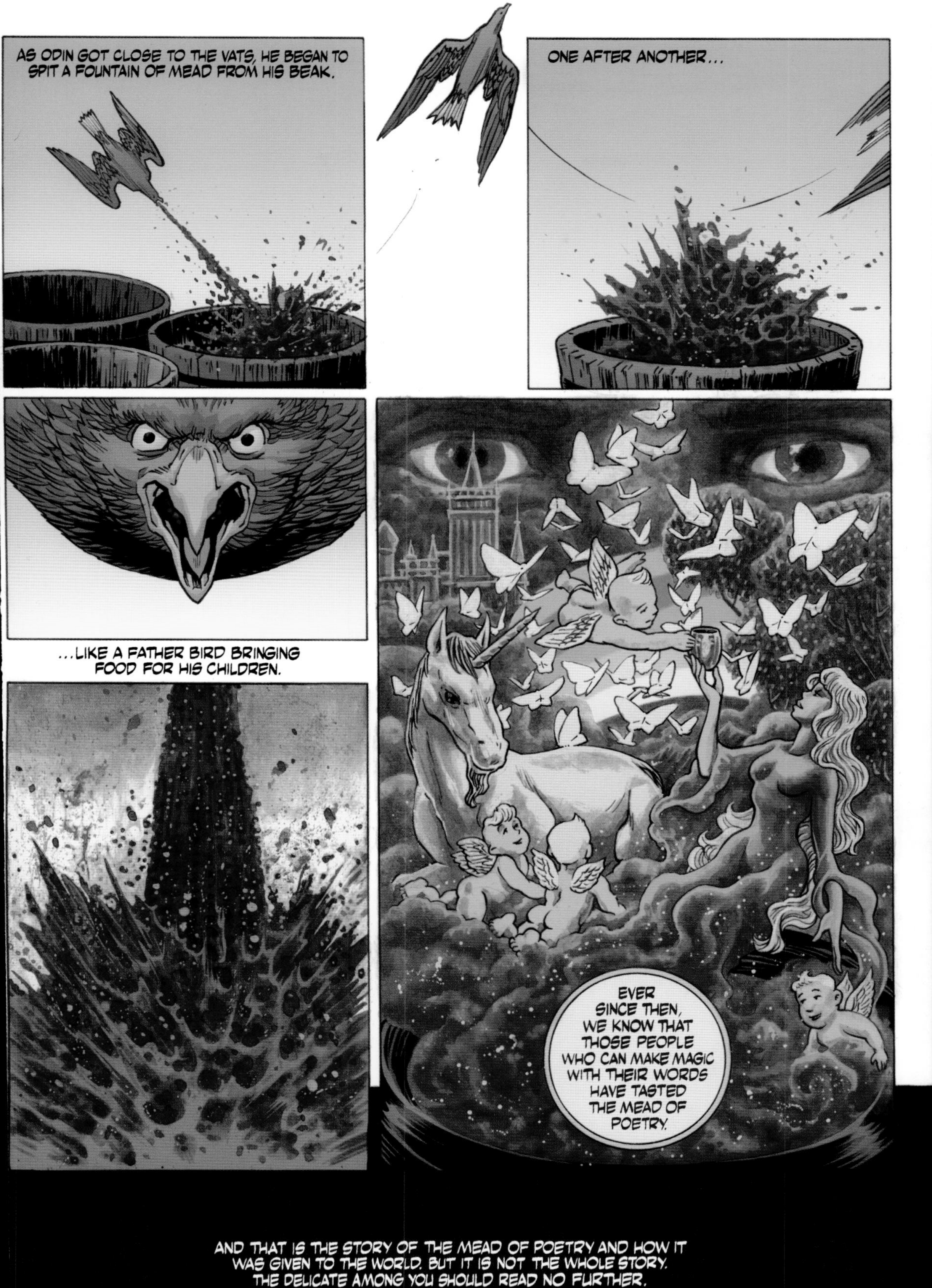
AS ODIN GOT CLOSE TO THE VATS, HE BEGAN TO SPIT A FOUNTAIN OF MEAD FROM HIS BEAK.
ONE AFTER ANOTHER...
...LIKE A FATHER BIRD BRINGING FOOD FOR HIS CHILDREN.
EVER SINCE THEN, WE KNOW THAT THOSE PEOPLE WHO CAN MAKE MAGIC WITH THEIR WORDS HAVE TASTED THE MEAD OF POETRY.
AND THAT IS THE STORY OF THE MEAD OF POETRY AND HOW IT WAS GIVEN TO THE WORLD. BUT IT IS NOT THE WHOLE STORY. THE DELICATE AMONG YOU SHOULD READ NO FURTHER.

HERE IS THE LAST THING, AND A SHAMEFUL ADMISSION IT IS. WHEN THE ALL-FATHER IN EAGLE FORM HAD ALMOST REACHED THE VATS, HE BLEW A SPLATTERY WET FART OF FOUL-SMELLING MEAD RIGHT IN SUTTUNG'S FACE.

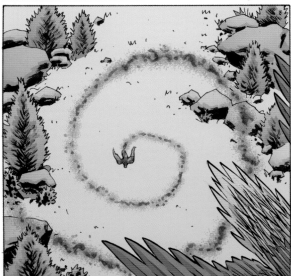

NO ONE, THEN OR NOW, WANTED TO DRINK THE MEAD THAT CAME OUT OF ODIN'S ASS.

BUT WHENEVER YOU HEAR BAD POETS DECLAIMING THEIR BAD POETRY, FILLED WITH FOOLISH SIMILES AND UGLY RHYMES, YOU WILL KNOW WHICH OF THE MEADS THEY HAVE TASTED.

Thor's Journey to the Land of the Giants

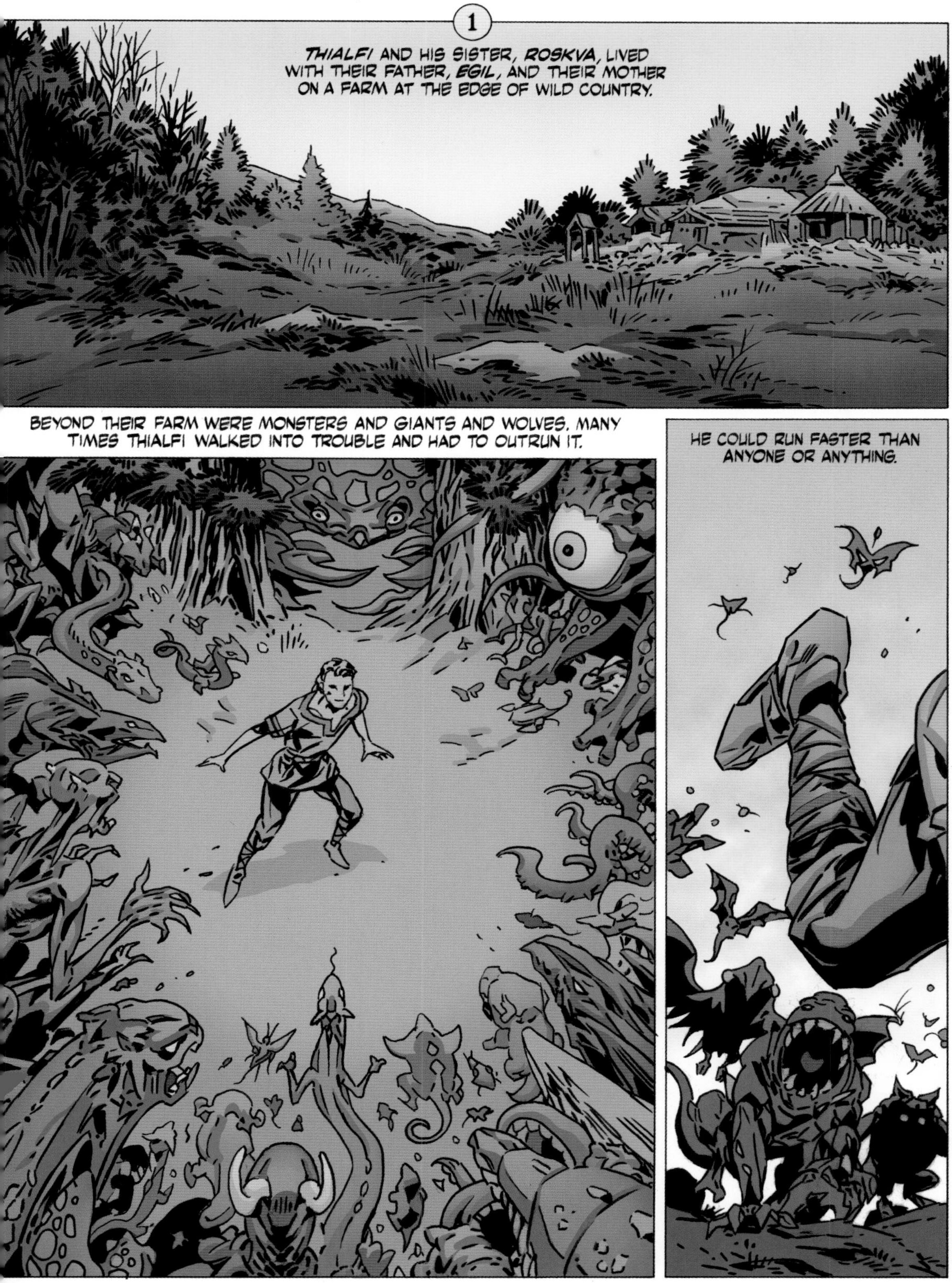
1
THIALFI AND HIS SISTER, ROSKVA, LIVED WITH THEIR FATHER, EGIL, AND THEIR MOTHER ON A FARM AT THE EDGE OF WILD COUNTRY.
BEYOND THEIR FARM WERE MONSTERS AND GIANTS AND WOLVES. MANY TIMES THIALFI WALKED INTO TROUBLE AND HAD TO OUTRUN IT.
HE COULD RUN FASTER THAN ANYONE OR ANYTHING.

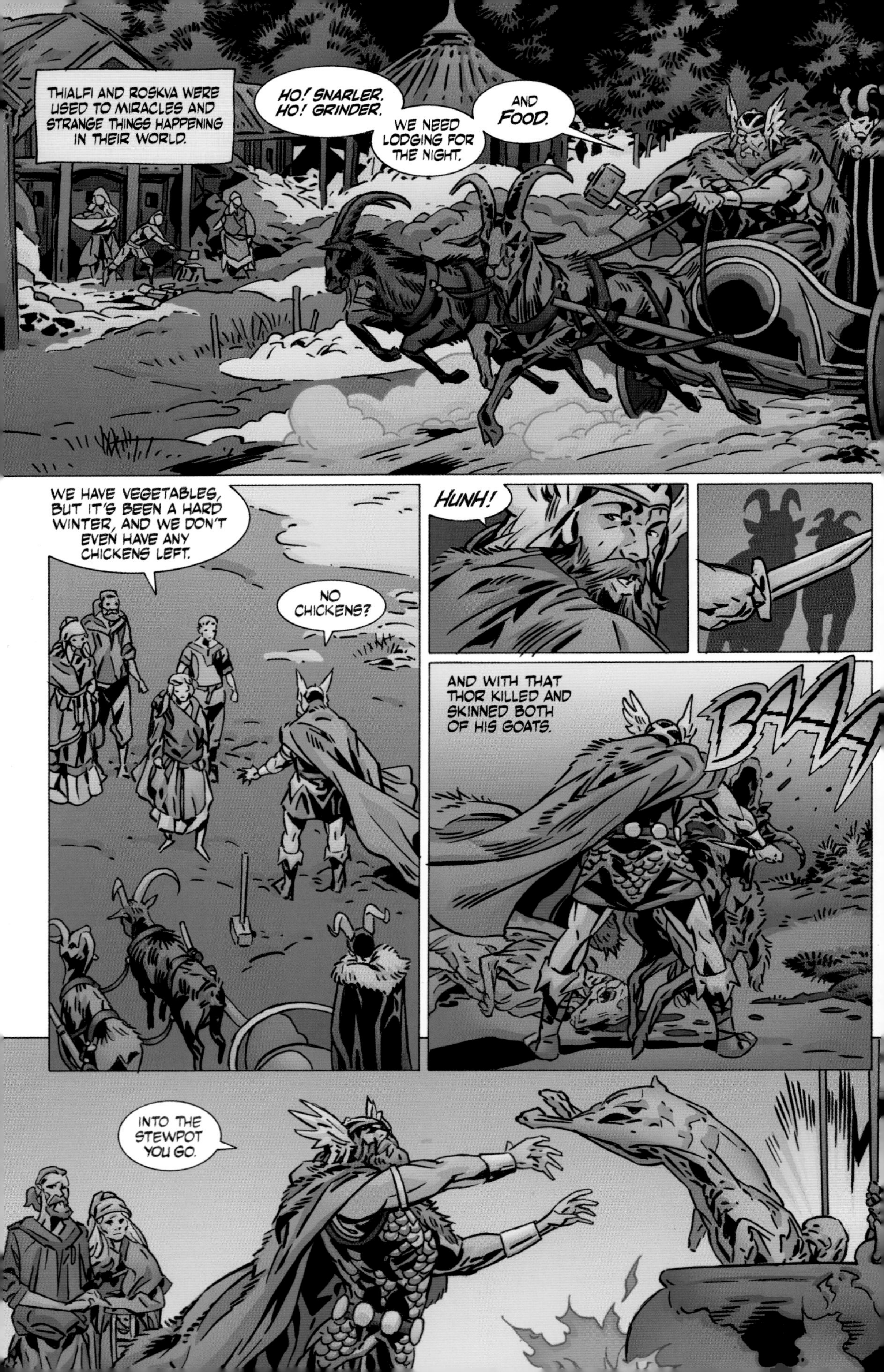
THIALFI AND ROSKVA WERE USED TO MIRACLES AND STRANGE THINGS HAPPENING IN THEIR WORLD.
HO! SNARLER. HO! GRINDER.
WE NEED LODGING FOR THE NIGHT.
AND FOOD.
WE HAVE VEGETABLES, BUT IT'S BEEN A HARD WINTER, AND WE DON'T EVEN HAVE ANY CHICKENS LEFT.
NO CHICKENS?
HUNH!
AND WITH THAT THOR KILLED AND SKINNED BOTH OF HIS GOATS.
BAAA
INTO THE STEWPOT YOU GO.

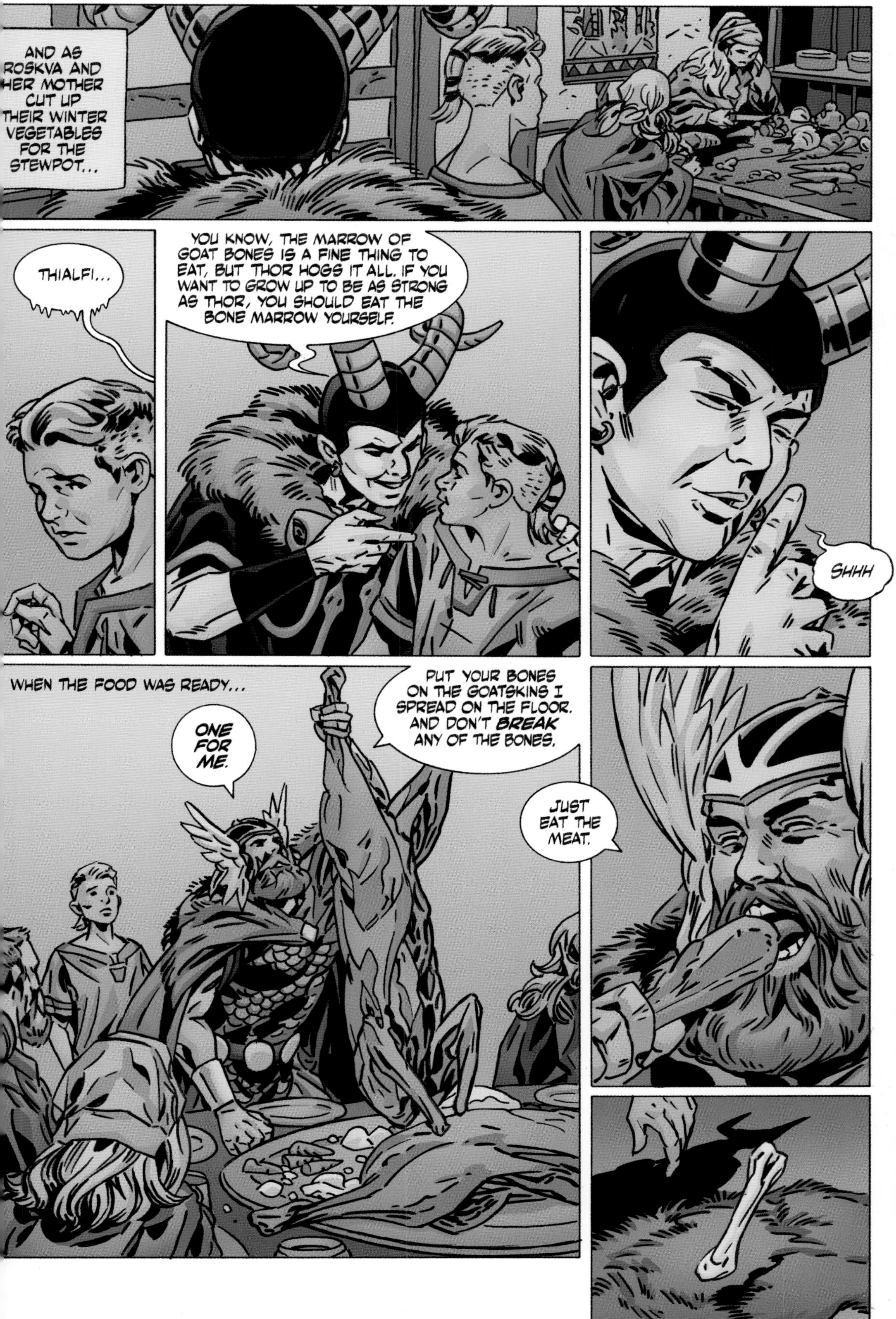
AND AS ROSKVA AND HER MOTHER CUT UP THEIR WINTER VEGETABLES FOR THE STEWPOT...
THIALFI...
YOU KNOW, THE MARROW OF GOAT BONES IS A FINE THING TO EAT, BUT THOR HOGS IT ALL. IF YOU WANT TO GROW UP TO BE AS STRONG AS THOR, YOU SHOULD EAT THE BONE MARROW YOURSELF.
SHHH
WHEN THE FOOD WAS READY...
ONE FOR ME.
PUT YOUR BONES ON THE GOATSKINS I SPREAD ON THE FLOOR. AND DON'T *BREAK* ANY OF THE BONES.
JUST EAT THE MEAT.

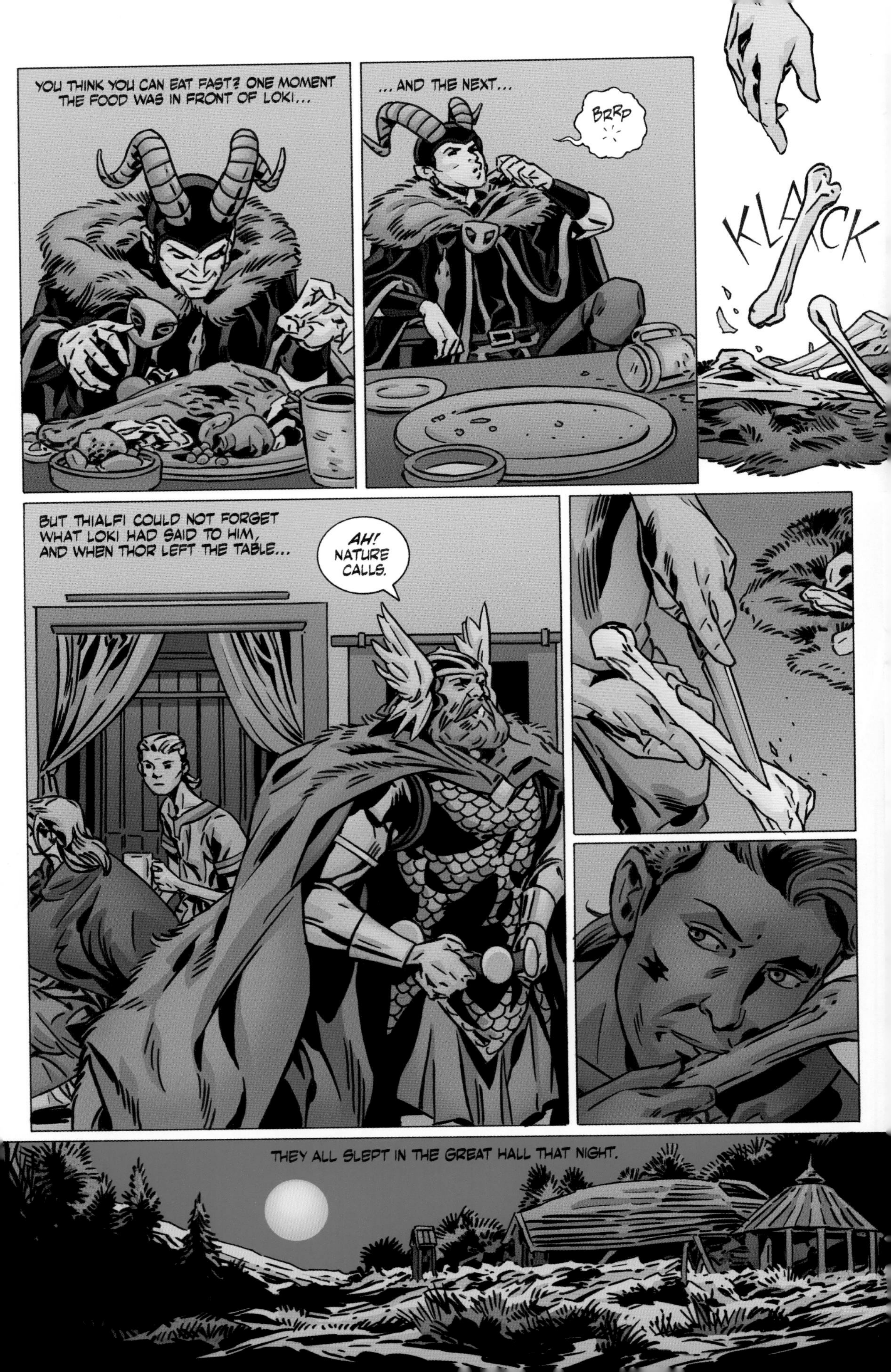
YOU THINK YOU CAN EAT FAST? ONE MOMENT THE FOOD WAS IN FRONT OF LOKI...
...AND THE NEXT...
BRRP
KLACK
BUT THIALFI COULD NOT FORGET WHAT LOKI HAD SAID TO HIM, AND WHEN THOR LEFT THE TABLE...
AH! NATURE CALLS.
THEY ALL SLEPT IN THE GREAT HALL THAT NIGHT.

IN THE MORNING, THOR COVERED THE BONES WITH THE GOATSKINS AND RAISED MJOLLNIR ON HIGH.

SNARLER AND GRINDER, BE WHOLE!

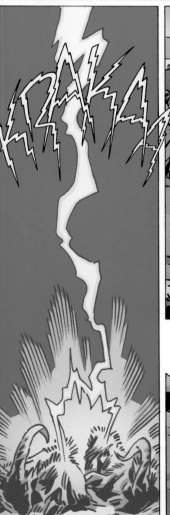

KRAKA

SNARLER STRETCHED ITSELF AND BEGAN TO GRAZE, BUT GRINDER STAGGERED ABOUT AS IF IT WERE IN PAIN.

BAA

BAA

GRINDER'S HIND LEG IS BROKEN. BRING ME WOOD AND CLOTH FOR A SPLINT.

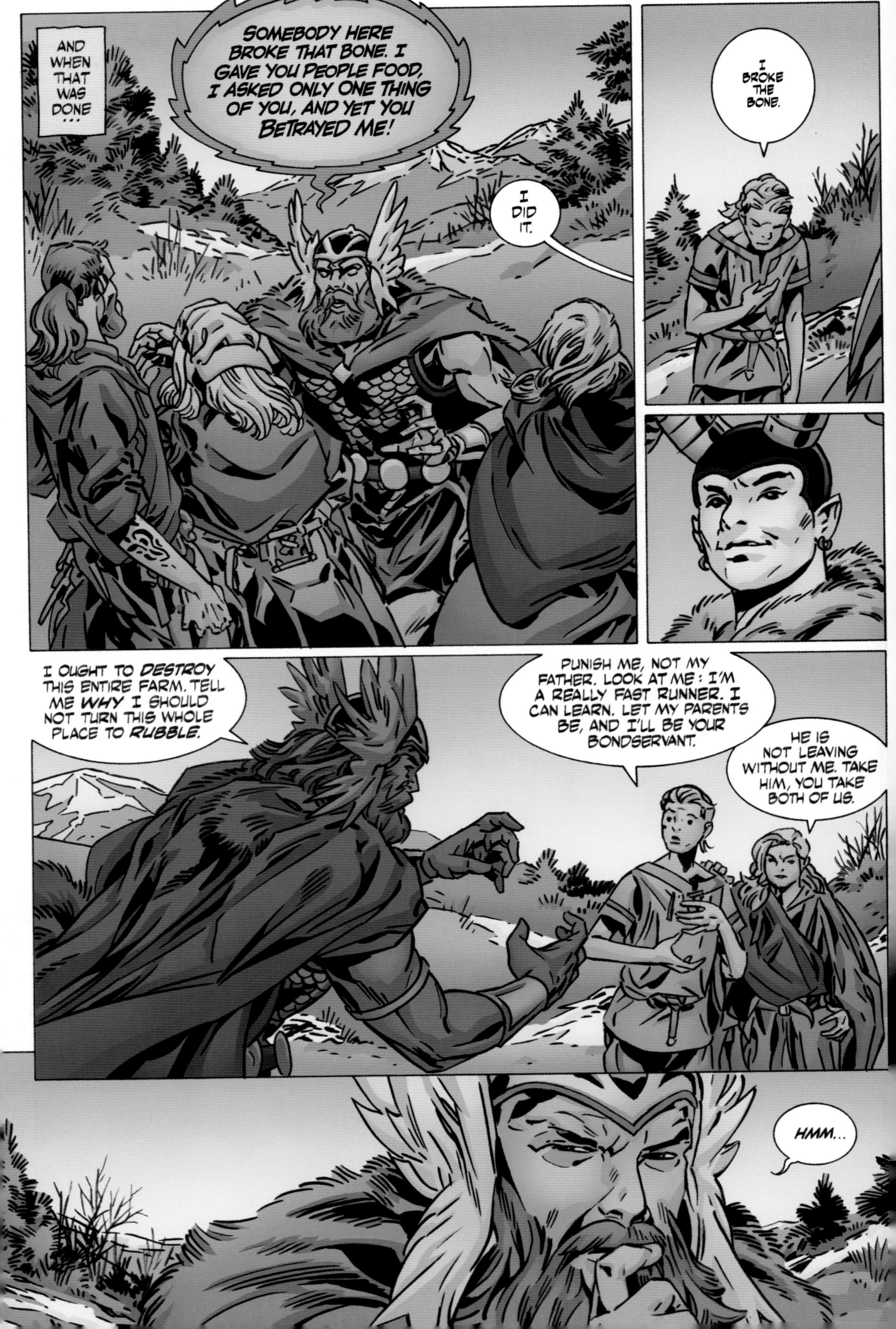
AND WHEN THAT WAS DONE . . .
SOMEBODY HERE BROKE THAT BONE. I GAVE YOU PEOPLE FOOD, I ASKED ONLY ONE THING OF YOU, AND YET YOU BETRAYED ME!
I DID IT.
I BROKE THE BONE.
I OUGHT TO DESTROY THIS ENTIRE FARM. TELL ME WHY I SHOULD NOT TURN THIS WHOLE PLACE TO RUBBLE.
PUNISH ME, NOT MY FATHER. LOOK AT ME : I'M A REALLY FAST RUNNER. I CAN LEARN. LET MY PARENTS BE, AND I'LL BE YOUR BONDSERVANT.
HE IS NOT LEAVING WITHOUT ME. TAKE HIM, YOU TAKE BOTH OF US.
HMM...

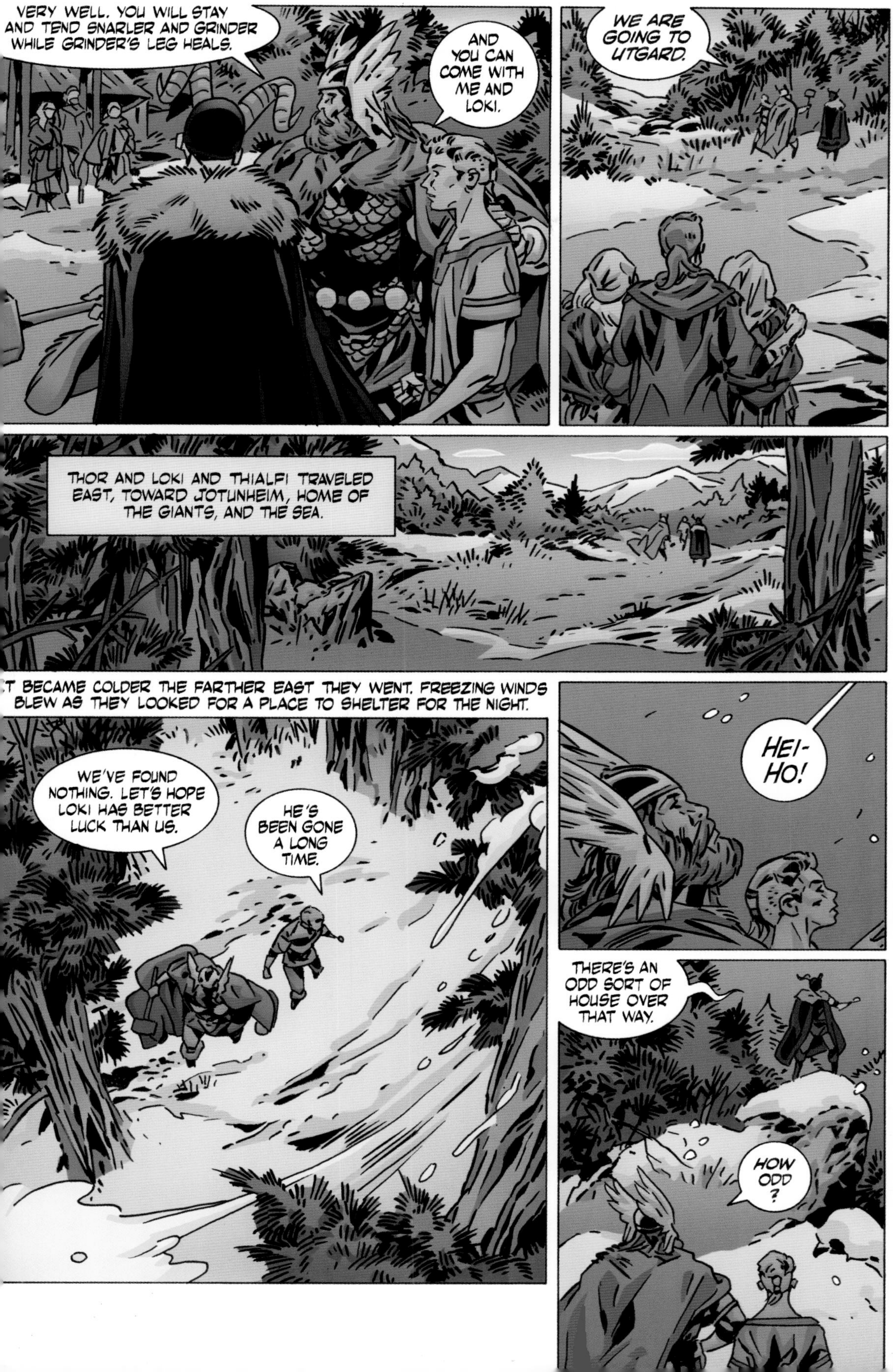

VERY WELL. YOU WILL STAY AND TEND SNARLER AND GRINDER WHILE GRINDER'S LEG HEALS.
AND YOU CAN COME WITH ME AND LOKI.
WE ARE GOING TO UTGARD.
THOR AND LOKI AND THIALFI TRAVELED EAST, TOWARD JOTUNHEIM, HOME OF THE GIANTS, AND THE SEA.
T BECAME COLDER THE FARTHER EAST THEY WENT. FREEZING WINDS BLEW AS THEY LOOKED FOR A PLACE TO SHELTER FOR THE NIGHT.
WE'VE FOUND NOTHING. LET'S HOPE LOKI HAS BETTER LUCK THAN US.
HE'S BEEN GONE A LONG TIME.
HEI-HO!
THERE'S AN ODD SORT OF HOUSE OVER THAT WAY.
HOW ODD?

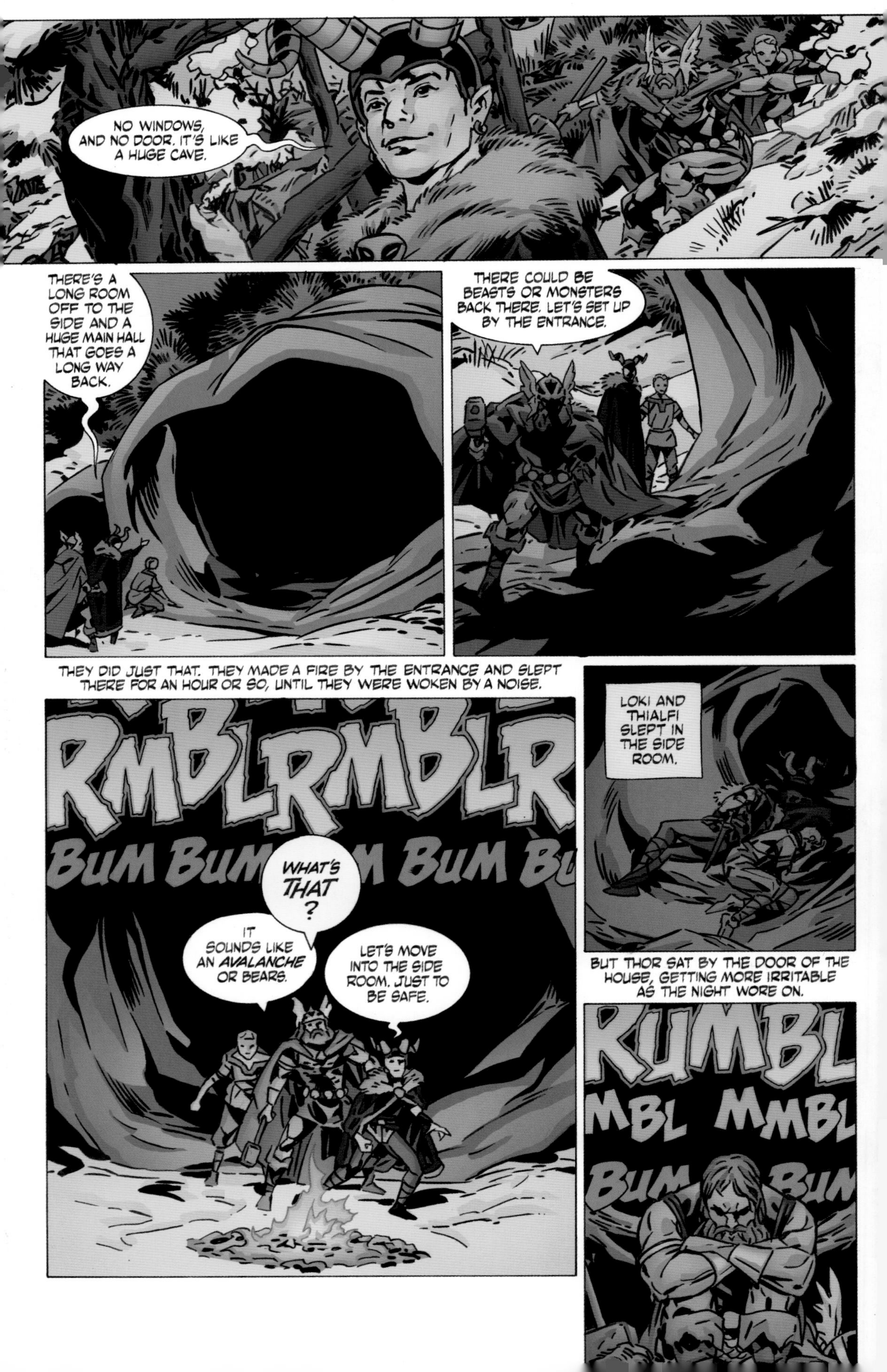

NO WINDOWS, AND NO DOOR. IT'S LIKE A HUGE CAVE.
THERE'S A LONG ROOM OFF TO THE SIDE AND A HUGE MAIN HALL THAT GOES A LONG WAY BACK.
THERE COULD BE BEASTS OR MONSTERS BACK THERE. LET'S SET UP BY THE ENTRANCE.
THEY DID JUST THAT. THEY MADE A FIRE BY THE ENTRANCE AND SLEPT THERE FOR AN HOUR OR SO, UNTIL THEY WERE WOKEN BY A NOISE.
RMBLRMBLR
BUM BUM BUM BUM
WHAT'S THAT?
IT SOUNDS LIKE AN AVALANCHE OR BEARS.
LET'S MOVE INTO THE SIDE ROOM. JUST TO BE SAFE.
LOKI AND THIALFI SLEPT IN THE SIDE ROOM.
BUT THOR SAT BY THE DOOR OF THE HOUSE, GETTING MORE IRRITABLE AS THE NIGHT WORE ON.
RUMBL
MMBL MMBL
BUM BUM

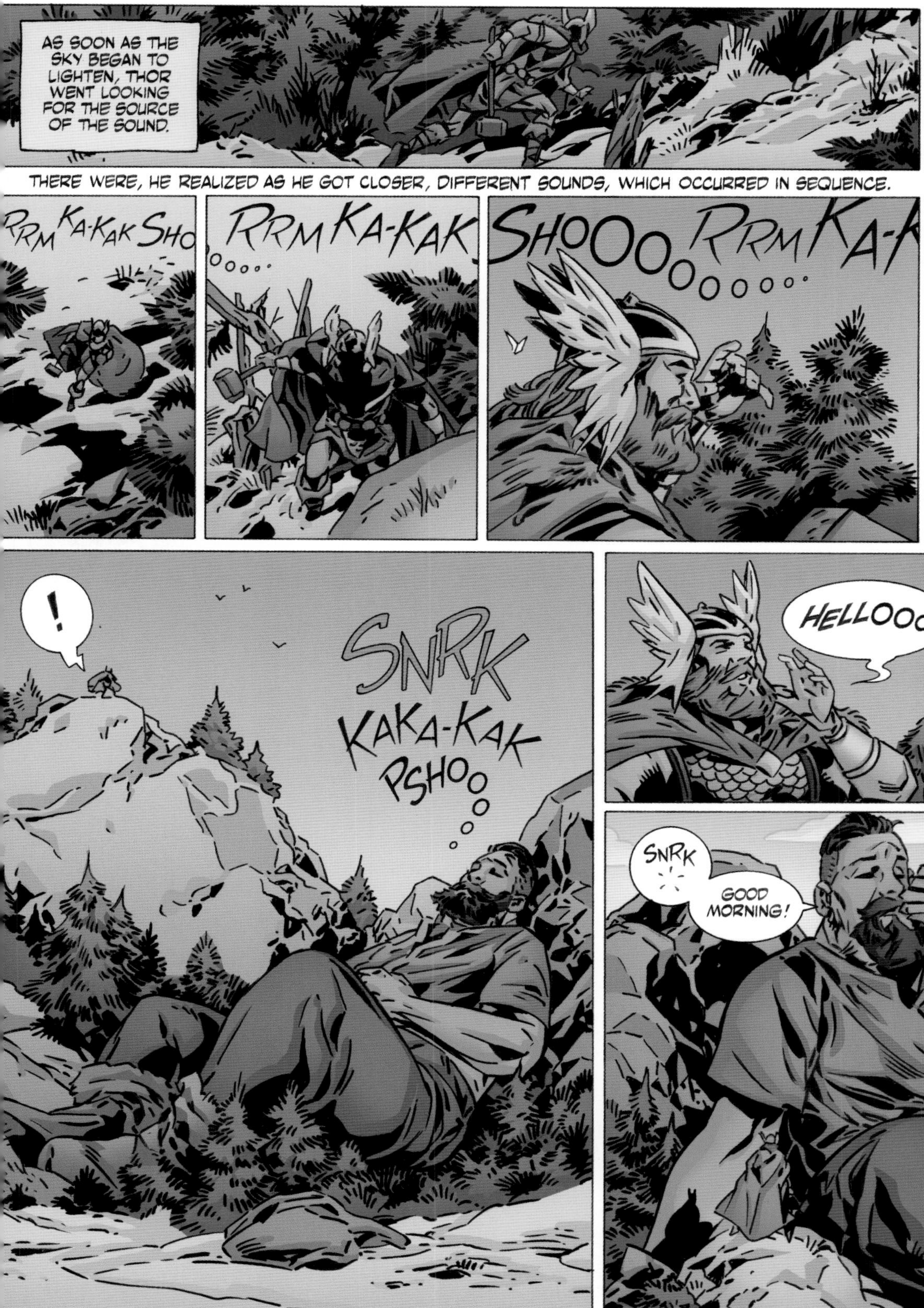
AS SOON AS THE SKY BEGAN TO LIGHTEN, THOR WENT LOOKING FOR THE SOURCE OF THE SOUND.
THERE WERE, HE REALIZED AS HE GOT CLOSER, DIFFERENT SOUNDS, WHICH OCCURRED IN SEQUENCE.
RRM KA-KAK SHO
RRM KA-KAK
ooooo
SHOOOOOOOOOOO RRM KA-K
!
SNRK
KAKA-KAK
PSHOOOO
HELLOOo
SNRK
GOOD MORNING!

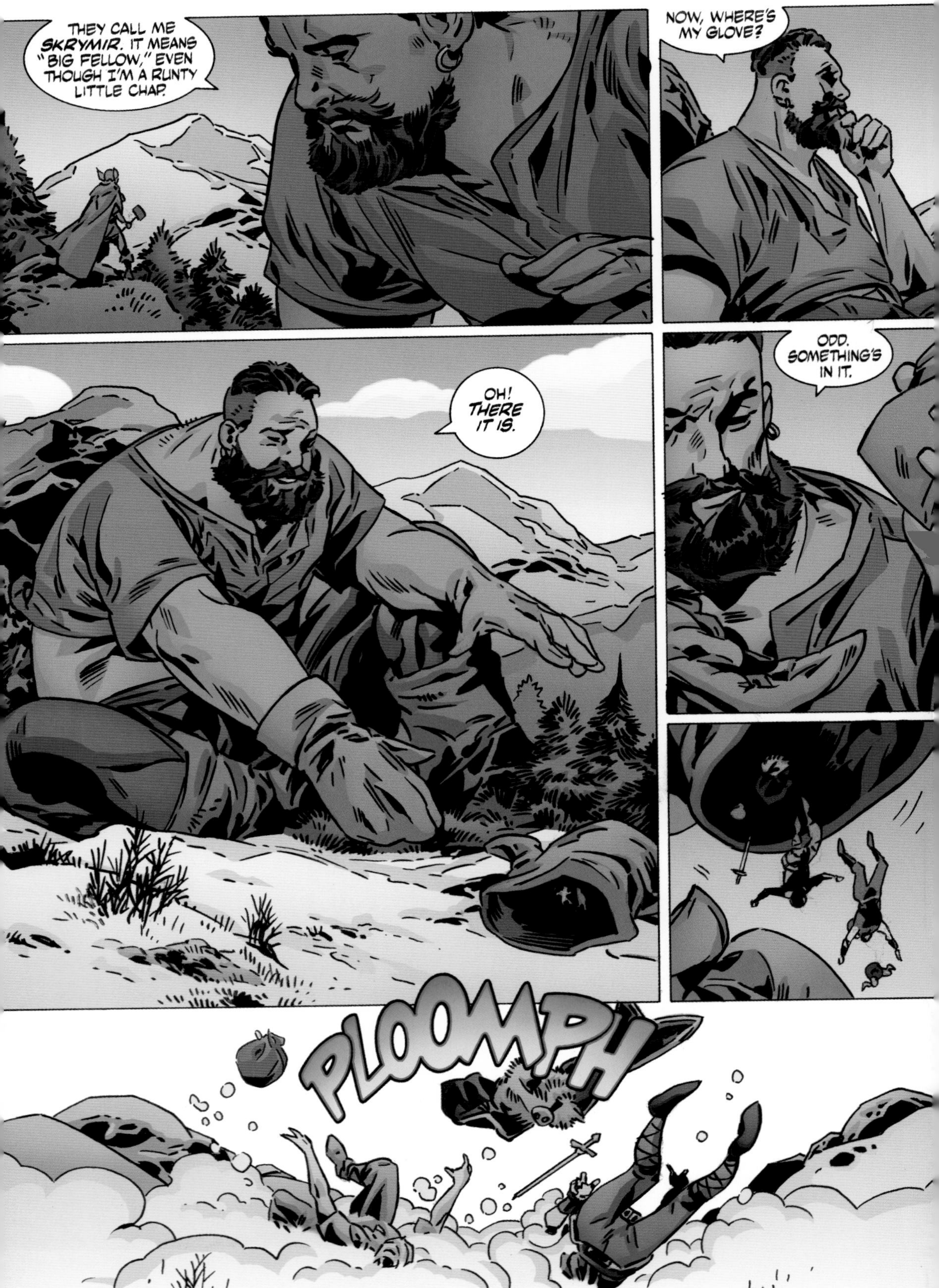
THEY CALL ME SKRYMIR. IT MEANS "BIG FELLOW," EVEN THOUGH I'M A RUNTY LITTLE CHAP.
NOW, WHERE'S MY GLOVE?
OH! THERE IT IS.
ODD. SOMETHING'S IN IT.
PLOOMPH

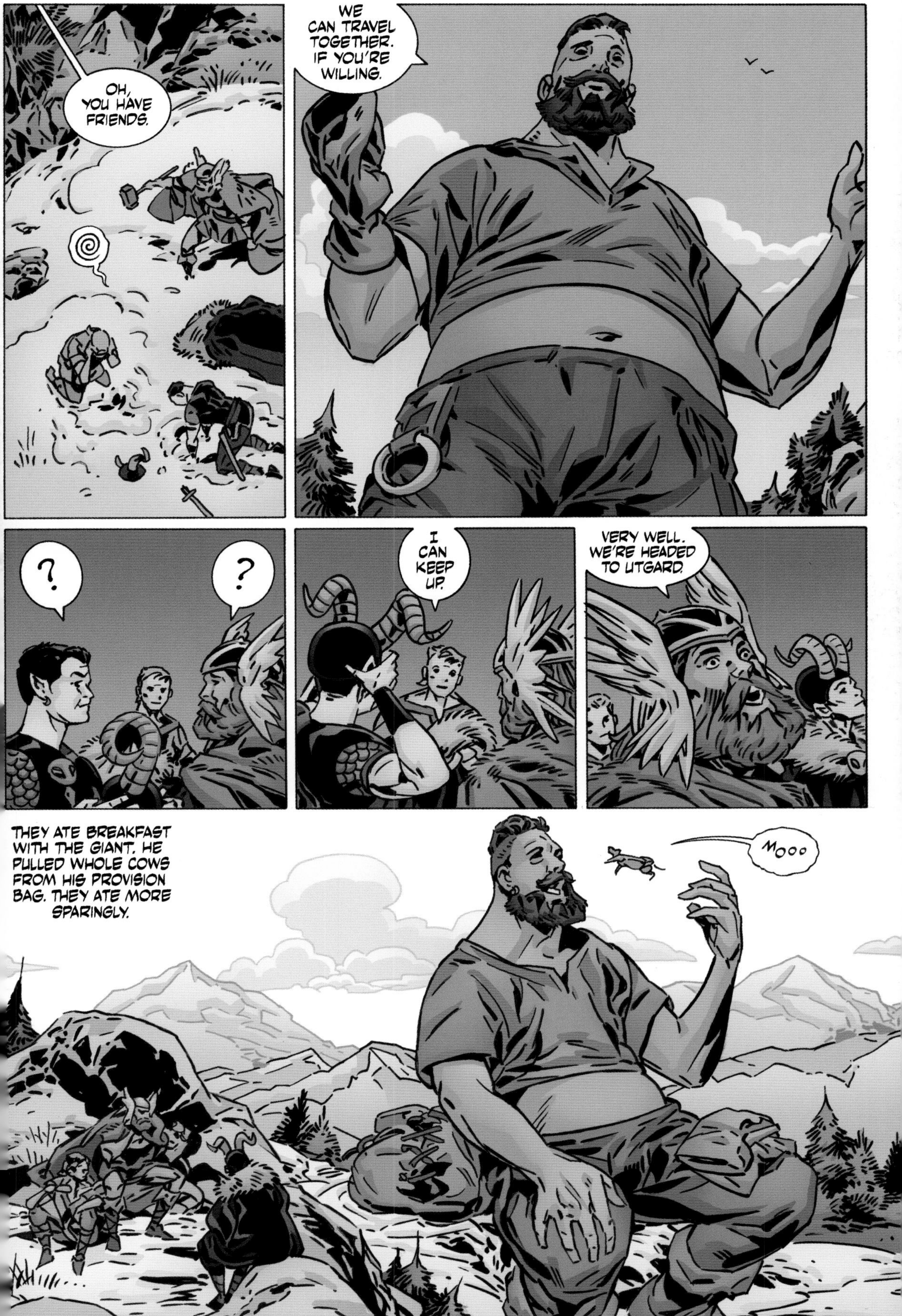
OH, YOU HAVE FRIENDS.
WE CAN TRAVEL TOGETHER. IF YOU'RE WILLING.
?
?
I CAN KEEP UP.
VERY WELL. WE'RE HEADED TO UTGARD.
THEY ATE BREAKFAST WITH THE GIANT. HE PULLED WHOLE COWS FROM HIS PROVISION BAG. THEY ATE MORE SPARINGLY.
MOOO

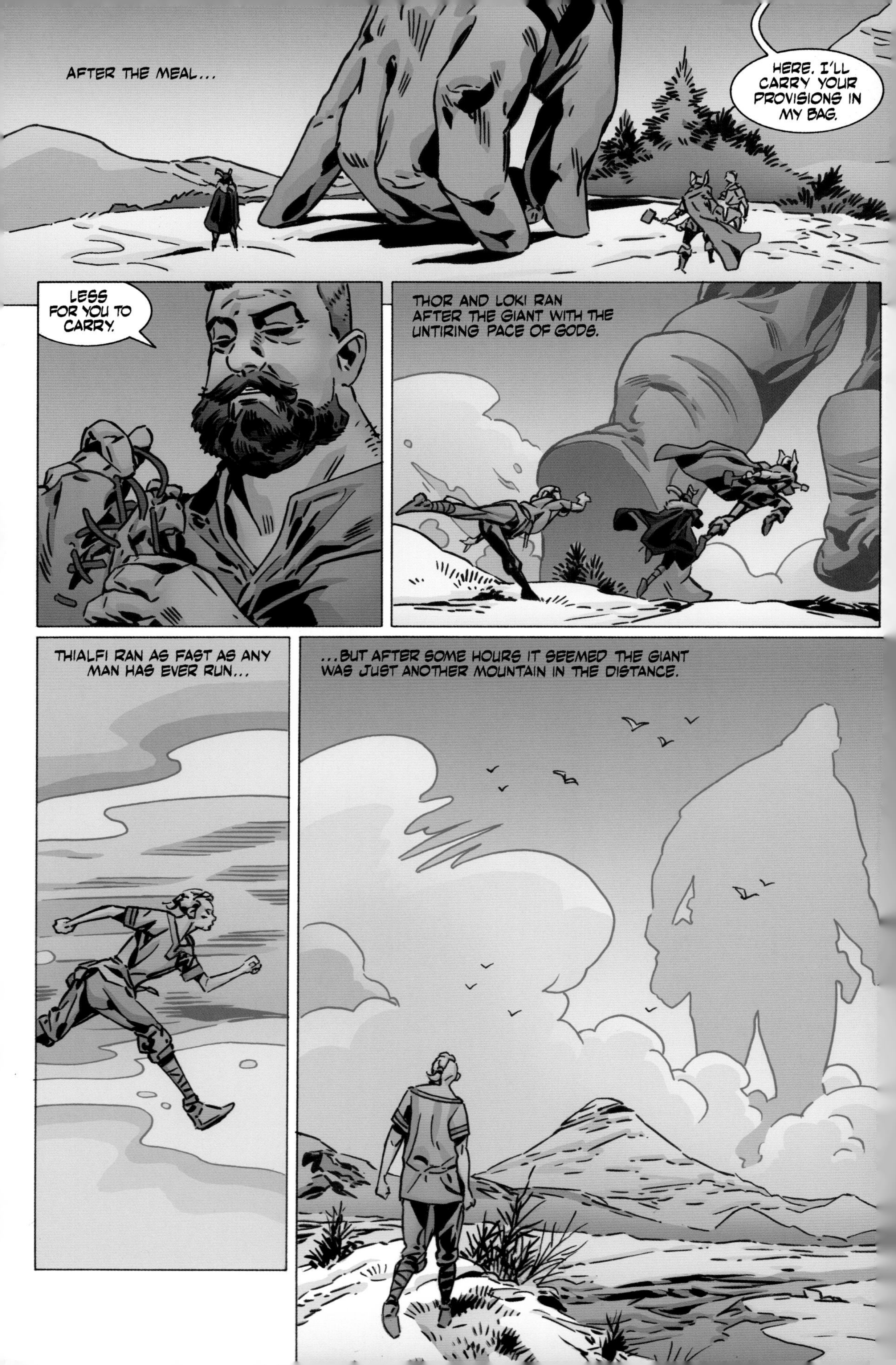
AFTER THE MEAL...
HERE. I'LL CARRY YOUR PROVISIONS IN MY BAG.
LESS FOR YOU TO CARRY.
THOR AND LOKI RAN AFTER THE GIANT WITH THE UNTIRING PACE OF GODS.
THIALFI RAN AS FAST AS ANY MAN HAS EVER RUN...
...BUT AFTER SOME HOURS IT SEEMED THE GIANT WAS JUST ANOTHER MOUNTAIN IN THE DISTANCE.

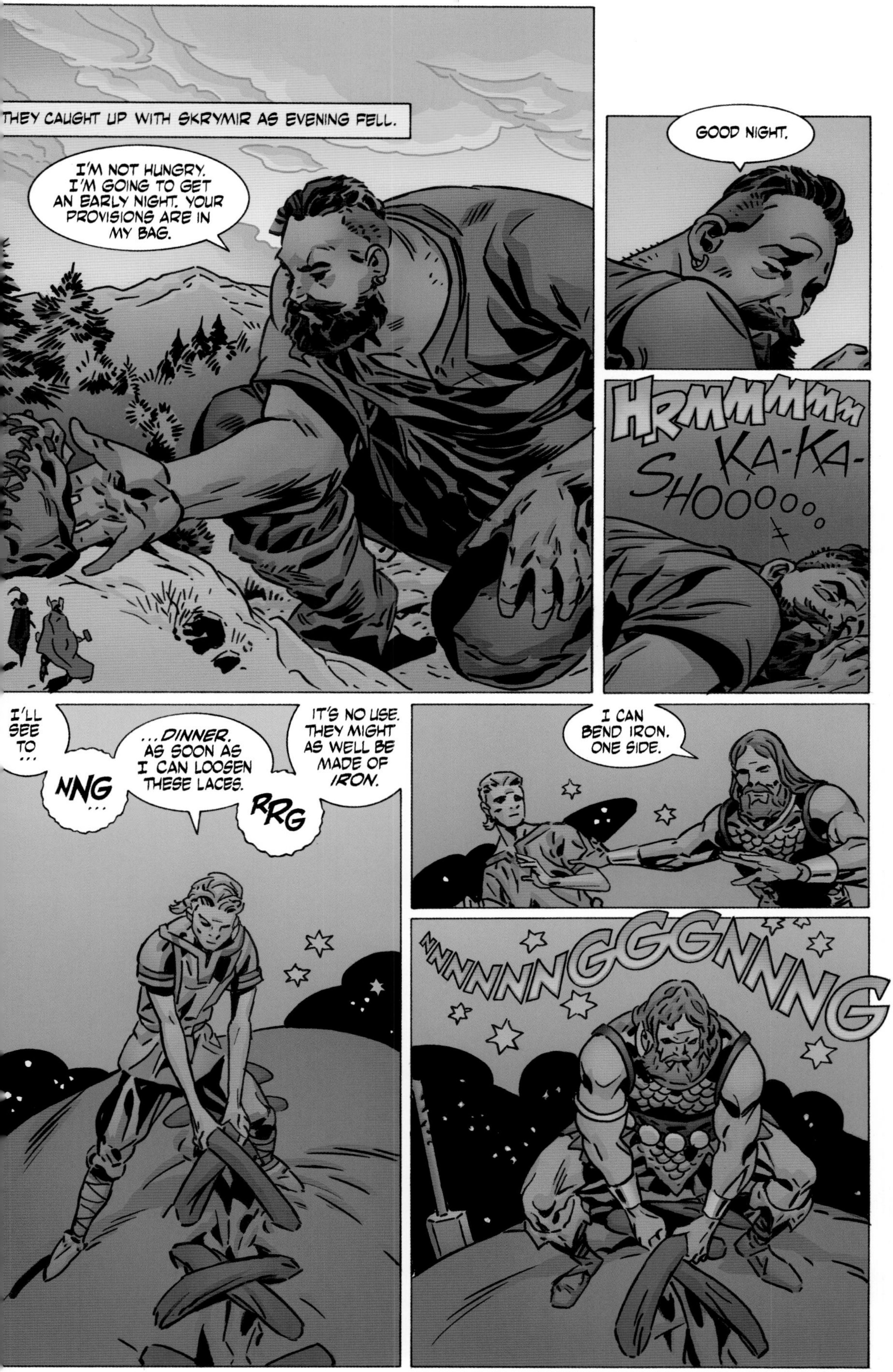
THEY CAUGHT UP WITH SKRYMIR AS EVENING FELL.
I'M NOT HUNGRY. I'M GOING TO GET AN EARLY NIGHT. YOUR PROVISIONS ARE IN MY BAG.
GOOD NIGHT.
HRMMMMMM
KA-KA-
SHOOOOOO
I'LL SEE TO...
NNG...
...DINNER. AS SOON AS I CAN LOOSEN THESE LACES.
RRG
IT'S NO USE. THEY MIGHT AS WELL BE MADE OF IRON.
I CAN BEND IRON. ONE SIDE.
NNNNNNGGGGNNNG

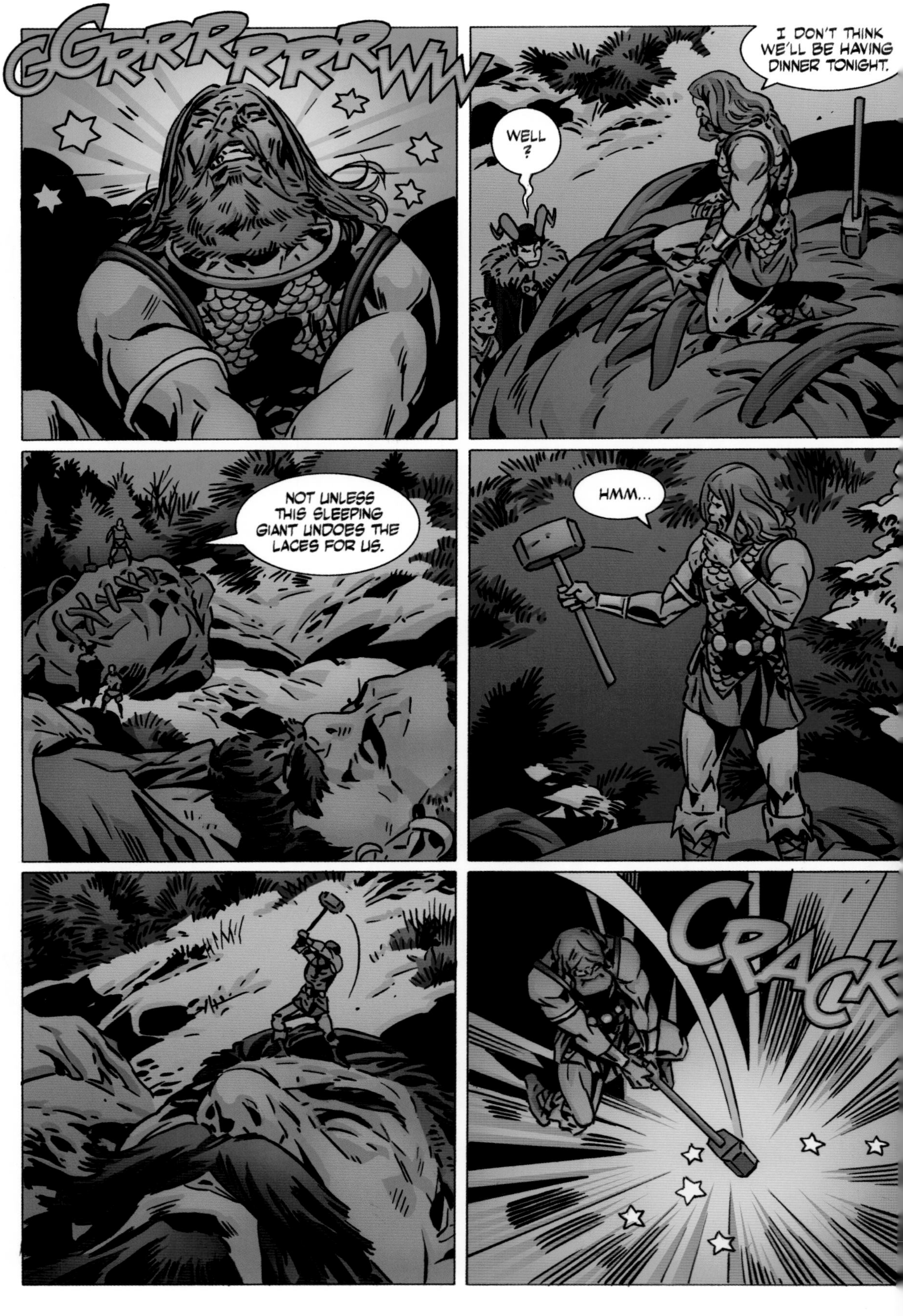
GGRRRRRRRWW
I DON'T THINK WE'LL BE HAVING DINNER TONIGHT.
WELL?
NOT UNLESS THIS SLEEPING GIANT UNDOES THE LACES FOR US.
HMM...
CRACK

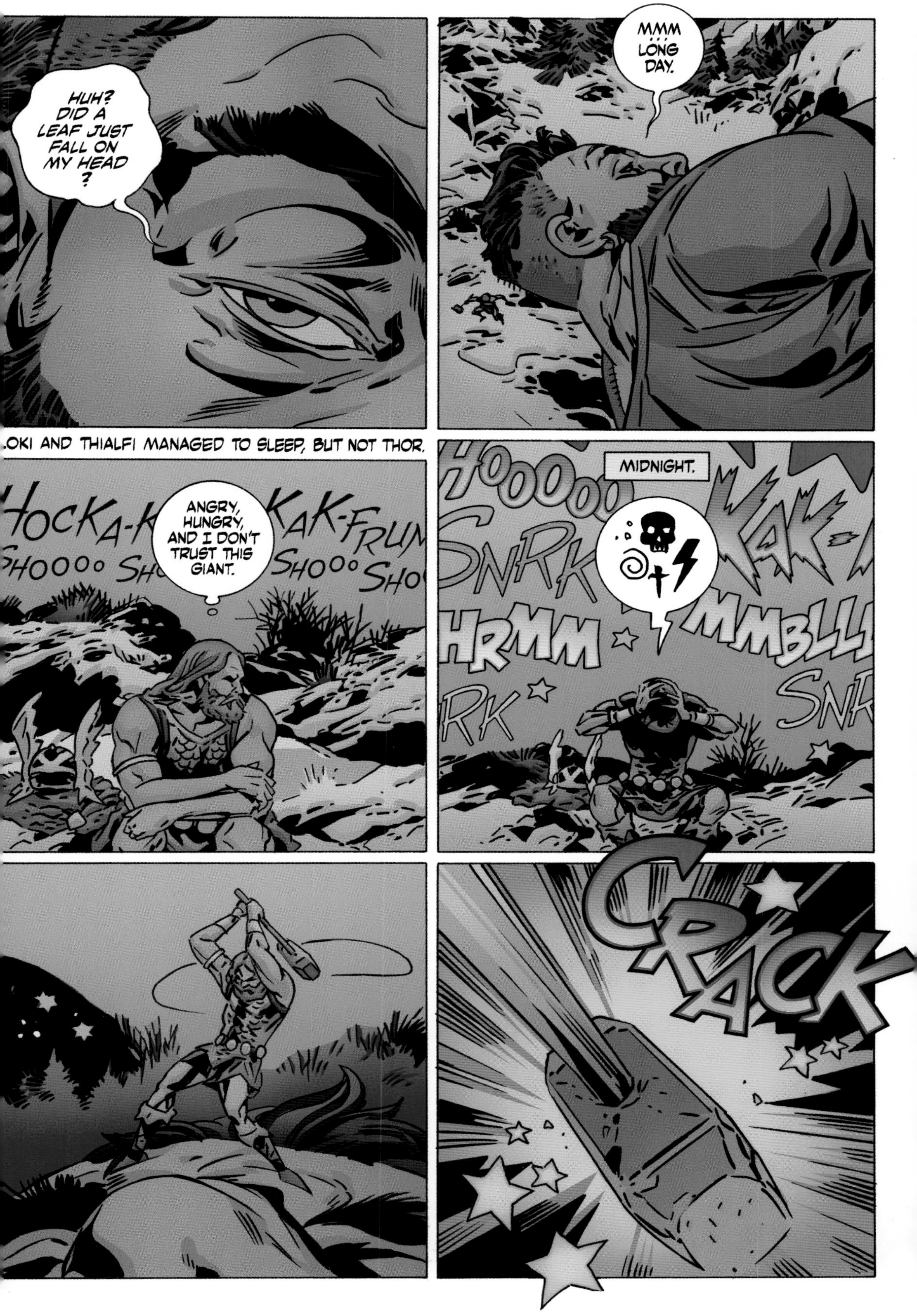
HUH? DID A LEAF JUST FALL ON MY HEAD ?
MMM ... LONG DAY.
LOKI AND THIALFI MANAGED TO SLEEP, BUT NOT THOR.
HOCKA-K KAK-FRUM
SHOOOO SHO SHOOO SHO
ANGRY, HUNGRY, AND I DON'T TRUST THIS GIANT.
MIDNIGHT.
HOOOOO
SNRK
KAK-
HRMM
MMBLL
RK
SNR
CRACK

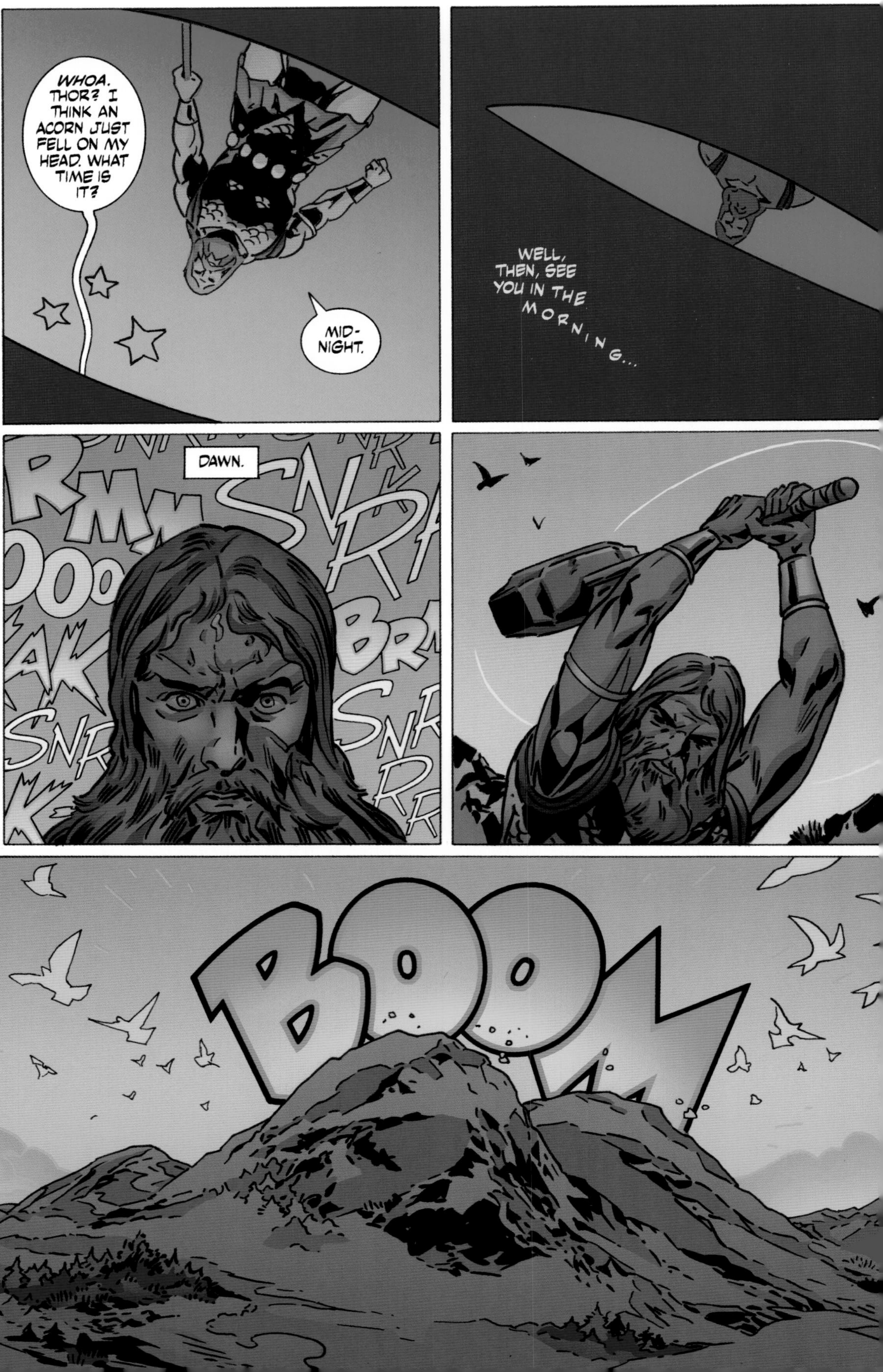
WHOA. THOR? I THINK AN ACORN JUST FELL ON MY HEAD. WHAT TIME IS IT?
MID-NIGHT.
WELL, THEN, SEE YOU IN THE MORNING...
DAWN.
BOOM

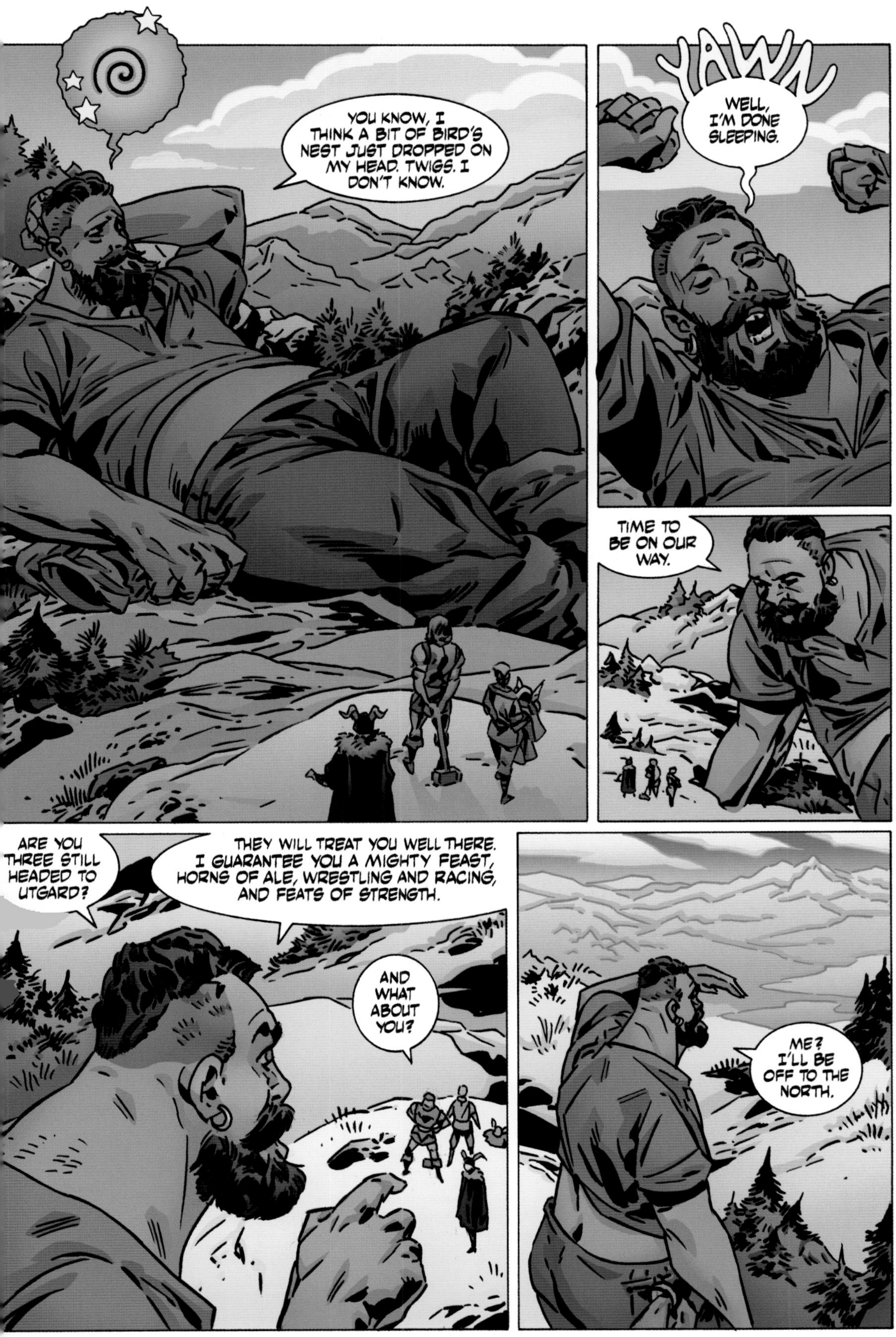
YOU KNOW, I THINK A BIT OF BIRD'S NEST JUST DROPPED ON MY HEAD. TWIGS. I DON'T KNOW.
YAWN
WELL, I'M DONE SLEEPING.
TIME TO BE ON OUR WAY.
ARE YOU THREE STILL HEADED TO UTGARD?
THEY WILL TREAT YOU WELL THERE. I GUARANTEE YOU A MIGHTY FEAST, HORNS OF ALE, WRESTLING AND RACING, AND FEATS OF STRENGTH.
AND WHAT ABOUT YOU?
ME? I'LL BE OFF TO THE NORTH.

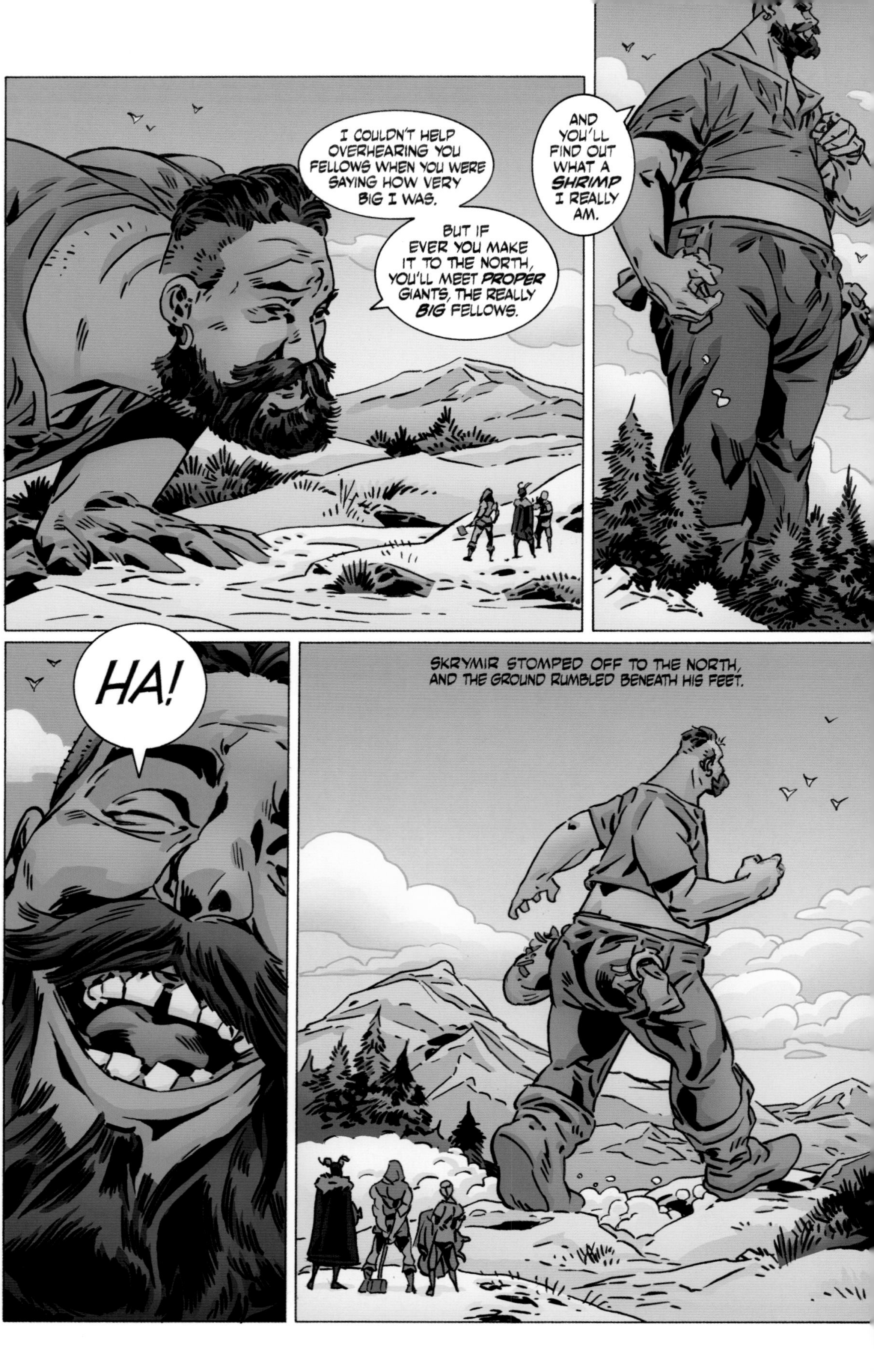
I COULDN'T HELP OVERHEARING YOU FELLOWS WHEN YOU WERE SAYING HOW VERY BIG I WAS.
BUT IF EVER YOU MAKE IT TO THE NORTH, YOU'LL MEET *PROPER* GIANTS, THE REALLY *BIG* FELLOWS.
AND YOU'LL FIND OUT WHAT A *SHRIMP* I REALLY AM.
HA!
SKRYMIR STOMPED OFF TO THE NORTH, AND THE GROUND RUMBLED BENEATH HIS FEET.

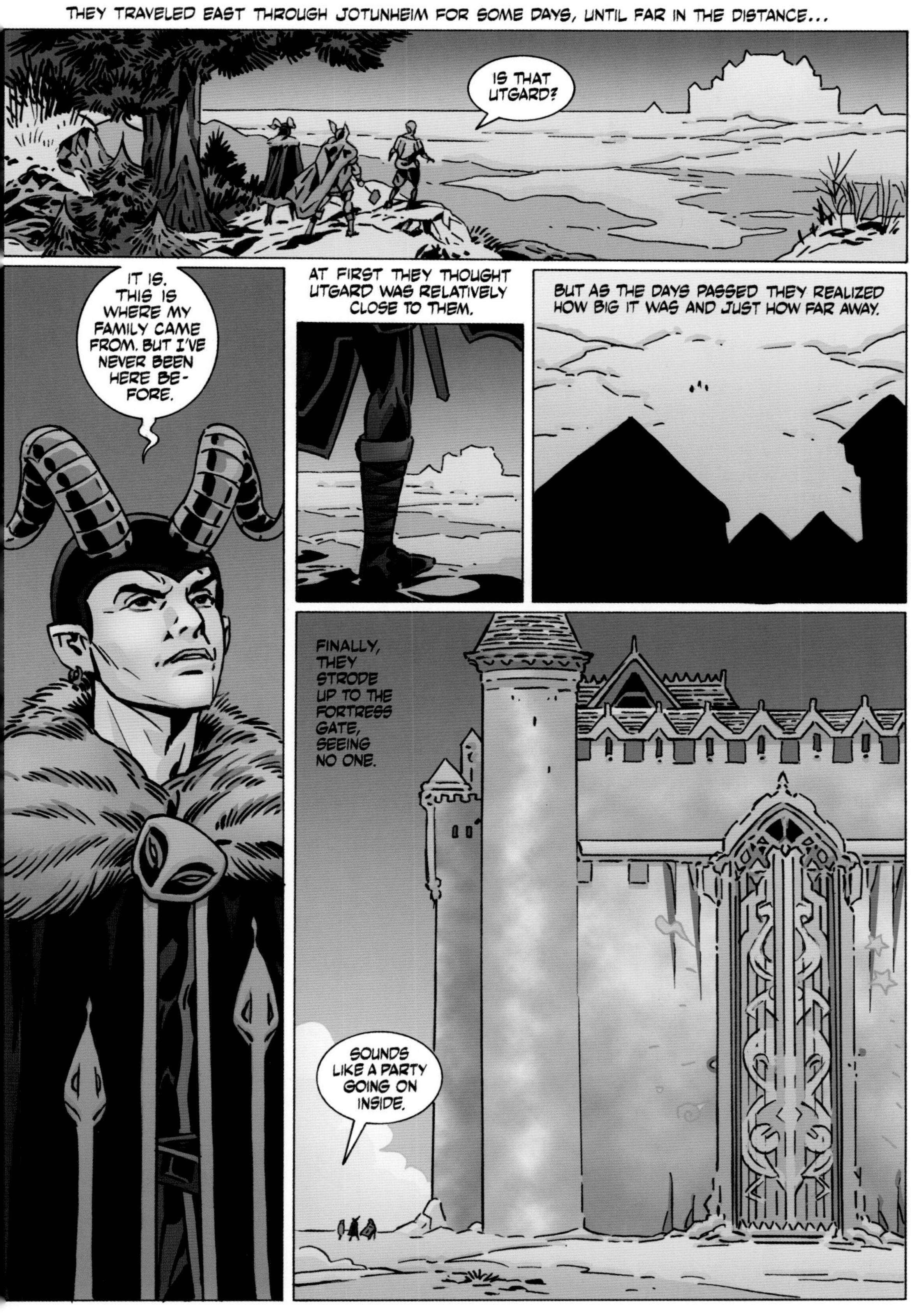
THEY TRAVELED EAST THROUGH JOTUNHEIM FOR SOME DAYS, UNTIL FAR IN THE DISTANCE...
IS THAT UTGARD?
IT IS. THIS IS WHERE MY FAMILY CAME FROM. BUT I'VE NEVER BEEN HERE BE-FORE.
AT FIRST THEY THOUGHT UTGARD WAS RELATIVELY CLOSE TO THEM.
BUT AS THE DAYS PASSED THEY REALIZED HOW BIG IT WAS AND JUST HOW FAR AWAY.
FINALLY, THEY STRODE UP TO THE FORTRESS GATE, SEEING NO ONE.
SOUNDS LIKE A PARTY GOING ON INSIDE.

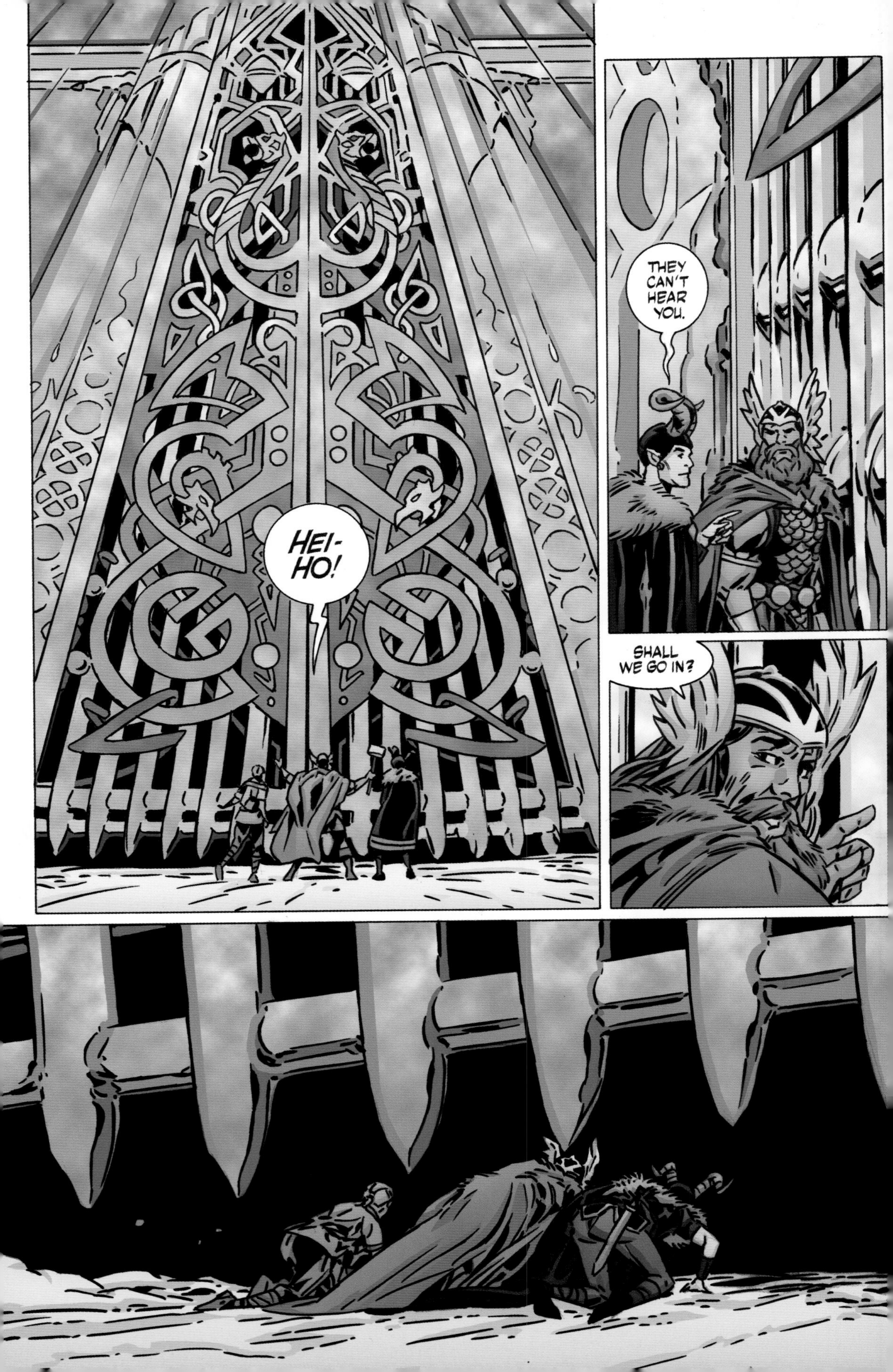
HEI-HO!
THEY CAN'T HEAR YOU.
SHALL WE GO IN?

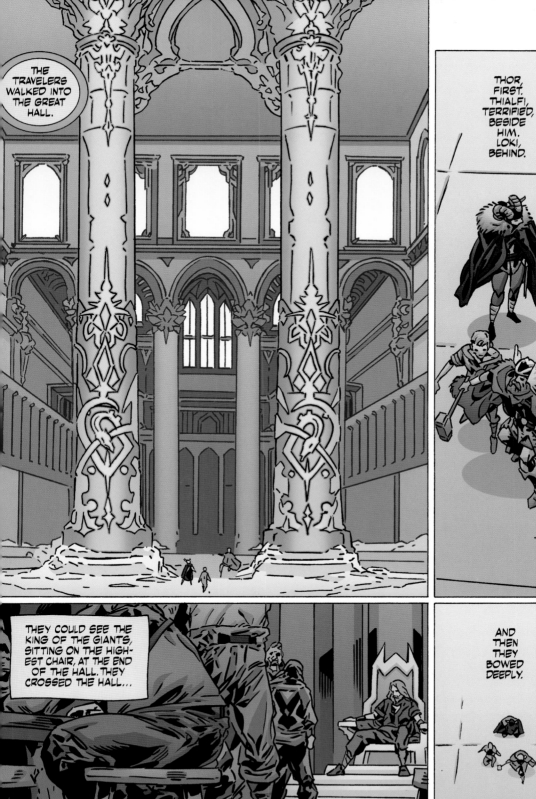

THE TRAVELERS WALKED INTO THE GREAT HALL.

THEY COULD SEE THE KING OF THE GIANTS, SITTING ON THE HIGHEST CHAIR, AT THE END OF THE HALL. THEY CROSSED THE HALL...

THOR, FIRST. THIALFI, TERRIFIED, BESIDE HIM. LOKI, BEHIND.

AND THEN THEY BOWED DEEPLY.

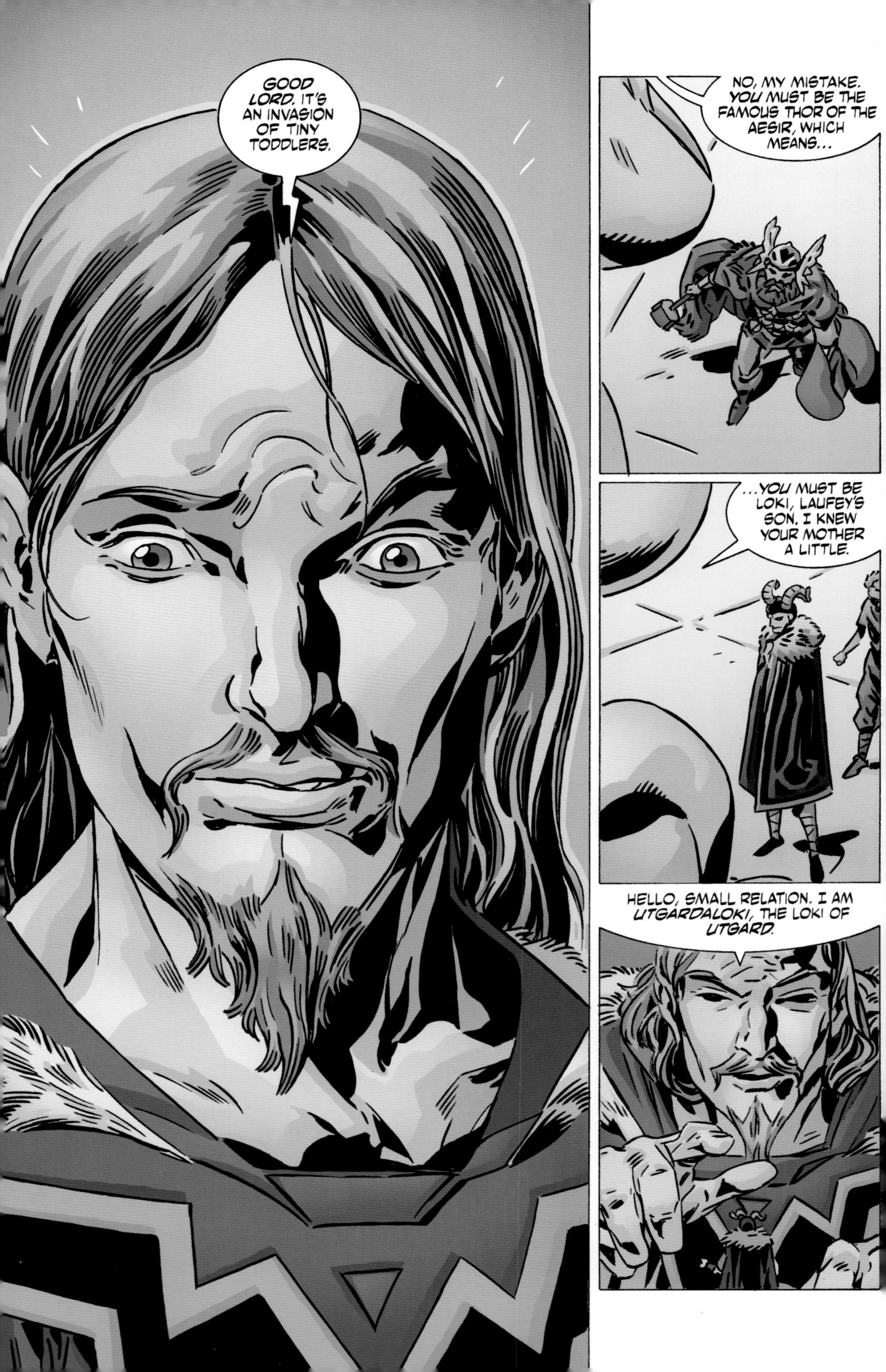
GOOD LORD. IT'S AN INVASION OF TINY TODDLERS.
NO, MY MISTAKE. YOU MUST BE THE FAMOUS THOR OF THE AESIR, WHICH MEANS...
...YOU MUST BE LOKI, LAUFEY'S SON. I KNEW YOUR MOTHER A LITTLE.
HELLO, SMALL RELATION. I AM UTGARDALOKI, THE LOKI OF UTGARD.

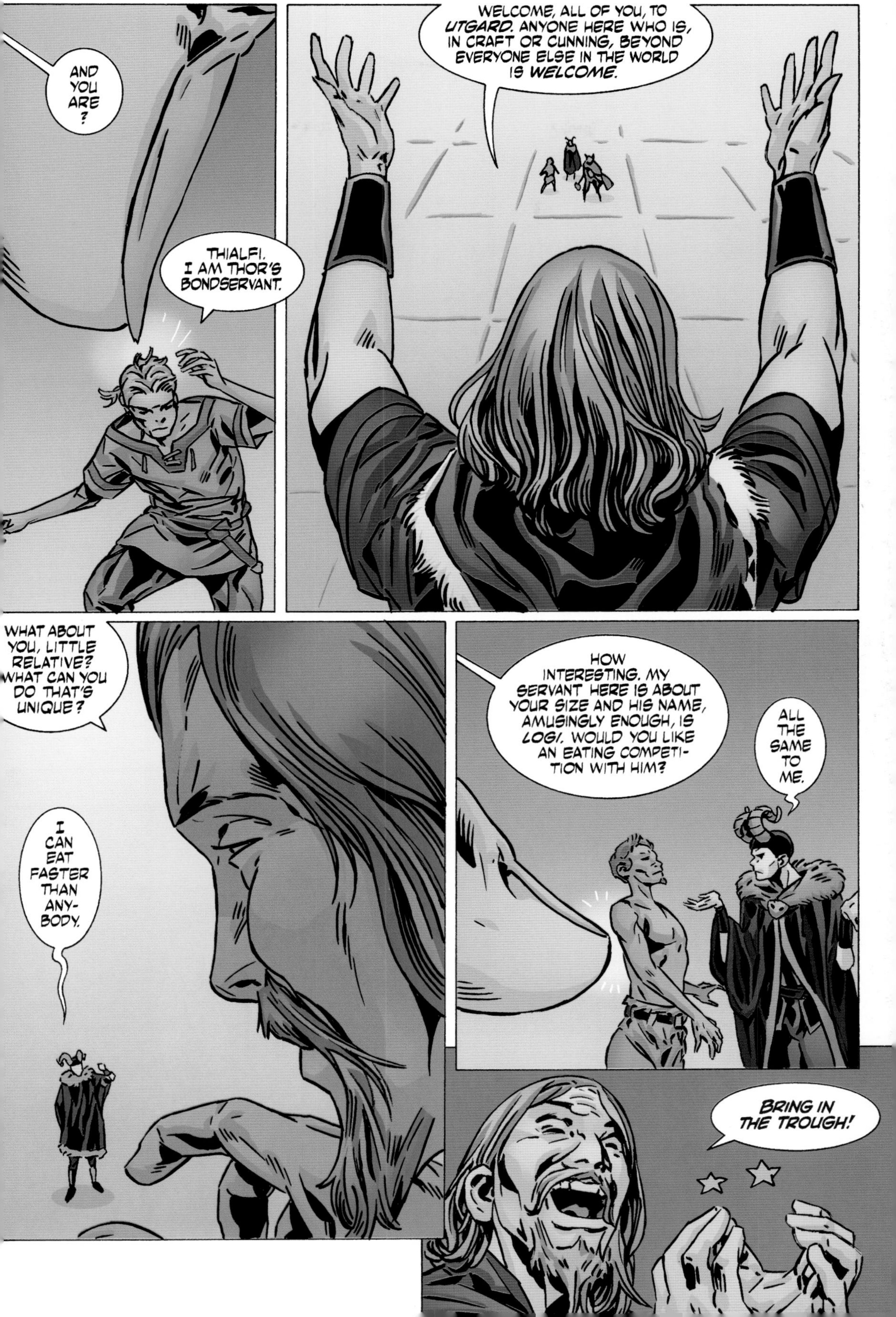
AND YOU ARE ?
THIALFI. I AM THOR'S BONDSERVANT.
WELCOME, ALL OF YOU, TO UTGARD. ANYONE HERE WHO IS, IN CRAFT OR CUNNING, BEYOND EVERYONE ELSE IN THE WORLD IS WELCOME.
WHAT ABOUT YOU, LITTLE RELATIVE? WHAT CAN YOU DO THAT'S UNIQUE?
I CAN EAT FASTER THAN ANY-BODY.
HOW INTERESTING. MY SERVANT HERE IS ABOUT YOUR SIZE AND HIS NAME, AMUSINGLY ENOUGH, IS LOGI. WOULD YOU LIKE AN EATING COMPETI-TION WITH HIM?
ALL THE SAME TO ME.
BRING IN THE TROUGH!

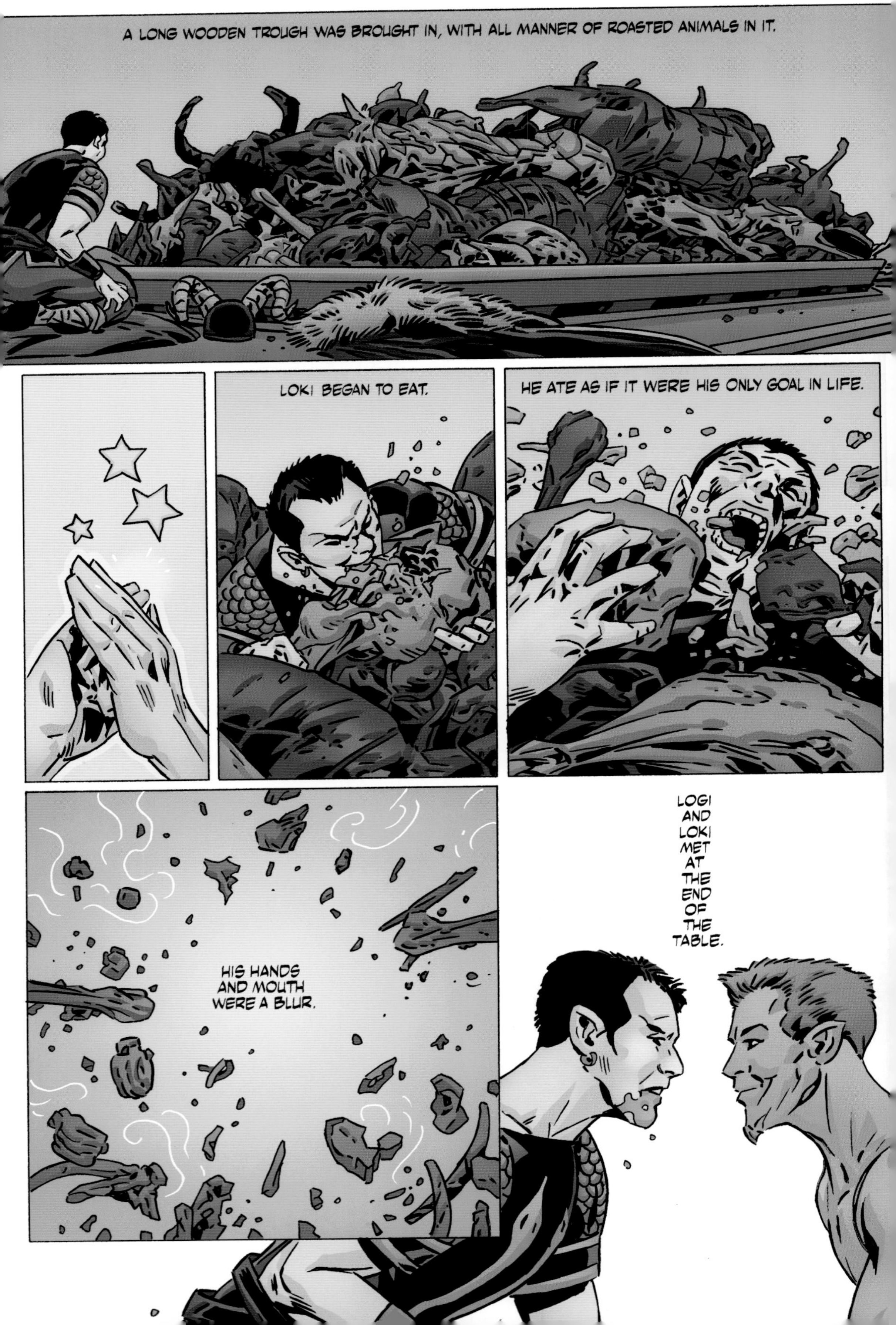
A LONG WOODEN TROUGH WAS BROUGHT IN, WITH ALL MANNER OF ROASTED ANIMALS IN IT.
LOKI BEGAN TO EAT.
HE ATE AS IF IT WERE HIS ONLY GOAL IN LIFE.
HIS HANDS AND MOUTH WERE A BLUR.
LOGI AND LOKI MET AT THE END OF THE TABLE.

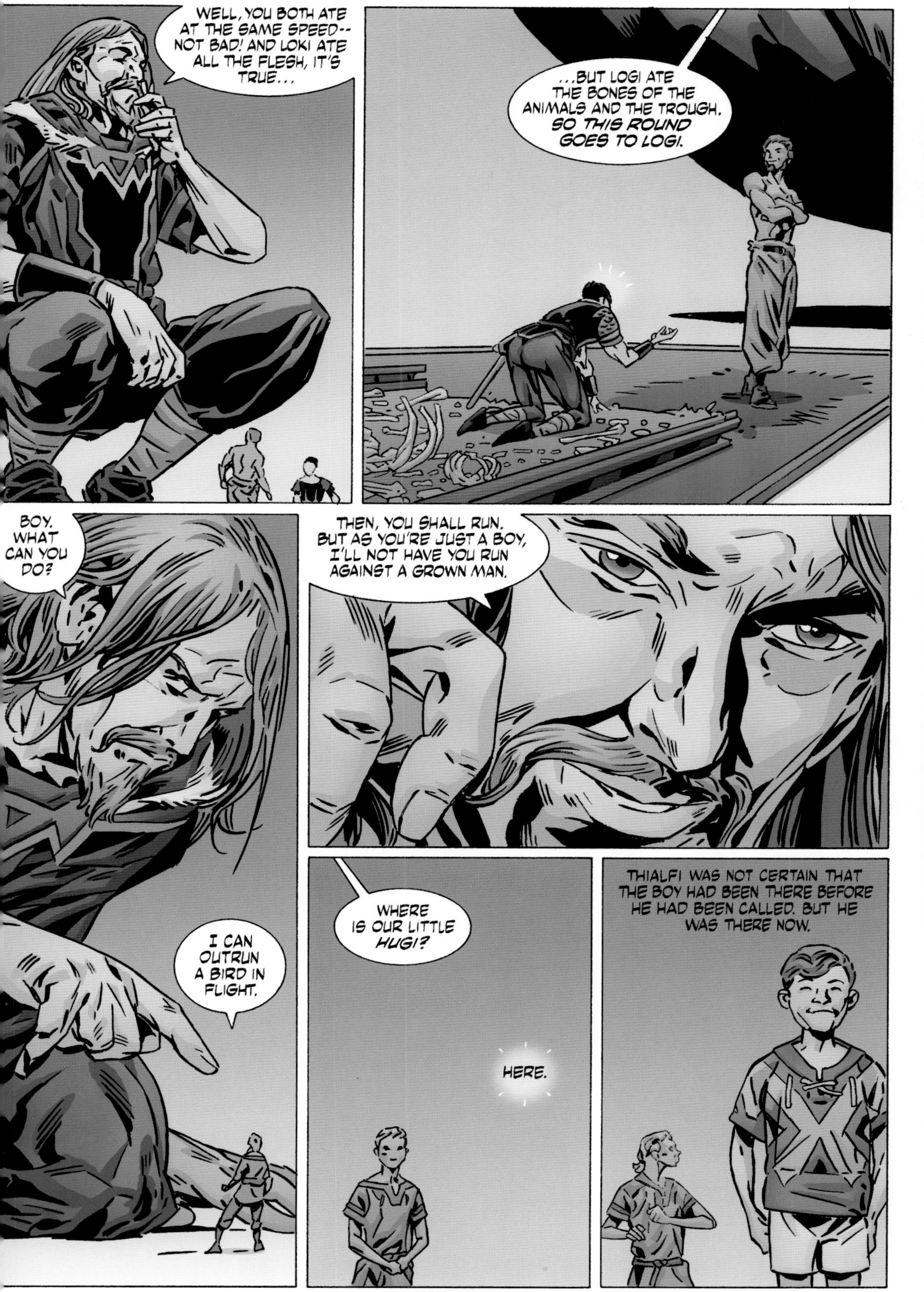
WELL, YOU BOTH ATE AT THE SAME SPEED-- NOT BAD! AND LOKI ATE ALL THE FLESH, IT'S TRUE...
...BUT LOGI ATE THE BONES OF THE ANIMALS AND THE TROUGH. SO THIS ROUND GOES TO LOGI.
BOY. WHAT CAN YOU DO?
I CAN OUTRUN A BIRD IN FLIGHT.
THEN, YOU SHALL RUN. BUT AS YOU'RE JUST A BOY, I'LL NOT HAVE YOU RUN AGAINST A GROWN MAN.
WHERE IS OUR LITTLE HUGI?
HERE.
THIALFI WAS NOT CERTAIN THAT THE BOY HAD BEEN THERE BEFORE HE HAD BEEN CALLED. BUT HE WAS THERE NOW.

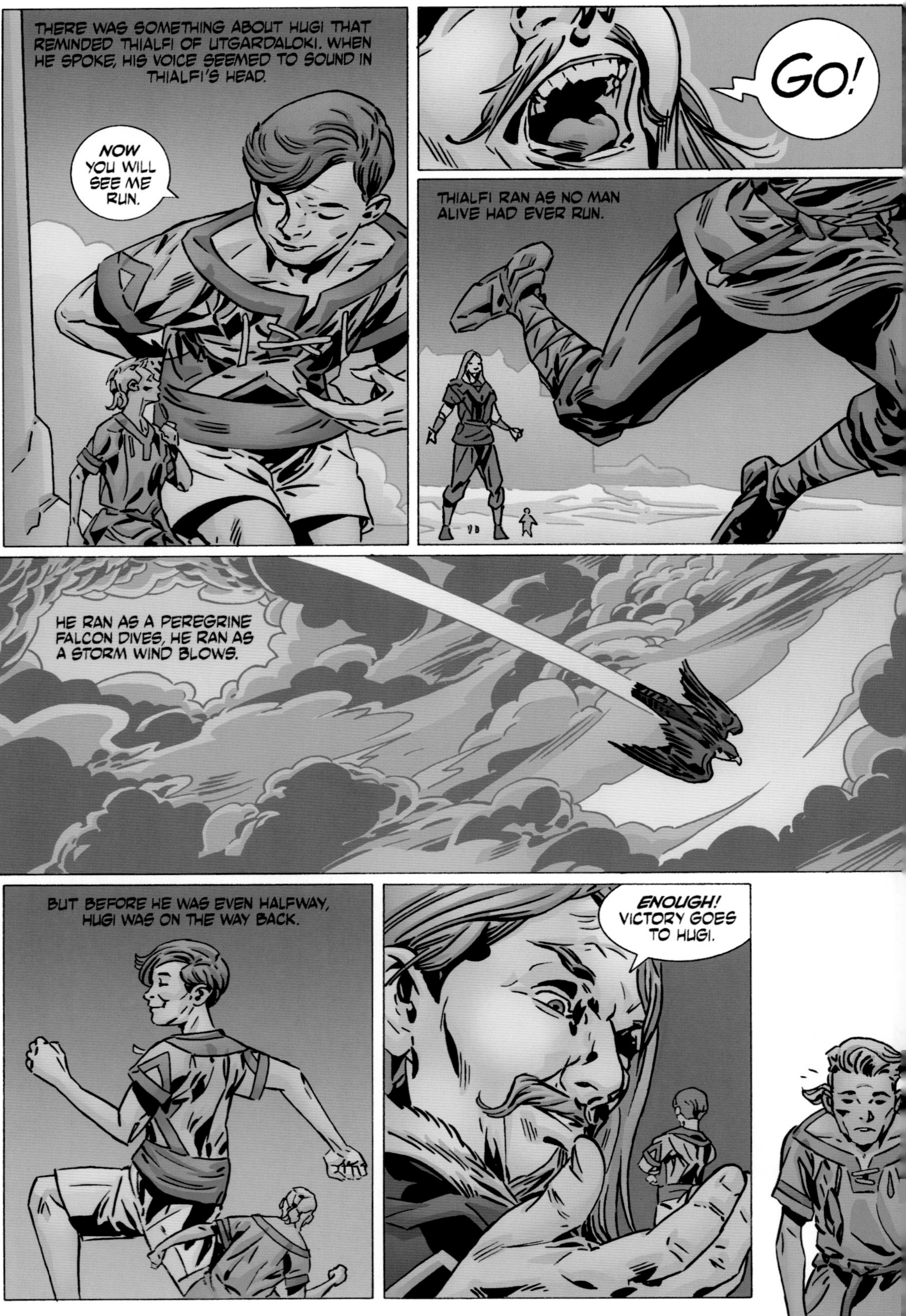
THERE WAS SOMETHING ABOUT HUGI THAT REMINDED THIALFI OF UTGARDALOKI. WHEN HE SPOKE, HIS VOICE SEEMED TO SOUND IN THIALFI'S HEAD.
NOW YOU WILL SEE ME RUN.
GO!
THIALFI RAN AS NO MAN ALIVE HAD EVER RUN.
HE RAN AS A PEREGRINE FALCON DIVES, HE RAN AS A STORM WIND BLOWS.
BUT BEFORE HE WAS EVEN HALFWAY, HUGI WAS ON THE WAY BACK.
ENOUGH! VICTORY GOES TO HUGI.

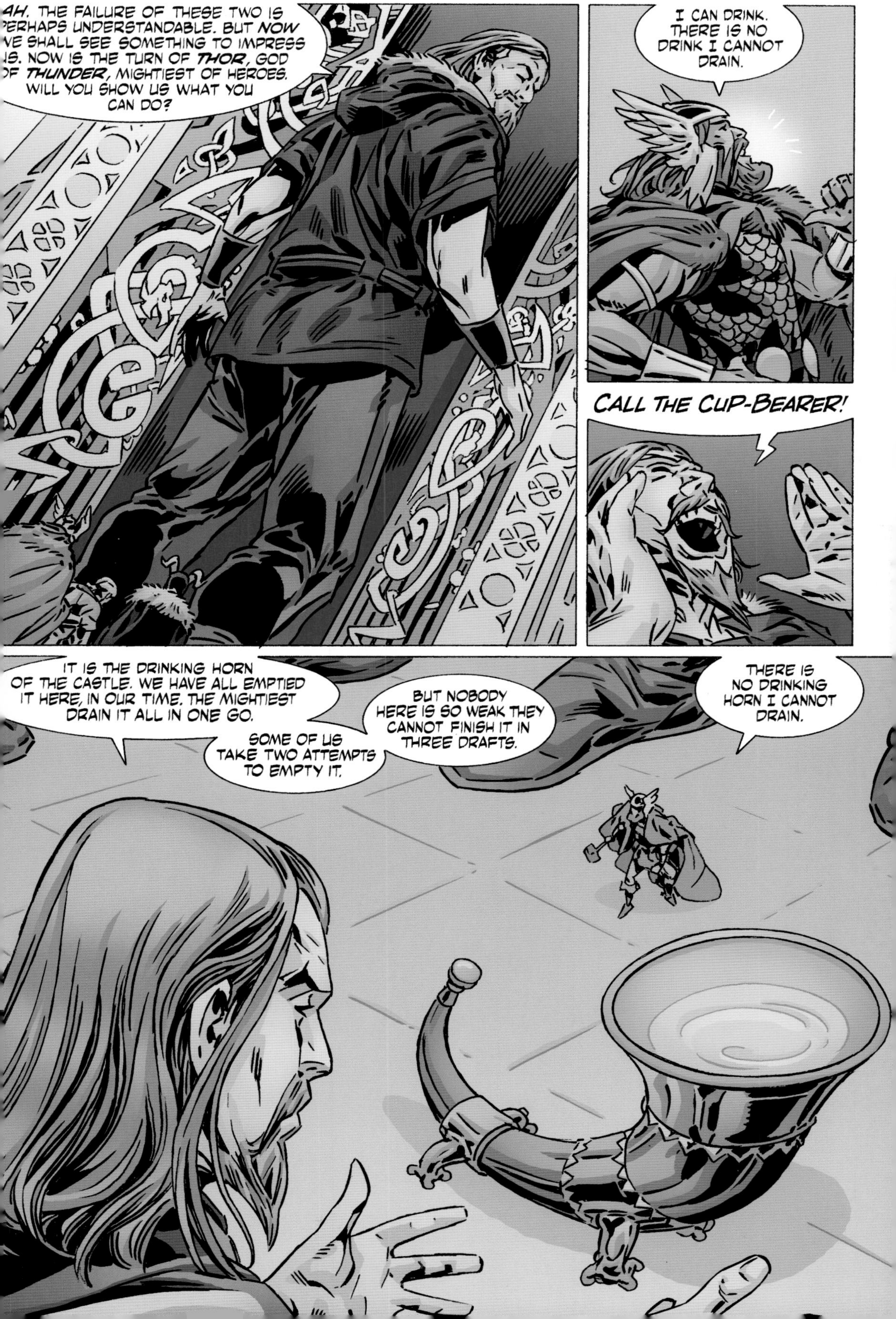
AH. THE FAILURE OF THESE TWO IS PERHAPS UNDERSTANDABLE. BUT NOW WE SHALL SEE SOMETHING TO IMPRESS US. NOW IS THE TURN OF THOR, GOD OF THUNDER, MIGHTIEST OF HEROES. WILL YOU SHOW US WHAT YOU CAN DO?
I CAN DRINK. THERE IS NO DRINK I CANNOT DRAIN.
CALL THE CUP-BEARER!
IT IS THE DRINKING HORN OF THE CASTLE. WE HAVE ALL EMPTIED IT HERE, IN OUR TIME. THE MIGHTIEST DRAIN IT ALL IN ONE GO.
SOME OF US TAKE TWO ATTEMPTS TO EMPTY IT.
BUT NOBODY HERE IS SO WEAK THEY CANNOT FINISH IT IN THREE DRAFTS.
THERE IS NO DRINKING HORN I CANNOT DRAIN.

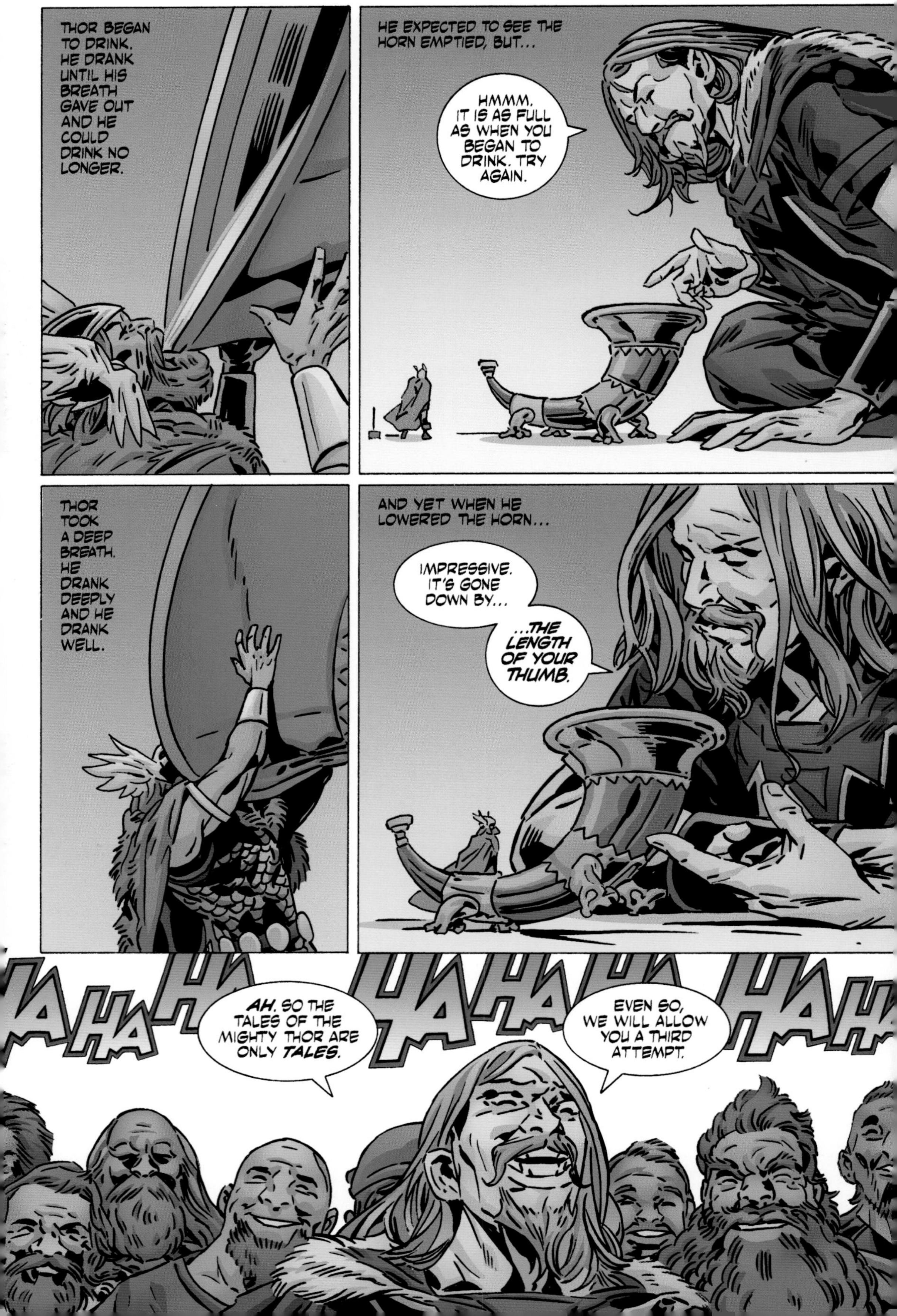
THOR BEGAN TO DRINK. HE DRANK UNTIL HIS BREATH GAVE OUT AND HE COULD DRINK NO LONGER.
HE EXPECTED TO SEE THE HORN EMPTIED, BUT...
HMMM. IT IS AS FULL AS WHEN YOU BEGAN TO DRINK. TRY AGAIN.
THOR TOOK A DEEP BREATH. HE DRANK DEEPLY AND HE DRANK WELL.
AND YET WHEN HE LOWERED THE HORN...
IMPRESSIVE. IT'S GONE DOWN BY...
...THE LENGTH OF YOUR THUMB.
HAHAHA HAHAHAHA HAHA
AH. SO THE TALES OF THE MIGHTY THOR ARE ONLY TALES.
EVEN SO, WE WILL ALLOW YOU A THIRD ATTEMPT.

THOR RAISED THE HORN TO HIS LIPS AND HE DRANK LIKE A GOD DRINKS, LONG AND DEEPLY.
BUT WHEN HE LOWERED THE HORN...
I AM DONE WITH THIS.
AND I AM NOT CONVINCED THAT IT IS ONLY A LITTLE MEAD.
IT IS TIME FOR A TEST OF STRENGTH. CAN YOU PICK UP A CAT?
WHAT KIND OF A QUES... OF COURSE I CAN PICK UP A CAT.
I SHOULD WARN YOU, MY CAT IS A GIANT'S CAT, SO I WILL UNDERSTAND IF YOU CANNOT PICK HER UP.
I WILL PICK UP YOUR CAT.
GOOD, SHE IS SLEEPING BY THE FIRE. LET'S GO.
SHE IS AS BIG AS A MAN, BUT I AM MIGHTIER THAN ANY MAN.

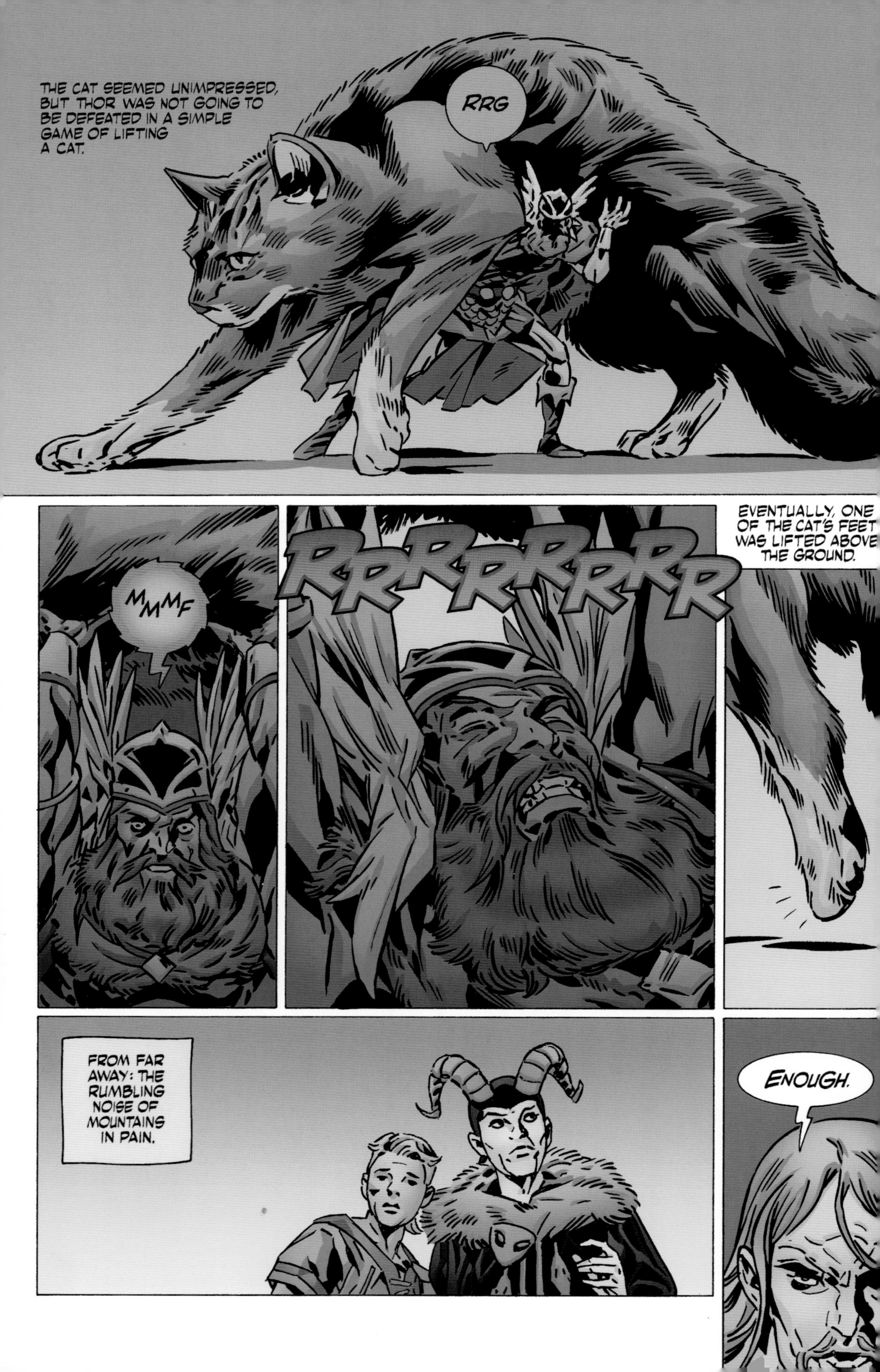
THE CAT SEEMED UNIMPRESSED, BUT THOR WAS NOT GOING TO BE DEFEATED IN A SIMPLE GAME OF LIFTING A CAT.
RRG
MMMF
RRRRRRRRR
EVENTUALLY, ONE OF THE CAT'S FEET WAS LIFTED ABOVE THE GROUND.
FROM FAR AWAY: THE RUMBLING NOISE OF MOUNTAINS IN PAIN.
ENOUGH.

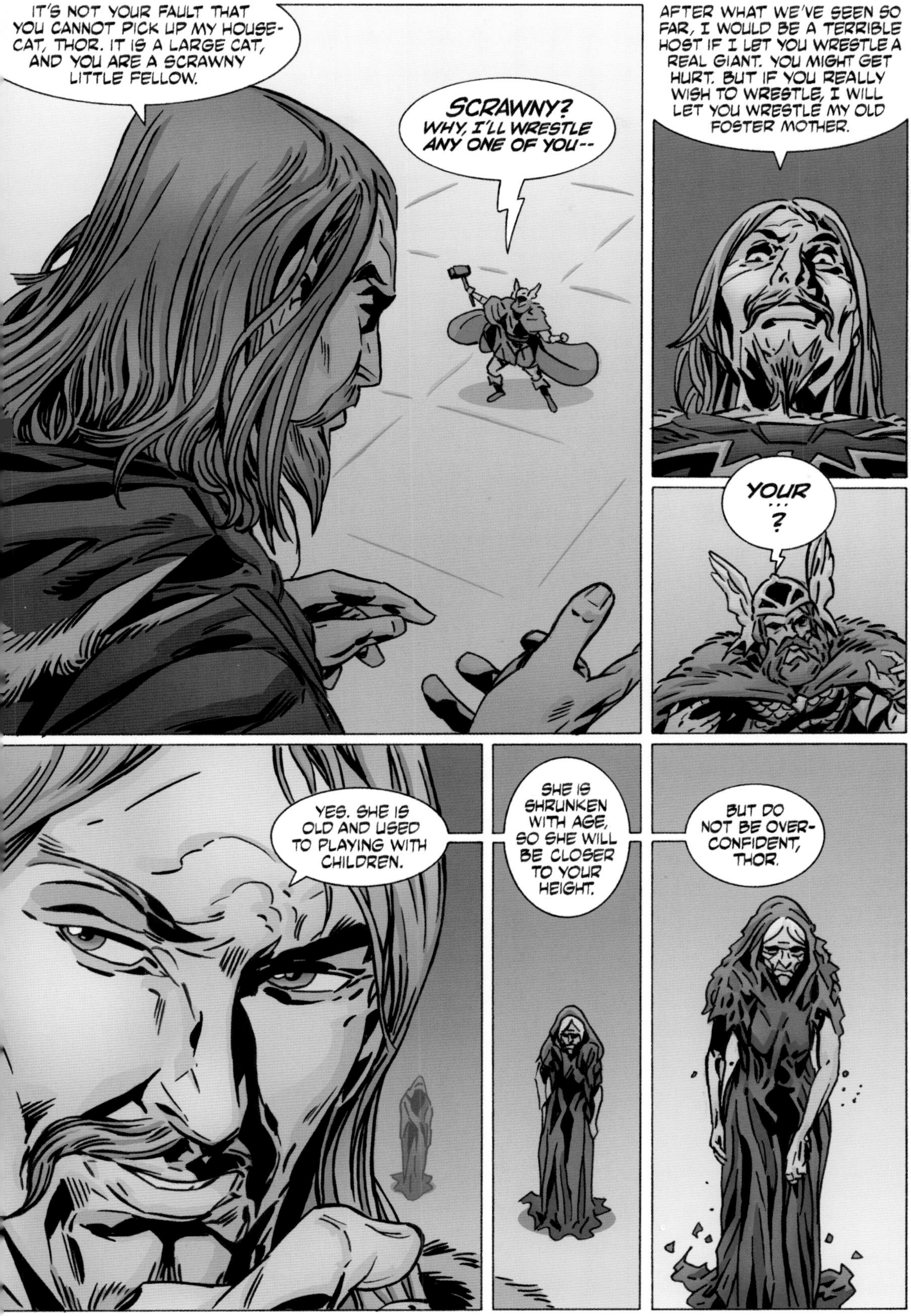
IT'S NOT YOUR FAULT THAT YOU CANNOT PICK UP MY HOUSE-CAT, THOR. IT IS A LARGE CAT, AND YOU ARE A SCRAWNY LITTLE FELLOW.
SCRAWNY? WHY, I'LL WRESTLE ANY ONE OF YOU--
AFTER WHAT WE'VE SEEN SO FAR, I WOULD BE A TERRIBLE HOST IF I LET YOU WRESTLE A REAL GIANT. YOU MIGHT GET HURT. BUT IF YOU REALLY WISH TO WRESTLE, I WILL LET YOU WRESTLE MY OLD FOSTER MOTHER.
YOUR ... ?
YES. SHE IS OLD AND USED TO PLAYING WITH CHILDREN.
SHE IS SHRUNKEN WITH AGE, SO SHE WILL BE CLOSER TO YOUR HEIGHT.
BUT DO NOT BE OVER-CONFIDENT, THOR.

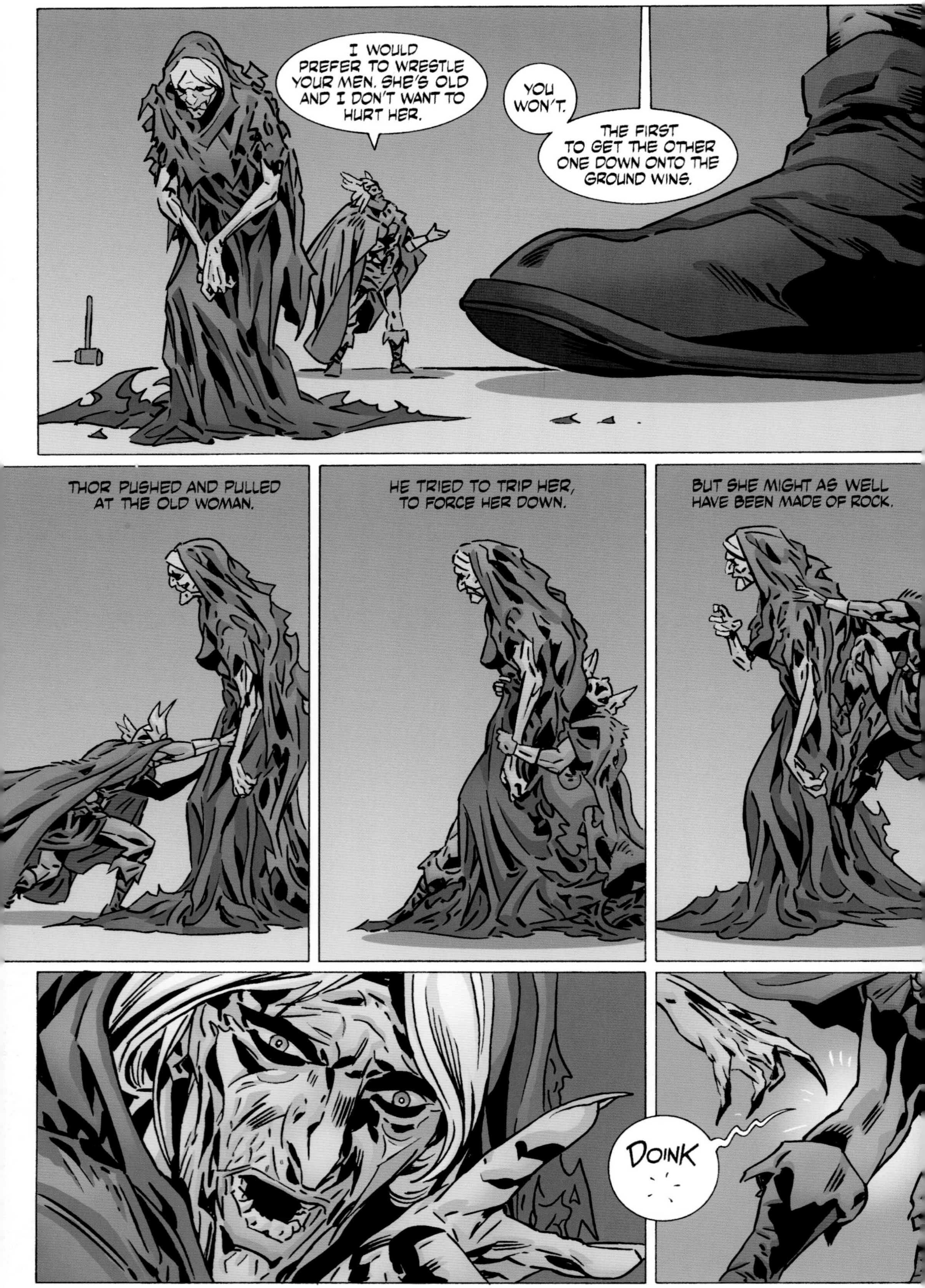
I WOULD PREFER TO WRESTLE YOUR MEN. SHE'S OLD AND I DON'T WANT TO HURT HER.
YOU WON'T.
THE FIRST TO GET THE OTHER ONE DOWN ONTO THE GROUND WINS.
THOR PUSHED AND PULLED AT THE OLD WOMAN.
HE TRIED TO TRIP HER, TO FORCE HER DOWN.
BUT SHE MIGHT AS WELL HAVE BEEN MADE OF ROCK.
DOINK

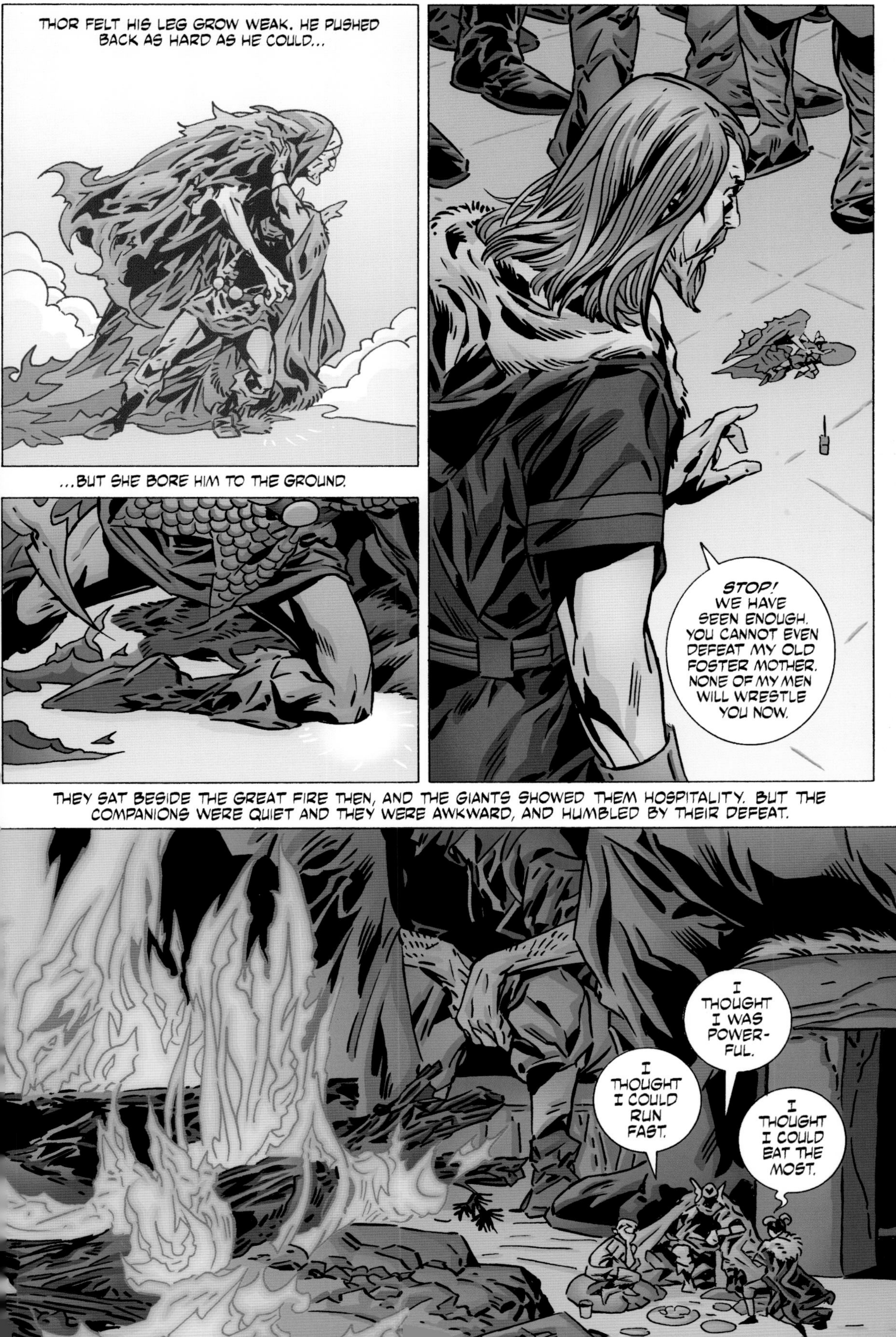
THOR FELT HIS LEG GROW WEAK. HE PUSHED BACK AS HARD AS HE COULD...
...BUT SHE BORE HIM TO THE GROUND.
STOP! WE HAVE SEEN ENOUGH. YOU CANNOT EVEN DEFEAT MY OLD FOSTER MOTHER. NONE OF MY MEN WILL WRESTLE YOU NOW.
THEY SAT BESIDE THE GREAT FIRE THEN, AND THE GIANTS SHOWED THEM HOSPITALITY. BUT THE COMPANIONS WERE QUIET AND THEY WERE AWKWARD, AND HUMBLED BY THEIR DEFEAT.
I THOUGHT I WAS POWER-FUL.
I THOUGHT I COULD RUN FAST.
I THOUGHT I COULD EAT THE MOST.

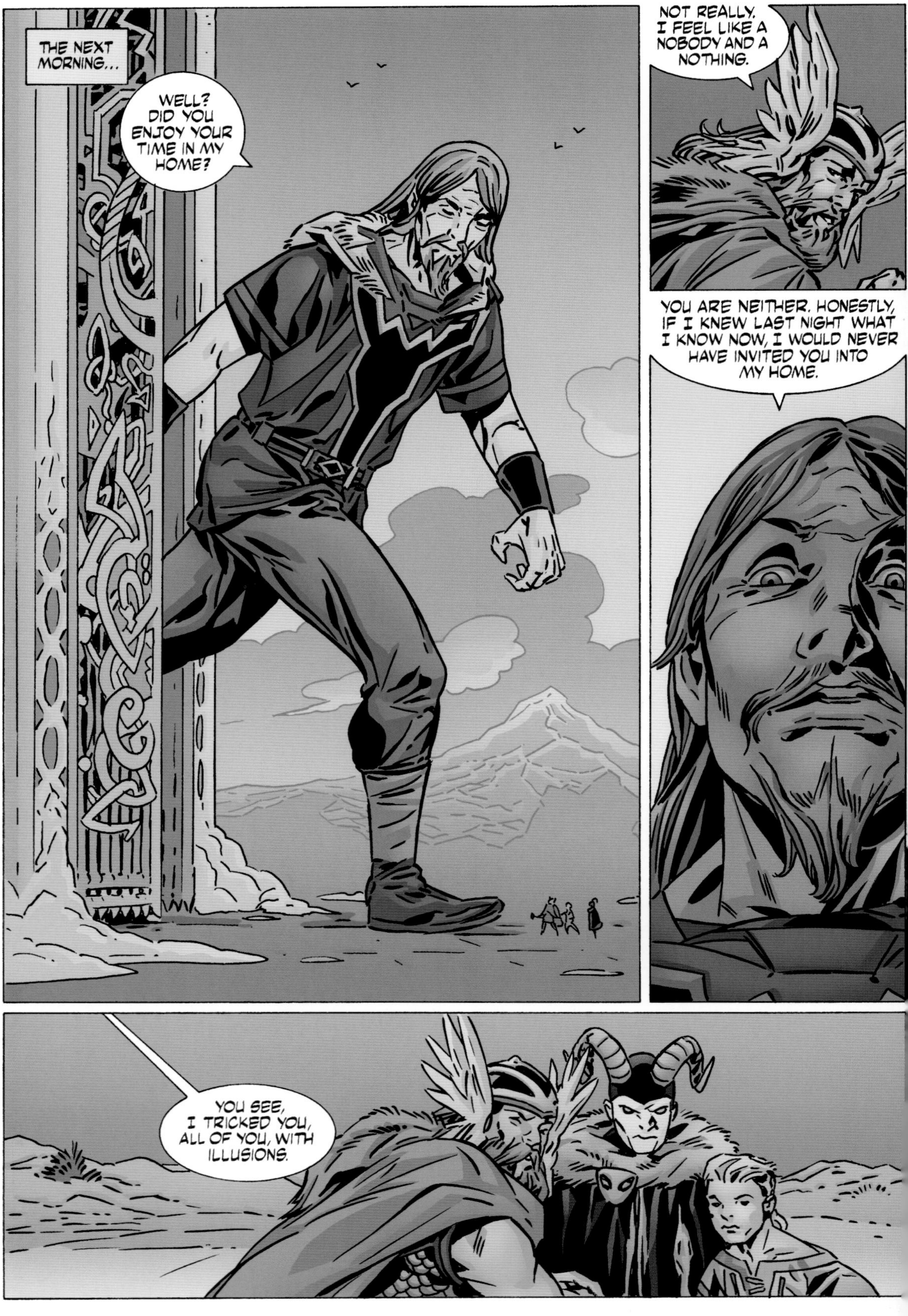
THE NEXT MORNING...
WELL? DID YOU ENJOY YOUR TIME IN MY HOME?
NOT REALLY. I FEEL LIKE A NOBODY AND A NOTHING.
YOU ARE NEITHER. HONESTLY, IF I KNEW LAST NIGHT WHAT I KNOW NOW, I WOULD NEVER HAVE INVITED YOU INTO MY HOME.
YOU SEE, I TRICKED YOU, ALL OF YOU, WITH ILLUSIONS.

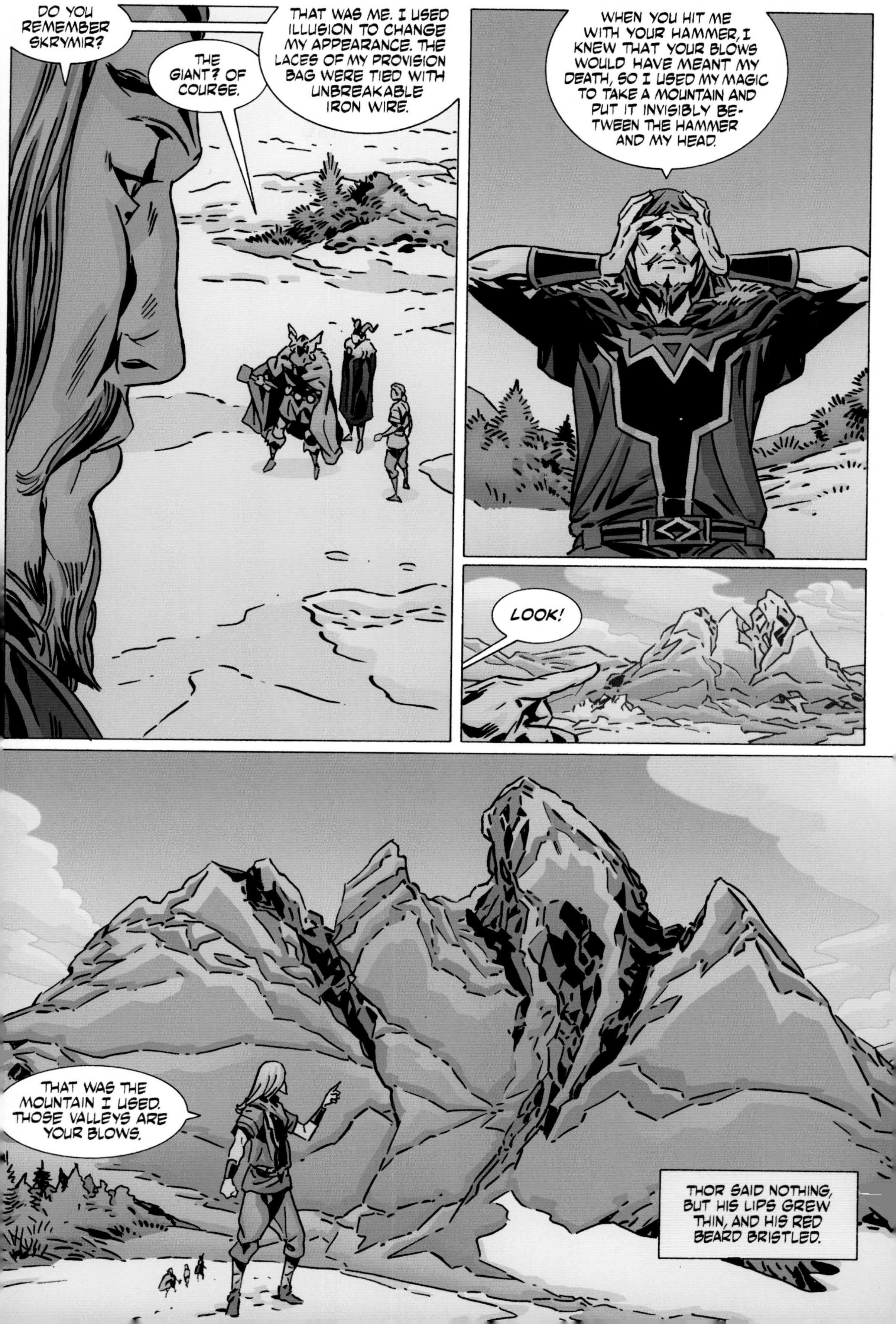
DO YOU REMEMBER SKRYMIR?
THE GIANT? OF COURSE.
THAT WAS ME. I USED ILLUSION TO CHANGE MY APPEARANCE. THE LACES OF MY PROVISION BAG WERE TIED WITH UNBREAKABLE IRON WIRE.
WHEN YOU HIT ME WITH YOUR HAMMER, I KNEW THAT YOUR BLOWS WOULD HAVE MEANT MY DEATH, SO I USED MY MAGIC TO TAKE A MOUNTAIN AND PUT IT INVISIBLY BE-TWEEN THE HAMMER AND MY HEAD.
LOOK!
THAT WAS THE MOUNTAIN I USED. THOSE VALLEYS ARE YOUR BLOWS.
THOR SAID NOTHING, BUT HIS LIPS GREW THIN, AND HIS RED BEARD BRISTLED.

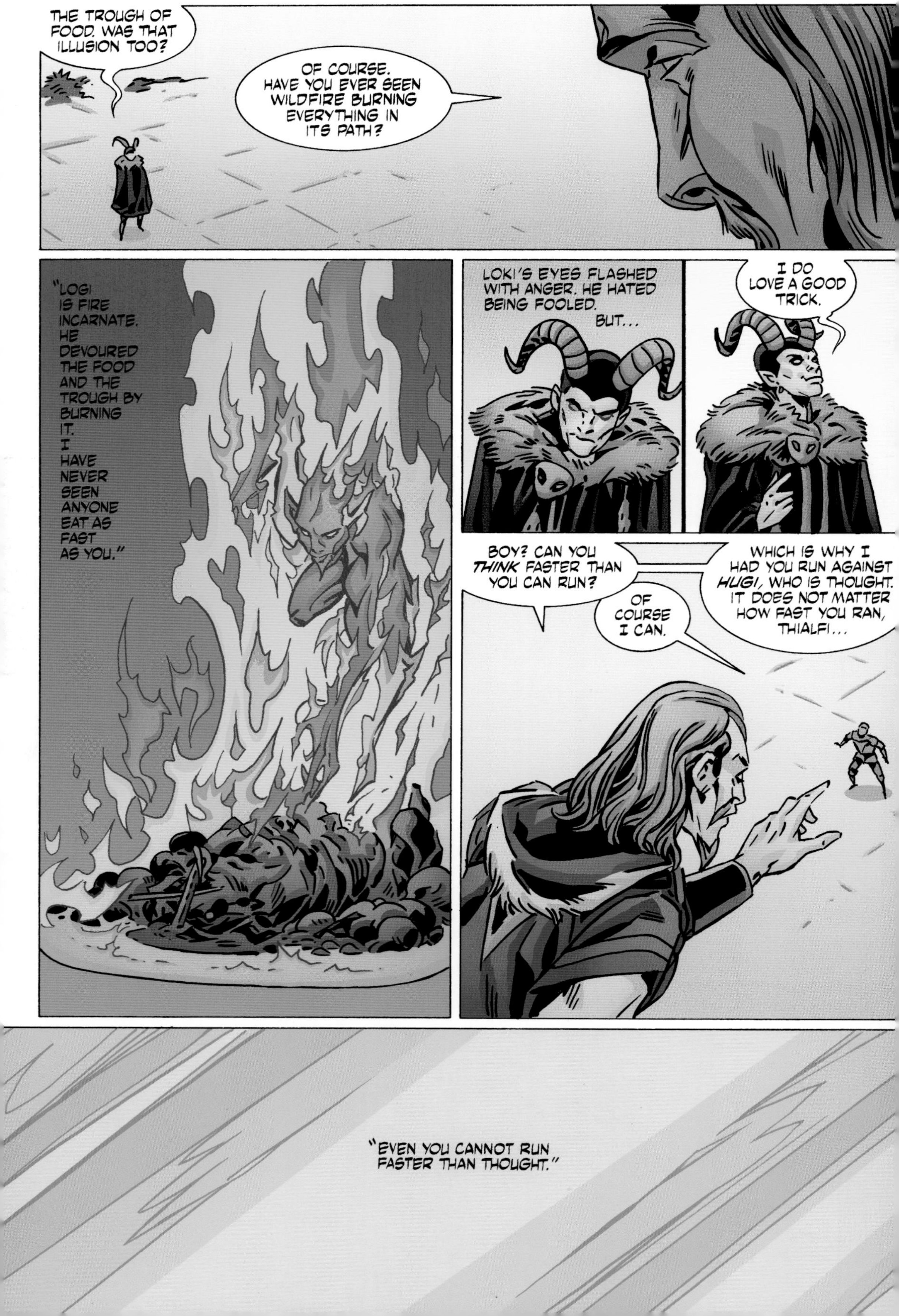
THE TROUGH OF FOOD. WAS THAT ILLUSION TOO?
OF COURSE. HAVE YOU EVER SEEN WILDFIRE BURNING EVERYTHING IN ITS PATH?
"LOGI IS FIRE INCARNATE. HE DEVOURED THE FOOD AND THE TROUGH BY BURNING IT. I HAVE NEVER SEEN ANYONE EAT AS FAST AS YOU."
LOKI'S EYES FLASHED WITH ANGER. HE HATED BEING FOOLED.
BUT...
I DO LOVE A GOOD TRICK.
BOY? CAN YOU *THINK* FASTER THAN YOU CAN RUN?
OF COURSE I CAN.
WHICH IS WHY I HAD YOU RUN AGAINST *HUGI*, WHO IS THOUGHT. IT DOES NOT MATTER HOW FAST YOU RAN, THIALFI...
"EVEN YOU CANNOT RUN FASTER THAN THOUGHT."

AND ME? WHAT DID I DO LAST NIGHT?

YOU DID THE IMPOSSIBLE.

"YOU COULD NOT PERCEIVE IT, BUT THE END OF THE DRINKING HORN WAS IN THE DEEPEST PART OF THE SEA. YOU DRANK ENOUGH TO TAKE THE OCEAN LEVEL DOWN, TO MAKE TIDES.

"BECAUSE OF YOU, THOR, THE SEAWATER WILL RISE AND EBB FOREVERMORE.

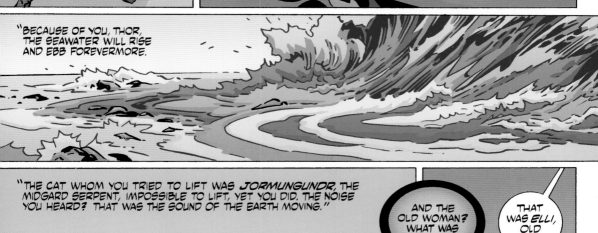

"THE CAT WHOM YOU TRIED TO LIFT WAS *JORMUNGUNDR*, THE MIDGARD SERPENT, IMPOSSIBLE TO LIFT, YET YOU DID. THE NOISE YOU HEARD? THAT WAS THE SOUND OF THE EARTH MOVING."

AND THE OLD WOMAN? WHAT WAS SHE?

THAT WAS *ELLI*, OLD AGE.

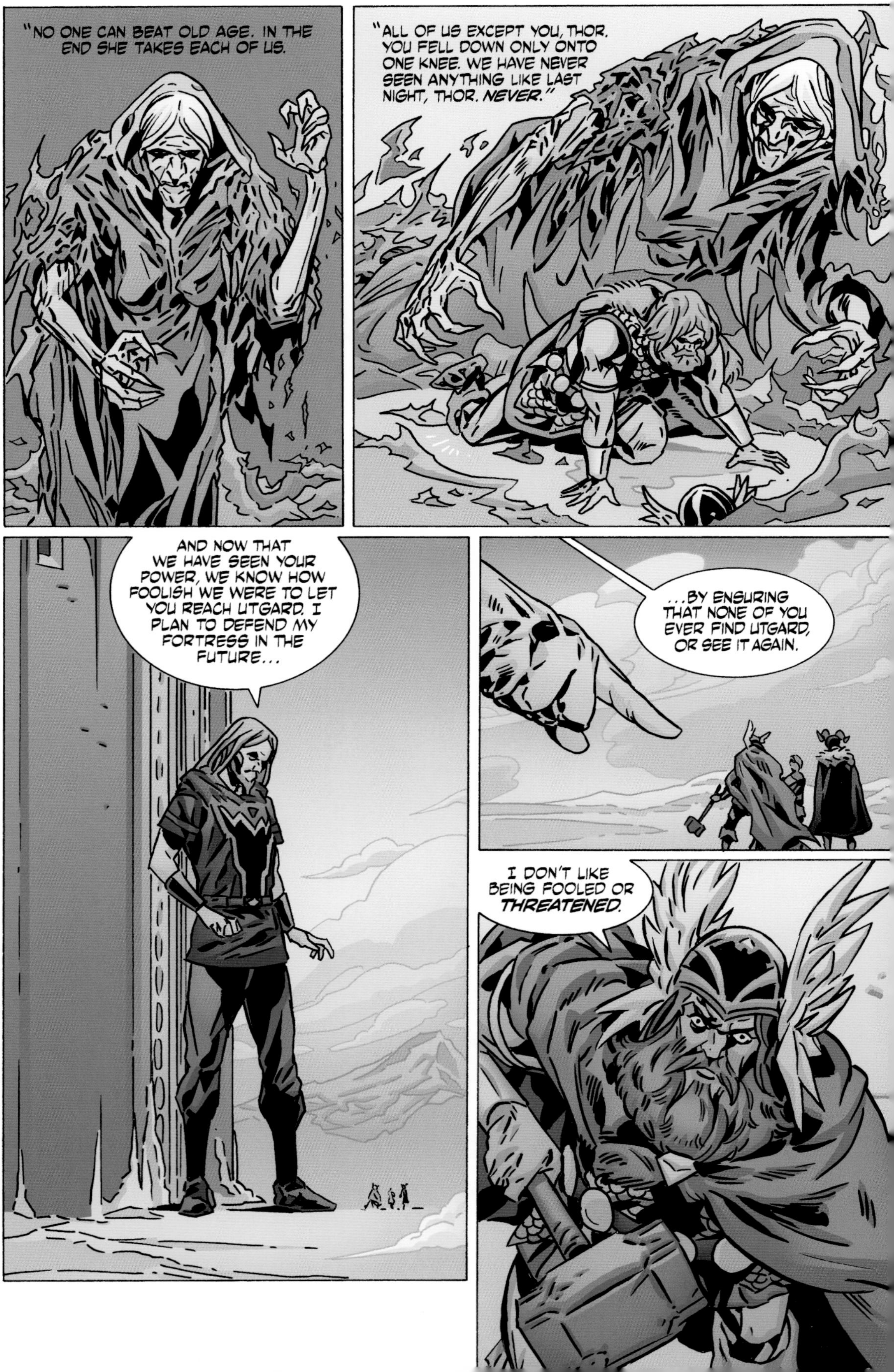
"NO ONE CAN BEAT OLD AGE. IN THE END SHE TAKES EACH OF US.
"ALL OF US EXCEPT YOU, THOR. YOU FELL DOWN ONLY ONTO ONE KNEE. WE HAVE NEVER SEEN ANYTHING LIKE LAST NIGHT, THOR. NEVER."
AND NOW THAT WE HAVE SEEN YOUR POWER, WE KNOW HOW FOOLISH WE WERE TO LET YOU REACH UTGARD. I PLAN TO DEFEND MY FORTRESS IN THE FUTURE...
...BY ENSURING THAT NONE OF YOU EVER FIND UTGARD, OR SEE IT AGAIN.
I DON'T LIKE BEING FOOLED OR THREATENED.

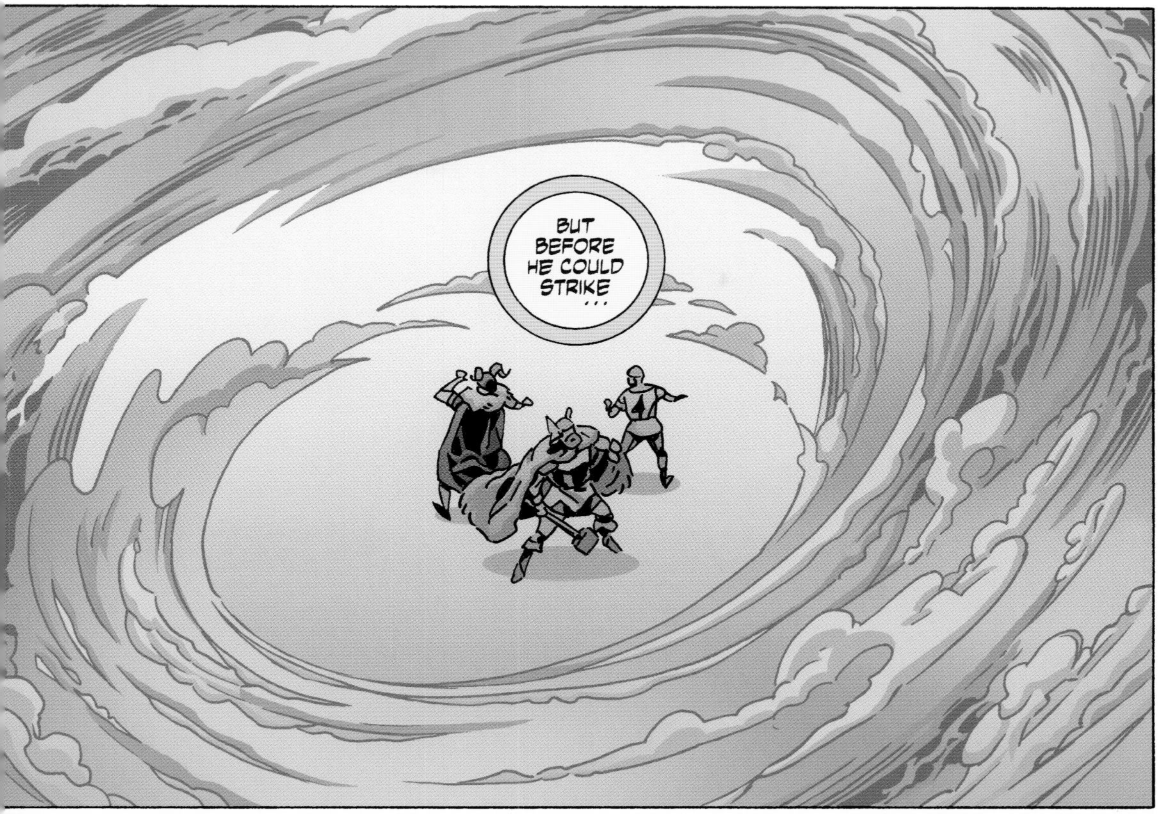
BUT BEFORE HE COULD STRIKE . . .

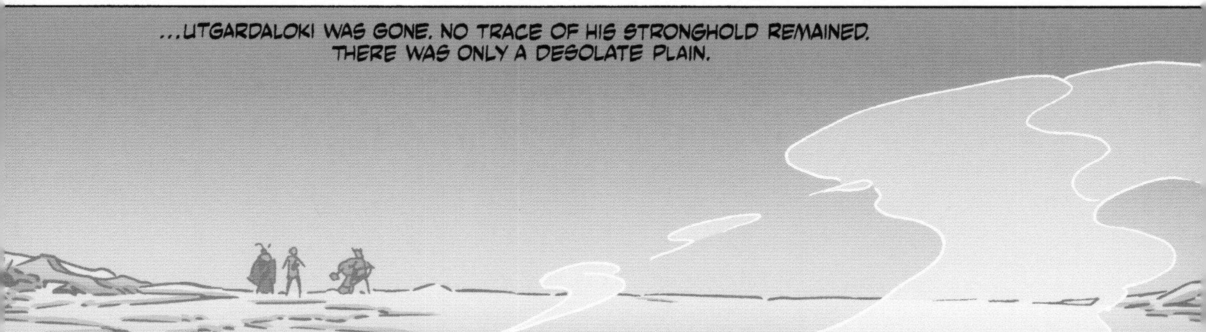
. . . UTGARDALOKI WAS GONE. NO TRACE OF HIS STRONGHOLD REMAINED. THERE WAS ONLY A DESOLATE PLAIN.

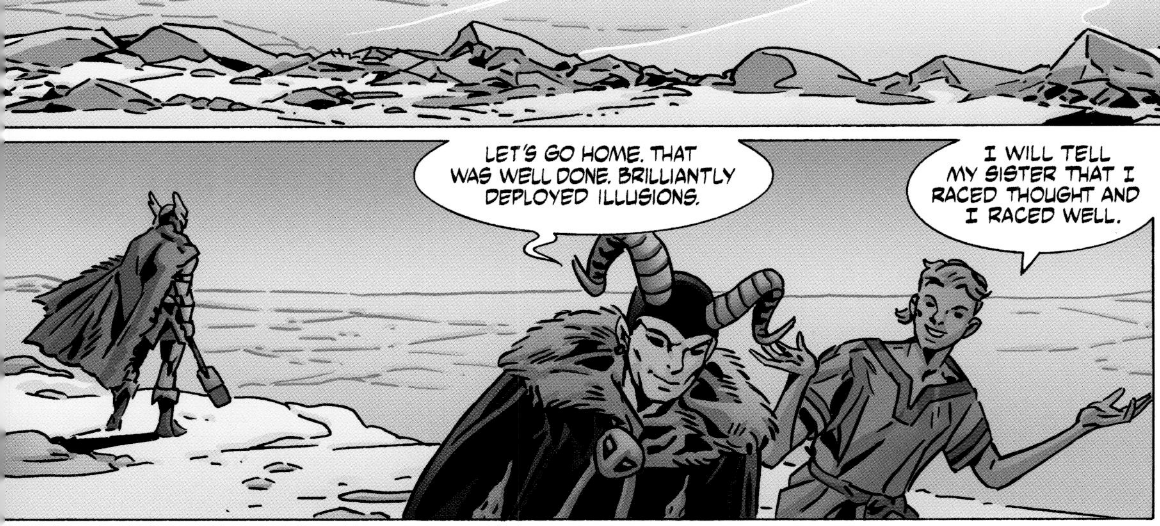
LET'S GO HOME. THAT WAS WELL DONE. BRILLIANTLY DEPLOYED ILLUSIONS.
I WILL TELL MY SISTER THAT I RACED THOUGHT AND I RACED WELL.

BUT THOR SAID NOTHING. HE WAS THINKING ABOUT THE NIGHT BEFORE, OF WRESTLING OLD AGE, OF DRINKING THE SE

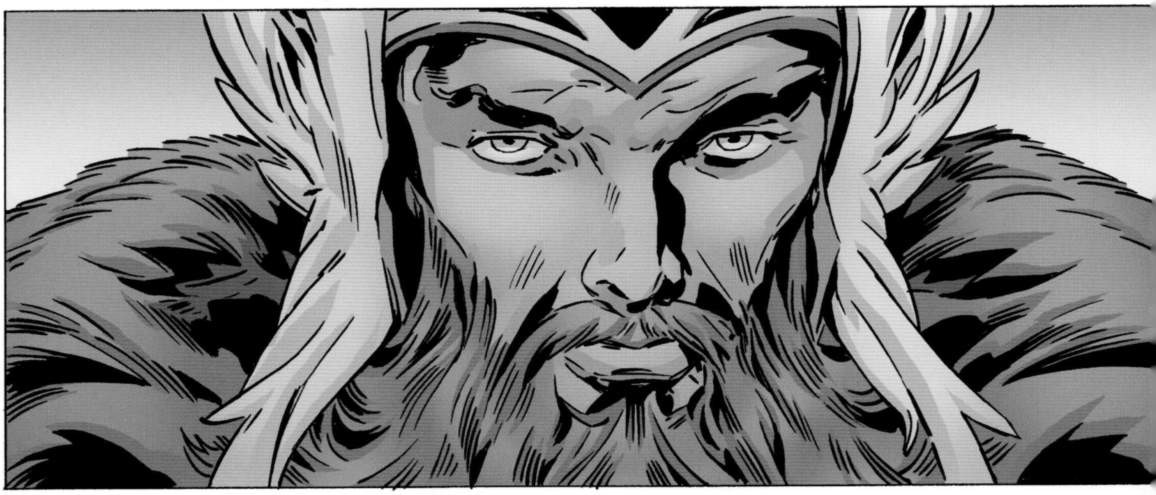

HE WAS THINKING ABOUT THE MIDGARD SERPENT.

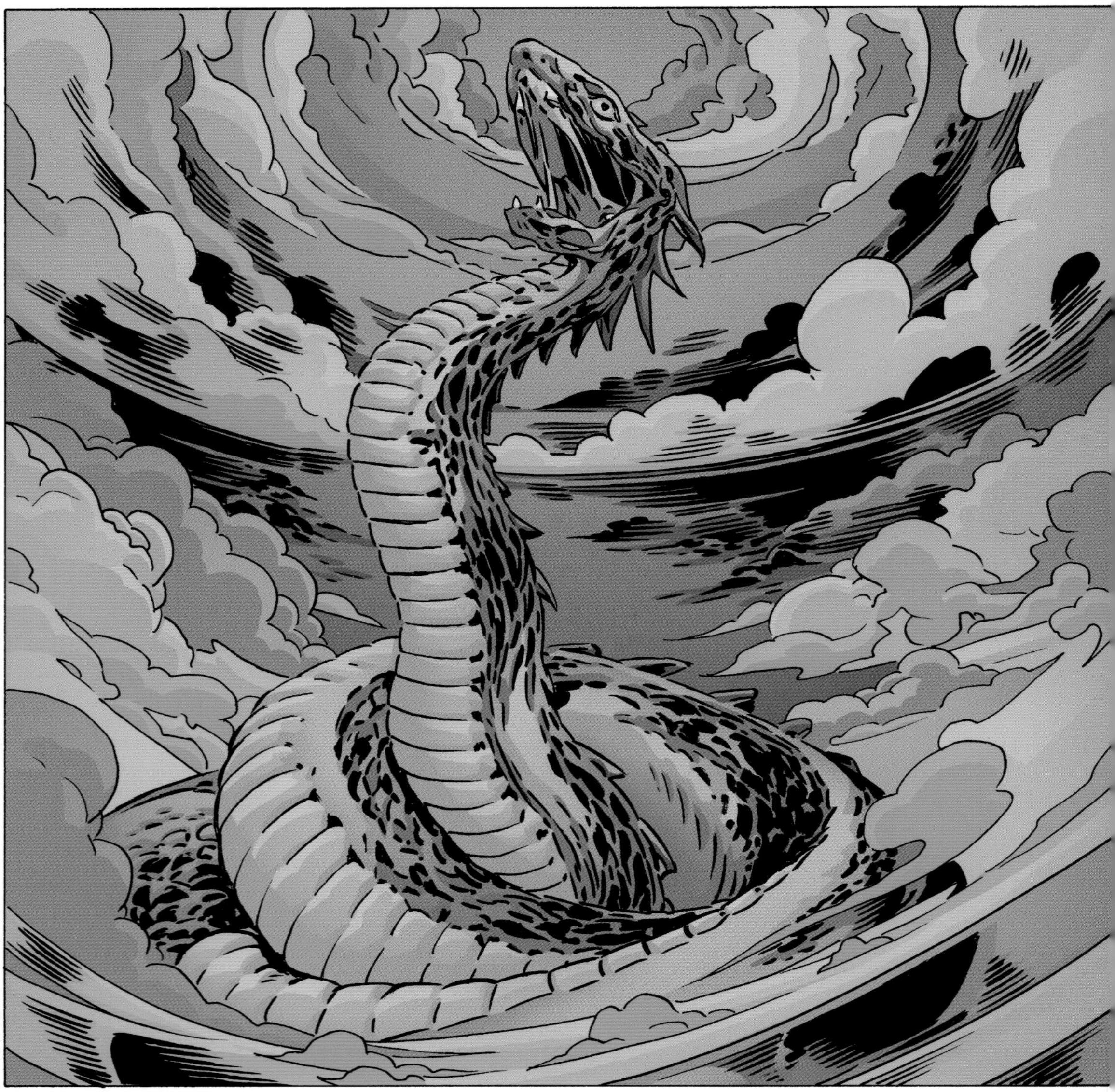

The Apples of Immortality

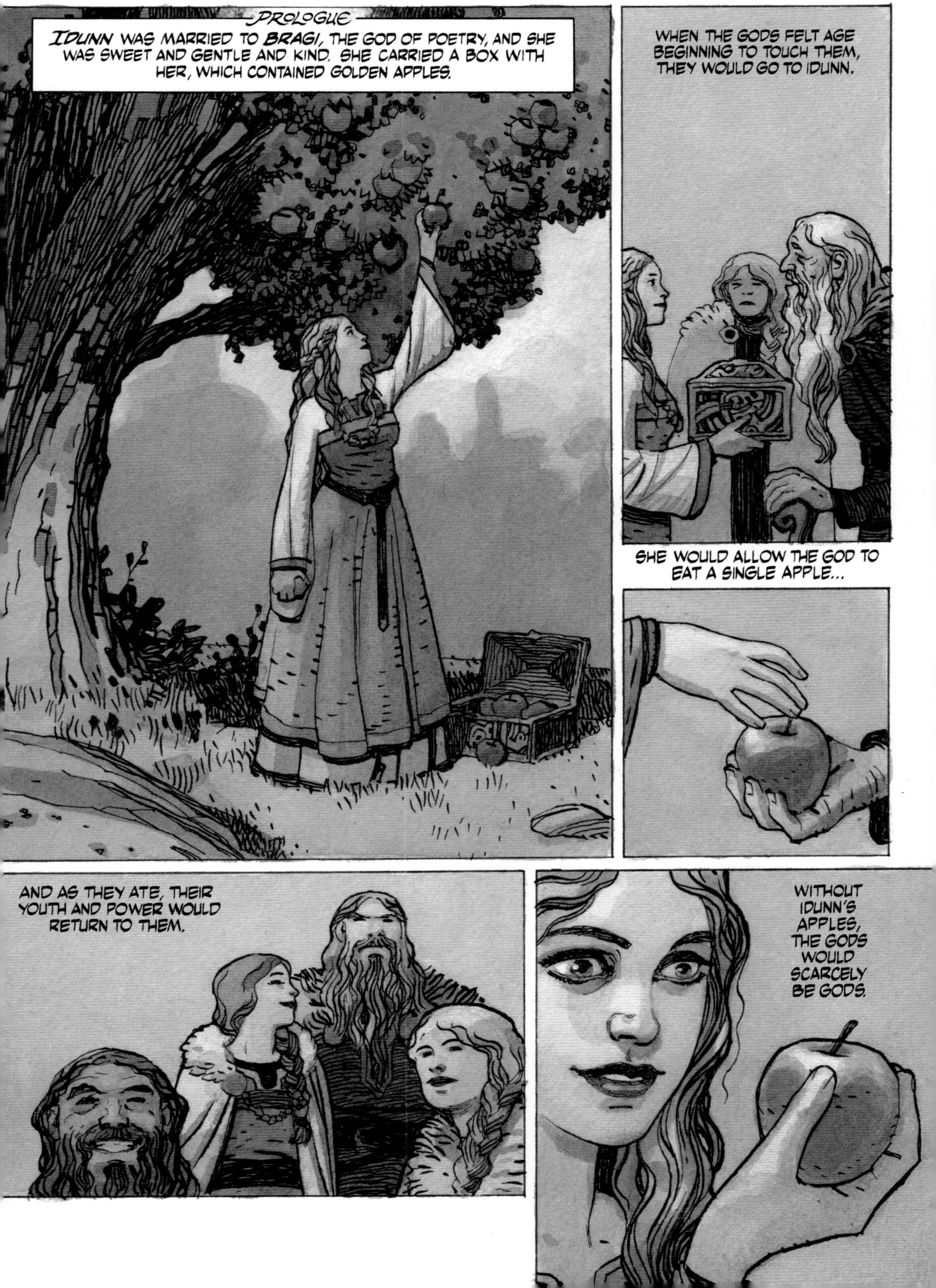
PROLOGUE
IDUNN WAS MARRIED TO BRAGI, THE GOD OF POETRY, AND SHE WAS SWEET AND GENTLE AND KIND. SHE CARRIED A BOX WITH HER, WHICH CONTAINED GOLDEN APPLES.
WHEN THE GODS FELT AGE BEGINNING TO TOUCH THEM, THEY WOULD GO TO IDUNN.
SHE WOULD ALLOW THE GOD TO EAT A SINGLE APPLE...
AND AS THEY ATE, THEIR YOUTH AND POWER WOULD RETURN TO THEM.
WITHOUT IDUNN'S APPLES, THE GODS WOULD SCARCELY BE GODS.

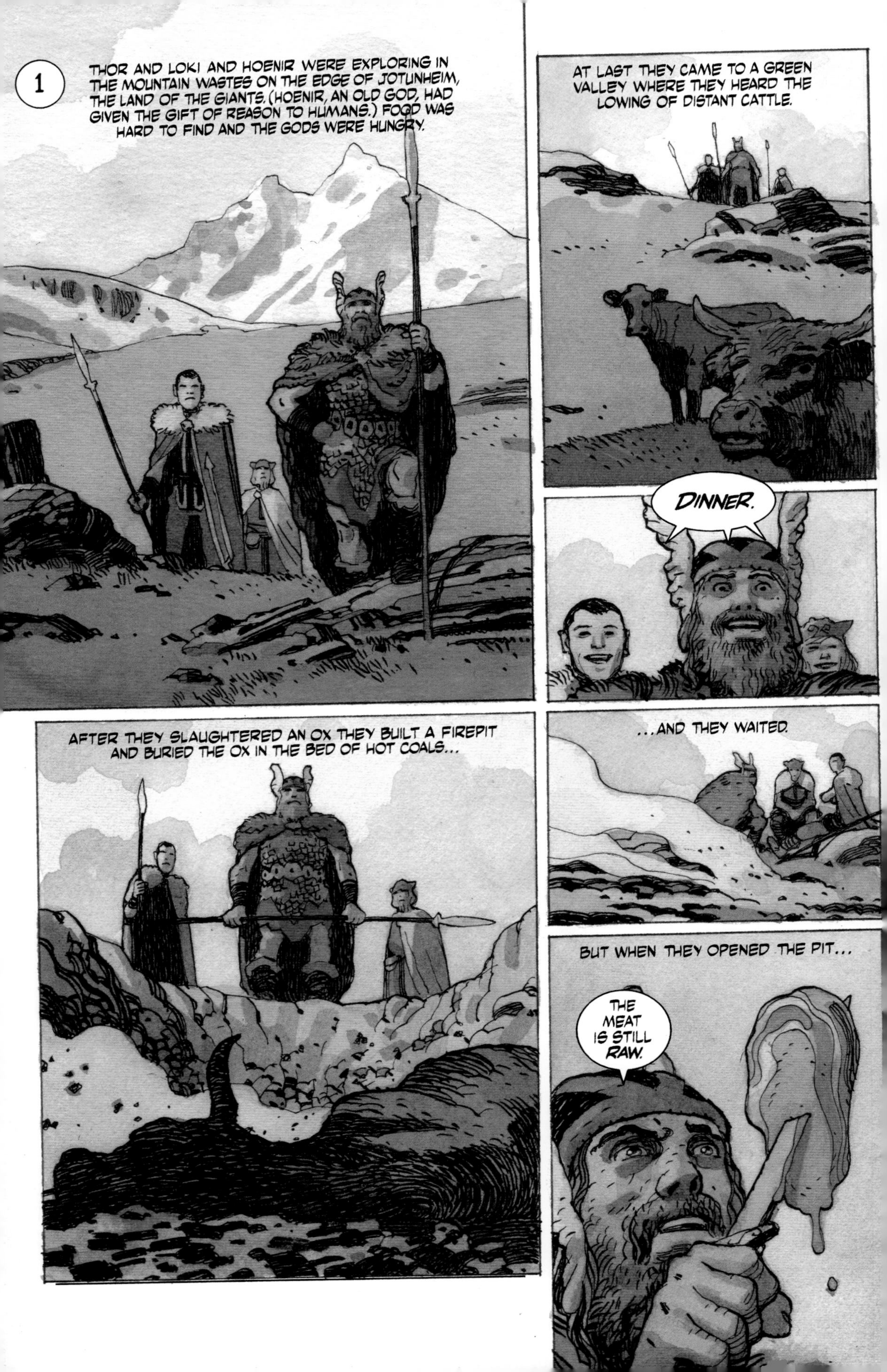
1
THOR AND LOKI AND HOENIR WERE EXPLORING IN THE MOUNTAIN WASTES ON THE EDGE OF JOTUNHEIM, THE LAND OF THE GIANTS. (HOENIR, AN OLD GOD, HAD GIVEN THE GIFT OF REASON TO HUMANS.) FOOD WAS HARD TO FIND AND THE GODS WERE HUNGRY.
AT LAST THEY CAME TO A GREEN VALLEY WHERE THEY HEARD THE LOWING OF DISTANT CATTLE.
DINNER.
AFTER THEY SLAUGHTERED AN OX THEY BUILT A FIREPIT AND BURIED THE OX IN THE BED OF HOT COALS...
...AND THEY WAITED.
BUT WHEN THEY OPENED THE PIT...
THE MEAT IS STILL RAW.

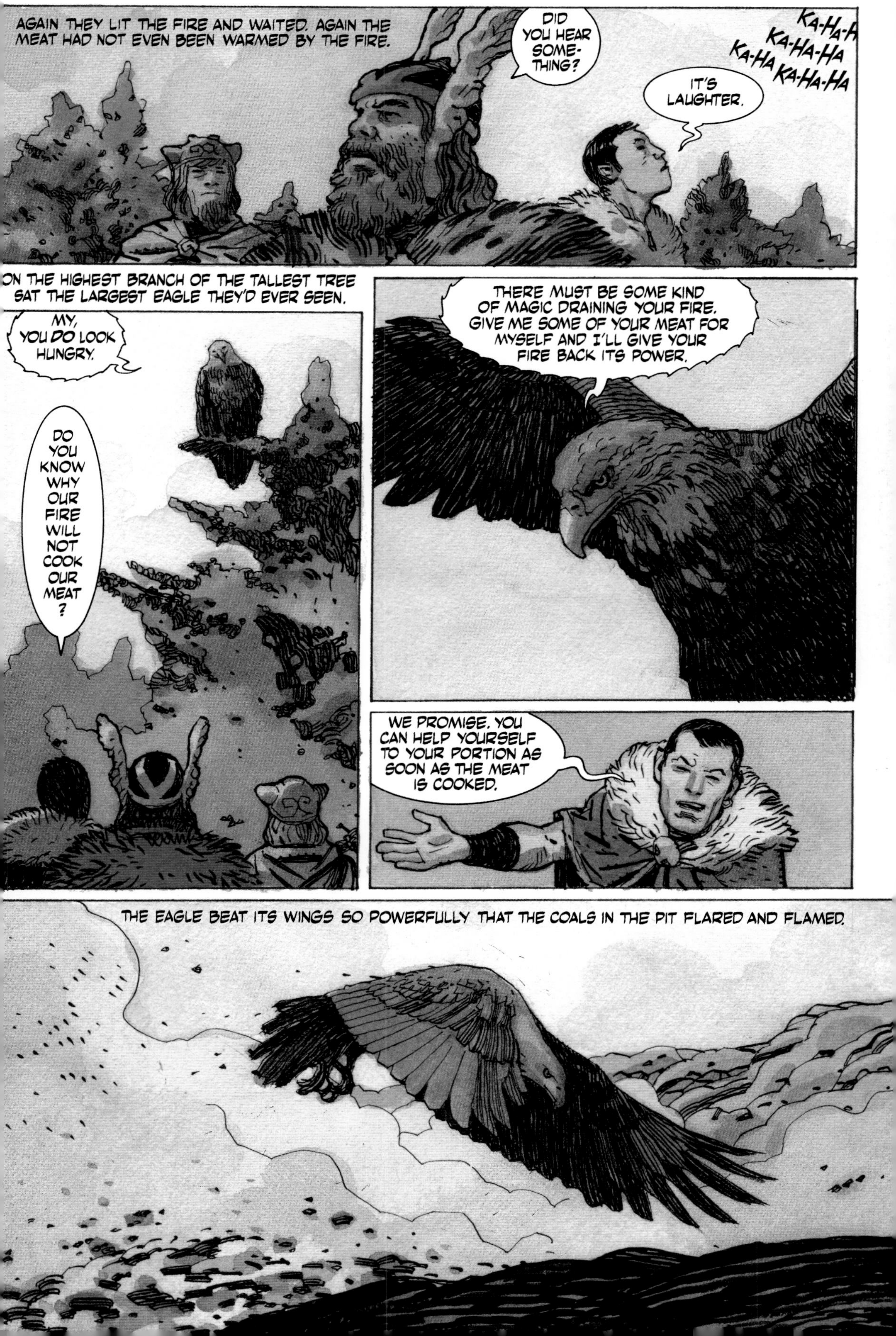

AGAIN THEY LIT THE FIRE AND WAITED. AGAIN THE MEAT HAD NOT EVEN BEEN WARMED BY THE FIRE.
DID YOU HEAR SOME-THING?
KA-HA-HA KA-HA-HA KA-HA KA-HA-HA
IT'S LAUGHTER.
ON THE HIGHEST BRANCH OF THE TALLEST TREE SAT THE LARGEST EAGLE THEY'D EVER SEEN.
MY, YOU DO LOOK HUNGRY.
DO YOU KNOW WHY OUR FIRE WILL NOT COOK OUR MEAT?
THERE MUST BE SOME KIND OF MAGIC DRAINING YOUR FIRE. GIVE ME SOME OF YOUR MEAT FOR MYSELF AND I'LL GIVE YOUR FIRE BACK ITS POWER.
WE PROMISE. YOU CAN HELP YOURSELF TO YOUR PORTION AS SOON AS THE MEAT IS COOKED.
THE EAGLE BEAT ITS WINGS SO POWERFULLY THAT THE COALS IN THE PIT FLARED AND FLAMED.

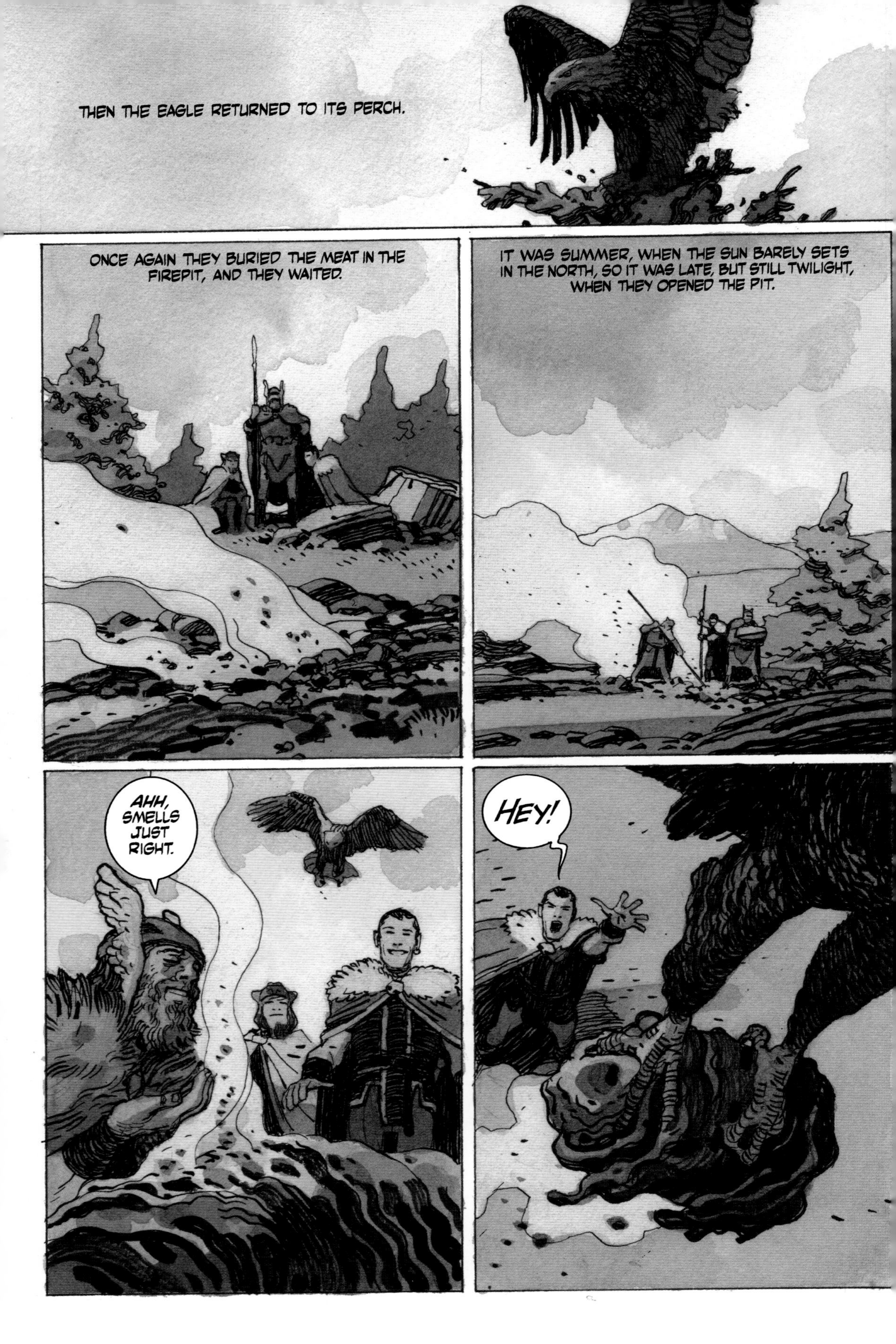
THEN THE EAGLE RETURNED TO ITS PERCH.
ONCE AGAIN THEY BURIED THE MEAT IN THE FIREPIT, AND THEY WAITED.
IT WAS SUMMER, WHEN THE SUN BARELY SETS IN THE NORTH, SO IT WAS LATE, BUT STILL TWILIGHT, WHEN THEY OPENED THE PIT.
AHH, SMELLS JUST RIGHT.
HEY!

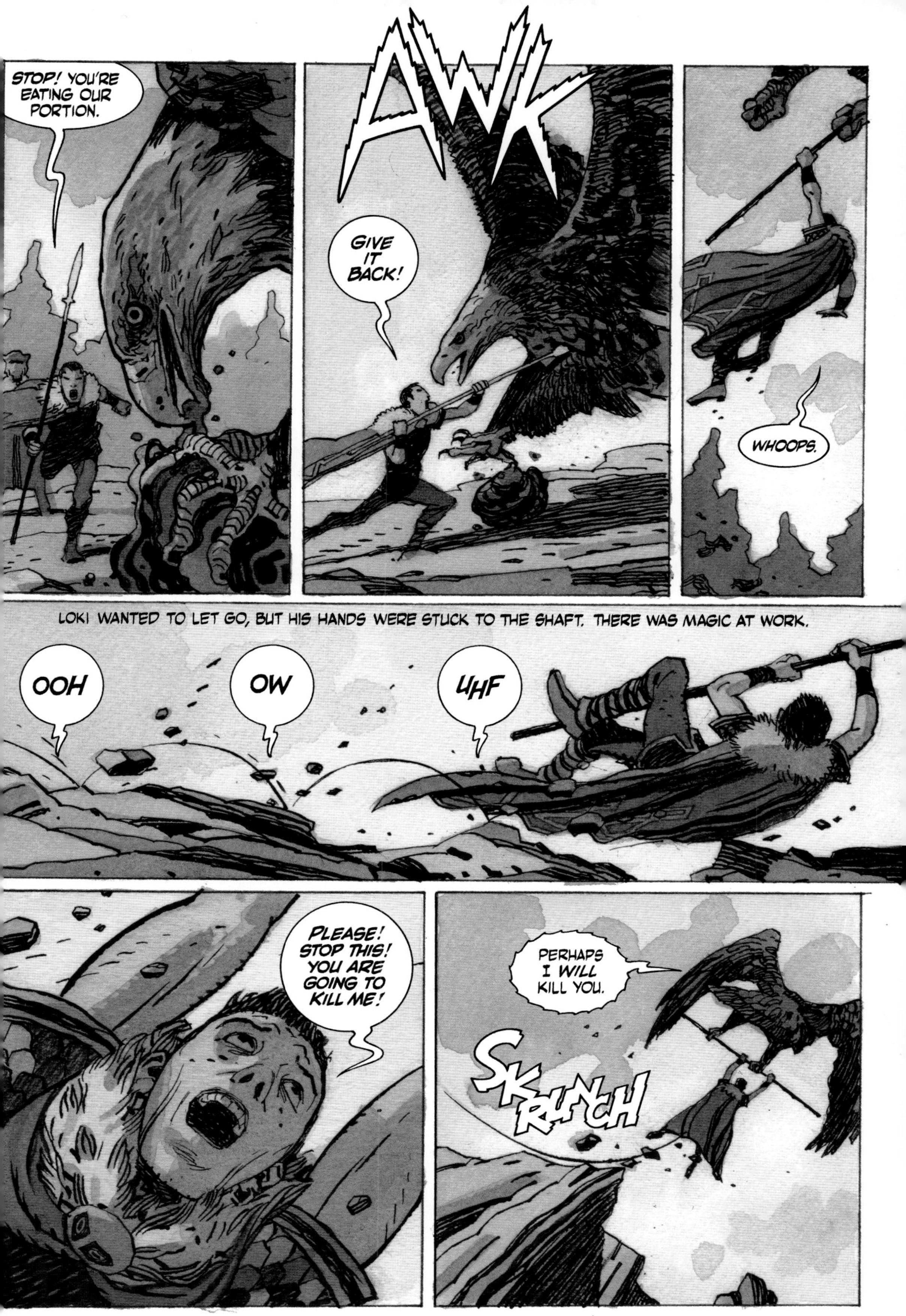
AWK
STOP! YOU'RE EATING OUR PORTION.
GIVE IT BACK!
WHOOPS.
LOKI WANTED TO LET GO, BUT HIS HANDS WERE STUCK TO THE SHAFT. THERE WAS MAGIC AT WORK.
OOH
OW
UHF
PLEASE! STOP THIS! YOU ARE GOING TO KILL ME!
PERHAPS I WILL KILL YOU.
SKRUNCH

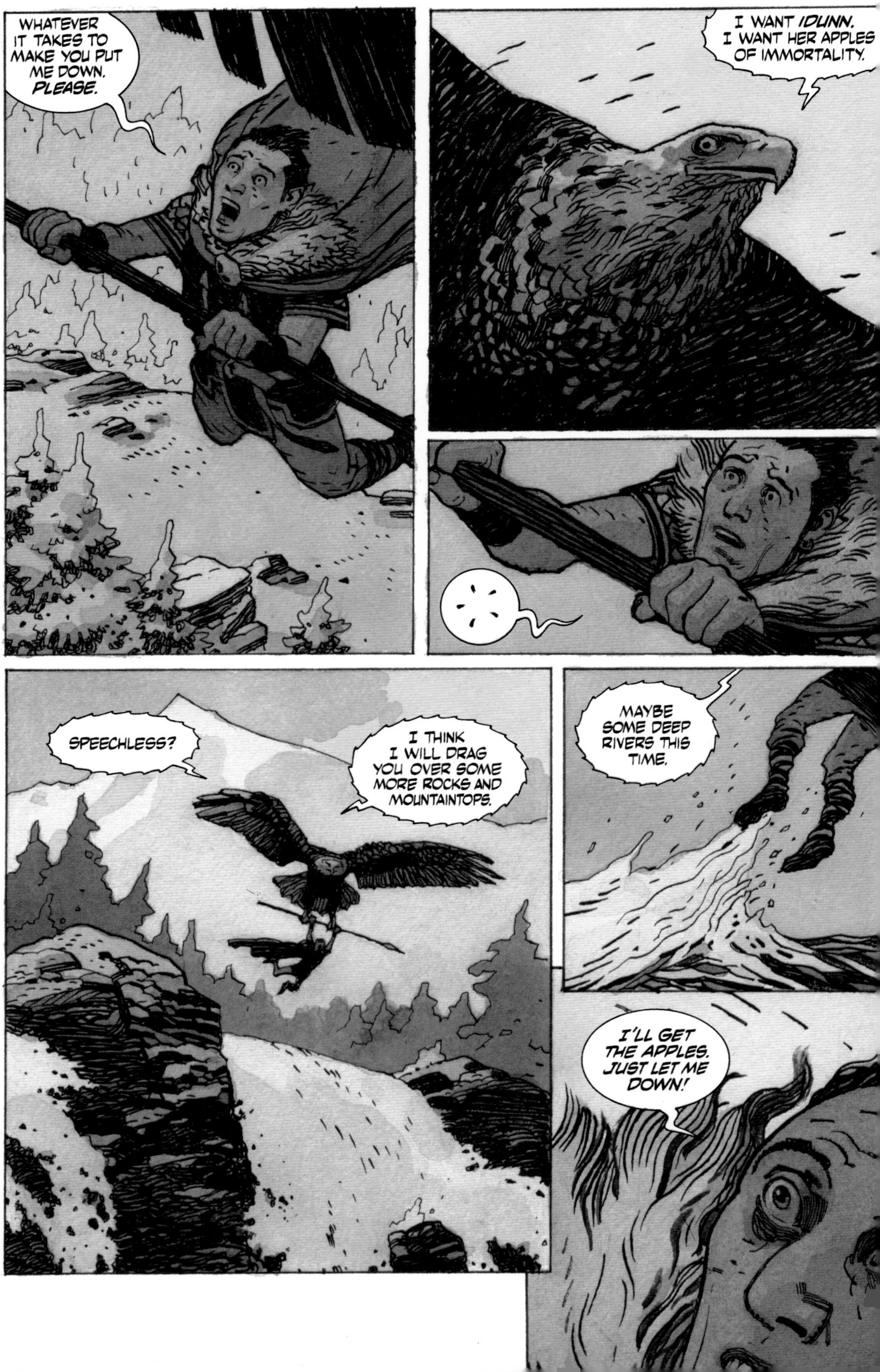
WHATEVER IT TAKES TO MAKE YOU PUT ME DOWN. PLEASE.
I WANT IDUNN. I WANT HER APPLES OF IMMORTALITY.
SPEECHLESS?
I THINK I WILL DRAG YOU OVER SOME MORE ROCKS AND MOUNTAINTOPS.
MAYBE SOME DEEP RIVERS THIS TIME.
I'LL GET THE APPLES. JUST LET ME DOWN!

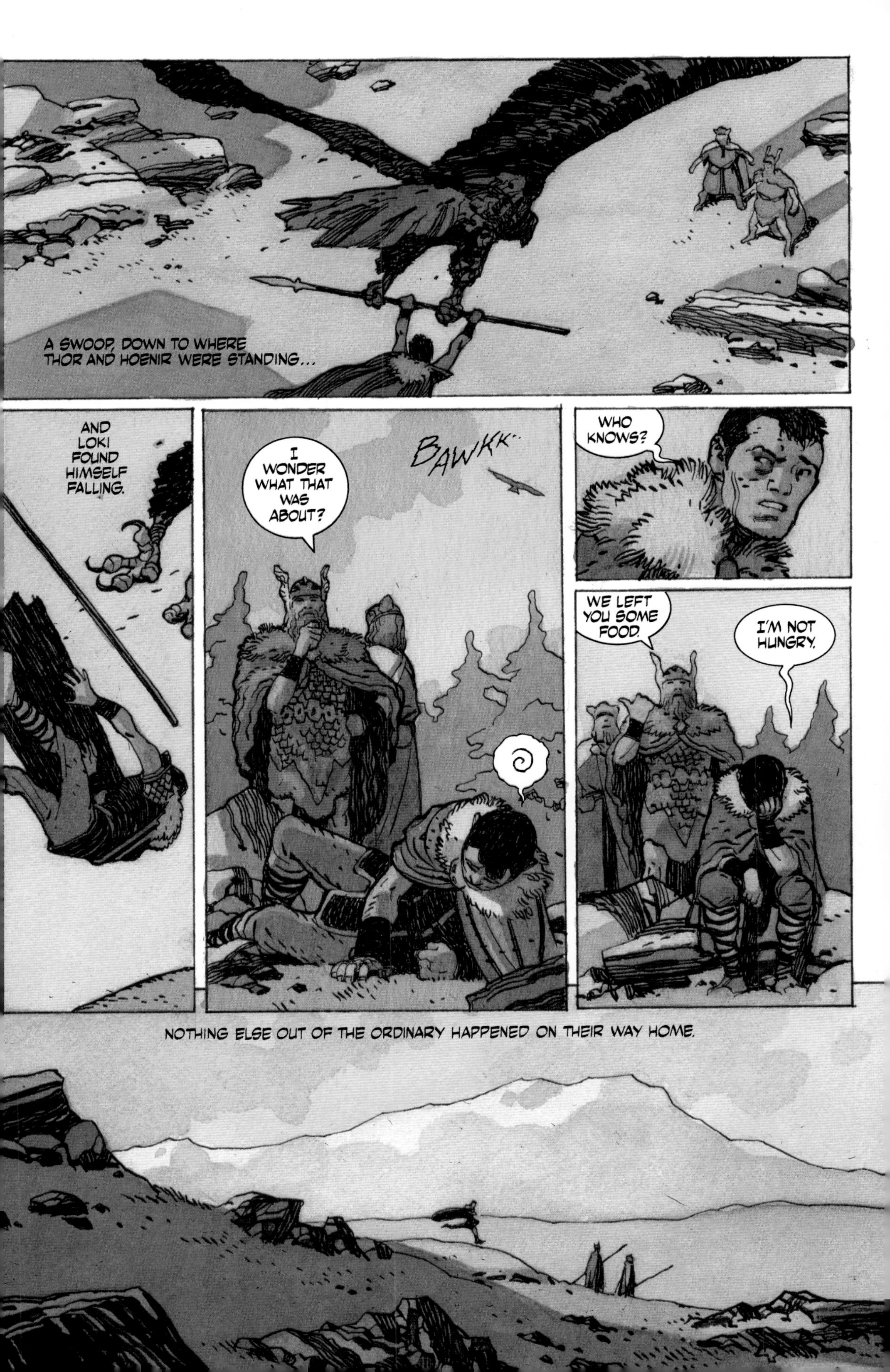
A SWOOP, DOWN TO WHERE THOR AND HOENIR WERE STANDING...
AND LOKI FOUND HIMSELF FALLING.
BAWKK
I WONDER WHAT THAT WAS ABOUT?
WHO KNOWS?
WE LEFT YOU SOME FOOD.
I'M NOT HUNGRY.
NOTHING ELSE OUT OF THE ORDINARY HAPPENED ON THEIR WAY HOME.

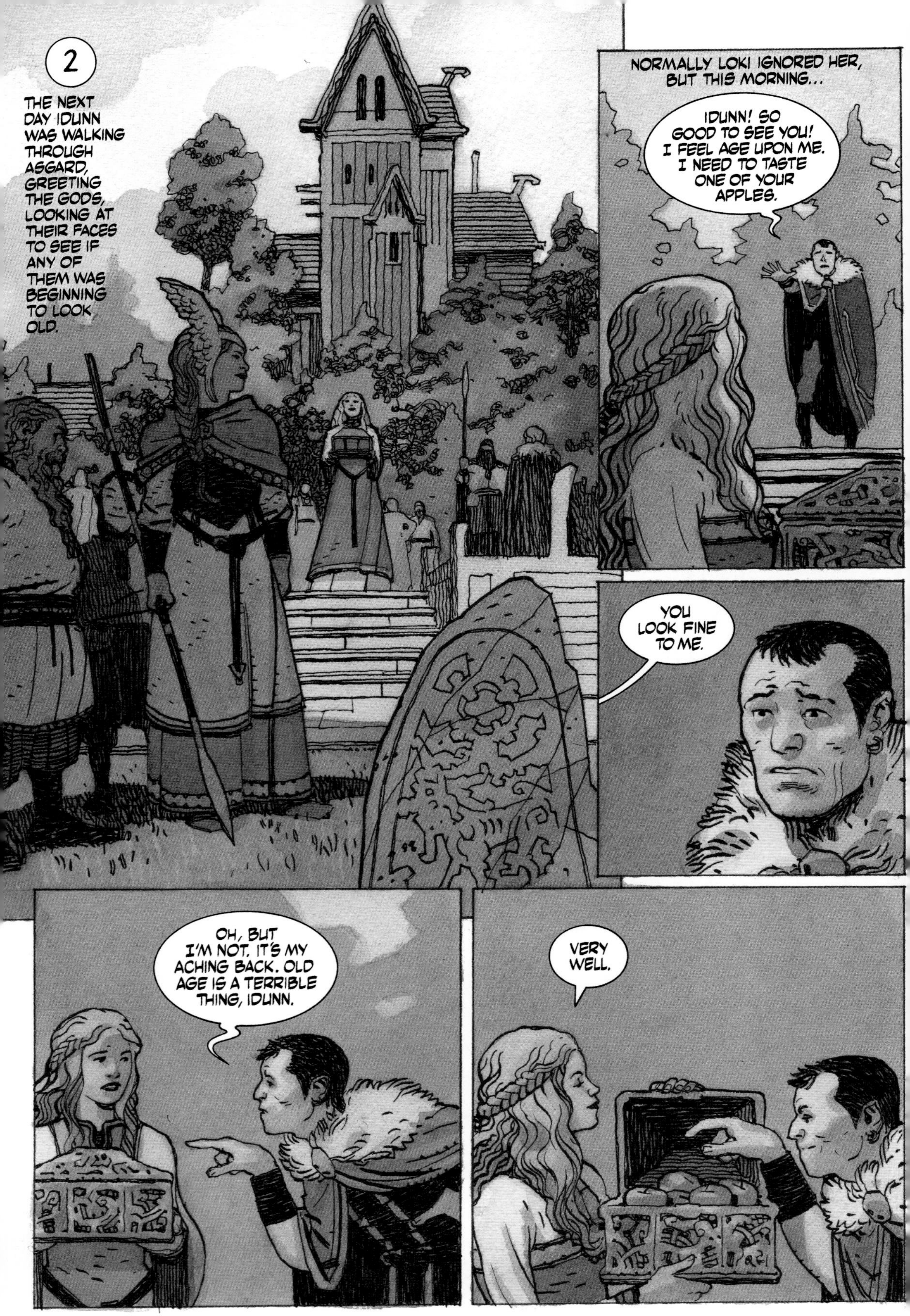
2
THE NEXT DAY IDUNN WAS WALKING THROUGH ASGARD, GREETING THE GODS, LOOKING AT THEIR FACES TO SEE IF ANY OF THEM WAS BEGINNING TO LOOK OLD.
NORMALLY LOKI IGNORED HER, BUT THIS MORNING...
IDUNN! SO GOOD TO SEE YOU! I FEEL AGE UPON ME. I NEED TO TASTE ONE OF YOUR APPLES.
YOU LOOK FINE TO ME.
OH, BUT I'M NOT. IT'S MY ACHING BACK. OLD AGE IS A TERRIBLE THING, IDUNN.
VERY WELL.

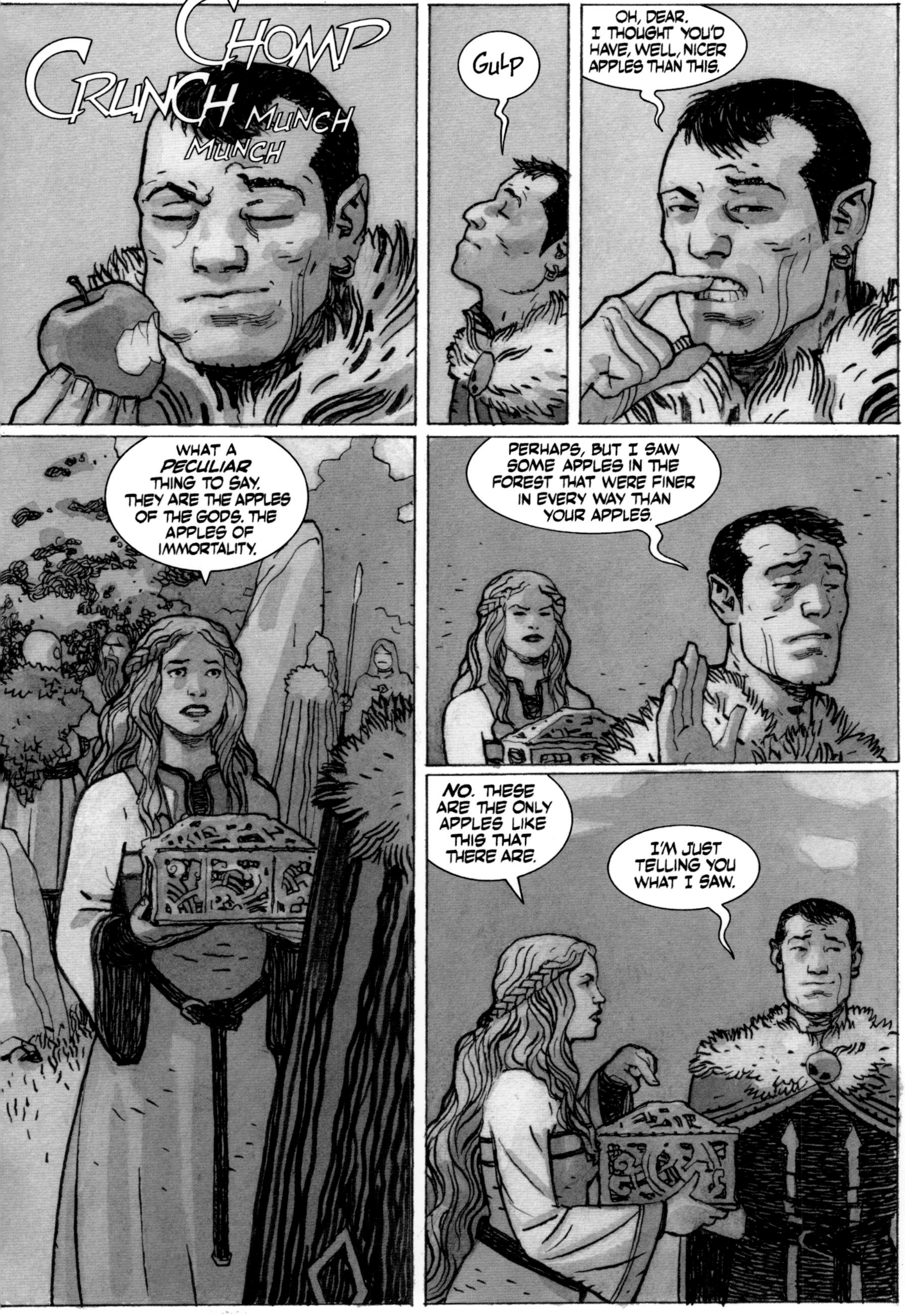
CHOMP
CRUNCH MUNCH
MUNCH
GULP
OH, DEAR. I THOUGHT YOU'D HAVE, WELL, NICER APPLES THAN THIS.
WHAT A PECULIAR THING TO SAY. THEY ARE THE APPLES OF THE GODS. THE APPLES OF IMMORTALITY.
PERHAPS, BUT I SAW SOME APPLES IN THE FOREST THAT WERE FINER IN EVERY WAY THAN YOUR APPLES.
NO. THESE ARE THE ONLY APPLES LIKE THIS THAT THERE ARE.
I'M JUST TELLING YOU WHAT I SAW.

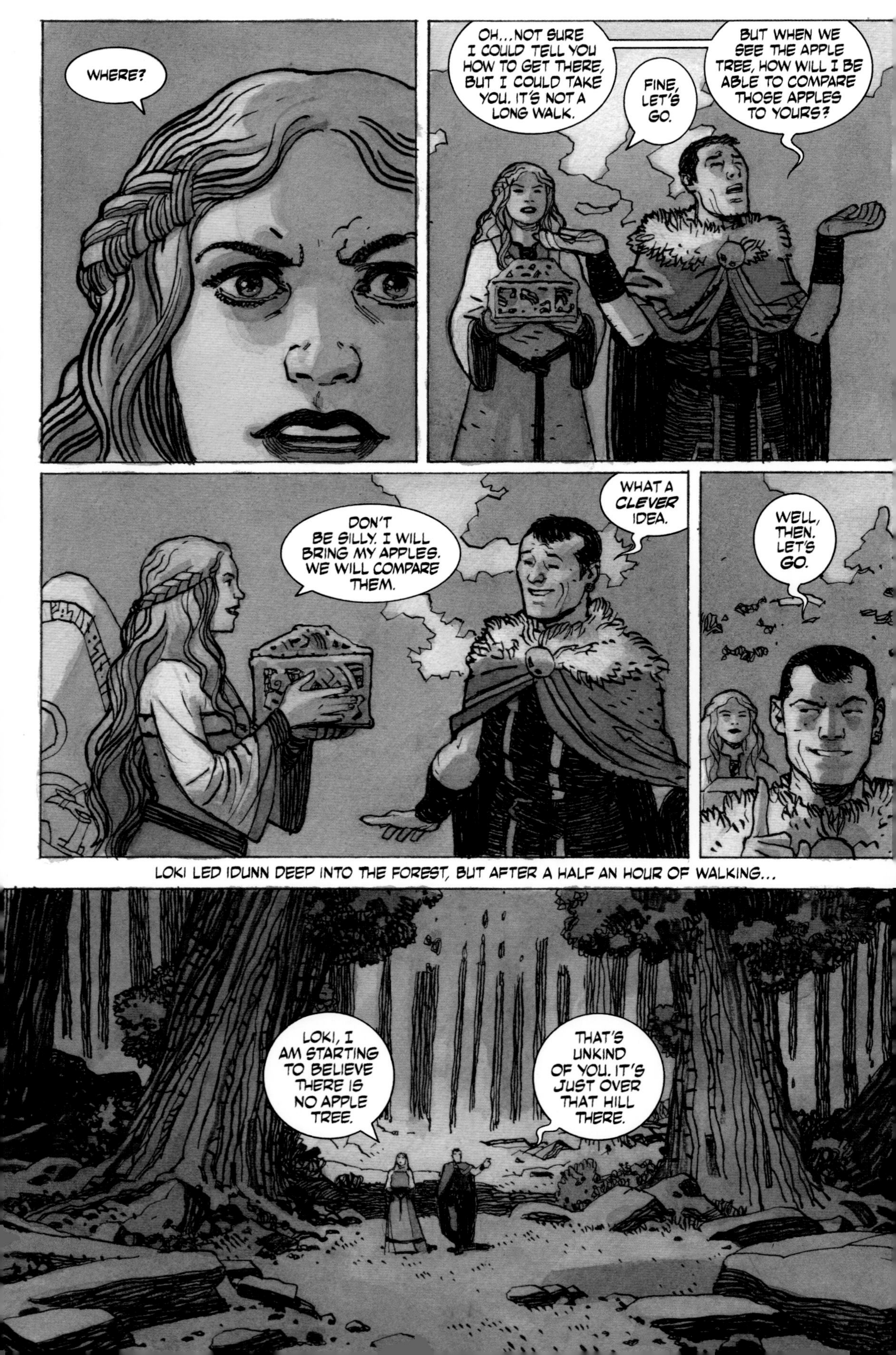
WHERE?
OH...NOT SURE I COULD TELL YOU HOW TO GET THERE, BUT I COULD TAKE YOU. IT'S NOT A LONG WALK.
FINE, LET'S GO.
BUT WHEN WE SEE THE APPLE TREE, HOW WILL I BE ABLE TO COMPARE THOSE APPLES TO YOURS?
DON'T BE SILLY. I WILL BRING MY APPLES. WE WILL COMPARE THEM.
WHAT A CLEVER IDEA.
WELL, THEN. LET'S GO.
LOKI LED IDUNN DEEP INTO THE FOREST, BUT AFTER A HALF AN HOUR OF WALKING...
LOKI, I AM STARTING TO BELIEVE THERE IS NO APPLE TREE.
THAT'S UNKIND OF YOU. IT'S JUST OVER THAT HILL THERE.

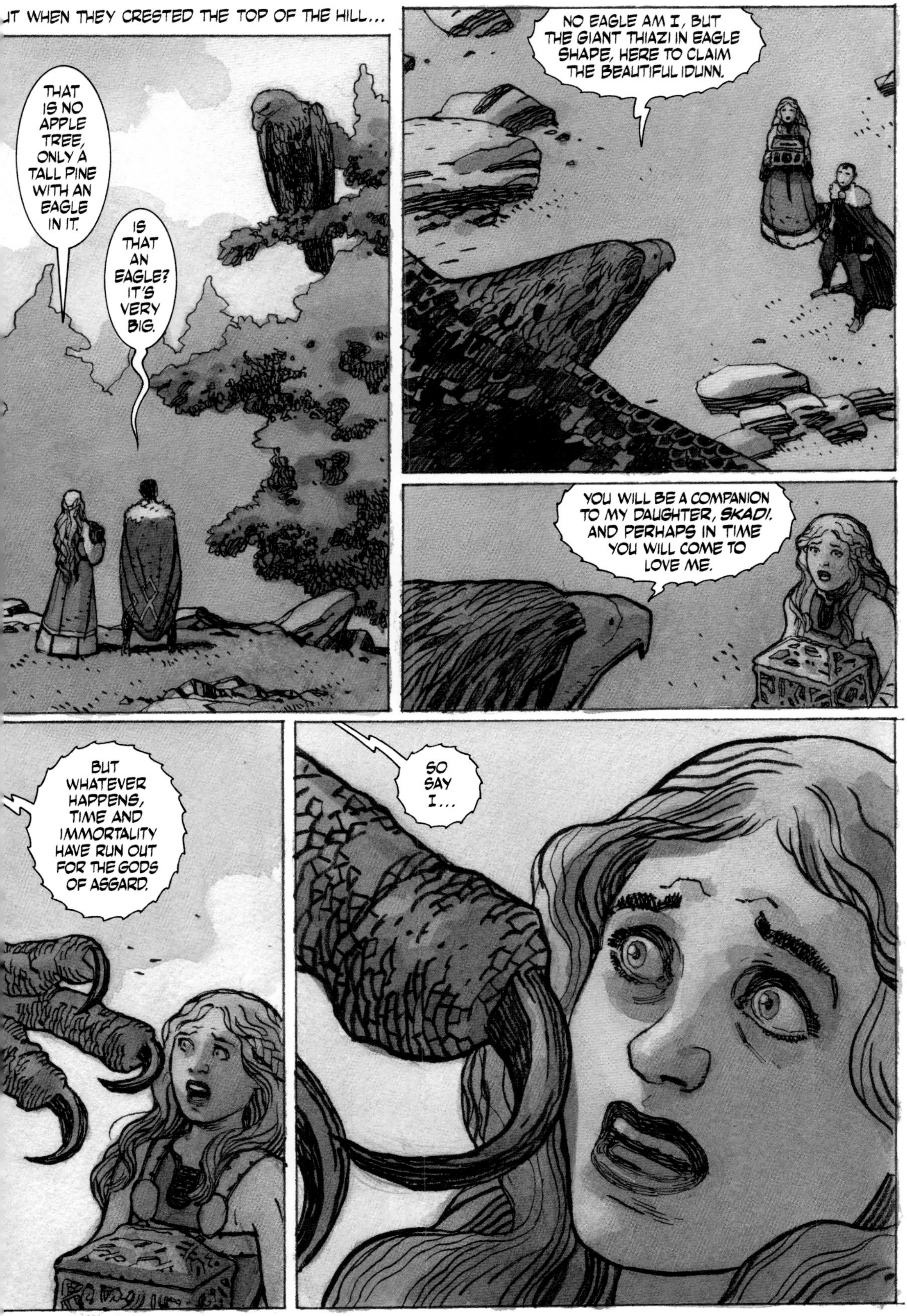

UT WHEN THEY CRESTED THE TOP OF THE HILL...
THAT IS NO APPLE TREE, ONLY A TALL PINE WITH AN EAGLE IN IT.
IS THAT AN EAGLE? IT'S VERY BIG.
NO EAGLE AM I, BUT THE GIANT THIAZI IN EAGLE SHAPE, HERE TO CLAIM THE BEAUTIFUL IDUNN.
YOU WILL BE A COMPANION TO MY DAUGHTER, SKADI. AND PERHAPS IN TIME YOU WILL COME TO LOVE ME.
BUT WHATEVER HAPPENS, TIME AND IMMORTALITY HAVE RUN OUT FOR THE GODS OF ASGARD.
SO SAY I...

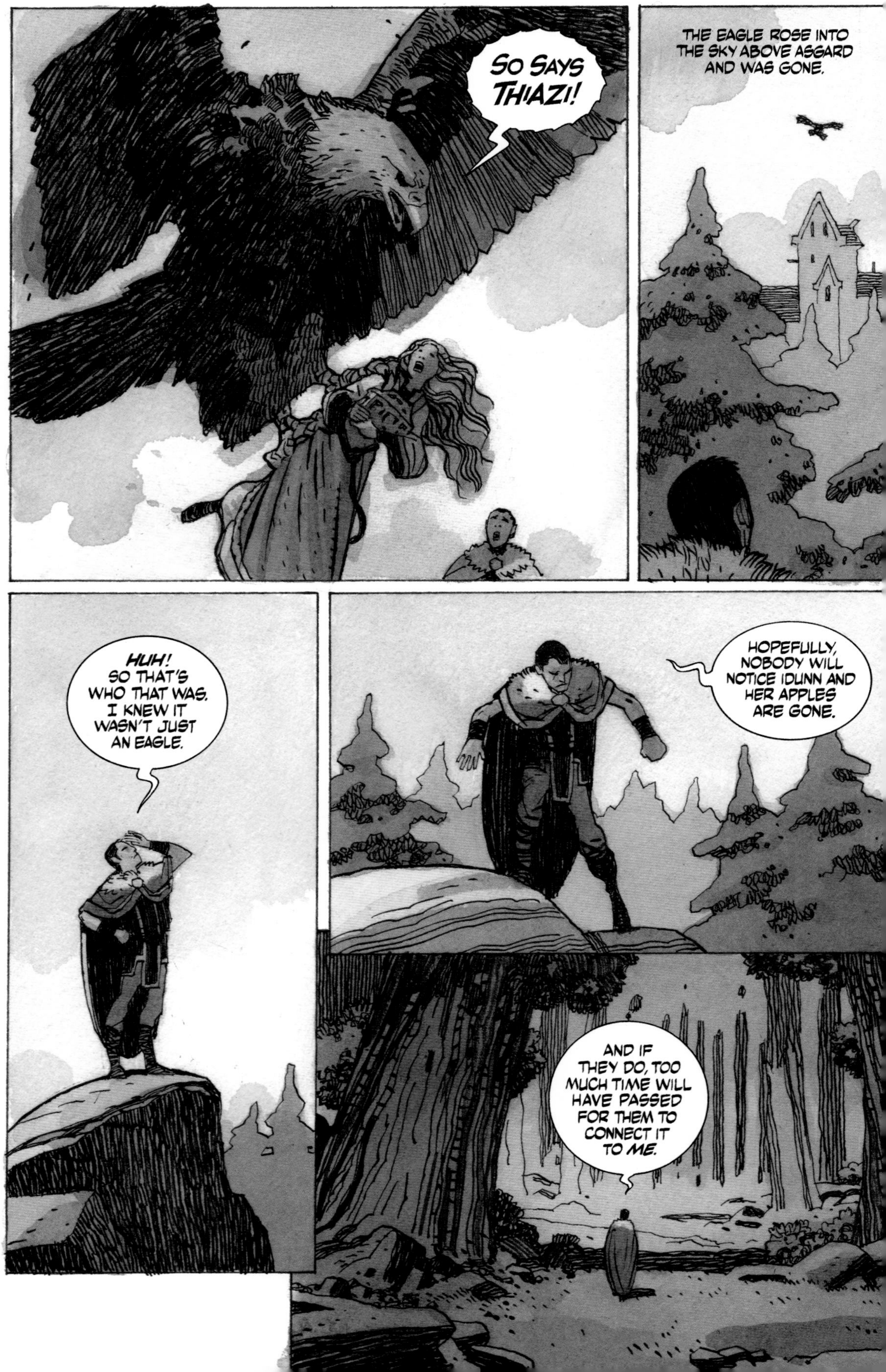
SO SAYS THIAZI!
THE EAGLE ROSE INTO THE SKY ABOVE ASGARD AND WAS GONE.
HUH! SO THAT'S WHO THAT WAS. I KNEW IT WASN'T JUST AN EAGLE.
HOPEFULLY, NOBODY WILL NOTICE IDUNN AND HER APPLES ARE GONE.
AND IF THEY DO, TOO MUCH TIME WILL HAVE PASSED FOR THEM TO CONNECT IT TO ME.

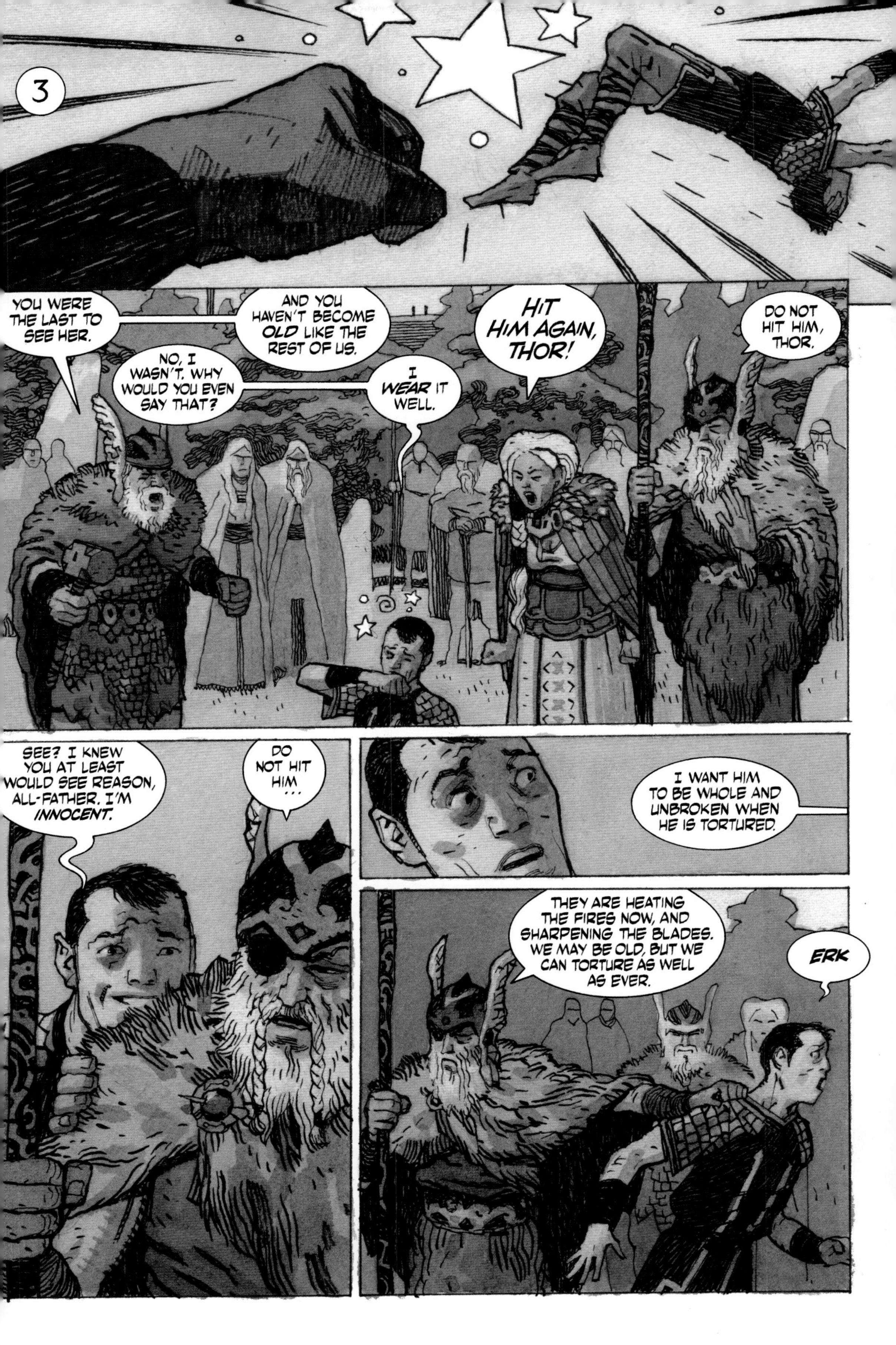
3
YOU WERE THE LAST TO SEE HER.
NO, I WASN'T. WHY WOULD YOU EVEN SAY THAT?
AND YOU HAVEN'T BECOME OLD LIKE THE REST OF US.
I WEAR IT WELL.
HIT HIM AGAIN, THOR!
DO NOT HIT HIM, THOR.
SEE? I KNEW YOU AT LEAST WOULD SEE REASON, ALL-FATHER. I'M INNOCENT.
DO NOT HIT HIM . . .
I WANT HIM TO BE WHOLE AND UNBROKEN WHEN HE IS TORTURED.
THEY ARE HEATING THE FIRES NOW, AND SHARPENING THE BLADES. WE MAY BE OLD, BUT WE CAN TORTURE AS WELL AS EVER.
ERK

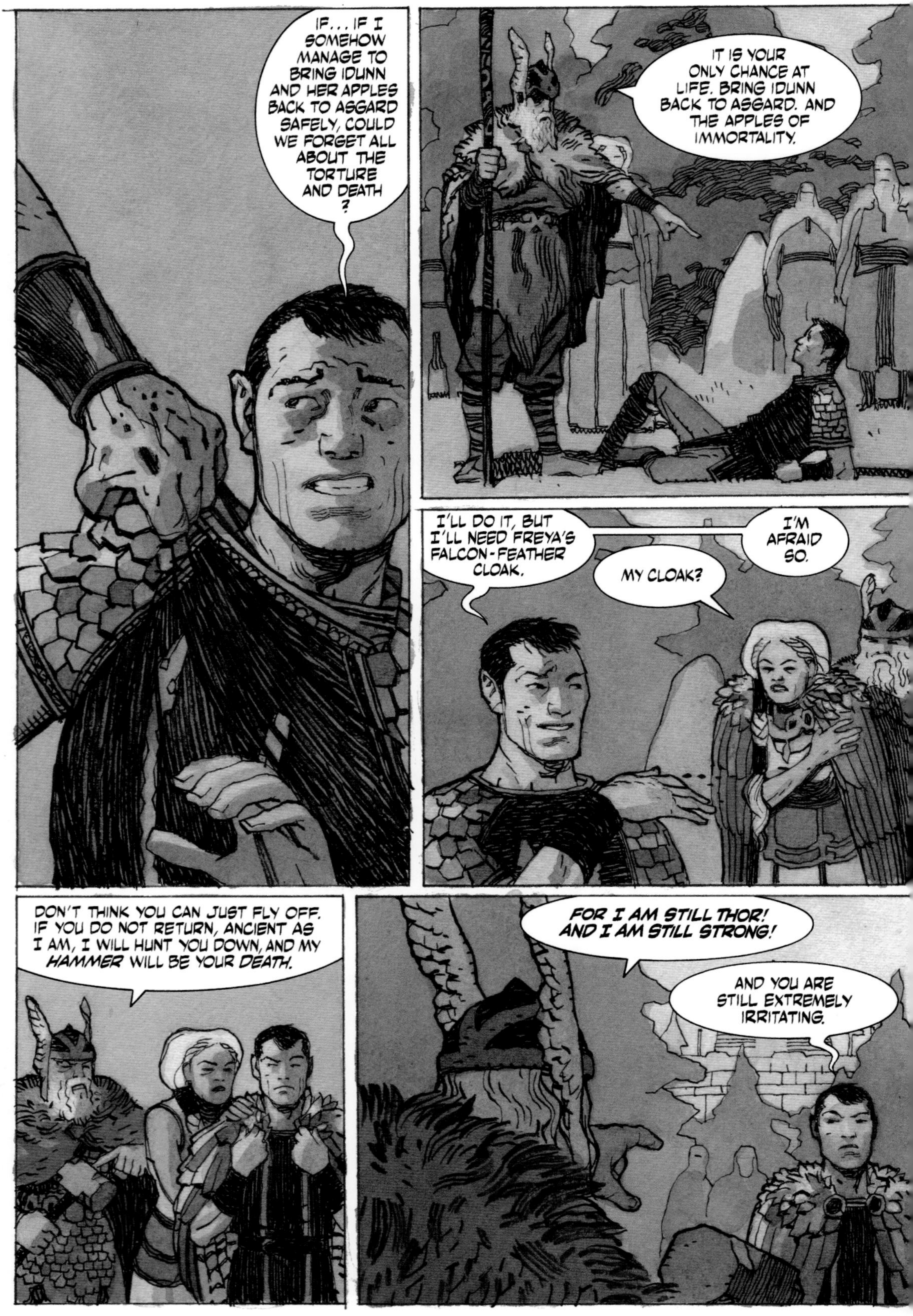
IF... IF I SOMEHOW MANAGE TO BRING IDUNN AND HER APPLES BACK TO ASGARD SAFELY, COULD WE FORGET ALL ABOUT THE TORTURE AND DEATH ?
IT IS YOUR ONLY CHANCE AT LIFE. BRING IDUNN BACK TO ASGARD. AND THE APPLES OF IMMORTALITY.
I'LL DO IT, BUT I'LL NEED FREYA'S FALCON-FEATHER CLOAK.
MY CLOAK?
I'M AFRAID SO.
DON'T THINK YOU CAN JUST FLY OFF. IF YOU DO NOT RETURN, ANCIENT AS I AM, I WILL HUNT YOU DOWN, AND MY *HAMMER* WILL BE YOUR *DEATH*.
FOR I AM STILL THOR! AND I AM STILL STRONG!
AND YOU ARE STILL EXTREMELY IRRITATING.

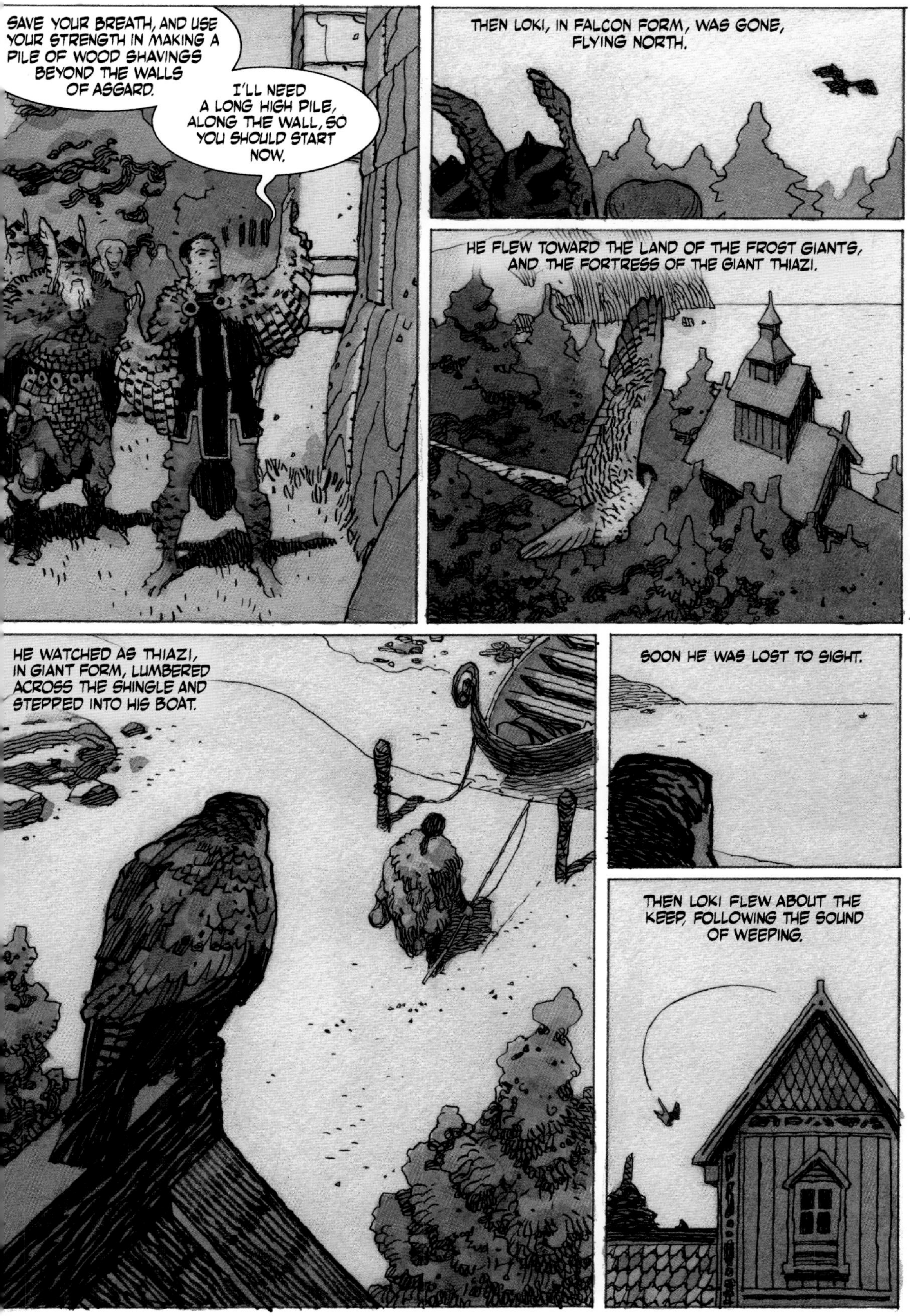
SAVE YOUR BREATH, AND USE YOUR STRENGTH IN MAKING A PILE OF WOOD SHAVINGS BEYOND THE WALLS OF ASGARD.
I'LL NEED A LONG HIGH PILE, ALONG THE WALL, SO YOU SHOULD START NOW.
THEN LOKI, IN FALCON FORM, WAS GONE, FLYING NORTH.
HE FLEW TOWARD THE LAND OF THE FROST GIANTS, AND THE FORTRESS OF THE GIANT THIAZI.
HE WATCHED AS THIAZI, IN GIANT FORM, LUMBERED ACROSS THE SHINGLE AND STEPPED INTO HIS BOAT.
SOON HE WAS LOST TO SIGHT.
THEN LOKI FLEW ABOUT THE KEEP, FOLLOWING THE SOUND OF WEEPING.

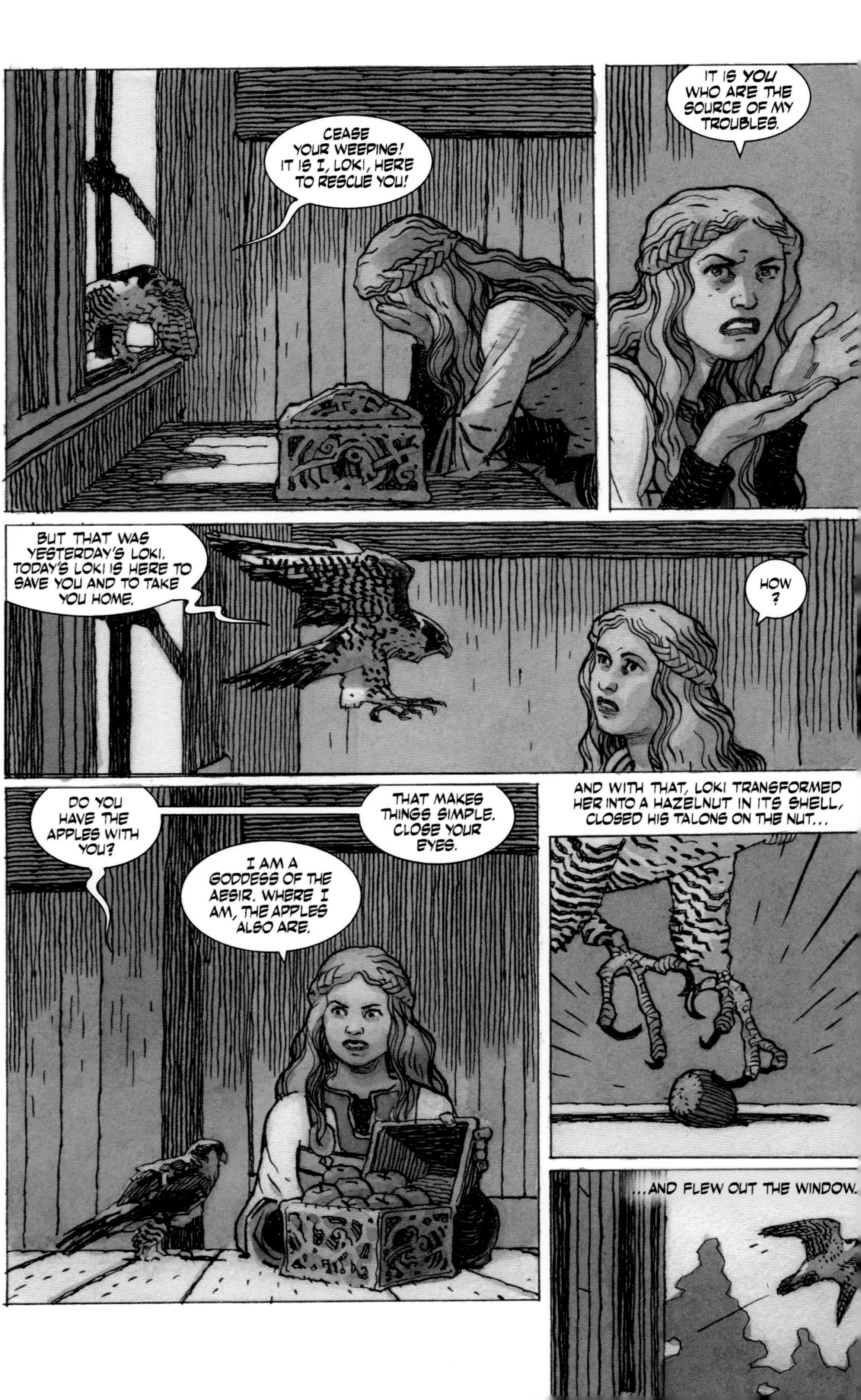
CEASE YOUR WEEPING! IT IS I, LOKI, HERE TO RESCUE YOU!
IT IS YOU WHO ARE THE SOURCE OF MY TROUBLES.
BUT THAT WAS YESTERDAY'S LOKI. TODAY'S LOKI IS HERE TO SAVE YOU AND TO TAKE YOU HOME.
HOW?
DO YOU HAVE THE APPLES WITH YOU?
I AM A GODDESS OF THE AESIR. WHERE I AM, THE APPLES ALSO ARE.
THAT MAKES THINGS SIMPLE. CLOSE YOUR EYES.
AND WITH THAT, LOKI TRANSFORMED HER INTO A HAZELNUT IN ITS SHELL, CLOSED HIS TALONS ON THE NUT...
...AND FLEW OUT THE WINDOW.

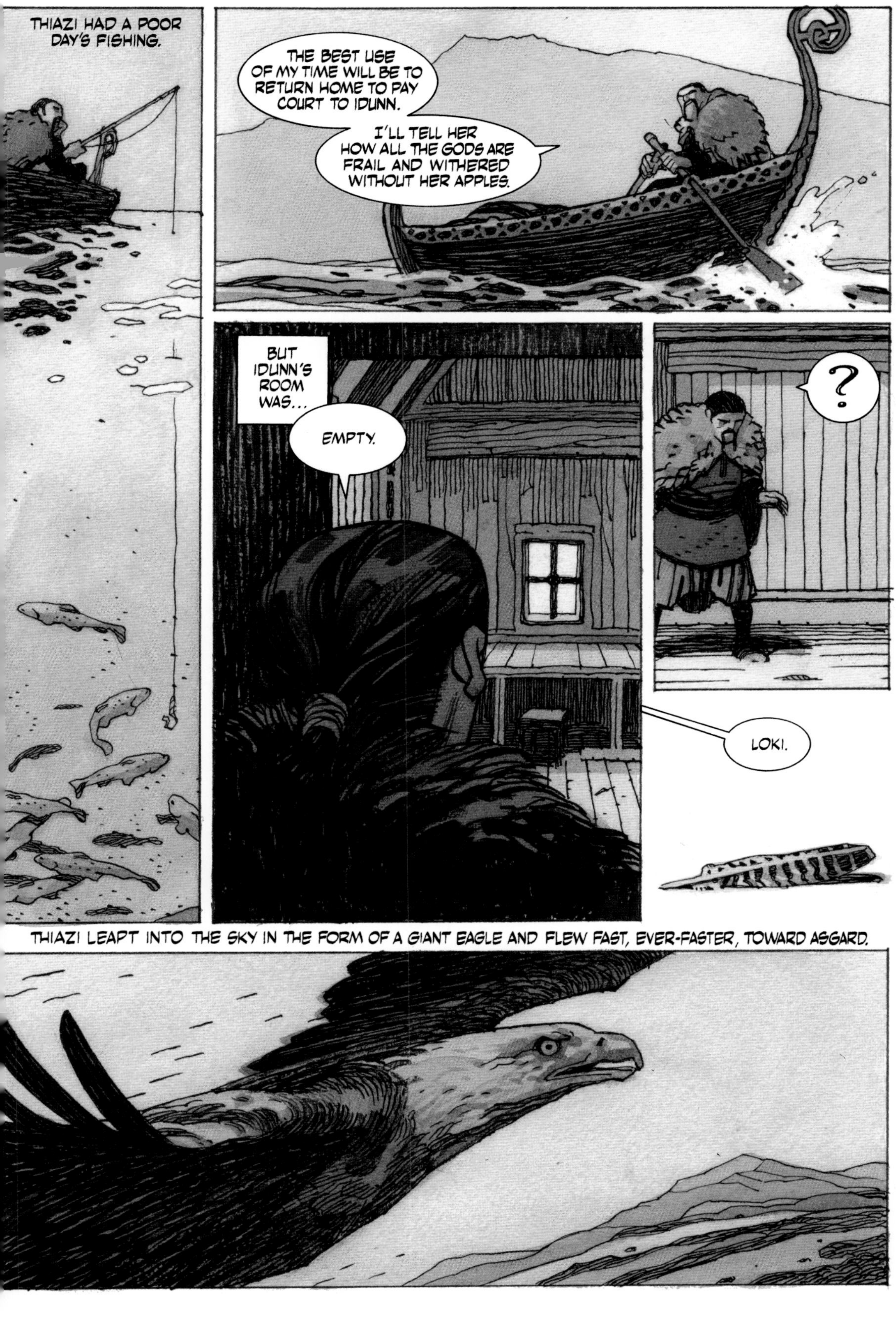
THIAZI HAD A POOR DAY'S FISHING.
THE BEST USE OF MY TIME WILL BE TO RETURN HOME TO PAY COURT TO IDUNN.
I'LL TELL HER HOW ALL THE GODS ARE FRAIL AND WITHERED WITHOUT HER APPLES.
BUT IDUNN'S ROOM WAS...
EMPTY.
?
LOKI.
THIAZI LEAPT INTO THE SKY IN THE FORM OF A GIANT EAGLE AND FLEW FAST, EVER-FASTER, TOWARD ASGARD.

HE FLEW SO FAST THAT THE AIR ITSELF...

BOOM

SKRAAAW

NOW
?

NOW.

NOW!

WHOOOMPH

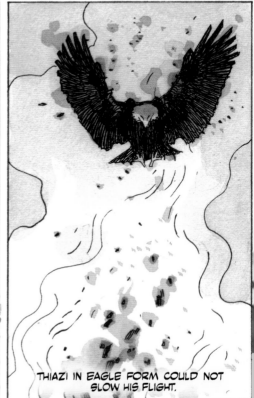

THIAZI IN EAGLE FORM COULD NOT SLOW HIS FLIGHT.

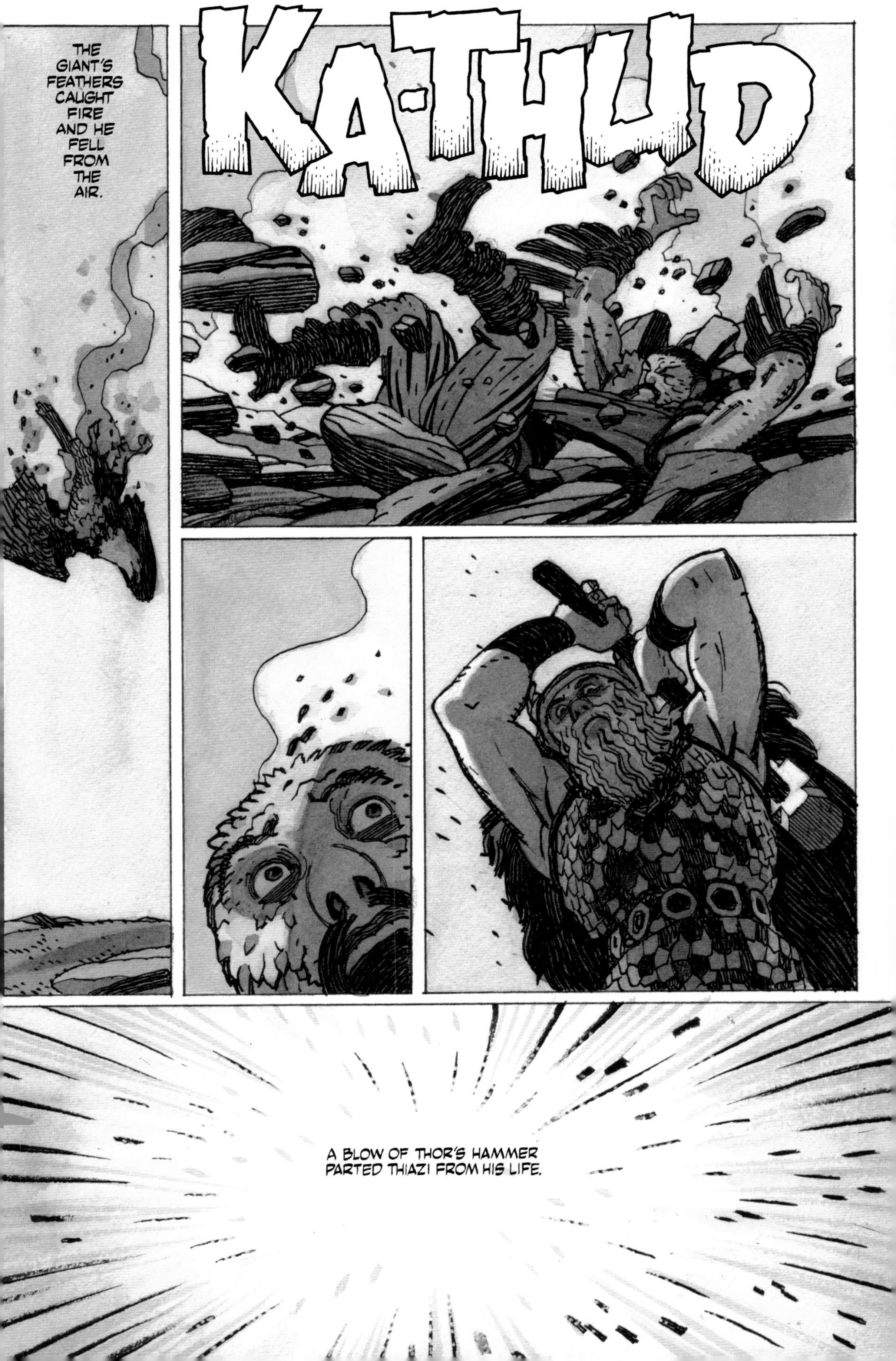
THE GIANT'S FEATHERS CAUGHT FIRE AND HE FELL FROM THE AIR.
KA-THUD
A BLOW OF THOR'S HAMMER PARTED THIAZI FROM HIS LIFE.

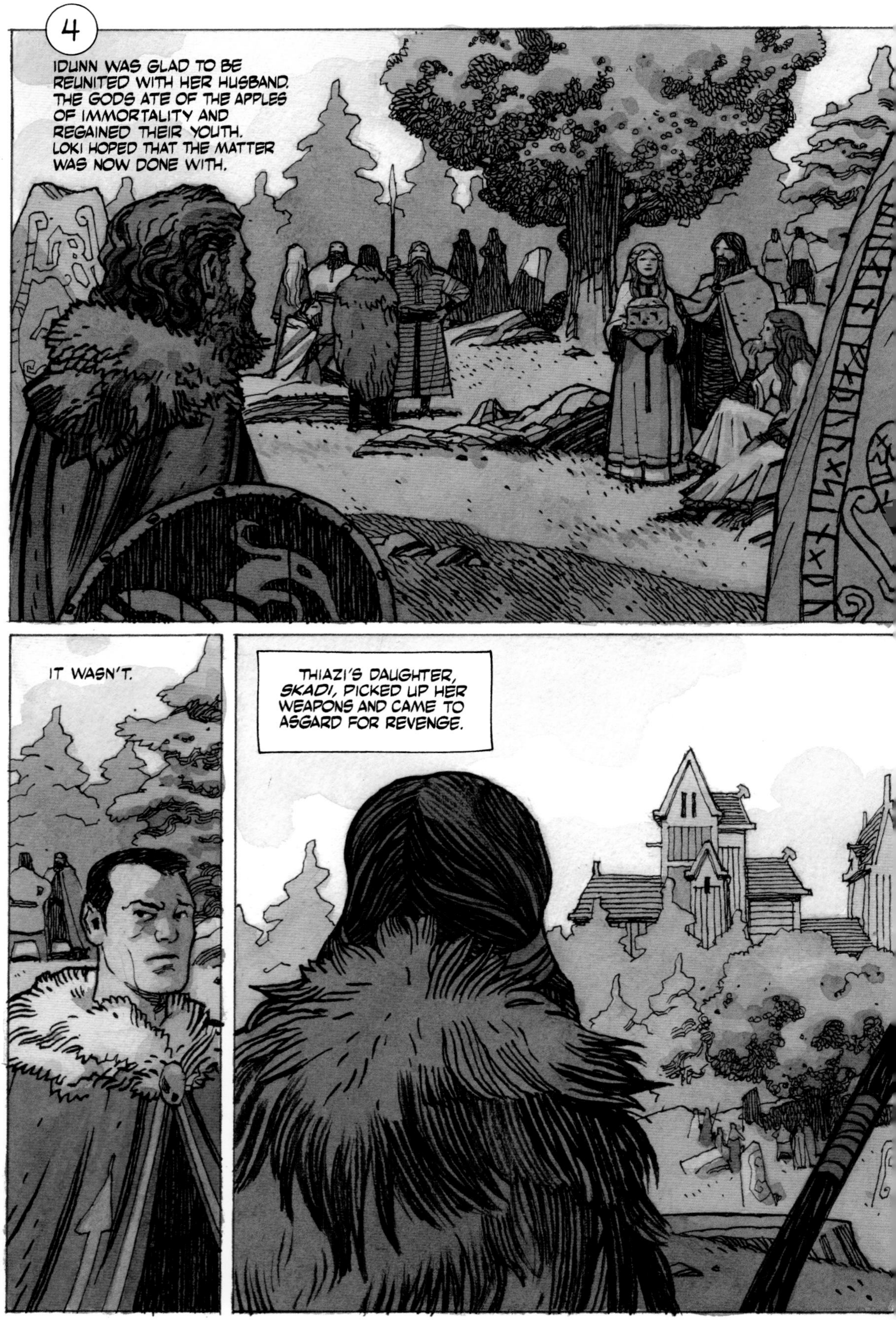
4
IDUNN WAS GLAD TO BE REUNITED WITH HER HUSBAND. THE GODS ATE OF THE APPLES OF IMMORTALITY AND REGAINED THEIR YOUTH. LOKI HOPED THAT THE MATTER WAS NOW DONE WITH.
IT WASN'T.
THIAZI'S DAUGHTER, *SKADI*, PICKED UP HER WEAPONS AND CAME TO ASGARD FOR REVENGE.

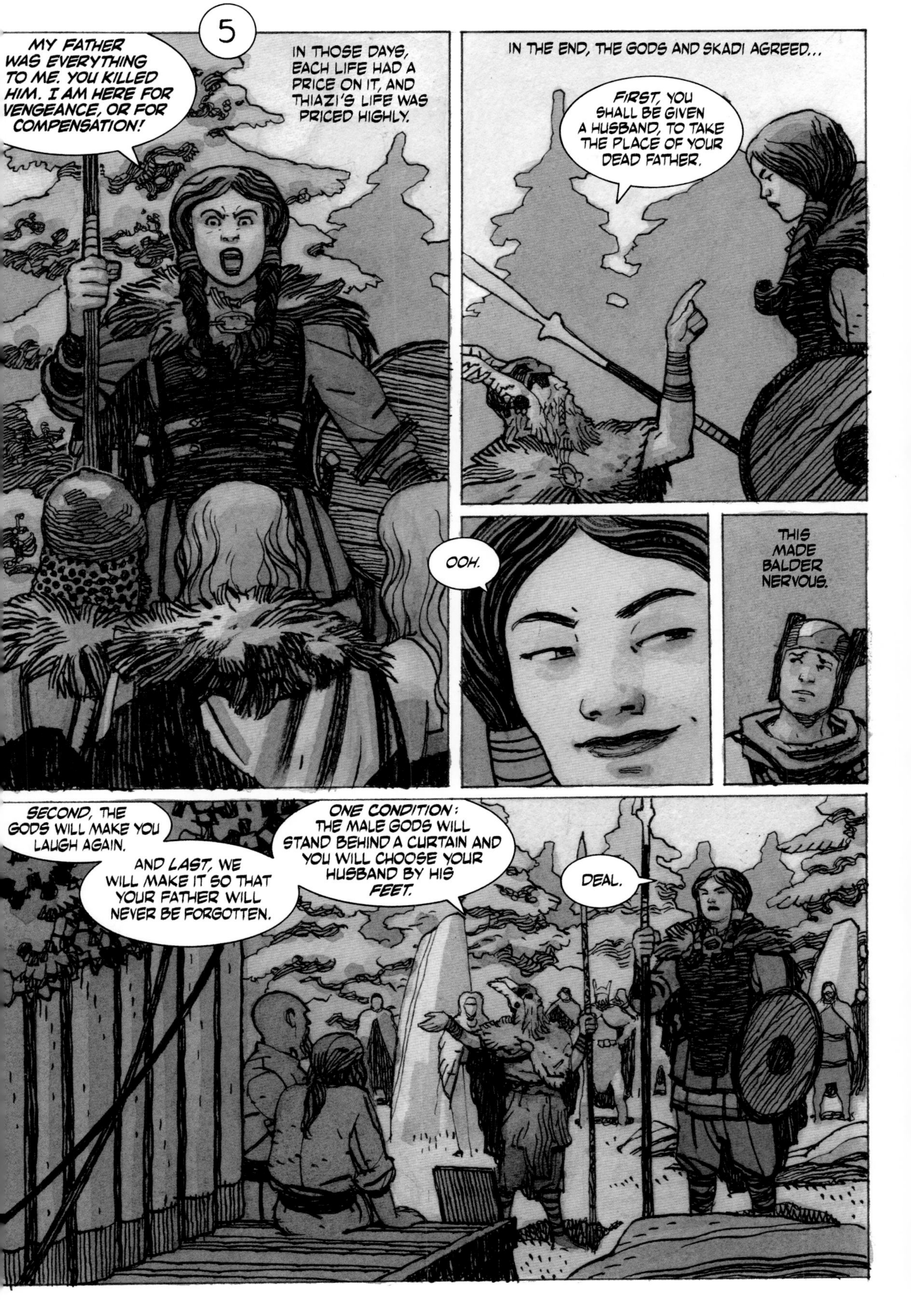
5
MY FATHER WAS EVERYTHING TO ME. YOU KILLED HIM. I AM HERE FOR VENGEANCE, OR FOR COMPENSATION!
IN THOSE DAYS, EACH LIFE HAD A PRICE ON IT, AND THIAZI'S LIFE WAS PRICED HIGHLY.
IN THE END, THE GODS AND SKADI AGREED...
FIRST, YOU SHALL BE GIVEN A HUSBAND, TO TAKE THE PLACE OF YOUR DEAD FATHER.
OOH.
THIS MADE BALDER NERVOUS.
SECOND, THE GODS WILL MAKE YOU LAUGH AGAIN.
AND LAST, WE WILL MAKE IT SO THAT YOUR FATHER WILL NEVER BE FORGOTTEN.
ONE CONDITION: THE MALE GODS WILL STAND BEHIND A CURTAIN AND YOU WILL CHOOSE YOUR HUSBAND BY HIS FEET.
DEAL.

ONE BY ONE THE GODS WALKED PAST THE CURTAIN.

UGLY FEET.

UGLY FEET.

UGLY FEET.

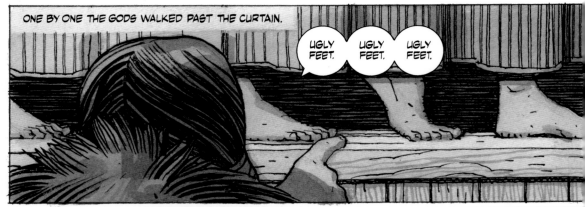

OH... BEAUTIFUL FEET. THEY MUST BE BALDER'S. NOTHING ON BALDER COULD BE UGLY.

BUT WHEN THE CURTAIN WAS LIFTED, THE FEET BELONGED TO NJORD, FATHER OF FREY AND FREYA.

SHE MARRIED HIM THEN AND THERE. AT THE WEDDING FEAST HER FACE WAS THE SADDEST ANY OF THE *AESIR* HAD EVER SEEN.

GO ON. MAKE HER LAUGH. THIS IS ALL YOUR FAULT ANYWAY.

REALLY?

REALLY.

LOKI LEFT THE WEDDING FEAST

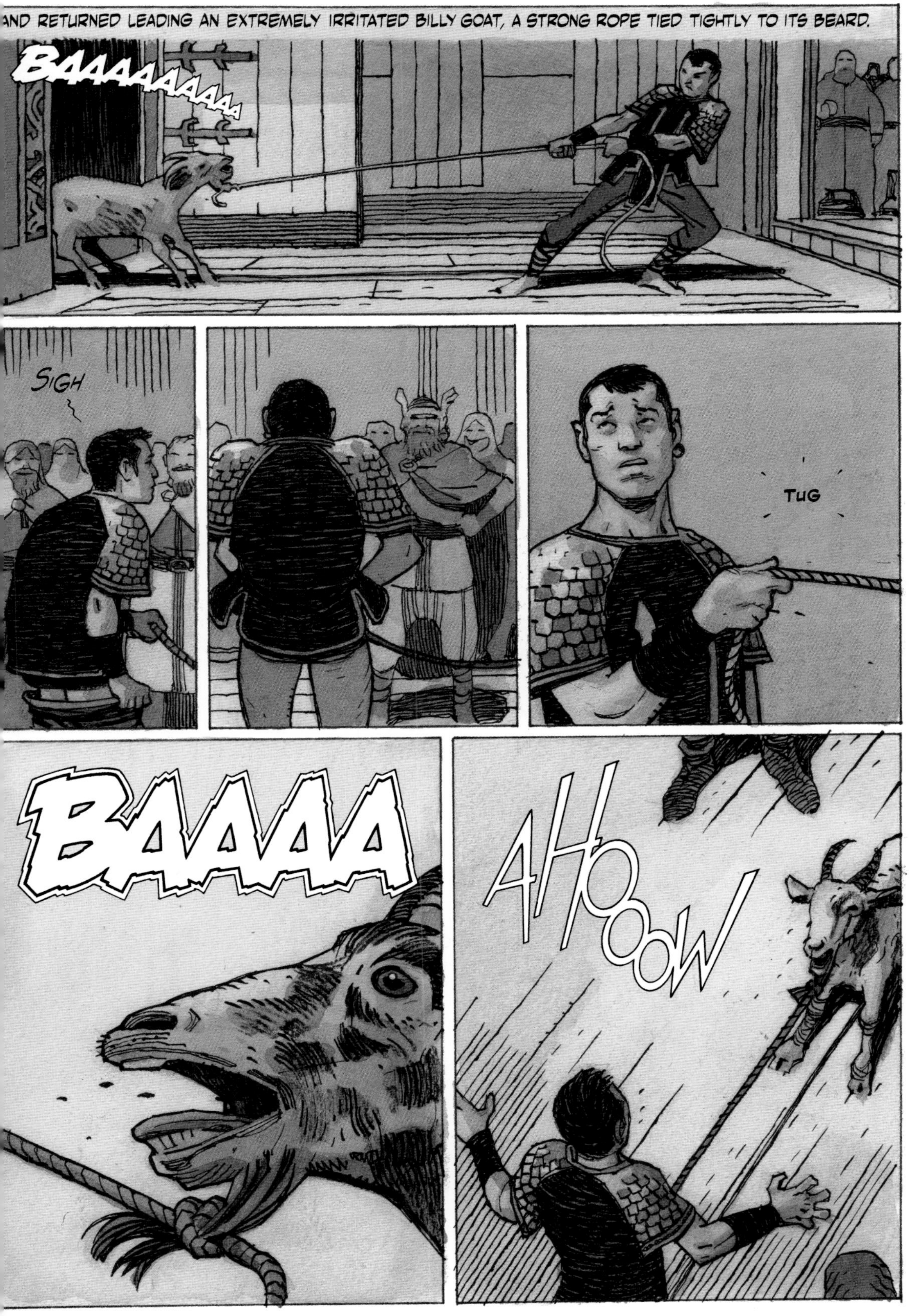
AND RETURNED LEADING AN EXTREMELY IRRITATED BILLY GOAT, A STRONG ROPE TIED TIGHTLY TO ITS BEARD.
BAAAAAAAAAA
SIGH
TUG
BAAAA
AHOOOW

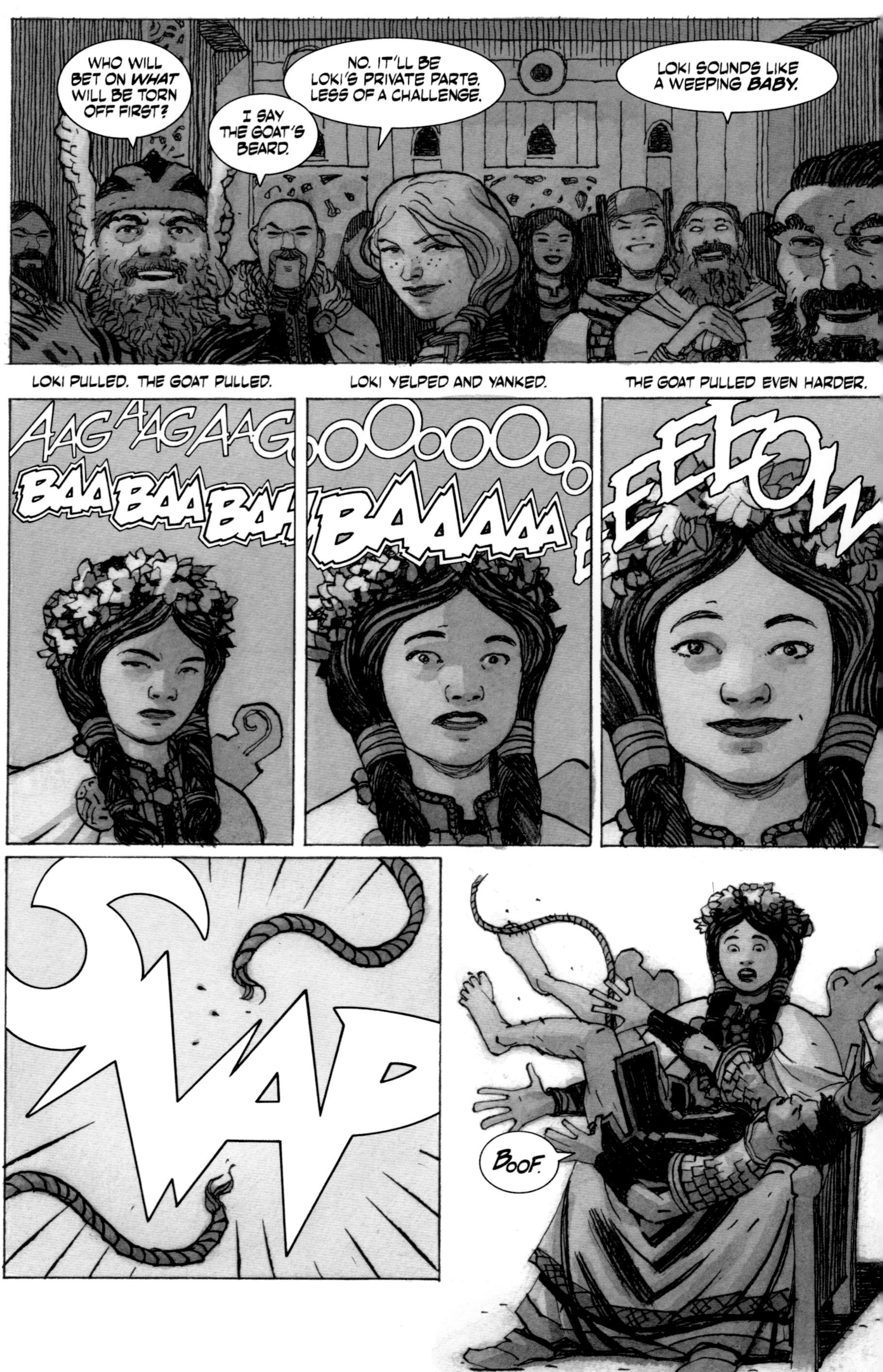
WHO WILL BET ON WHAT WILL BE TORN OFF FIRST?
I SAY THE GOAT'S BEARD.
NO. IT'LL BE LOKI'S PRIVATE PARTS. LESS OF A CHALLENGE.
LOKI SOUNDS LIKE A WEEPING BABY.
LOKI PULLED. THE GOAT PULLED.
AAG AAG AAG
BAA BAA BAH
LOKI YELPED AND YANKED.
OOOOOOOOO
BAAAAAA
THE GOAT PULLED EVEN HARDER.
EEEOW
SNAP
BOOF.

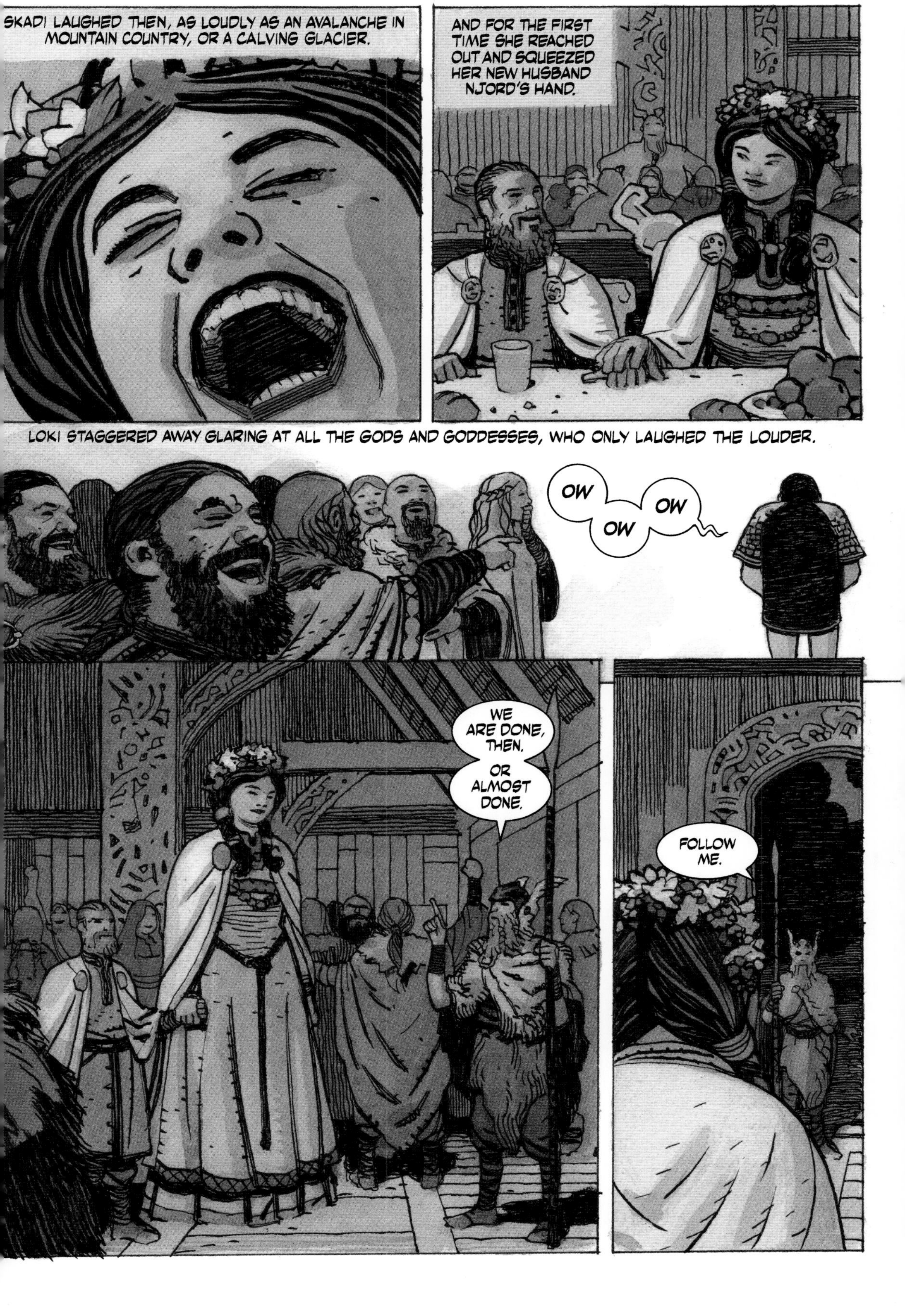
SKADI LAUGHED THEN, AS LOUDLY AS AN AVALANCHE IN MOUNTAIN COUNTRY, OR A CALVING GLACIER.
AND FOR THE FIRST TIME SHE REACHED OUT AND SQUEEZED HER NEW HUSBAND NJORD'S HAND.
LOKI STAGGERED AWAY GLARING AT ALL THE GODS AND GODDESSES, WHO ONLY LAUGHED THE LOUDER.
OW
OW
OW
WE ARE DONE, THEN.
OR ALMOST DONE.
FOLLOW ME.

ODIN LED SKADI TO THE FUNERAL PYRE THE GODS HAD MADE FOR THIAZI.

BESIDE IT WERE TWO ORBS, FILLED WITH LIGHT.

THESE WERE YOUR FATHER'S EYES.

THIAZI SHALL NEVER BE FORGOTTEN.

THE ALL-FATHER THREW THE TWO EYES UP INTO THE NIGHT SKY.

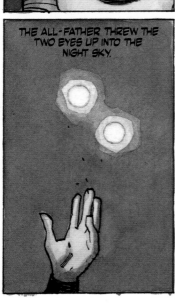

LOOK UP INTO THE NIGHT IN MIDWINTER. YOU CAN SEE THEM THERE, ONE BLAZING BESIDE THE OTHER. THEY ARE THIAZI'S EYES.

THEY ARE SHINING STILL.

The Story of Gerd and Frey

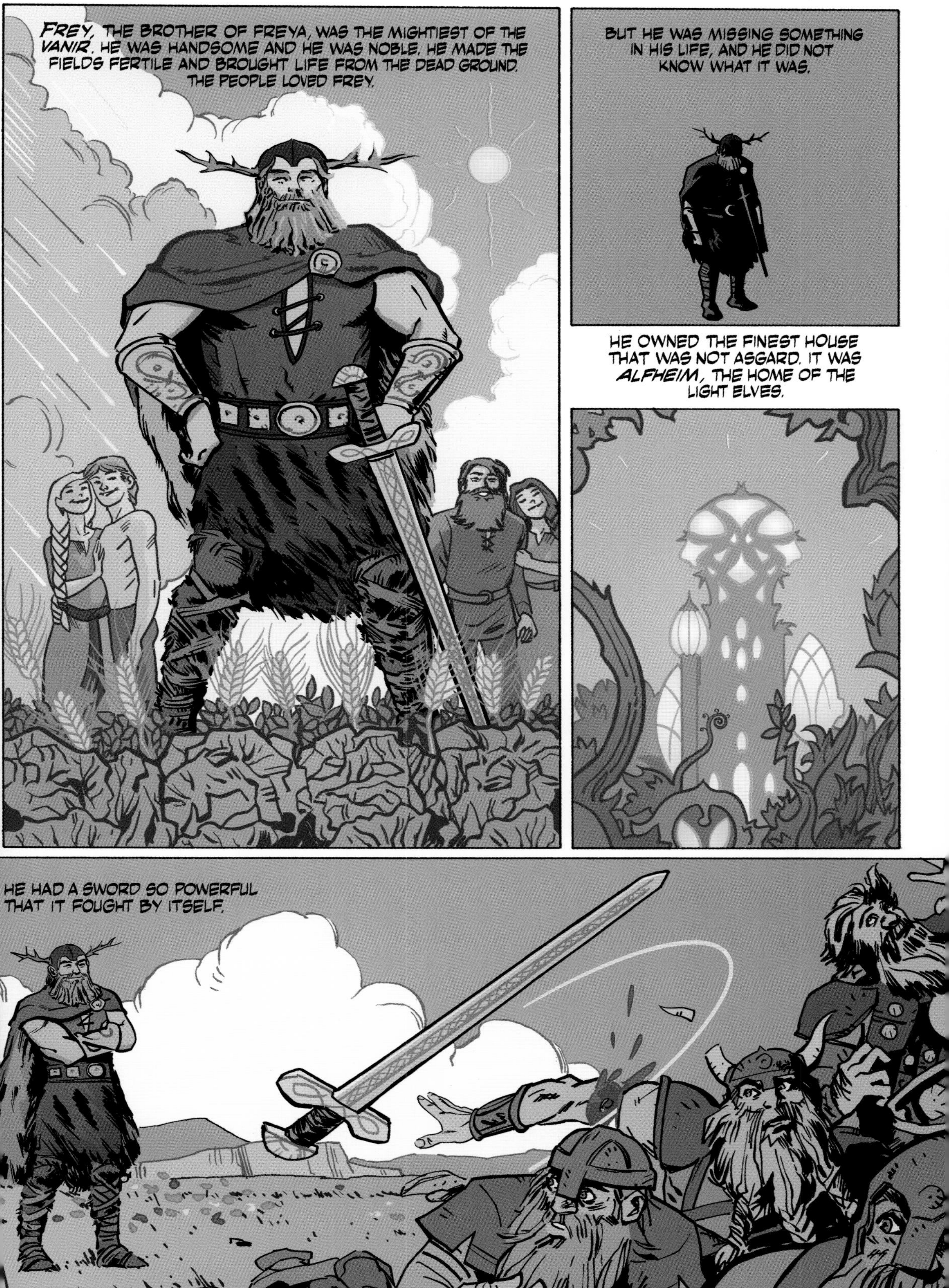

FREY, THE BROTHER OF FREYA, WAS THE MIGHTIEST OF THE VANIR. HE WAS HANDSOME AND HE WAS NOBLE. HE MADE THE FIELDS FERTILE AND BROUGHT LIFE FROM THE DEAD GROUND. THE PEOPLE LOVED FREY.
BUT HE WAS MISSING SOMETHING IN HIS LIFE, AND HE DID NOT KNOW WHAT IT WAS.
HE OWNED THE FINEST HOUSE THAT WAS NOT ASGARD. IT WAS ALFHEIM, THE HOME OF THE LIGHT ELVES.
HE HAD A SWORD SO POWERFUL THAT IT FOUGHT BY ITSELF.

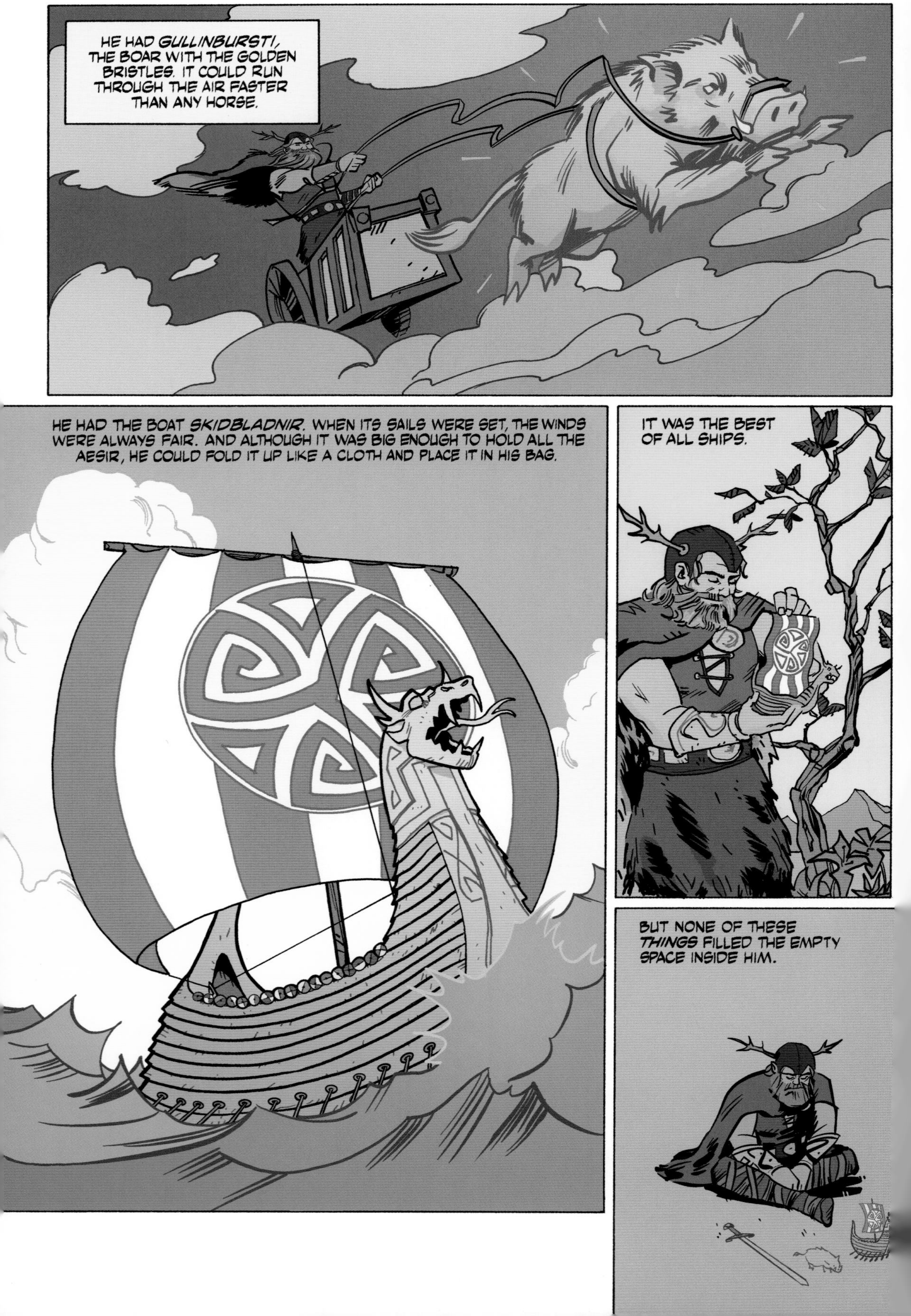
HE HAD *GULLINBURSTI*, THE BOAR WITH THE GOLDEN BRISTLES. IT COULD RUN THROUGH THE AIR FASTER THAN ANY HORSE.
HE HAD THE BOAT *SKIDBLADNIR*. WHEN ITS SAILS WERE SET, THE WINDS WERE ALWAYS FAIR. AND ALTHOUGH IT WAS BIG ENOUGH TO HOLD ALL THE AESIR, HE COULD FOLD IT UP LIKE A CLOTH AND PLACE IT IN HIS BAG.
IT WAS THE BEST OF ALL SHIPS.
BUT NONE OF THESE *THINGS* FILLED THE EMPTY SPACE INSIDE HIM.

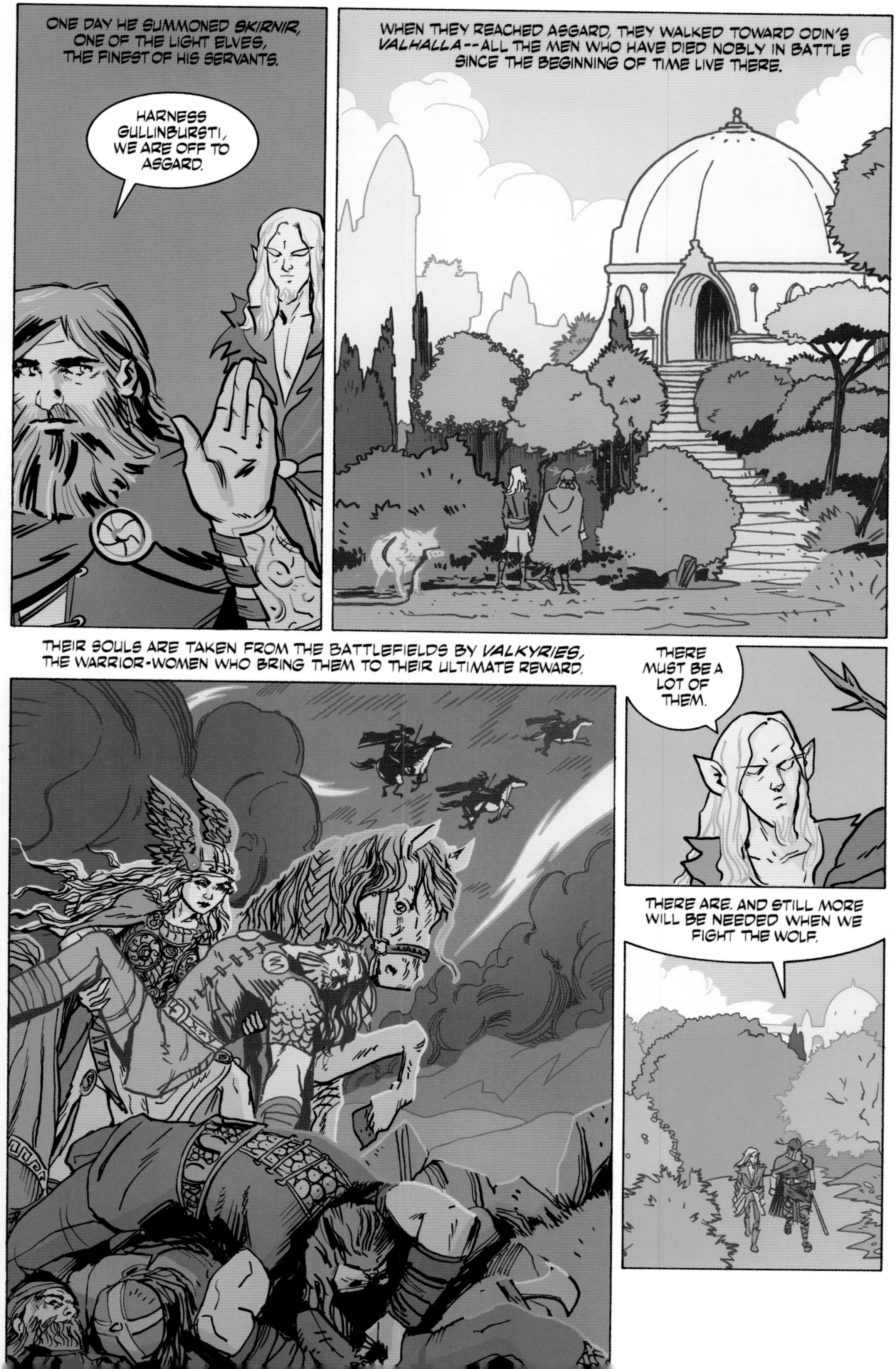
ONE DAY HE SUMMONED SKIRNIR, ONE OF THE LIGHT ELVES, THE FINEST OF HIS SERVANTS.
HARNESS GULLINBURSTI, WE ARE OFF TO ASGARD.
WHEN THEY REACHED ASGARD, THEY WALKED TOWARD ODIN'S VALHALLA--ALL THE MEN WHO HAVE DIED NOBLY IN BATTLE SINCE THE BEGINNING OF TIME LIVE THERE.
THEIR SOULS ARE TAKEN FROM THE BATTLEFIELDS BY VALKYRIES, THE WARRIOR-WOMEN WHO BRING THEM TO THEIR ULTIMATE REWARD.
THERE MUST BE A LOT OF THEM.
THERE ARE. AND STILL MORE WILL BE NEEDED WHEN WE FIGHT THE WOLF.

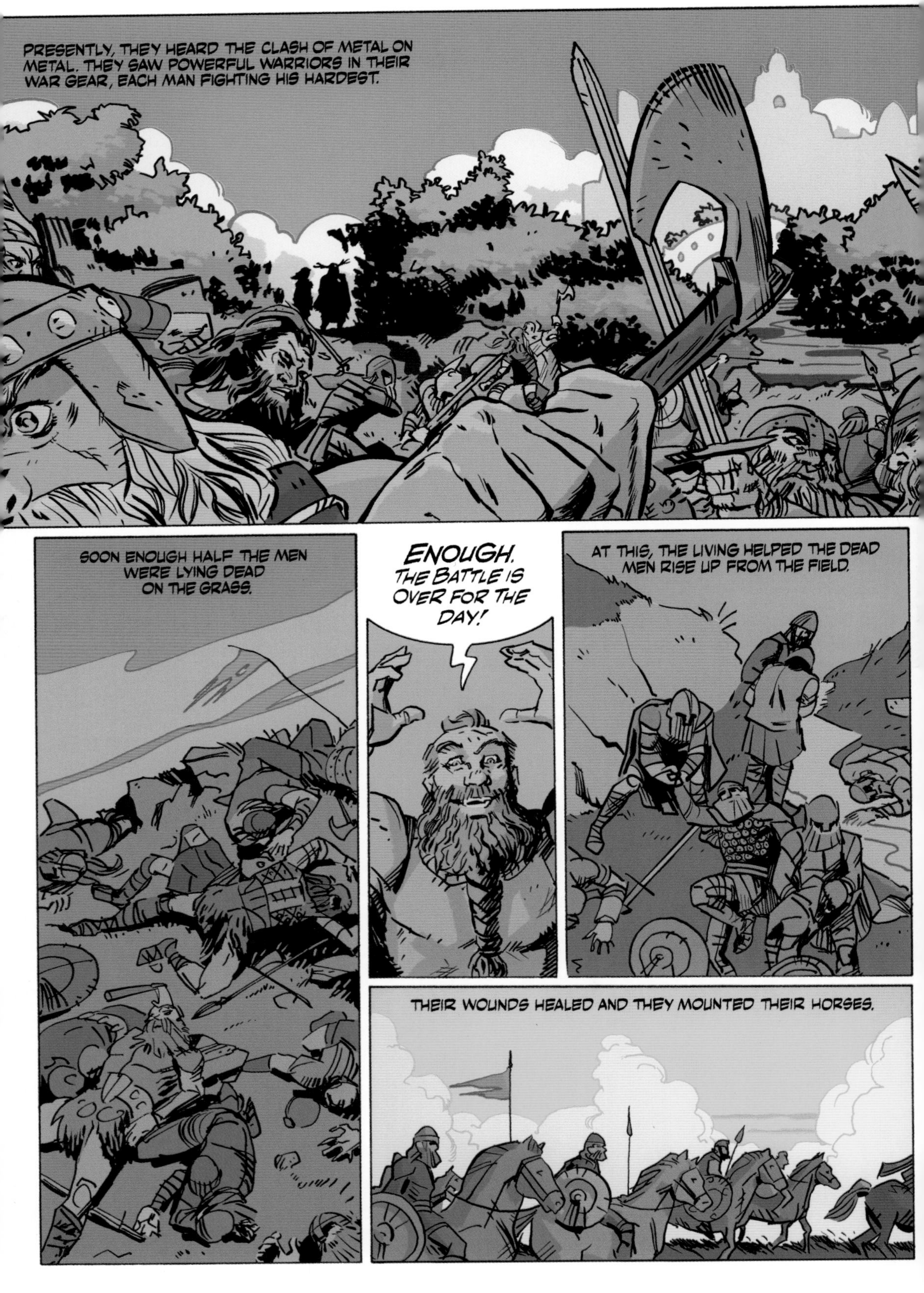
PRESENTLY, THEY HEARD THE CLASH OF METAL ON METAL. THEY SAW POWERFUL WARRIORS IN THEIR WAR GEAR, EACH MAN FIGHTING HIS HARDEST.
SOON ENOUGH HALF THE MEN WERE LYING DEAD ON THE GRASS.
ENOUGH. THE BATTLE IS OVER FOR THE DAY!
AT THIS, THE LIVING HELPED THE DEAD MEN RISE UP FROM THE FIELD.
THEIR WOUNDS HEALED AND THEY MOUNTED THEIR HORSES.

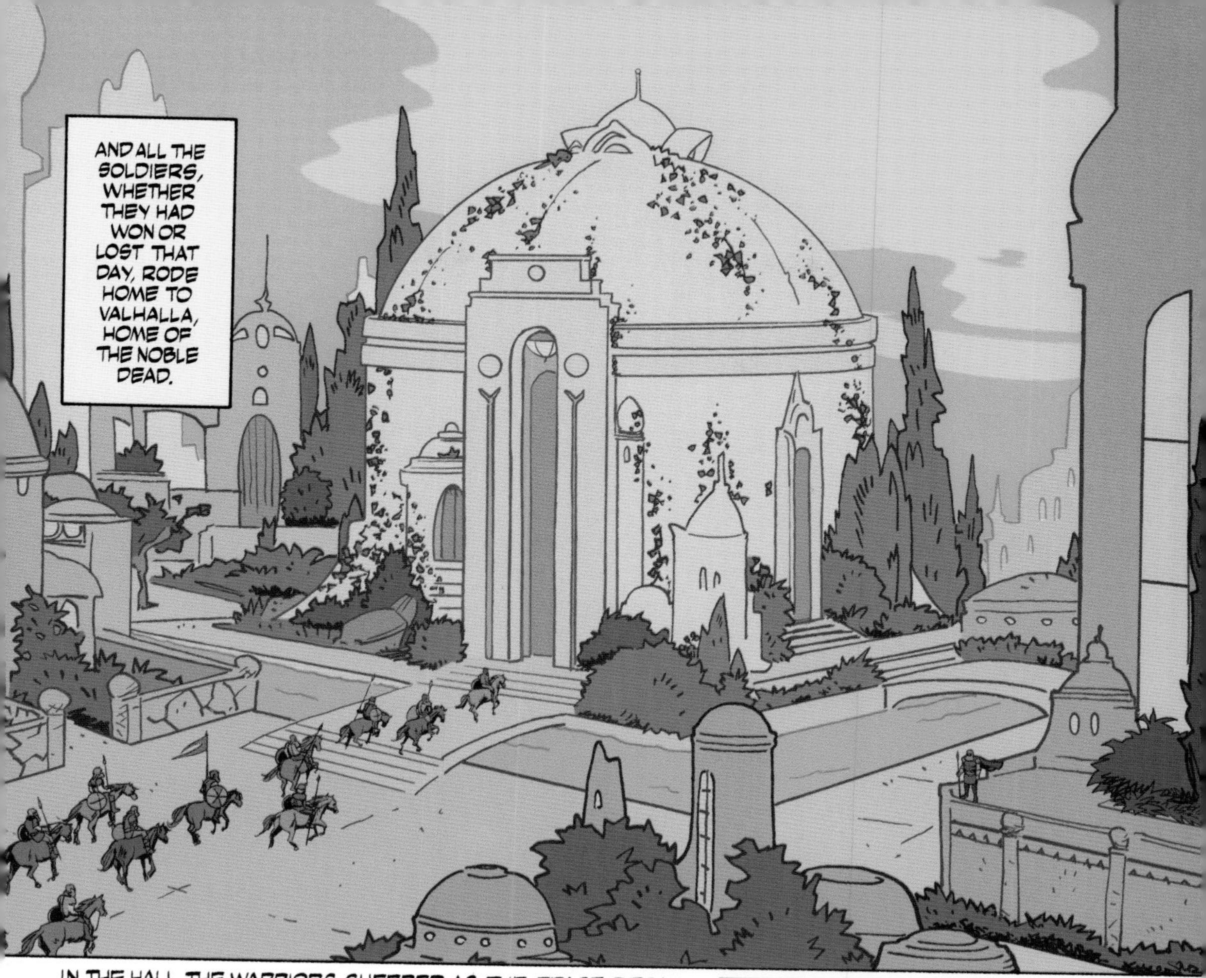
AND ALL THE SOLDIERS, WHETHER THEY HAD WON OR LOST THAT DAY, RODE HOME TO VALHALLA, HOME OF THE NOBLE DEAD.

IN THE HALL, THE WARRIORS CHEERED AS THE FEAST BEGAN. EVERY NIGHT THEY WOULD FEAST ON THE BOAR *SAERIMNIR*. EACH MORNING THE MONSTROUS BEAST WOULD BE ALIVE AGAIN.

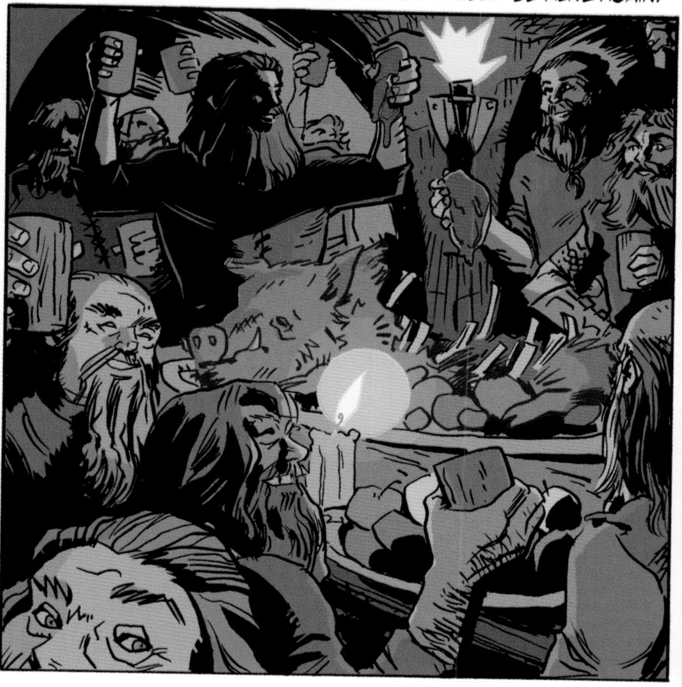

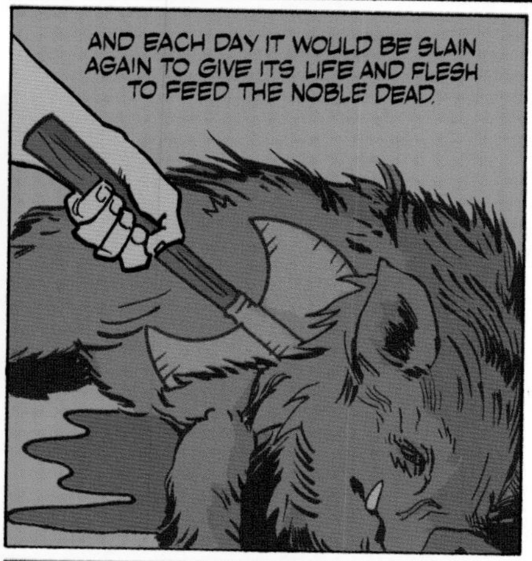
AND EACH DAY IT WOULD BE SLAIN AGAIN TO GIVE ITS LIFE AND FLESH TO FEED THE NOBLE DEAD.

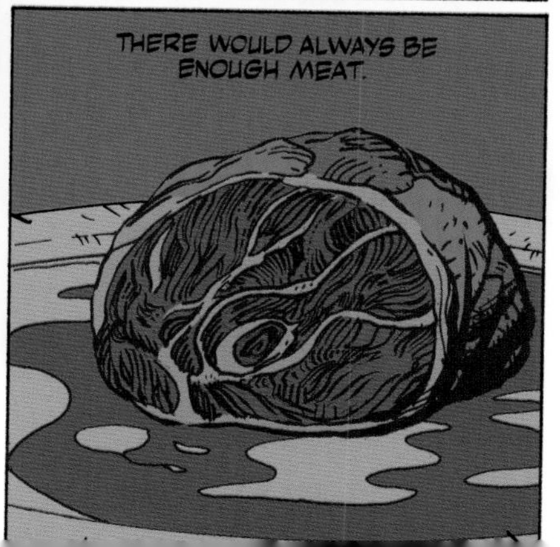
THERE WOULD ALWAYS BE ENOUGH MEAT.

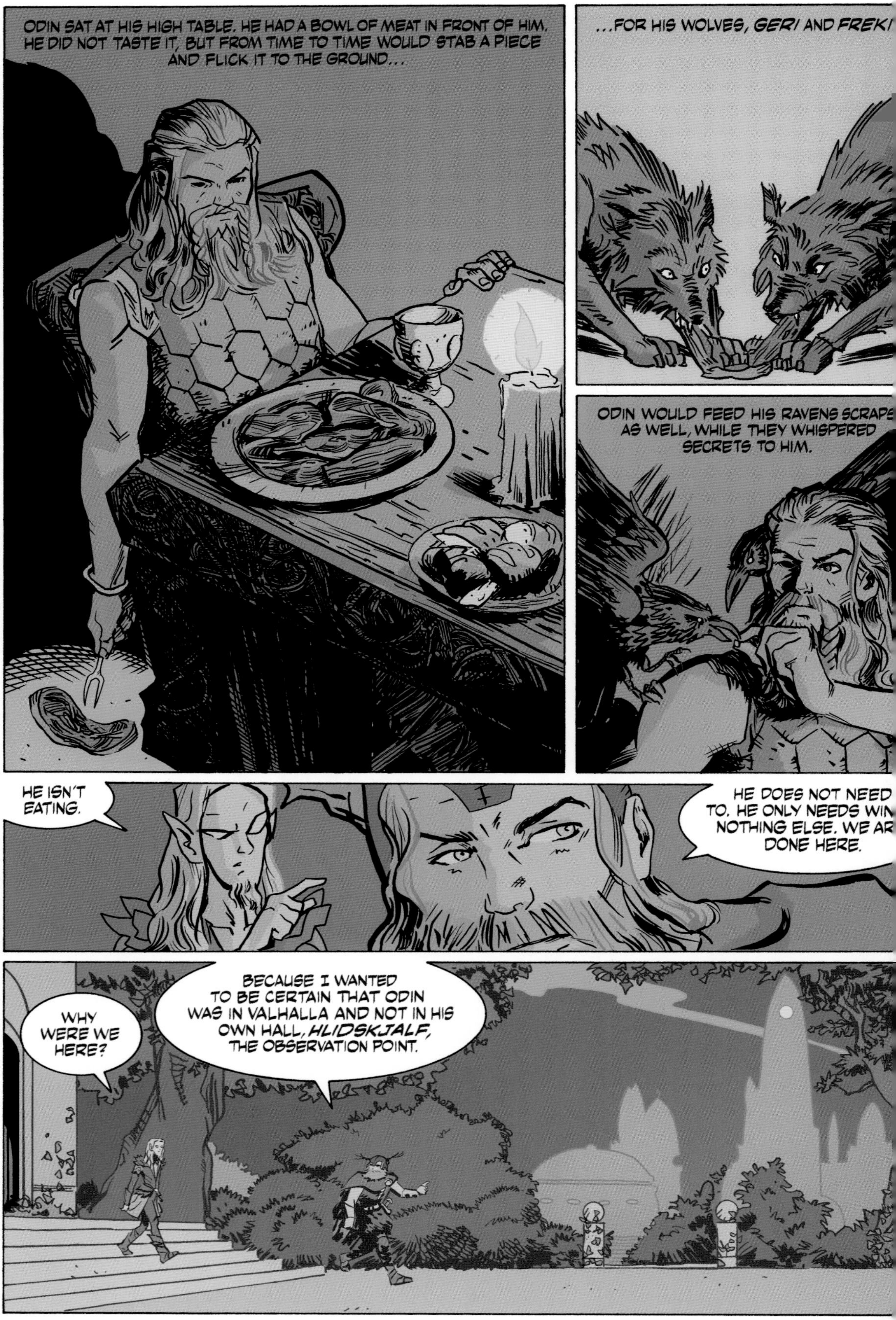
ODIN SAT AT HIS HIGH TABLE. HE HAD A BOWL OF MEAT IN FRONT OF HIM. HE DID NOT TASTE IT, BUT FROM TIME TO TIME WOULD STAB A PIECE AND FLICK IT TO THE GROUND...
...FOR HIS WOLVES, GERI AND FREKI
ODIN WOULD FEED HIS RAVENS SCRAPS AS WELL, WHILE THEY WHISPERED SECRETS TO HIM.
HE ISN'T EATING.
HE DOES NOT NEED TO. HE ONLY NEEDS WIN NOTHING ELSE. WE AR DONE HERE.
WHY WERE WE HERE?
BECAUSE I WANTED TO BE CERTAIN THAT ODIN WAS IN VALHALLA AND NOT IN HIS OWN HALL, HLIDSKJALF, THE OBSERVATION POINT.

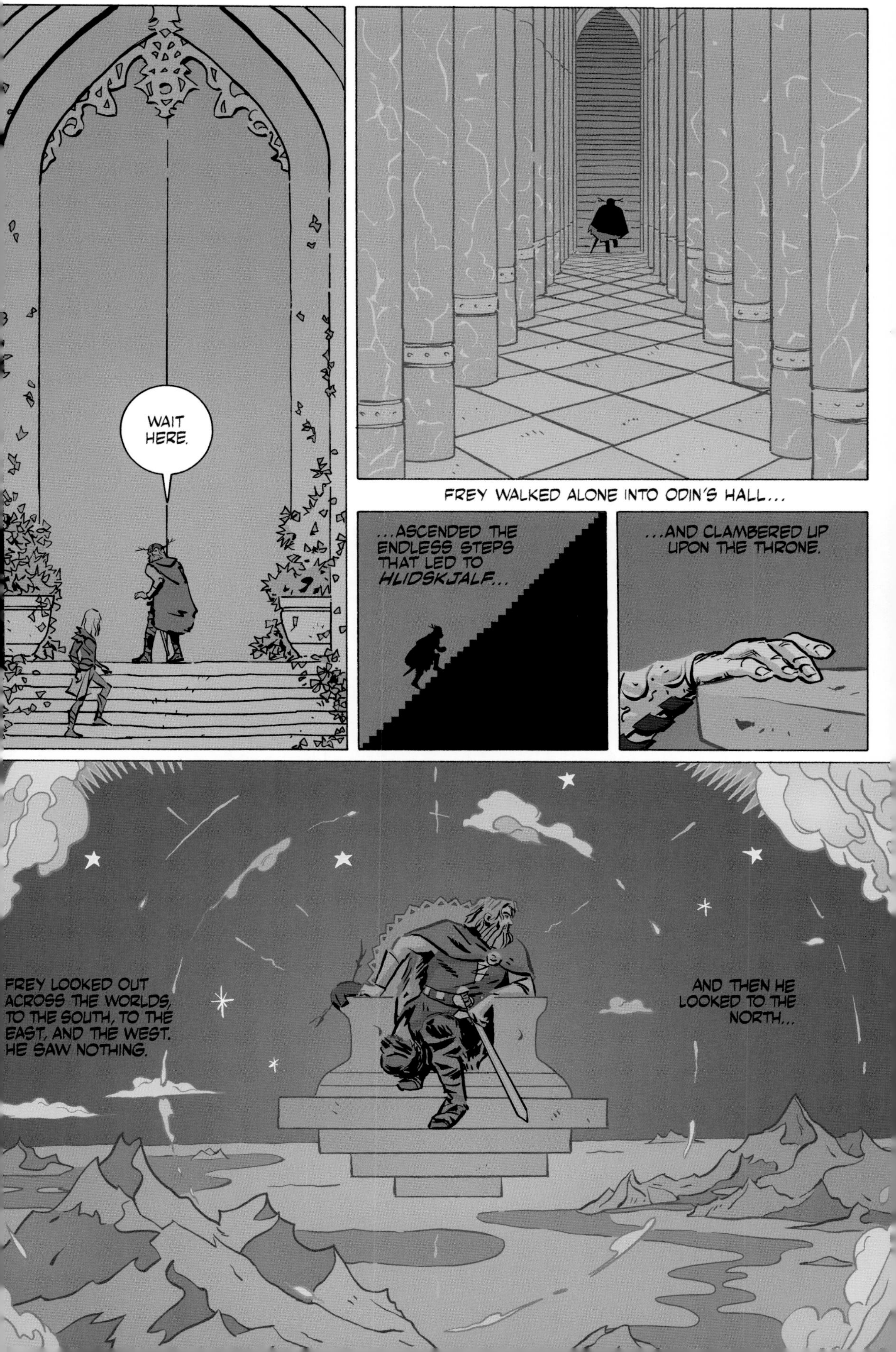
WAIT HERE.
FREY WALKED ALONE INTO ODIN'S HALL...
...ASCENDED THE ENDLESS STEPS THAT LED TO HLIDSKJALF...
...AND CLAMBERED UP UPON THE THRONE.
FREY LOOKED OUT ACROSS THE WORLDS, TO THE SOUTH, TO THE EAST, AND THE WEST. HE SAW NOTHING.
AND THEN HE LOOKED TO THE NORTH...

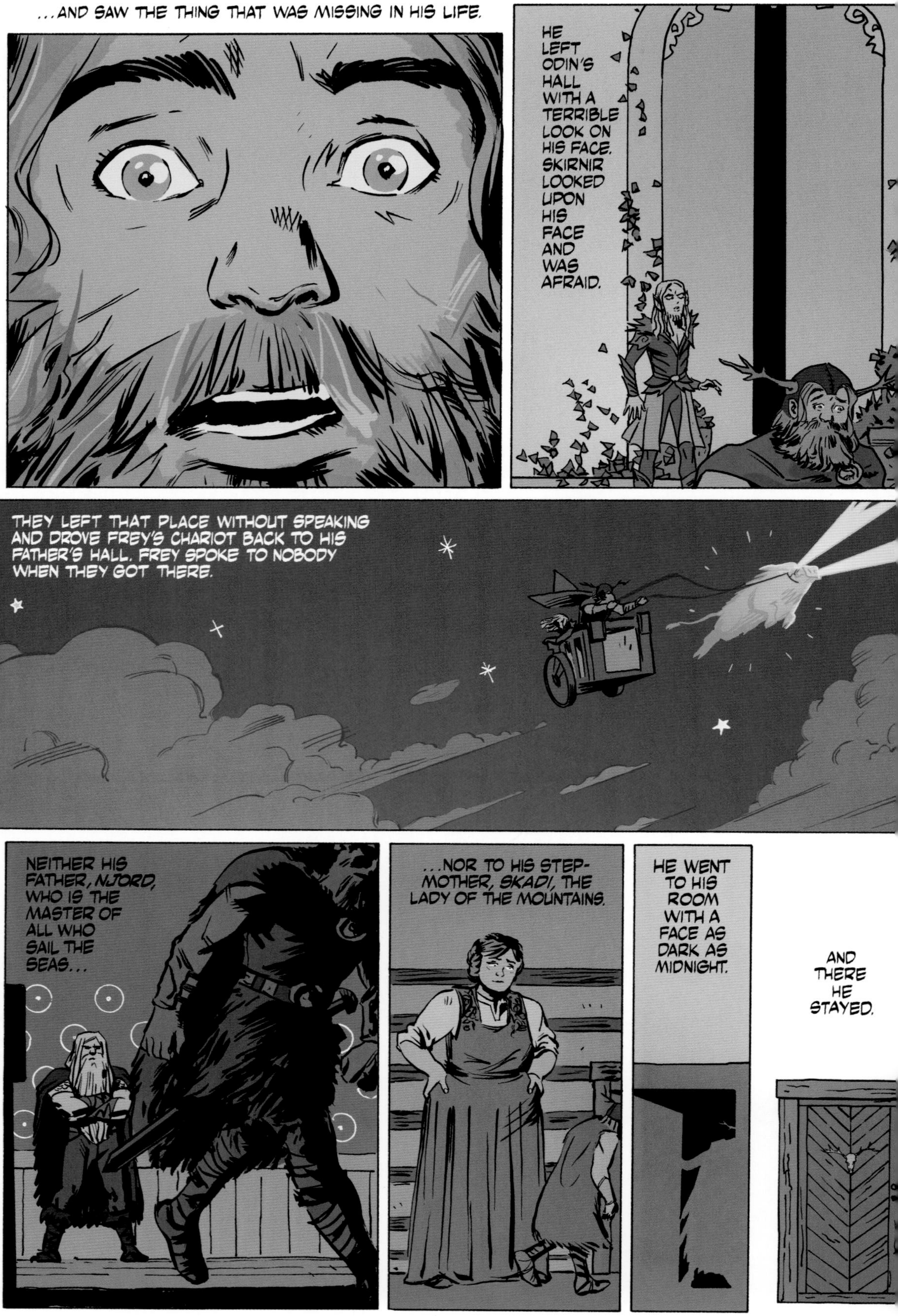
...AND SAW THE THING THAT WAS MISSING IN HIS LIFE.
HE LEFT ODIN'S HALL WITH A TERRIBLE LOOK ON HIS FACE. SKIRNIR LOOKED UPON HIS FACE AND WAS AFRAID.
THEY LEFT THAT PLACE WITHOUT SPEAKING AND DROVE FREY'S CHARIOT BACK TO HIS FATHER'S HALL. FREY SPOKE TO NOBODY WHEN THEY GOT THERE.
NEITHER HIS FATHER, NJORD, WHO IS THE MASTER OF ALL WHO SAIL THE SEAS...
...NOR TO HIS STEP-MOTHER, SKADI, THE LADY OF THE MOUNTAINS.
HE WENT TO HIS ROOM WITH A FACE AS DARK AS MIDNIGHT.
AND THERE HE STAYED.

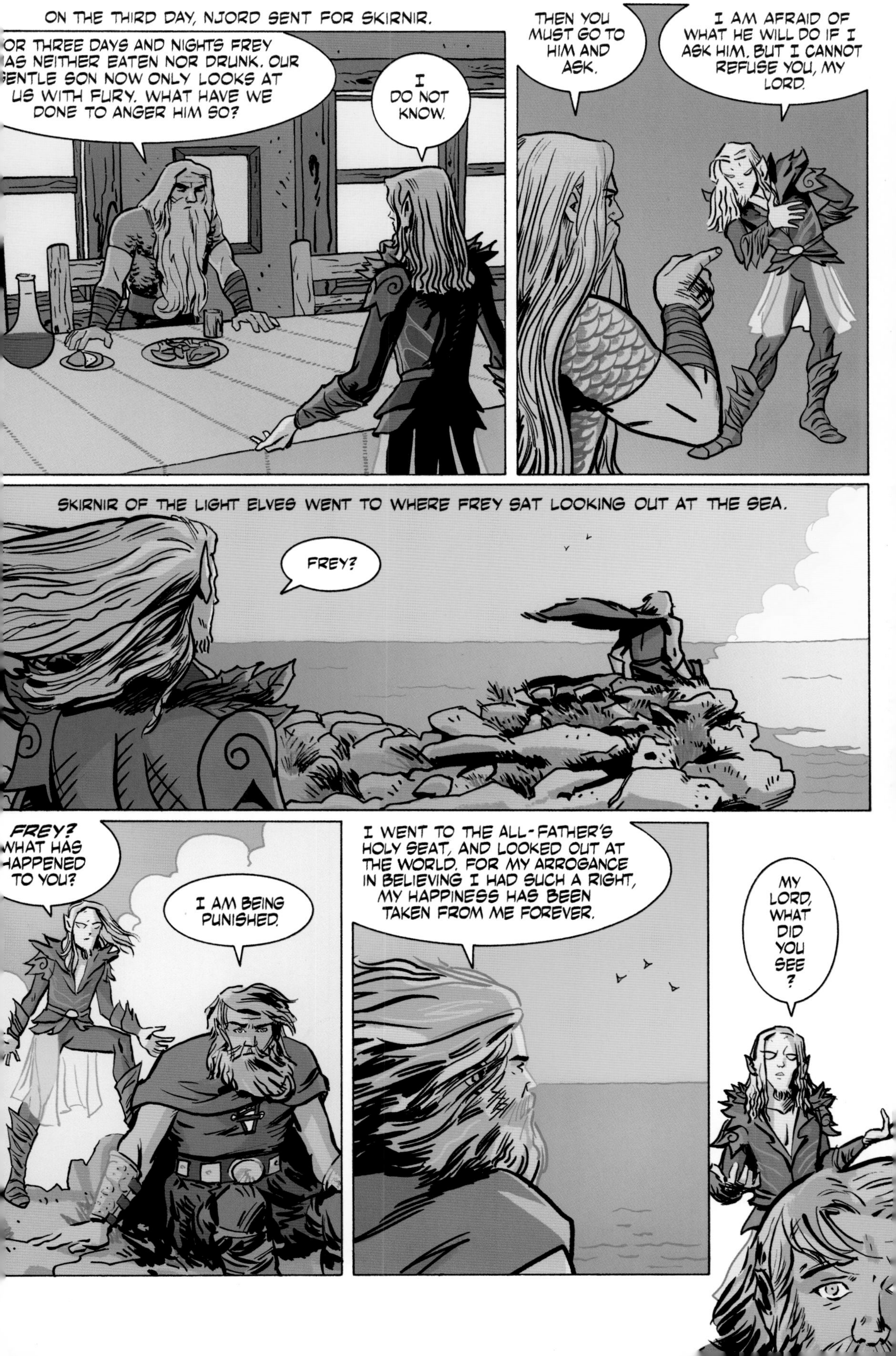
ON THE THIRD DAY, NJORD SENT FOR SKIRNIR.
FOR THREE DAYS AND NIGHTS FREY HAS NEITHER EATEN NOR DRUNK. OUR GENTLE SON NOW ONLY LOOKS AT US WITH FURY. WHAT HAVE WE DONE TO ANGER HIM SO?
I DO NOT KNOW.
THEN YOU MUST GO TO HIM AND ASK.
I AM AFRAID OF WHAT HE WILL DO IF I ASK HIM. BUT I CANNOT REFUSE YOU, MY LORD.
SKIRNIR OF THE LIGHT ELVES WENT TO WHERE FREY SAT LOOKING OUT AT THE SEA.
FREY?
FREY? WHAT HAS HAPPENED TO YOU?
I AM BEING PUNISHED.
I WENT TO THE ALL-FATHER'S HOLY SEAT, AND LOOKED OUT AT THE WORLD. FOR MY ARROGANCE IN BELIEVING I HAD SUCH A RIGHT, MY HAPPINESS HAS BEEN TAKEN FROM ME FOREVER.
MY LORD, WHAT DID YOU SEE?

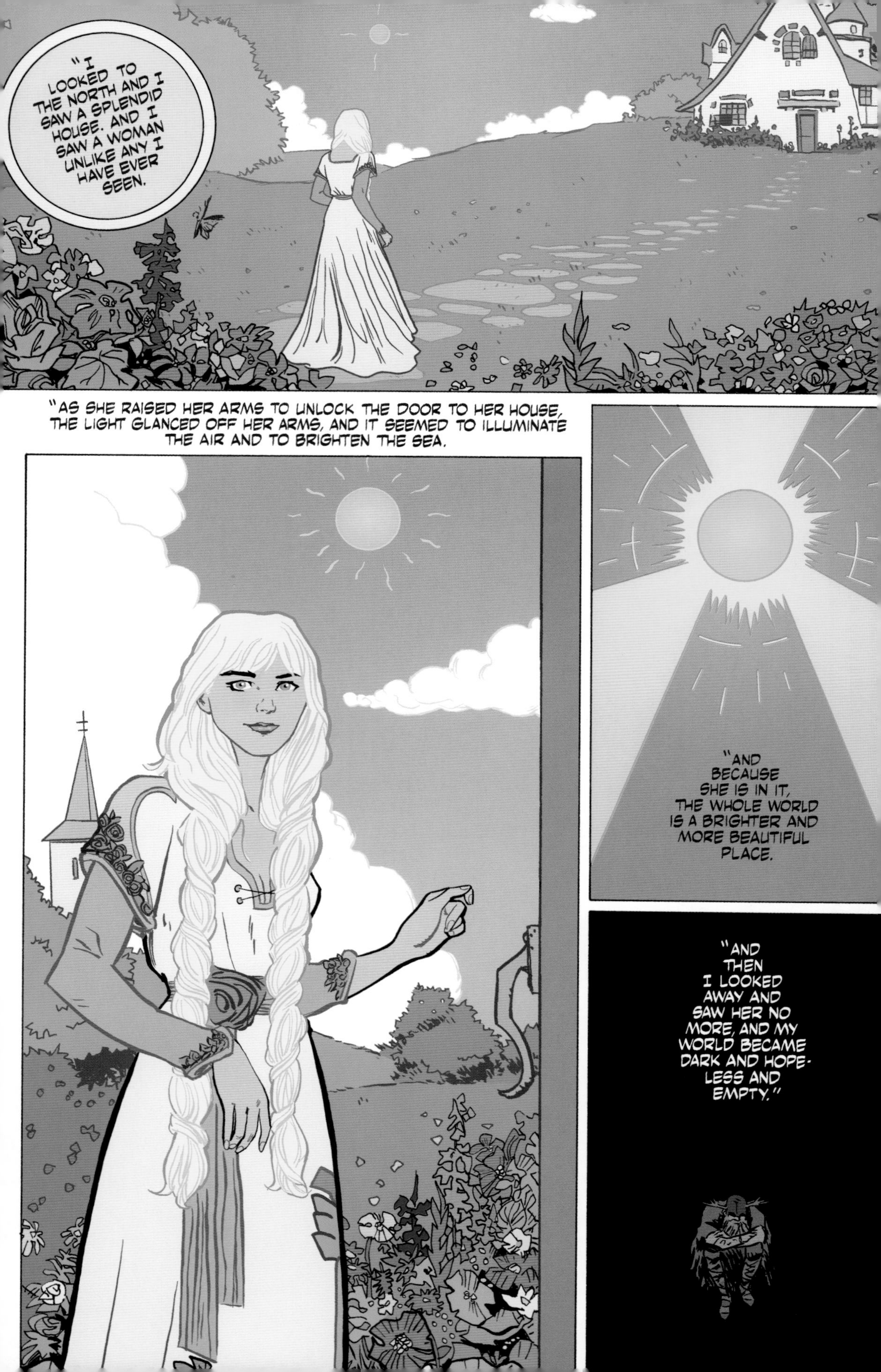
"I LOOKED TO THE NORTH AND I SAW A SPLENDID HOUSE. AND I SAW A WOMAN UNLIKE ANY I HAVE EVER SEEN.
"AS SHE RAISED HER ARMS TO UNLOCK THE DOOR TO HER HOUSE, THE LIGHT GLANCED OFF HER ARMS, AND IT SEEMED TO ILLUMINATE THE AIR AND TO BRIGHTEN THE SEA.
"AND BECAUSE SHE IS IN IT, THE WHOLE WORLD IS A BRIGHTER AND MORE BEAUTIFUL PLACE.
"AND THEN I LOOKED AWAY AND SAW HER NO MORE, AND MY WORLD BECAME DARK AND HOPE-LESS AND EMPTY."

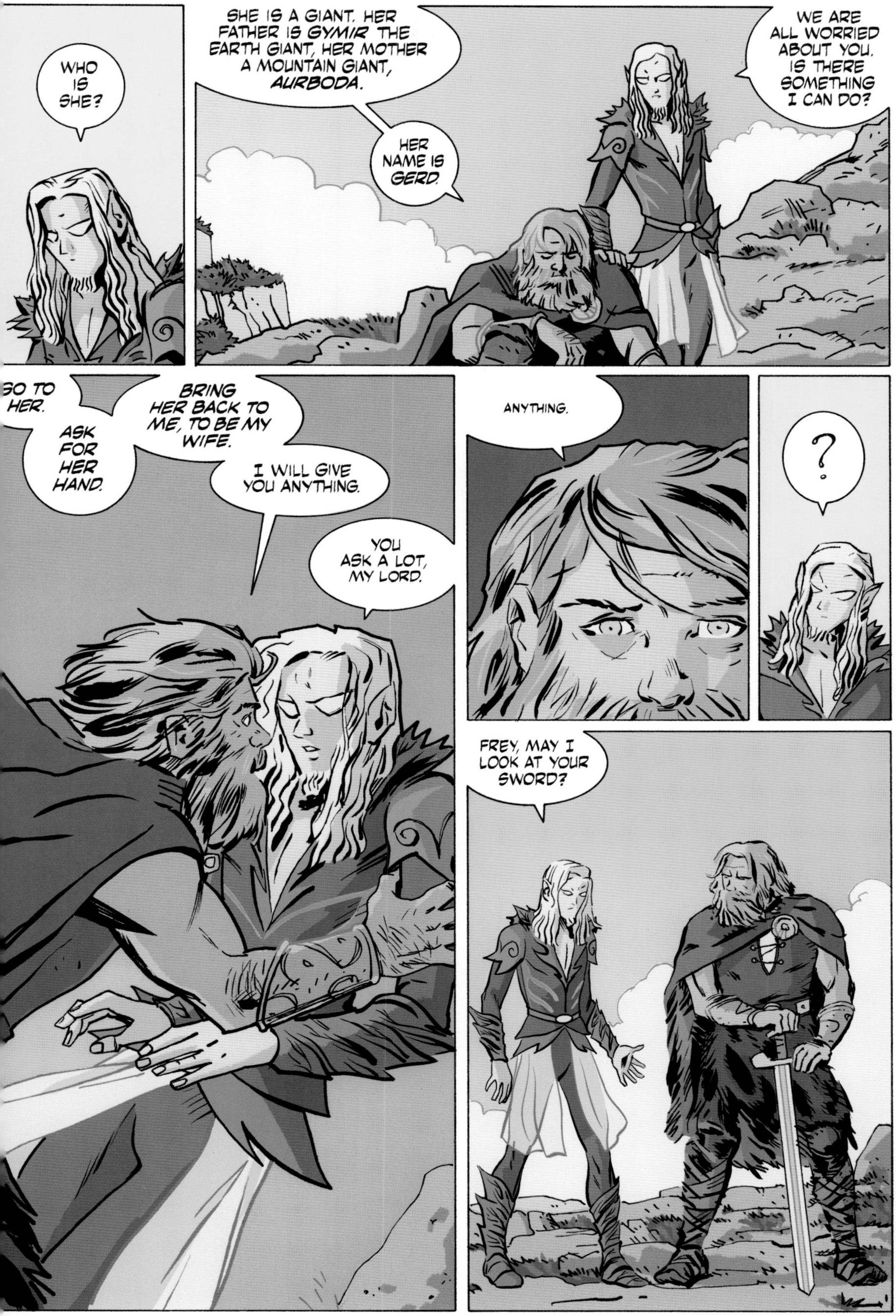
WHO IS SHE?
SHE IS A GIANT. HER FATHER IS GYMIR THE EARTH GIANT, HER MOTHER A MOUNTAIN GIANT, AURBODA.
HER NAME IS GERD.
WE ARE ALL WORRIED ABOUT YOU. IS THERE SOMETHING I CAN DO?
GO TO HER.
ASK FOR HER HAND.
BRING HER BACK TO ME, TO BE MY WIFE.
I WILL GIVE YOU ANYTHING.
YOU ASK A LOT, MY LORD.
ANYTHING.
?
FREY, MAY I LOOK AT YOUR SWORD?

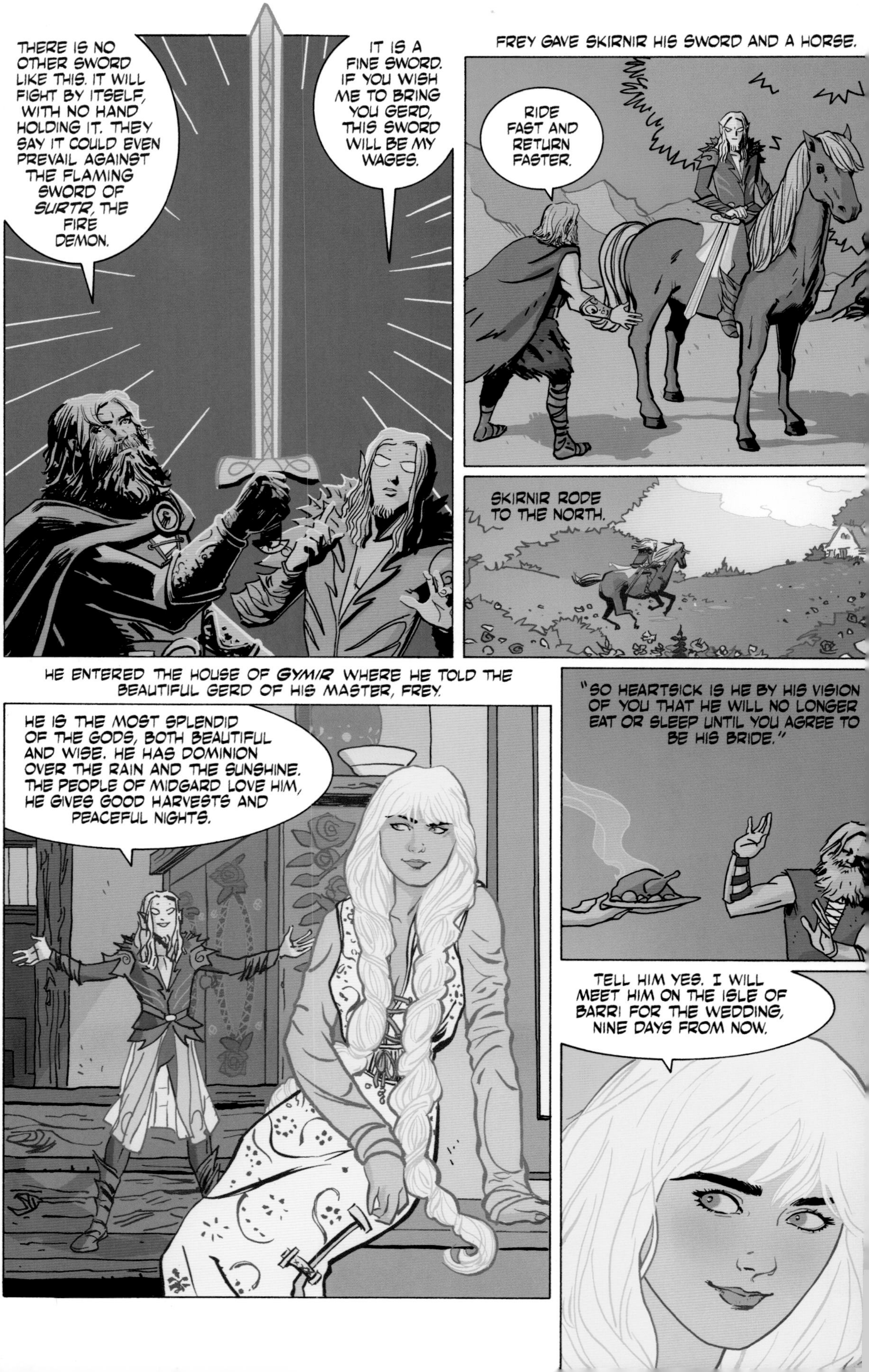
THERE IS NO OTHER SWORD LIKE THIS. IT WILL FIGHT BY ITSELF, WITH NO HAND HOLDING IT. THEY SAY IT COULD EVEN PREVAIL AGAINST THE FLAMING SWORD OF SURTR, THE FIRE DEMON.
IT IS A FINE SWORD. IF YOU WISH ME TO BRING YOU GERD, THIS SWORD WILL BE MY WAGES.
FREY GAVE SKIRNIR HIS SWORD AND A HORSE.
RIDE FAST AND RETURN FASTER.
SKIRNIR RODE TO THE NORTH.
HE ENTERED THE HOUSE OF GYMIR WHERE HE TOLD THE BEAUTIFUL GERD OF HIS MASTER, FREY.
HE IS THE MOST SPLENDID OF THE GODS, BOTH BEAUTIFUL AND WISE. HE HAS DOMINION OVER THE RAIN AND THE SUNSHINE. THE PEOPLE OF MIDGARD LOVE HIM, HE GIVES GOOD HARVESTS AND PEACEFUL NIGHTS.
"SO HEARTSICK IS HE BY HIS VISION OF YOU THAT HE WILL NO LONGER EAT OR SLEEP UNTIL YOU AGREE TO BE HIS BRIDE."
TELL HIM YES. I WILL MEET HIM ON THE ISLE OF BARRI FOR THE WEDDING, NINE DAYS FROM NOW.

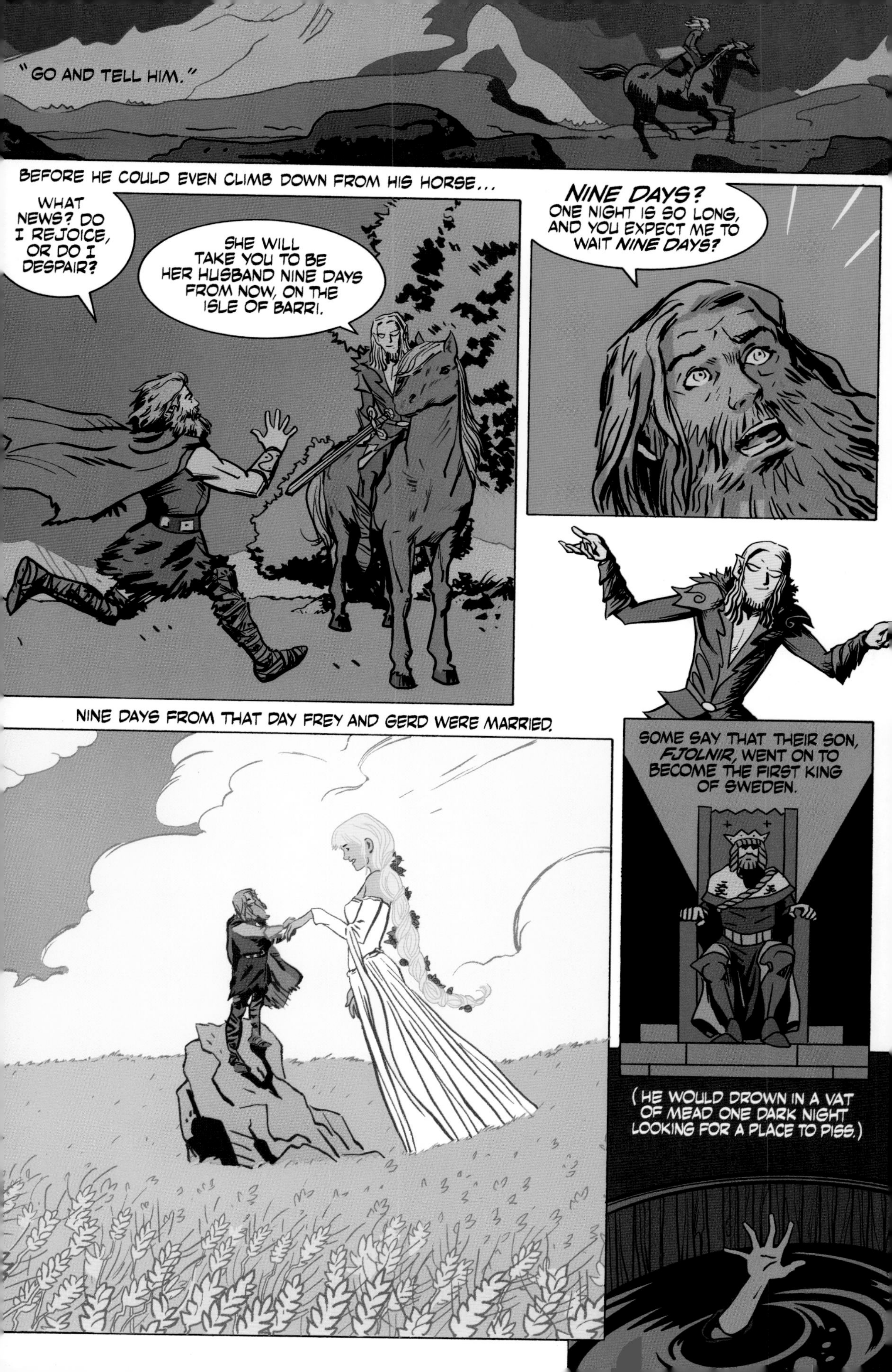
"GO AND TELL HIM."
BEFORE HE COULD EVEN CLIMB DOWN FROM HIS HORSE...
WHAT NEWS? DO I REJOICE, OR DO I DESPAIR?
SHE WILL TAKE YOU TO BE HER HUSBAND NINE DAYS FROM NOW, ON THE ISLE OF BARRI.
NINE DAYS? ONE NIGHT IS SO LONG, AND YOU EXPECT ME TO WAIT NINE DAYS?
NINE DAYS FROM THAT DAY FREY AND GERD WERE MARRIED.
SOME SAY THAT THEIR SON, FJOLNIR, WENT ON TO BECOME THE FIRST KING OF SWEDEN.
(HE WOULD DROWN IN A VAT OF MEAD ONE DARK NIGHT LOOKING FOR A PLACE TO PISS.)

SKIRNIR TOOK THE SWORD HE HAD BEEN GIVEN AND RODE BACK TO ALFHEIM WITH IT.

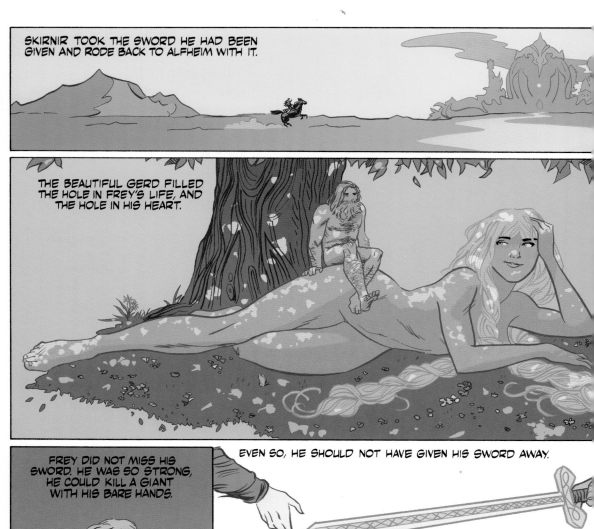

THE BEAUTIFUL GERD FILLED THE HOLE IN FREY'S LIFE, AND THE HOLE IN HIS HEART.

FREY DID NOT MISS HIS SWORD. HE WAS SO STRONG, HE COULD KILL A GIANT WITH HIS BARE HANDS.

EVEN SO, HE SHOULD NOT HAVE GIVEN HIS SWORD AWAY.

RAGNAROK IS COMING. WHEN THE DARK POWERS OF MUSPELL MARCH OUT, FREY WILL WISH HE STILL HAD HIS SWORD.

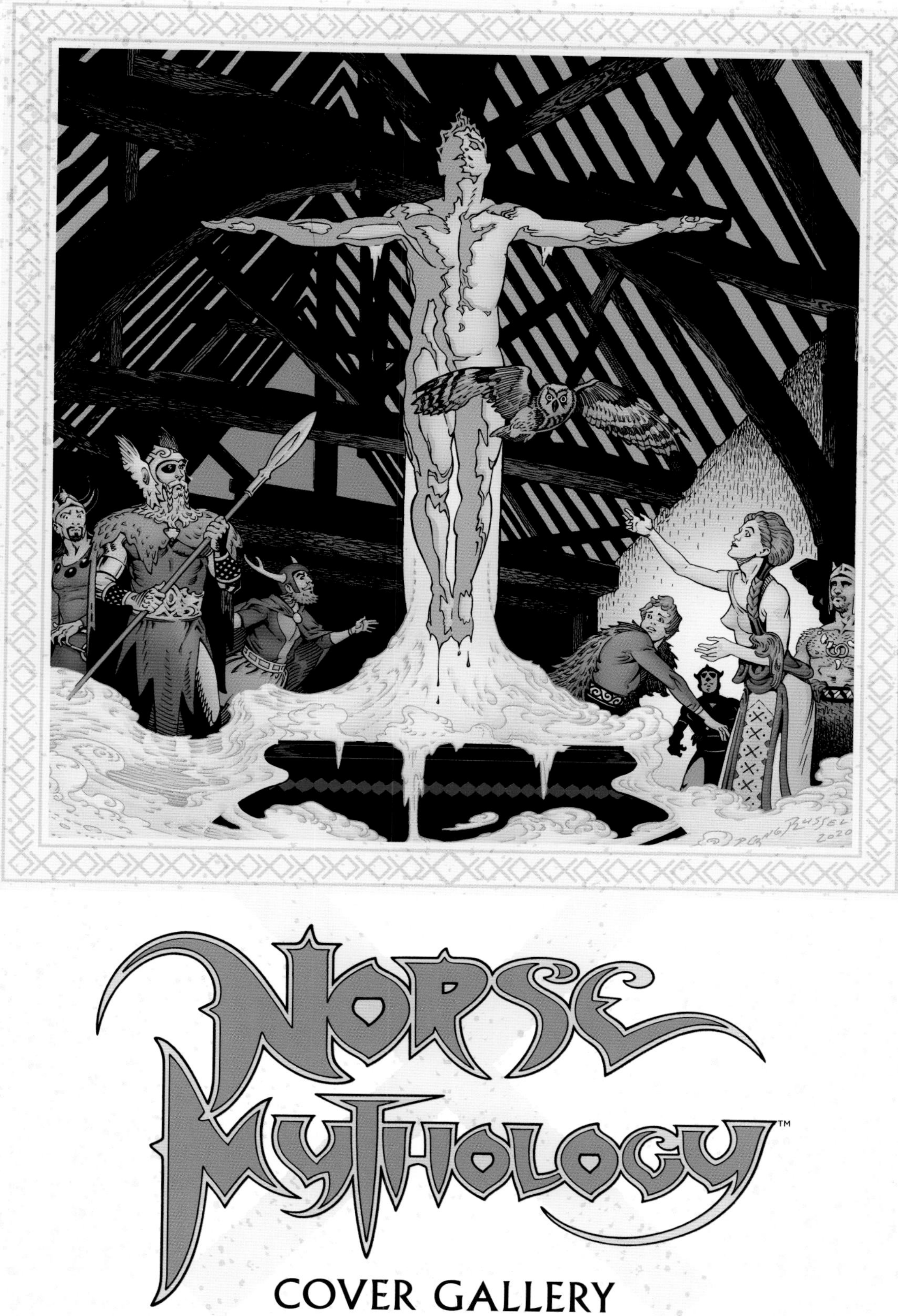
P. CRAIG RUSSELL
2020

NORSE MYTHOLOGY™

COVER GALLERY

Norse Mythology II #1 standard cover by
P. CRAIG RUSSELL
with
LOVERN KINDZIERSKI

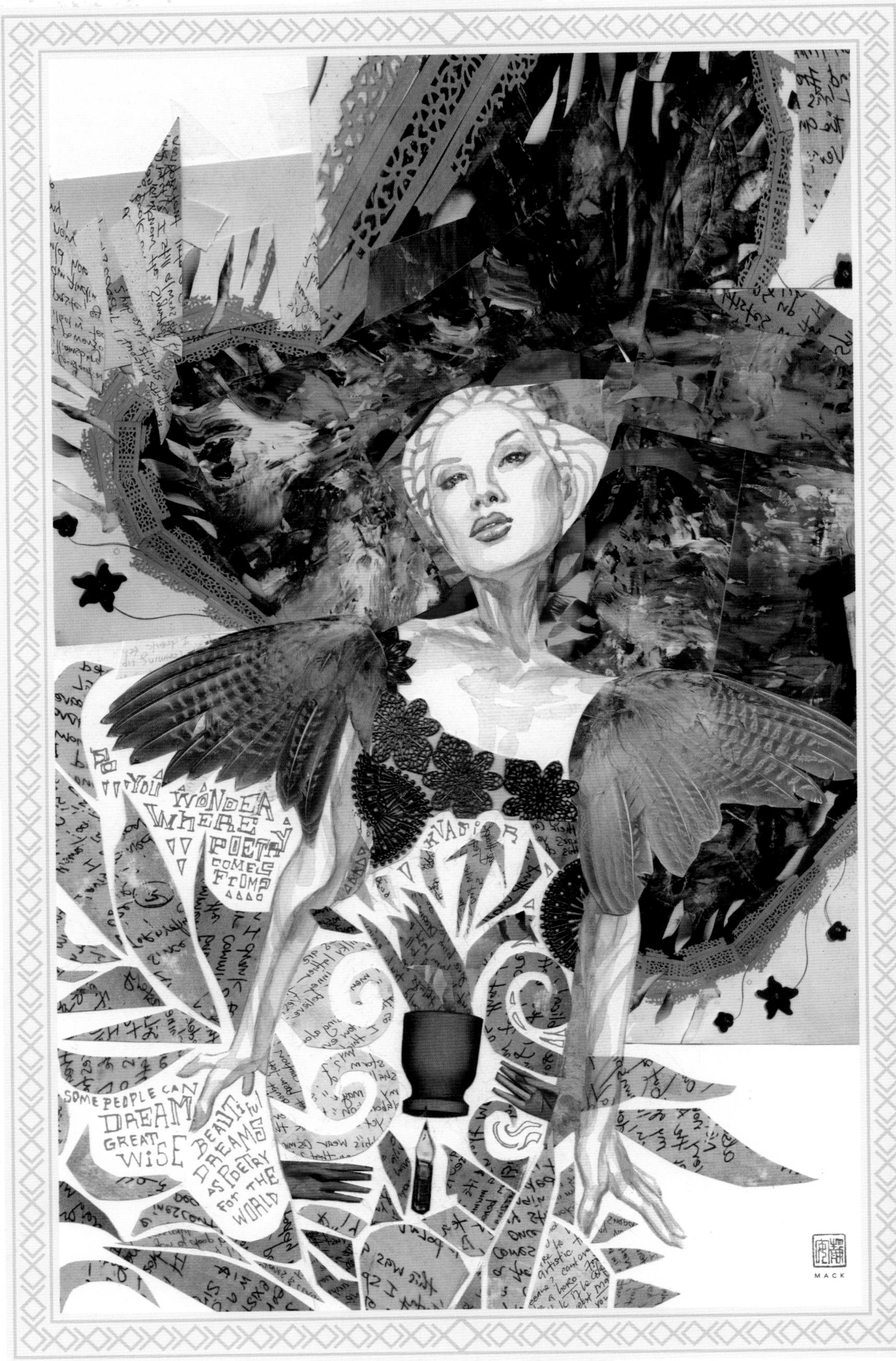
DO YOU WONDER WHERE POETRY COMES FROM?
KVASIR
SOME PEOPLE CAN DREAM GREAT WISE BEAUTIFUL DREAMS AS POETRY FOR THE WORLD
MACK

Norse Mythology II #1 variant cover by
DAVID MACK

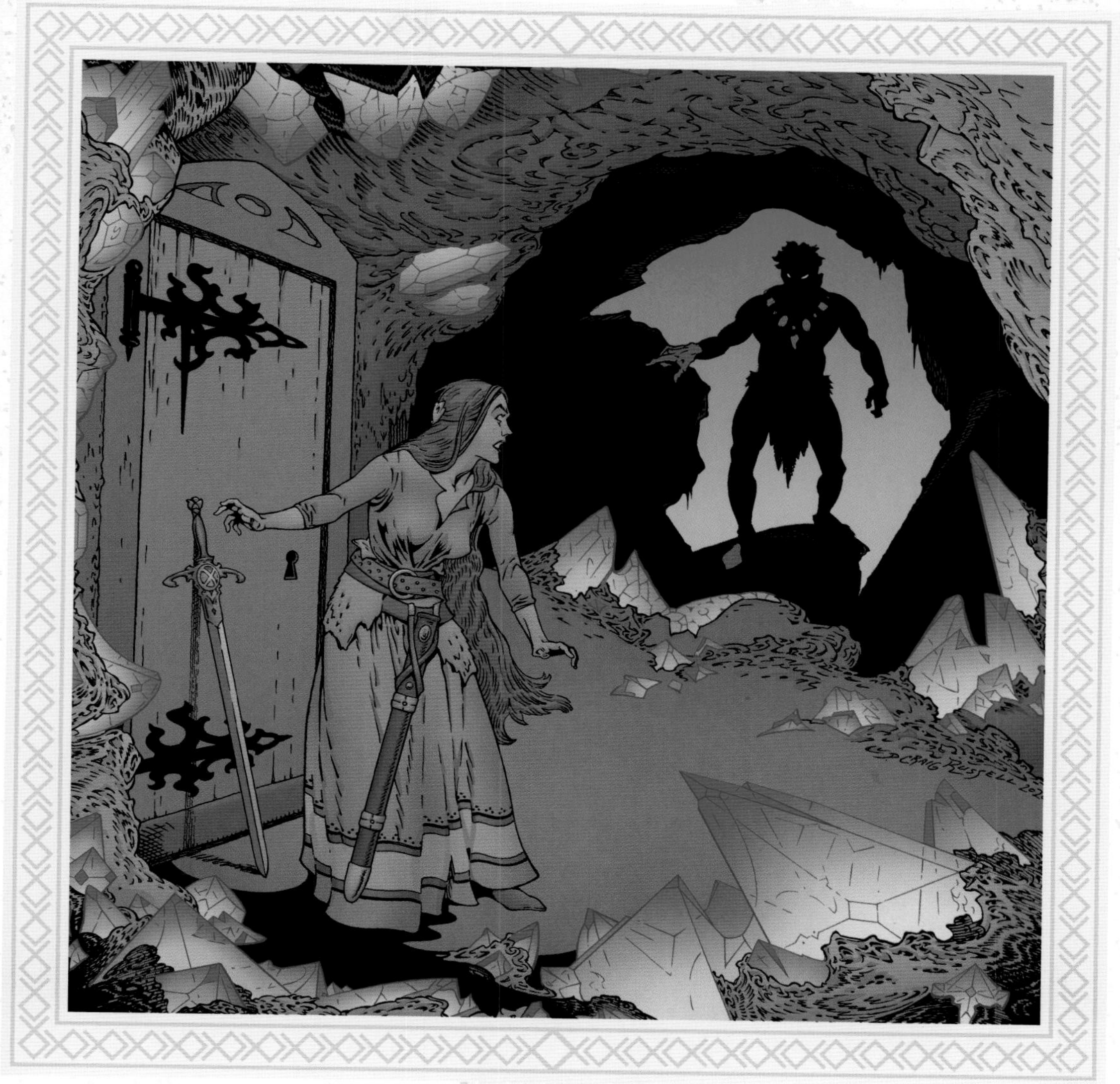
CRAIG RUSSELL

Norse Mythology II #2 standard cover by

P. CRAIG RUSSELL

with

LOVERN KINDZIERSKI

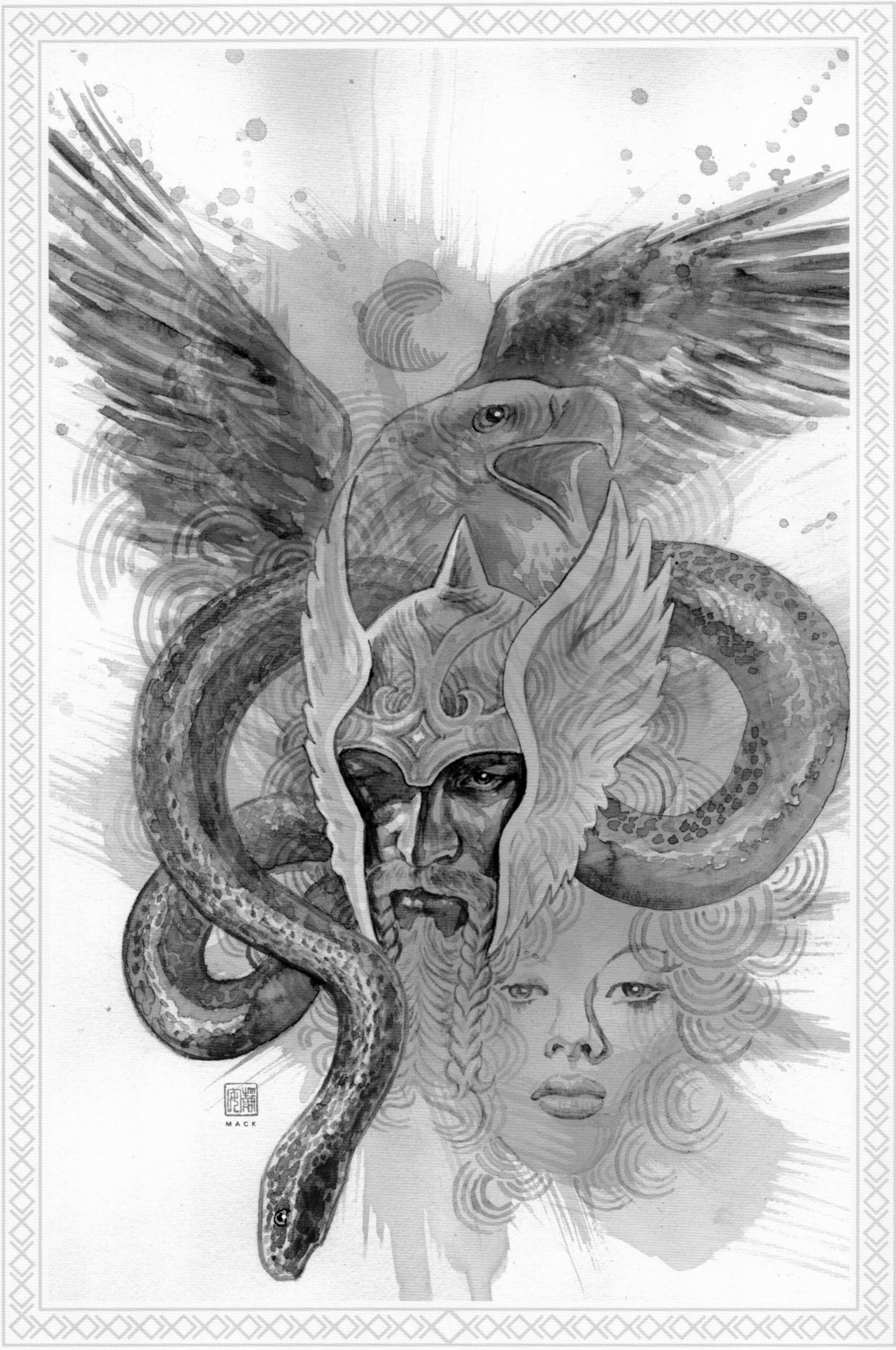
MACK

Norse Mythology II #2 variant cover by
DAVID MACK

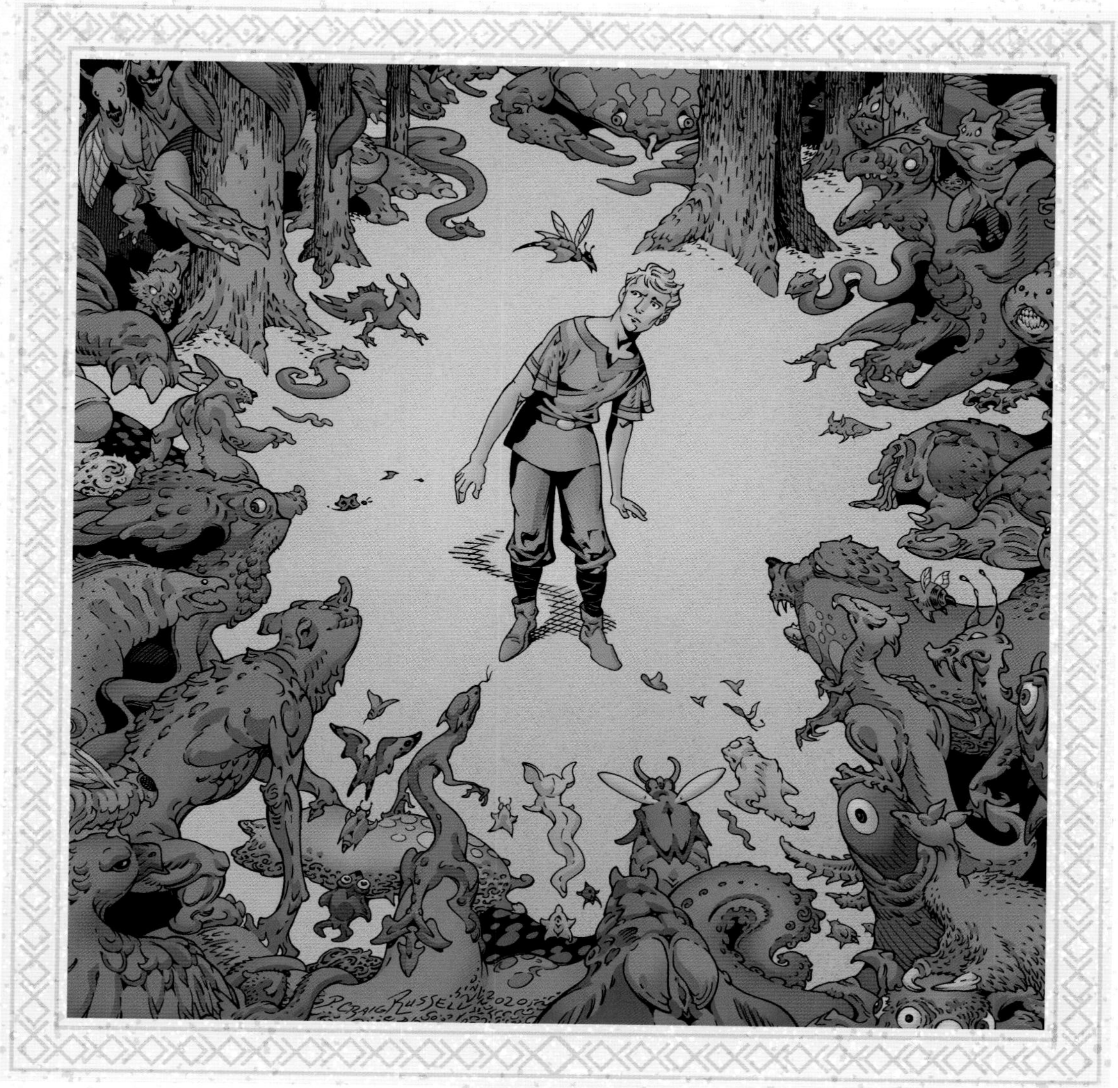

Norse Mythology II #3 standard cover by

P. CRAIG RUSSELL

with

LOVERN KINDZIERSKI

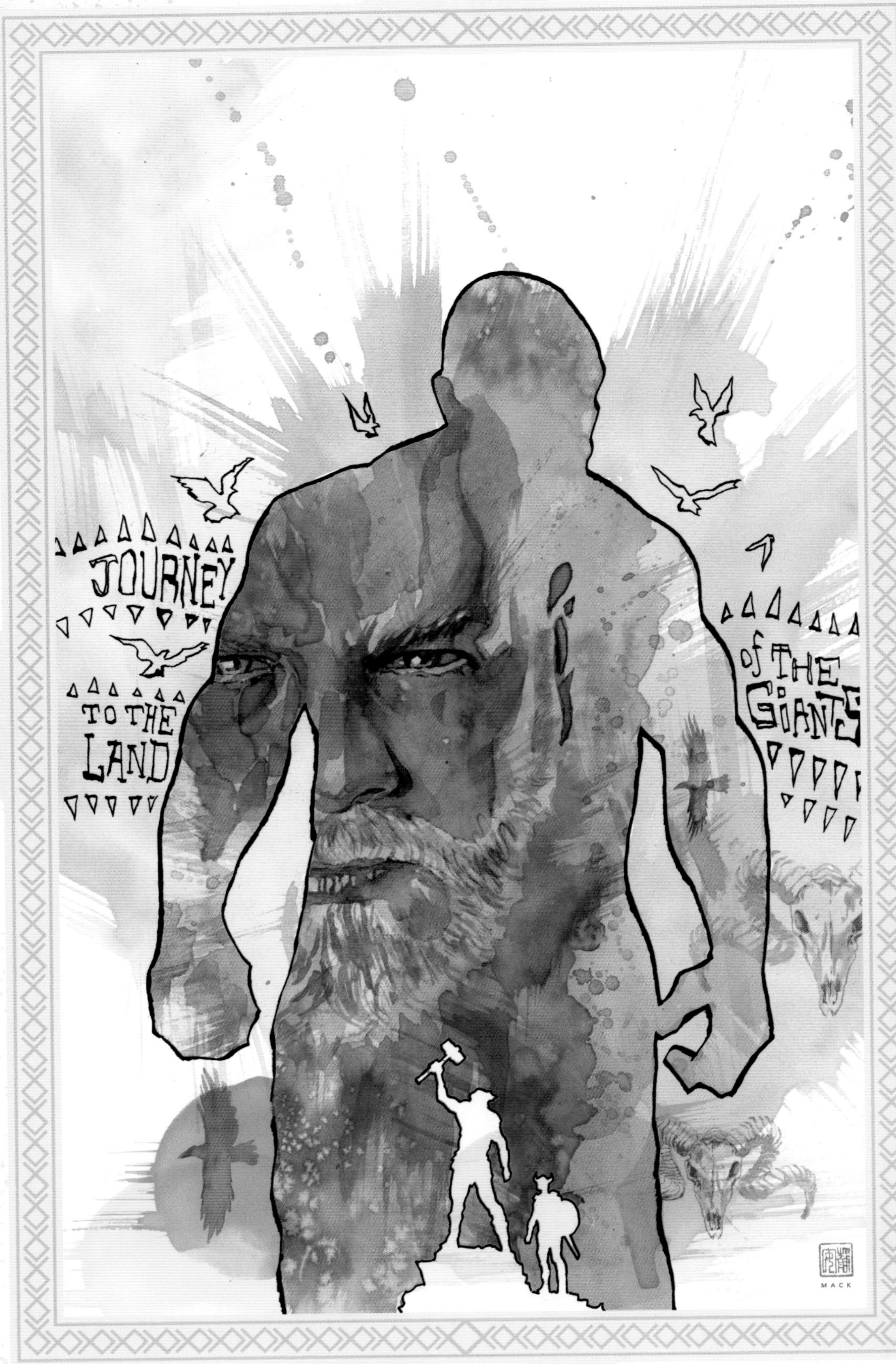
JOURNEY
TO THE
LAND
of THE
GIANTS
MACK

Norse Mythology II #3 variant cover by
DAVID MACK

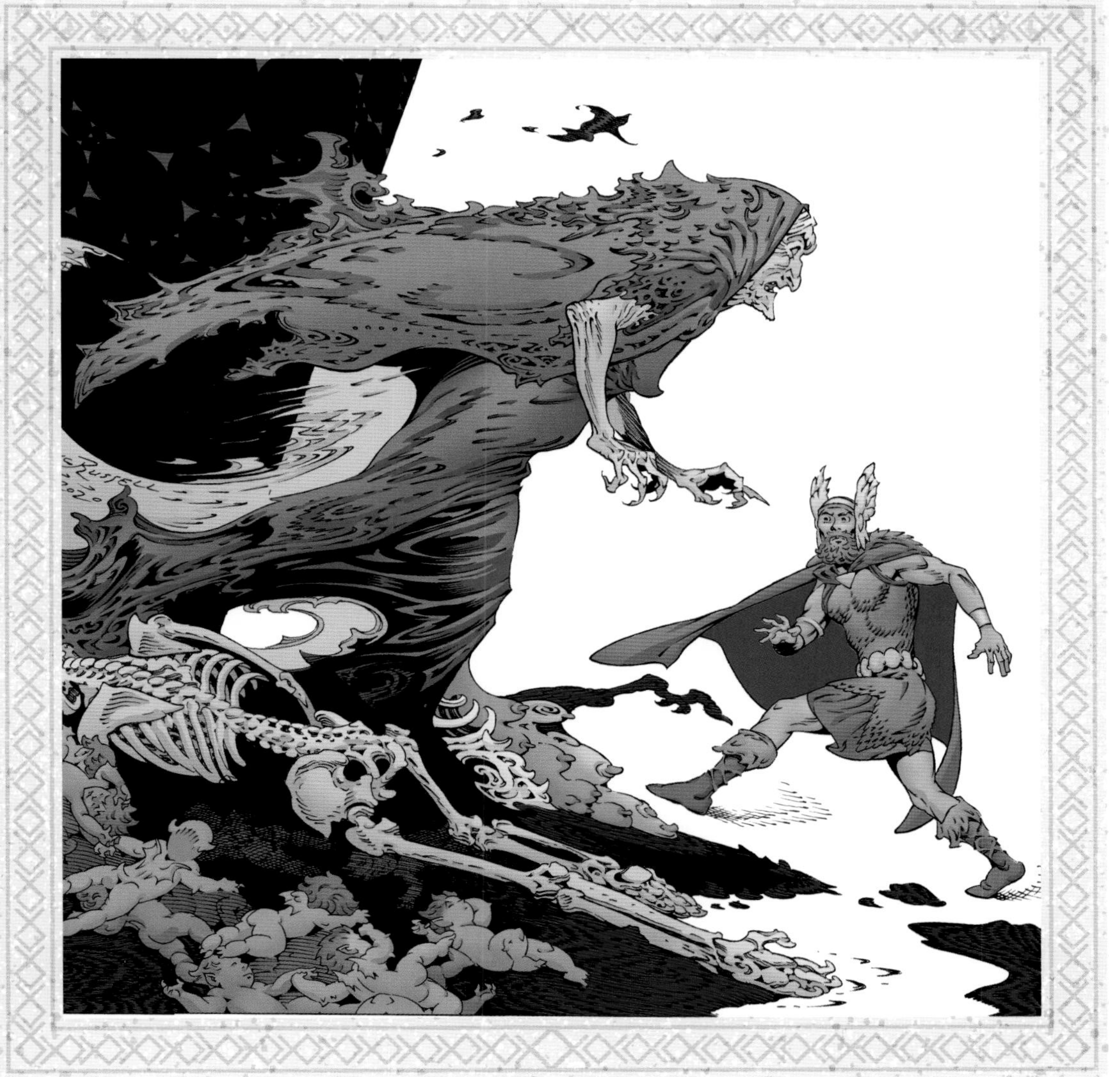

Norse Mythology II #4 standard cover by

P. CRAIG RUSSELL

with

LOVERN KINDZIERSKI

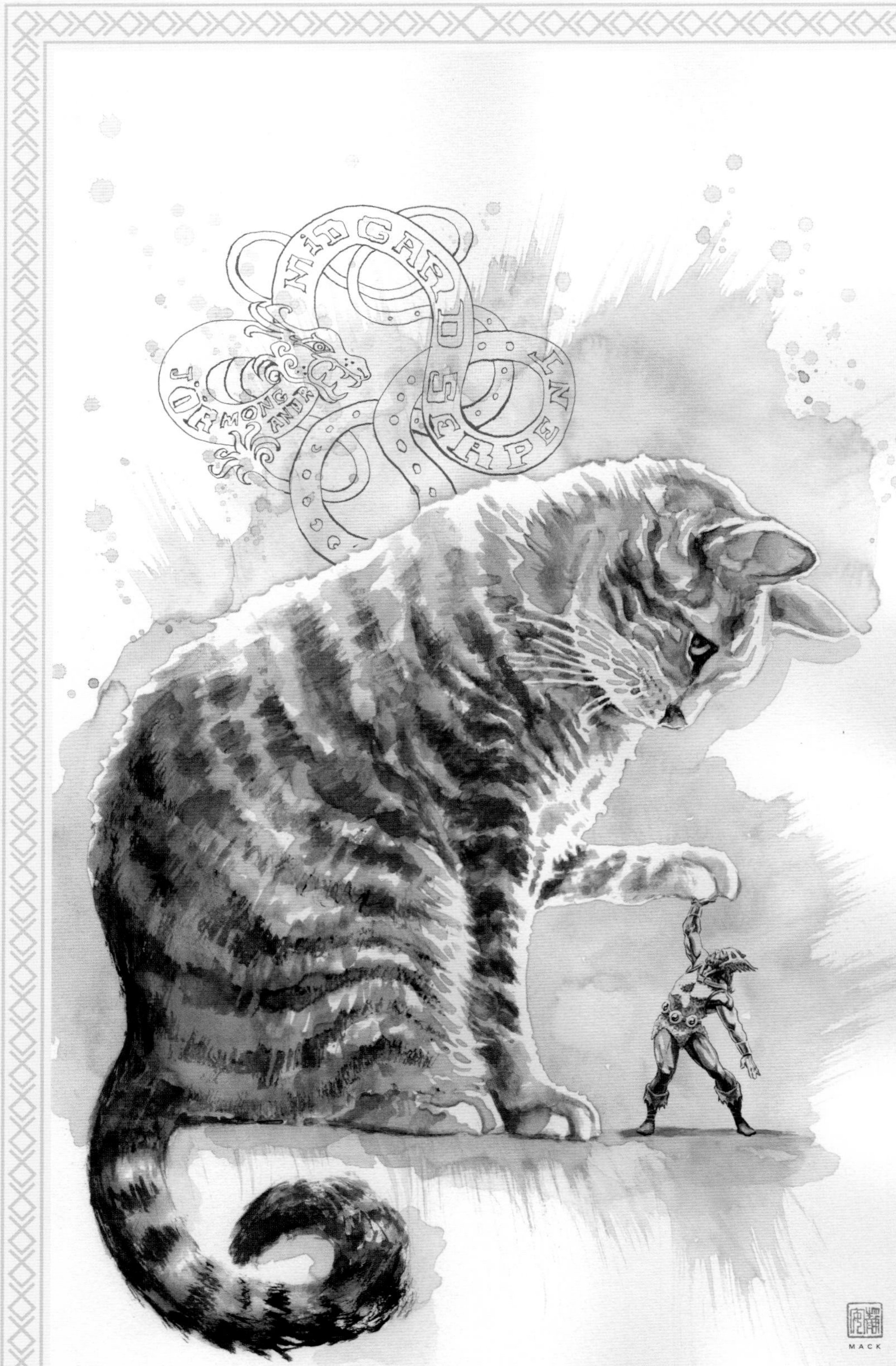
MIDGARD SERPENT
JÖRMONGANDR
MACK

Norse Mythology II #4 variant cover by
DAVID MACK

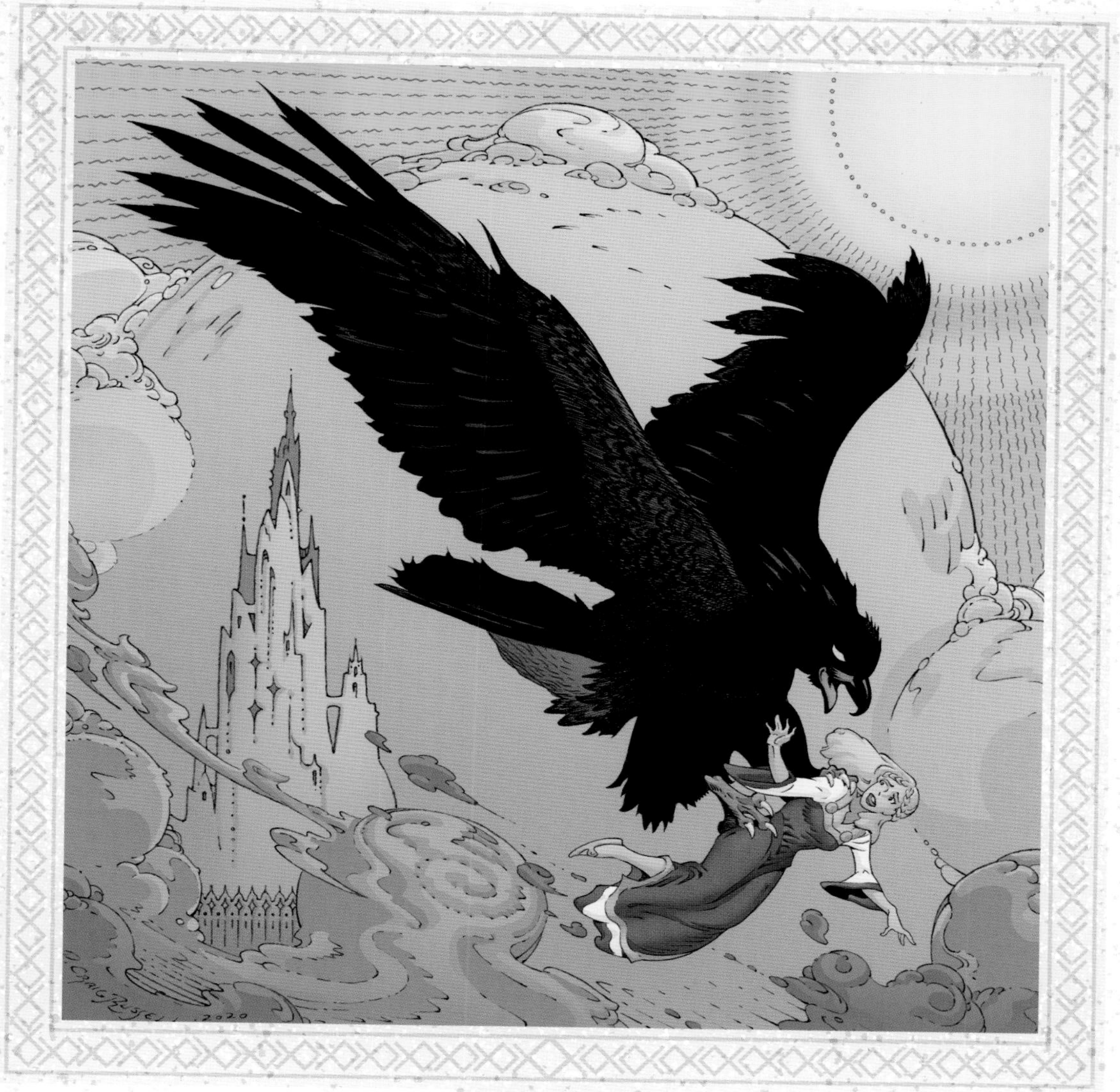

Norse Mythology II #5 standard cover by

P. CRAIG RUSSELL

with

LOVERN KINDZIERSKI

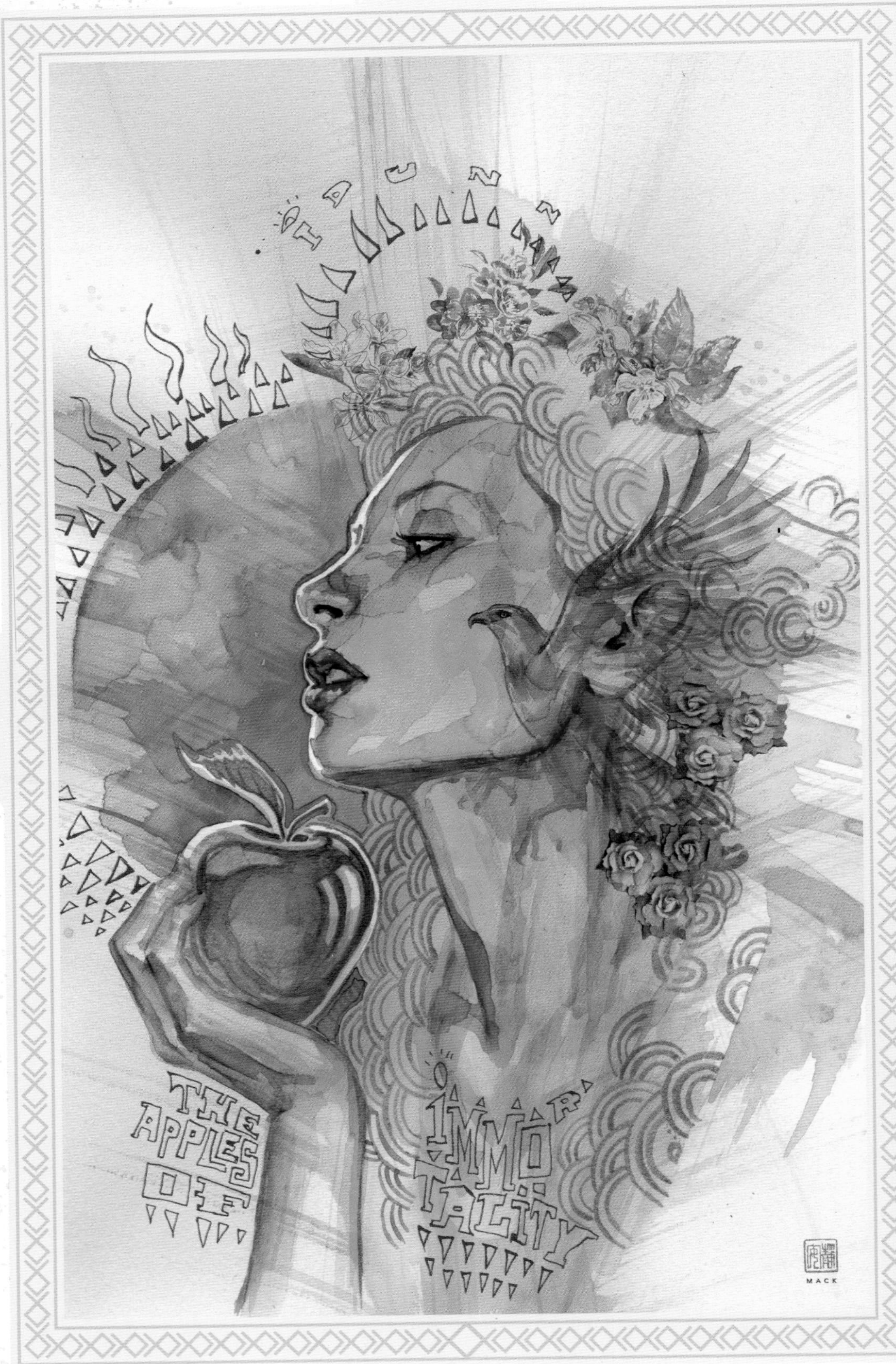
IDUNN
THE APPLES OF
IMMORTALITY
MACK

Norse Mythology II #5 variant cover by
DAVID MACK

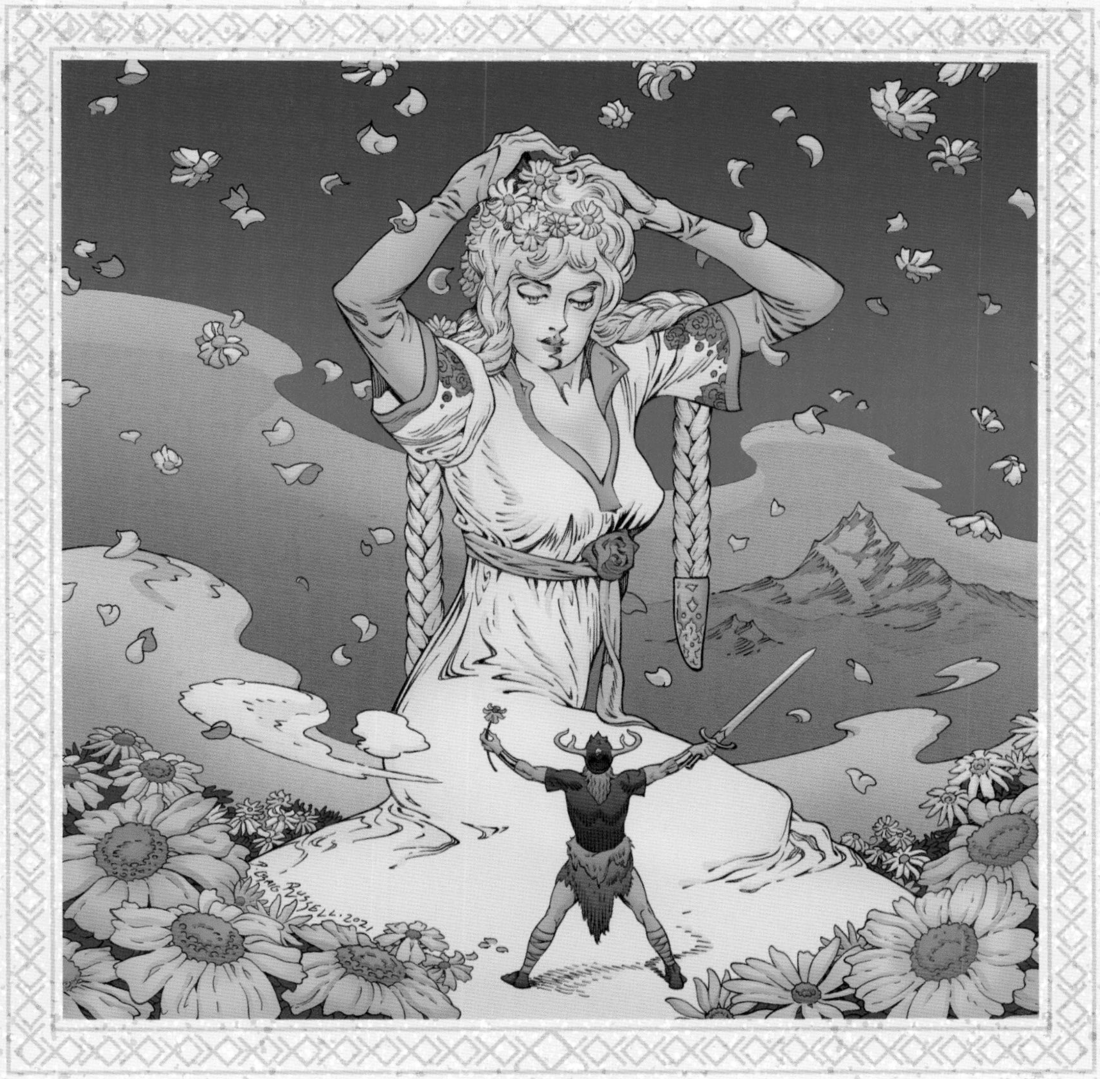
P. CRAIG RUSSELL · 2021

Norse Mythology II #6 standard cover by
P. CRAIG RUSSELL
with
LOVERN KINDZIERSKI

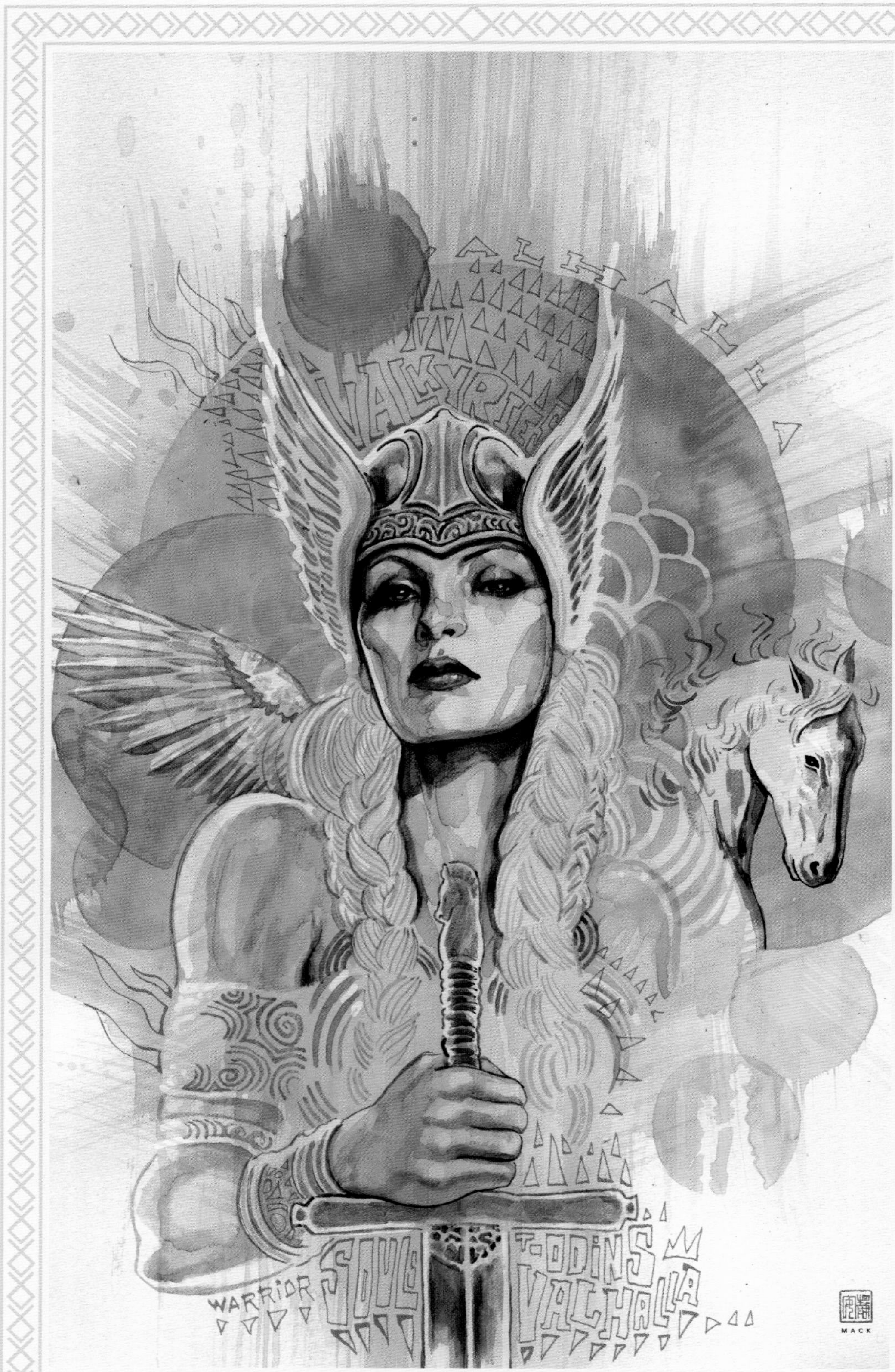
VALHALLA
VALKYRIES
WARRIOR SOUL
ODINS VALHALLA
MACK

Norse Mythology II #6 variant cover by
DAVID MACK

SKETCHBOOK

Notes by Sandy Jarrell, Mark Buckingham, Matt Horak, and Gabriel Hernández Walta.

FREY CHARACTER DESIGN

Two of my three character designs here are guys who appeared in the first arc, and with Frey I was following Jerry Ordway. I dressed him in mostly animal hides, and drew him as the big ol' friendly bear of a fellow that everyone wants to have a beer with. —Sandy Jarrell

SKIRNIR CHARACTER DESIGN

I wasn't the first to draw Skirnir, either. He's pretty much a mash-up of David Rubín's design and Craig's light elves—a cool guy dressed in salad. —SJ

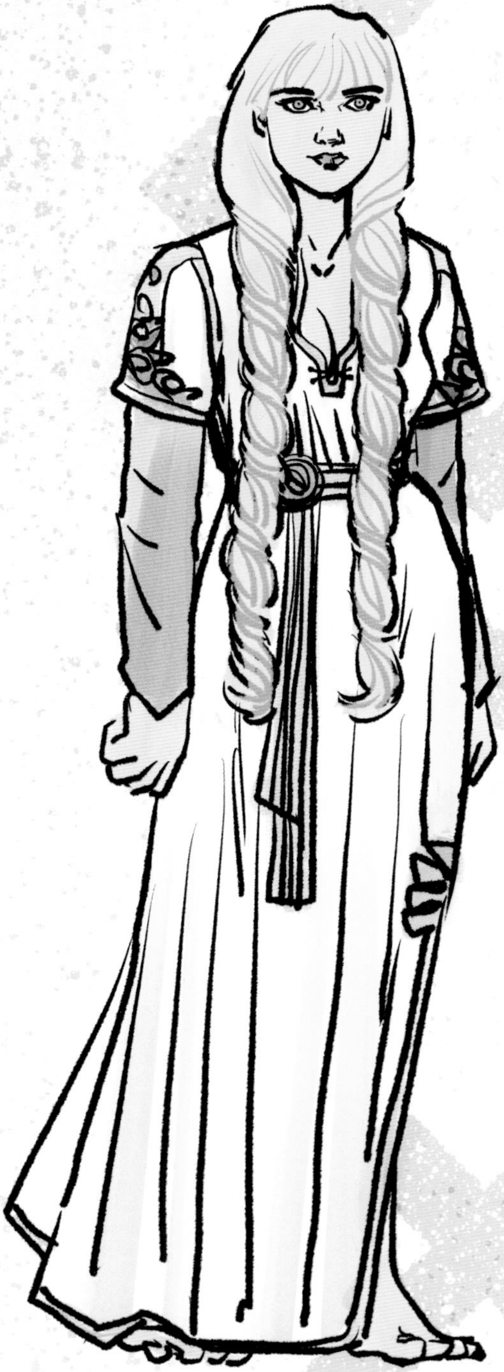

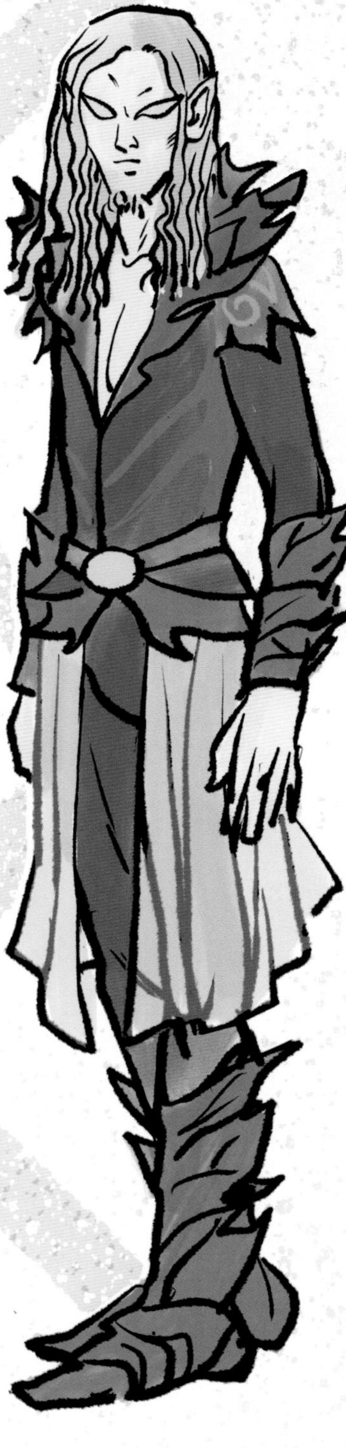

GERD CHARACTER DESIGN

Gerd is all mine, though she owes a lot to Kay Nielsen's designs in *East of the Sun, West of the Moon* (1913). I tried to make her so stunning that Frey couldn't live without her, no matter what the cost. —SJ

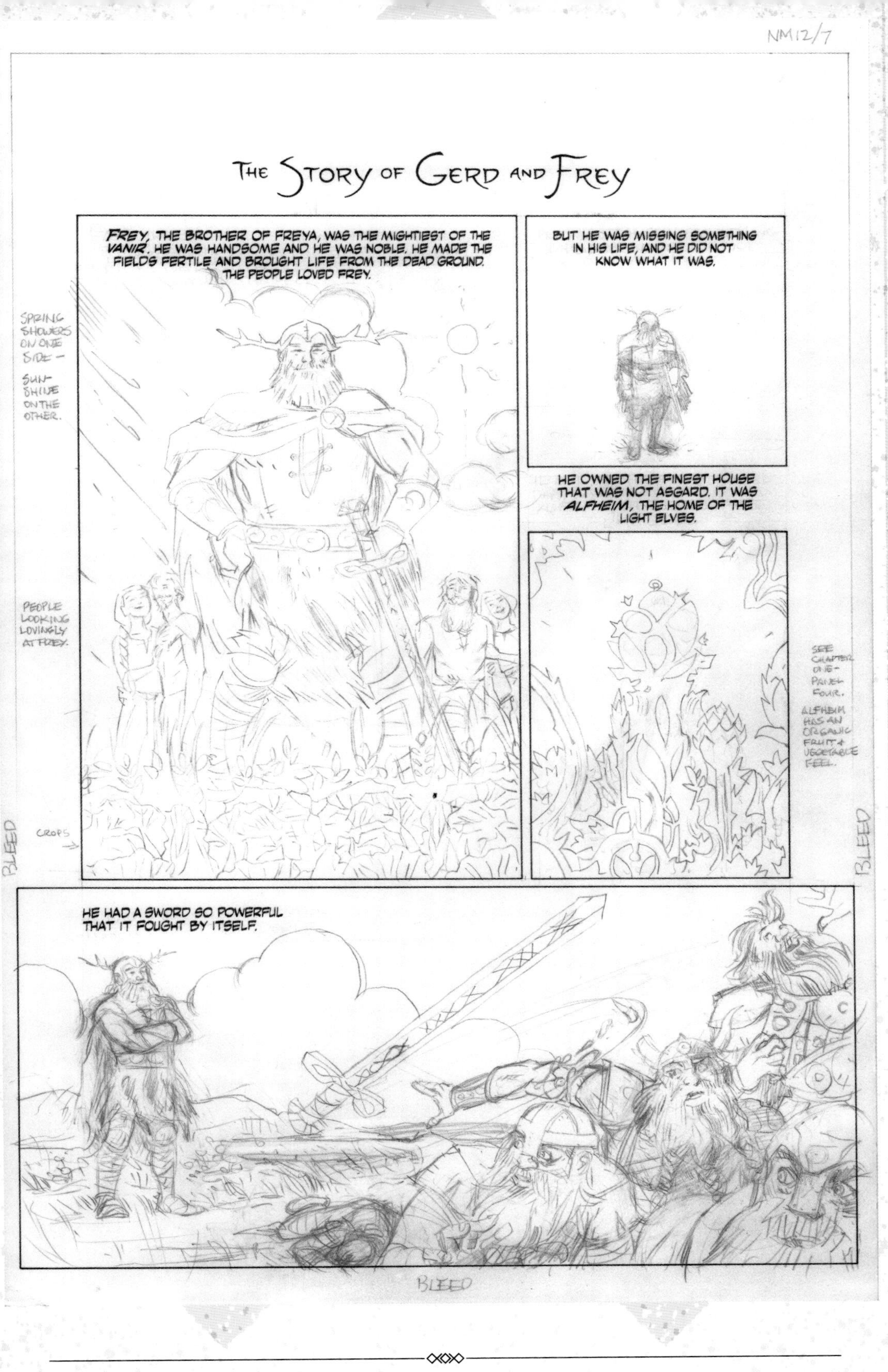
NM12/7
THE STORY OF GERD AND FREY
FREY, THE BROTHER OF FREYA, WAS THE MIGHTIEST OF THE VANIR. HE WAS HANDSOME AND HE WAS NOBLE. HE MADE THE FIELDS FERTILE AND BROUGHT LIFE FROM THE DEAD GROUND. THE PEOPLE LOVED FREY.
SPRING SHOWERS ON ONE SIDE — SUN-SHINE ON THE OTHER.
PEOPLE LOOKING LOVINGLY AT FREY.
CROPS
BUT HE WAS MISSING SOMETHING IN HIS LIFE, AND HE DID NOT KNOW WHAT IT WAS.
HE OWNED THE FINEST HOUSE THAT WAS NOT ASGARD. IT WAS ALFHEIM, THE HOME OF THE LIGHT ELVES.
SEE CHAPTER ONE — PANEL FOUR.
ALFHEIM HAS AN ORGANIC FRUIT & VEGETABLE FEEL.
BLEED
BLEED
HE HAD A SWORD SO POWERFUL THAT IT FOUGHT BY ITSELF.
BLEED

PENCILED PAGES

I've never worked on hand-lettered boards before! That made this doubly intimidating, because A) one false move would wreck them, and B) I was working over—and *erasing*—Craig's layouts, after being a fan for decades. —SJ

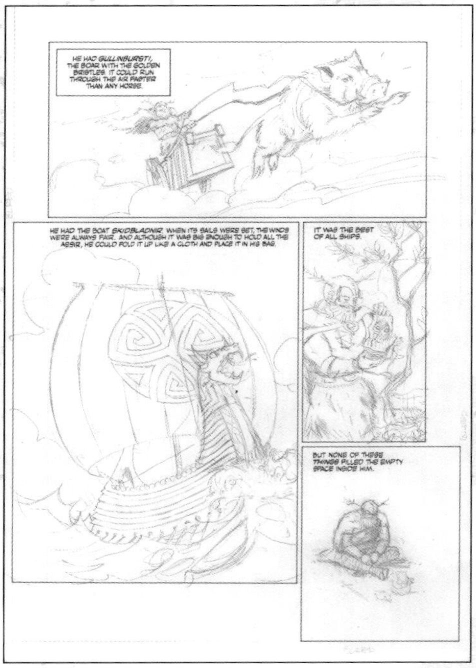
HE HAD GULLINBURSTI, THE BOAR WITH THE GOLDEN BRISTLES. IT COULD RUN THROUGH THE AIR FASTER THAN ANY HORSE.
HE HAD THE BOAT SKIDBLADNIR. WHEN ITS SAILS WERE SET, THE WINDS WERE ALWAYS FAIR. AND ALTHOUGH IT WAS BIG ENOUGH TO HOLD ALL THE AESIR, HE COULD FOLD IT UP LIKE A CLOTH AND PLACE IT IN HIS BAG.
IT WAS THE BEST OF ALL SHIPS.
BUT NONE OF THESE THINGS FILLED THE EMPTY SPACE INSIDE HIM.

ISSUE SIX, PAGE 8

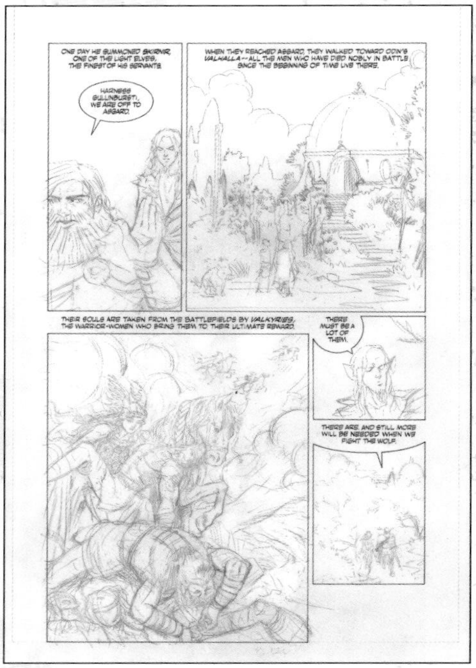
ONE DAY HE SUMMONED SKIRNIR, ONE OF THE LIGHT ELVES, THE FINEST OF HIS SERVANTS.
HARNESS GULLINBURSTI, WE ARE OFF TO ASGARD.
WHEN THEY REACHED ASGARD, THEY WALKED TOWARD ODIN'S VALHALLA--ALL THE MEN WHO HAVE DIED NOBLY IN BATTLE SINCE THE BEGINNING OF TIME LIVE THERE.
THEIR SOULS ARE TAKEN FROM THE BATTLEFIELDS BY VALKYRIES, THE WARRIOR-WOMEN WHO BRING THEM TO THEIR ULTIMATE REWARD.
THERE MUST BE A LOT OF THEM.
THERE ARE. AND STILL MORE WILL BE NEEDED WHEN WE FIGHT THE WOLF.

ISSUE SIX, PAGE 9

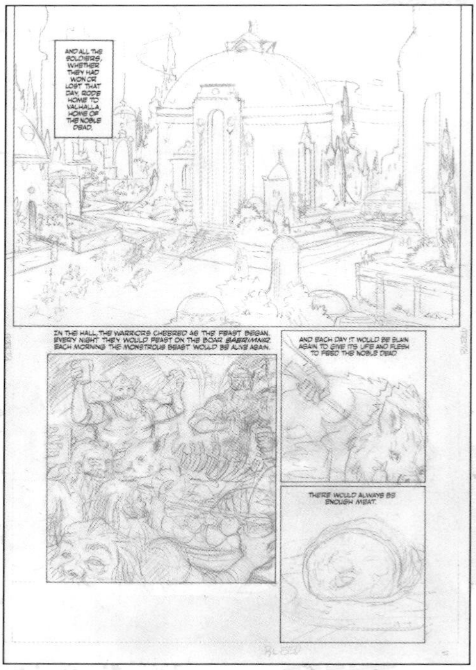
AND ALL THE SOLDIERS, WHETHER THEY HAD WON OR LOST THAT DAY, RODE HOME TO VALHALLA, HOME OF THE NOBLE DEAD.
IN THE HALL, THE WARRIORS CHEERED AS THE FEAST BEGAN. EVERY NIGHT THEY WOULD FEAST ON THE BOAR SAERIMNIR. EACH MORNING THE MONSTROUS BEAST WOULD BE ALIVE AGAIN.
AND EACH DAY IT WOULD BE SLAIN AGAIN TO GIVE ITS LIFE AND FLESH TO FEED THE NOBLE DEAD.
THERE WOULD ALWAYS BE ENOUGH MEAT.

ISSUE SIX, PAGE 10

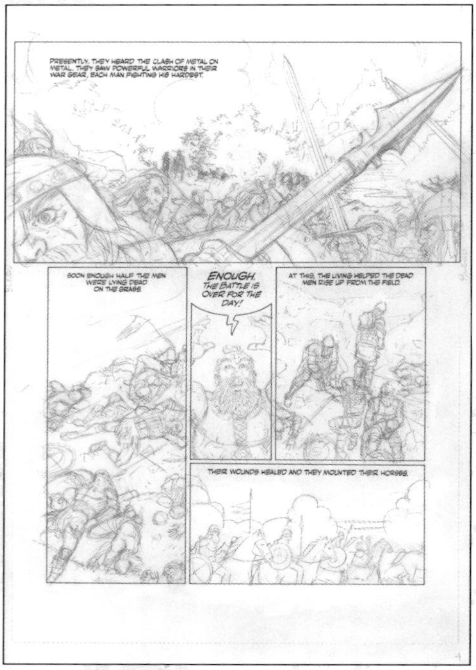
PRESENTLY, THEY HEARD THE CLASH OF METAL ON METAL. THEY SAW POWERFUL WARRIORS IN THEIR WAR GEAR, EACH MAN FIGHTING HIS HARDEST.
SOON ENOUGH HALF THE MEN WERE LYING DEAD ON THE GRASS.
ENOUGH. THE BATTLE IS OVER FOR THE DAY!
AT THIS, THE LIVING HELPED THE DEAD MEN RISE UP FROM THE FIELD.
THEIR WOUNDS HEALED AND THEY MOUNTED THEIR HORSES.

ISSUE SIX, PAGE 11

PENCILED PAGES

The Valkyrie on page 9 is totally Arthur Rackham's Brünnhilde from *The Rhinegold and the Valkyrie* (1910), one of a whole bunch of things I got to draw for this story that made me really happy (see also: the "ENOUGH" dude in the center of page 11).—SJ

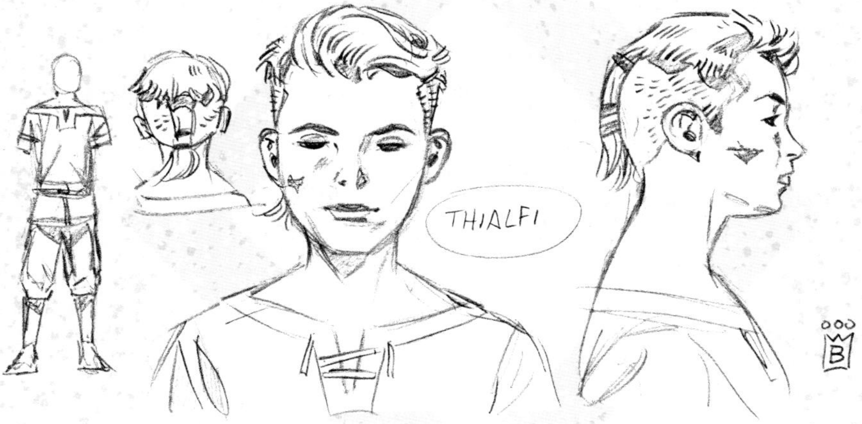
THIALFI

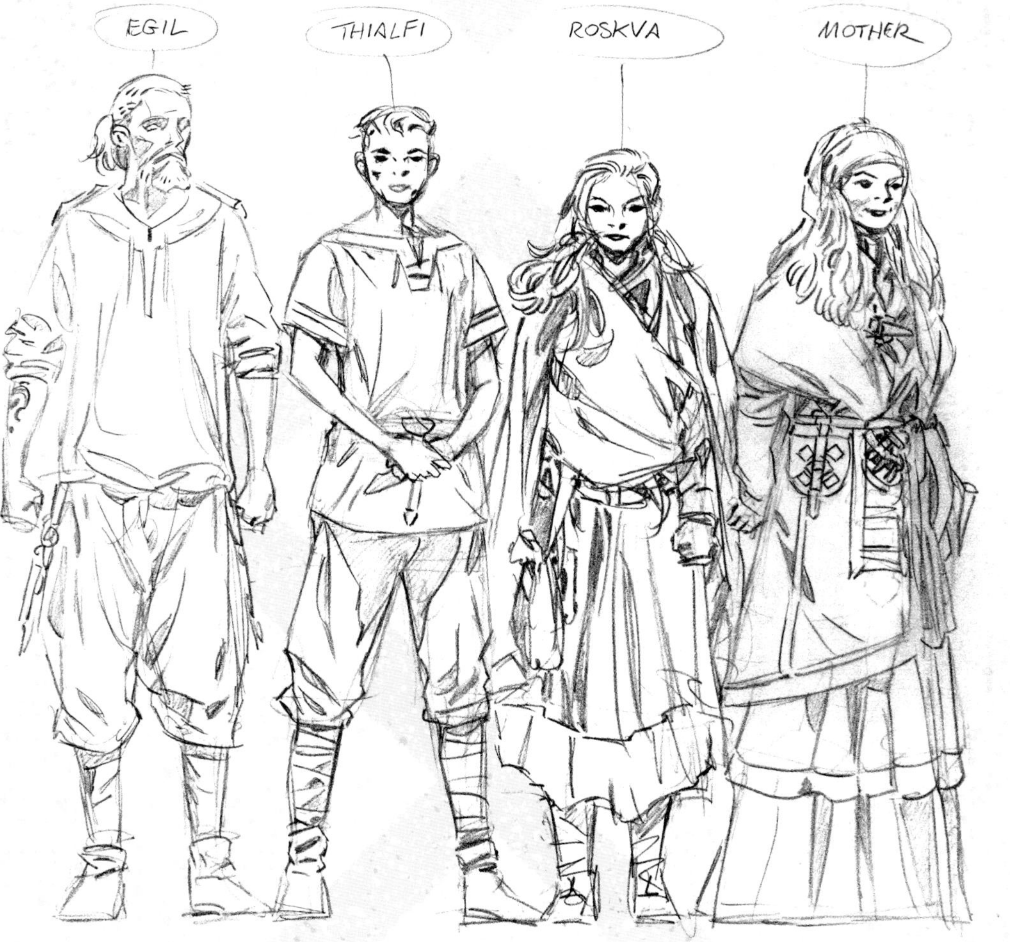
EGIL
THIALFI
ROSKVA
MOTHER

THIALFI, EGIL, ROSKVA, AND MOTHER CHARACTER DESIGNS

I had a lot of freedom with these characters, as Craig had only loosely indicated them in the layouts, giving me an opportunity to research Norse clothing, hair, buildings, and interior decorations, as well as images of wilder Nordic landscapes, to hopefully give the wild country, Jotenheim, the farm, and it's inhabitants, a little authenticity.

Thialfi has a Peregrine Falcon tattoo on his cheek which is drawn from the reference to his speed when he races against thought at Utgard. —Mark Buckingham

SKRYMIR DESIGN

I really liked the cartoony way Craig had indicated Skrymir in some of the layouts for the first episode . . . so I just ran with it! I liked that he didn't have a belt, but added some rings for him to tie gloves and bags too so he could keep his hands free when needed.

While revisiting Neil's original *Norse Mythology* novel, after drawing this sketch, I read that Skrymir had black hair, and that his gloves were in fact mittens, so I changed both of those as I set to work penciling the finished pages. —MB

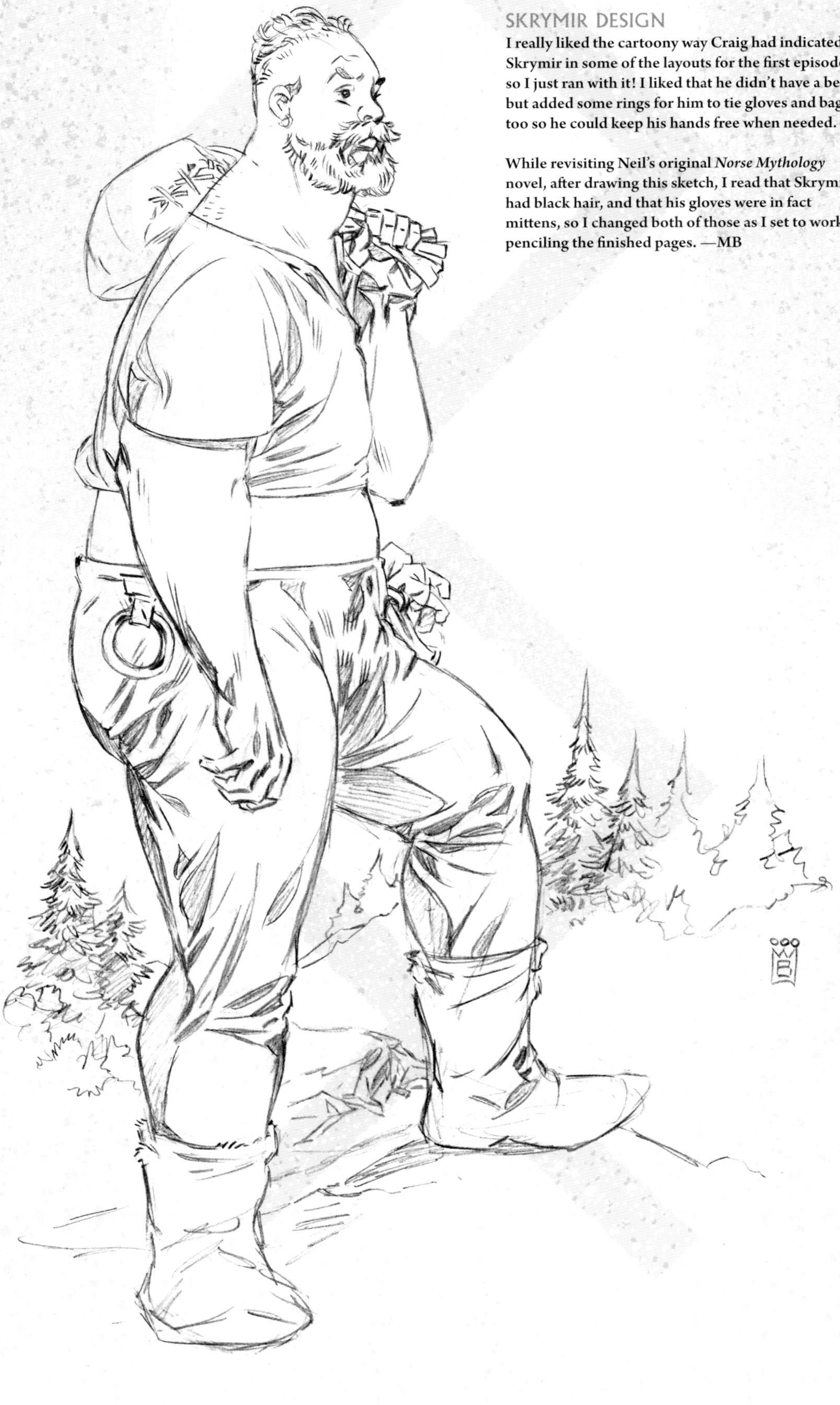

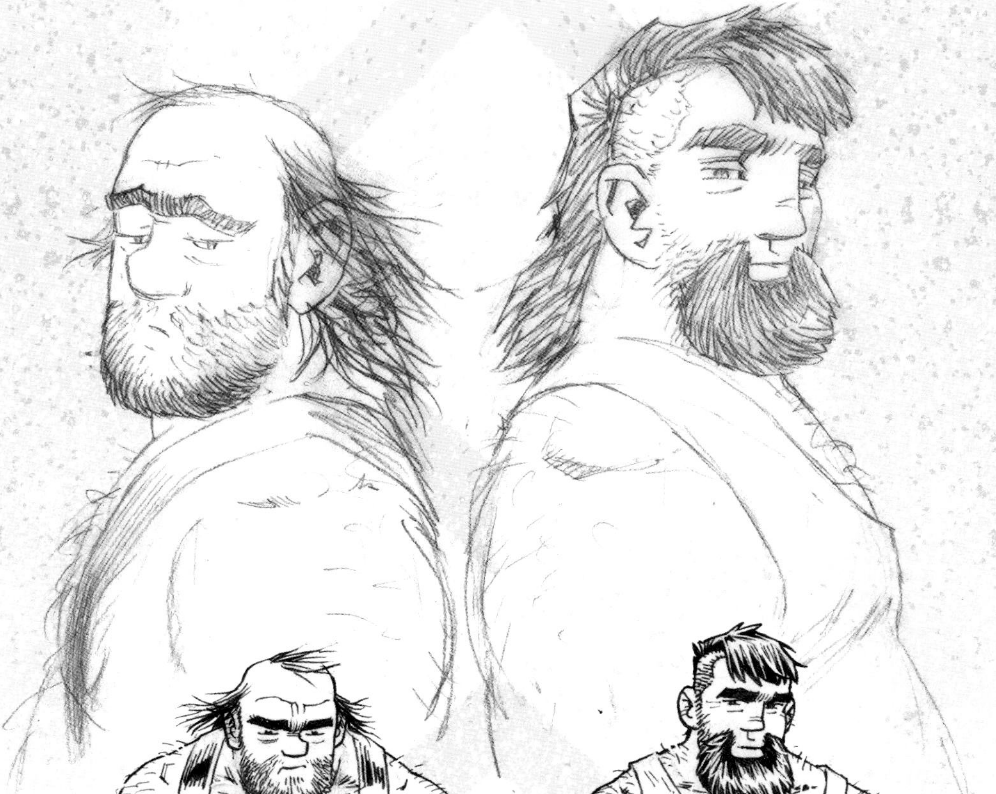
FJALAR
GALAR

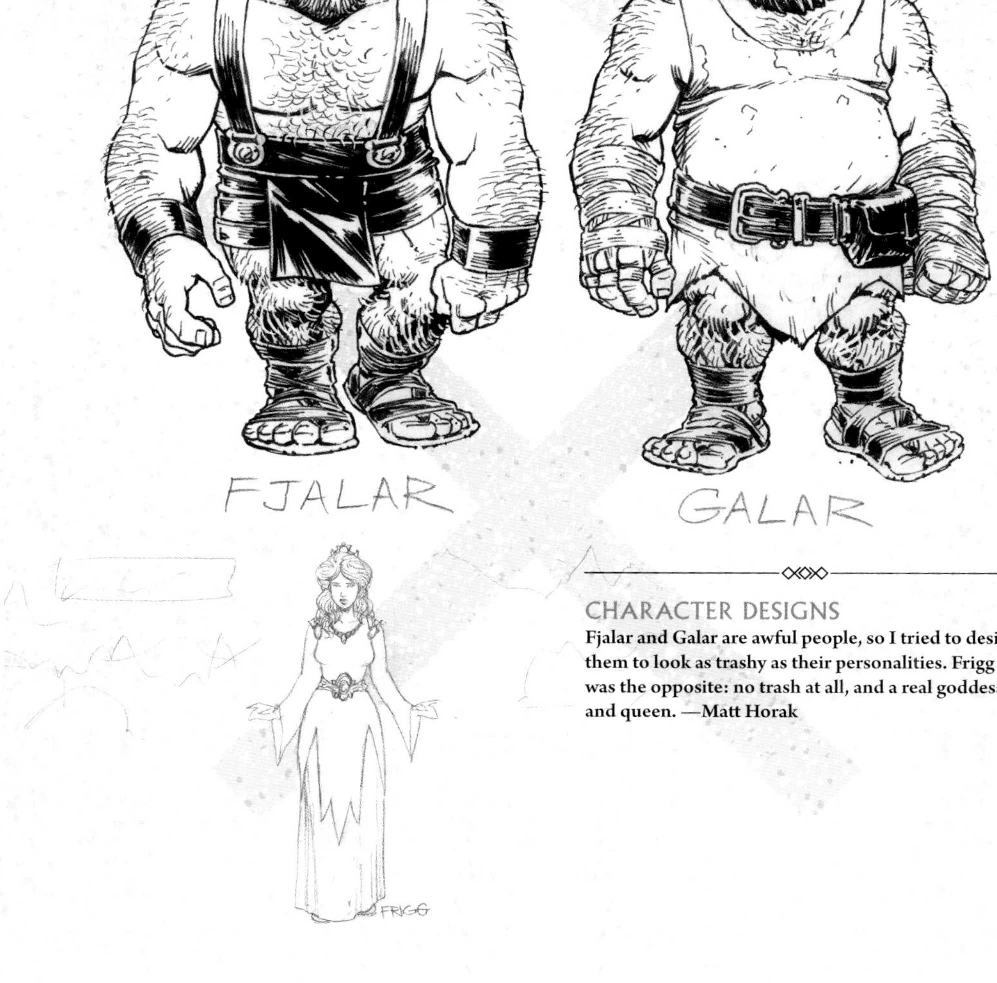
FRIGG

CHARACTER DESIGNS

Fjalar and Galar are awful people, so I tried to design them to look as trashy as their personalities. Frigg was the opposite: no trash at all, and a real goddess and queen. —Matt Horak

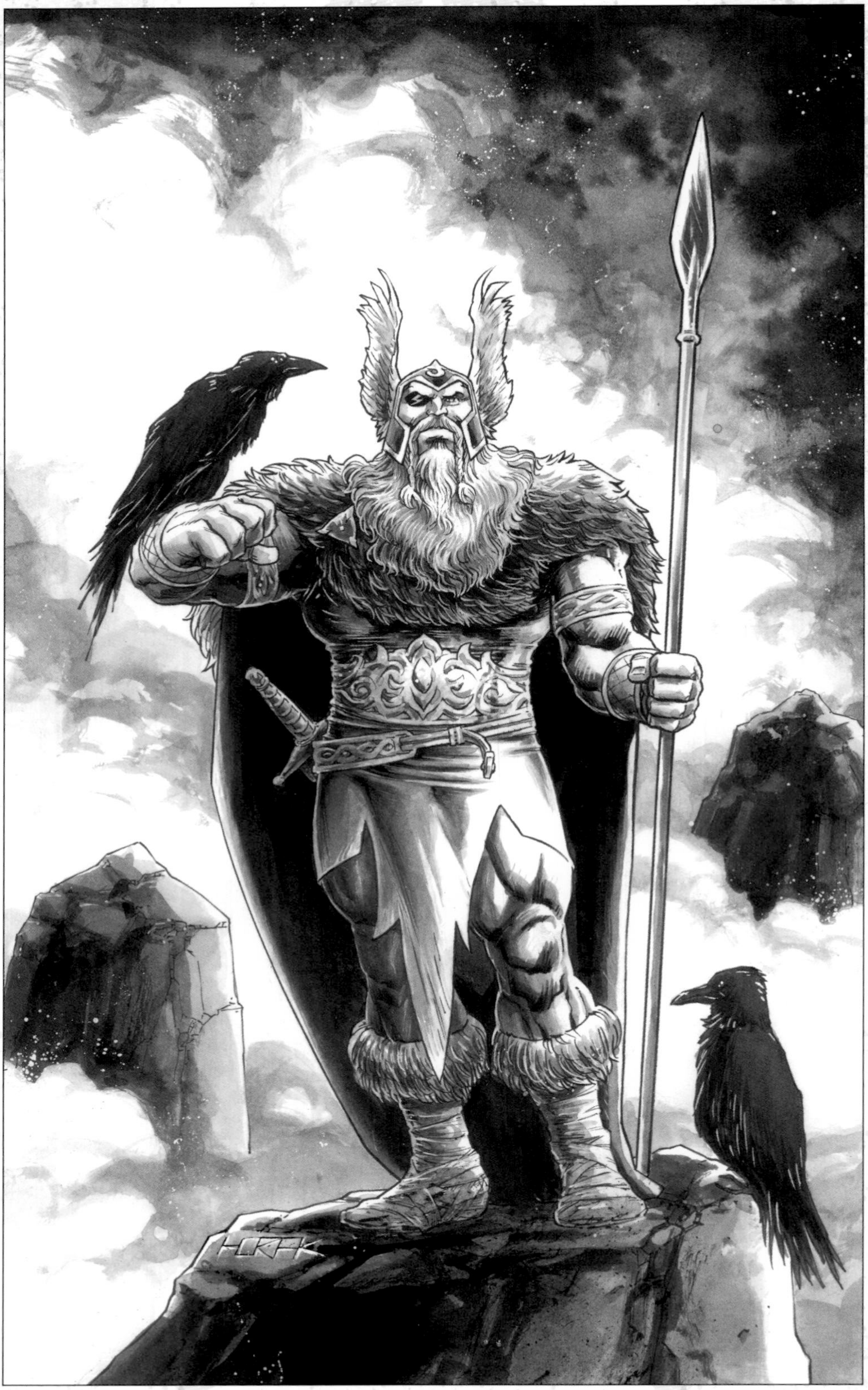

ODIN

This drawing was done to practice washes and work out the look of Odin and the ravens. I only ended up using the washes for clouds and water effects in the end.—MH

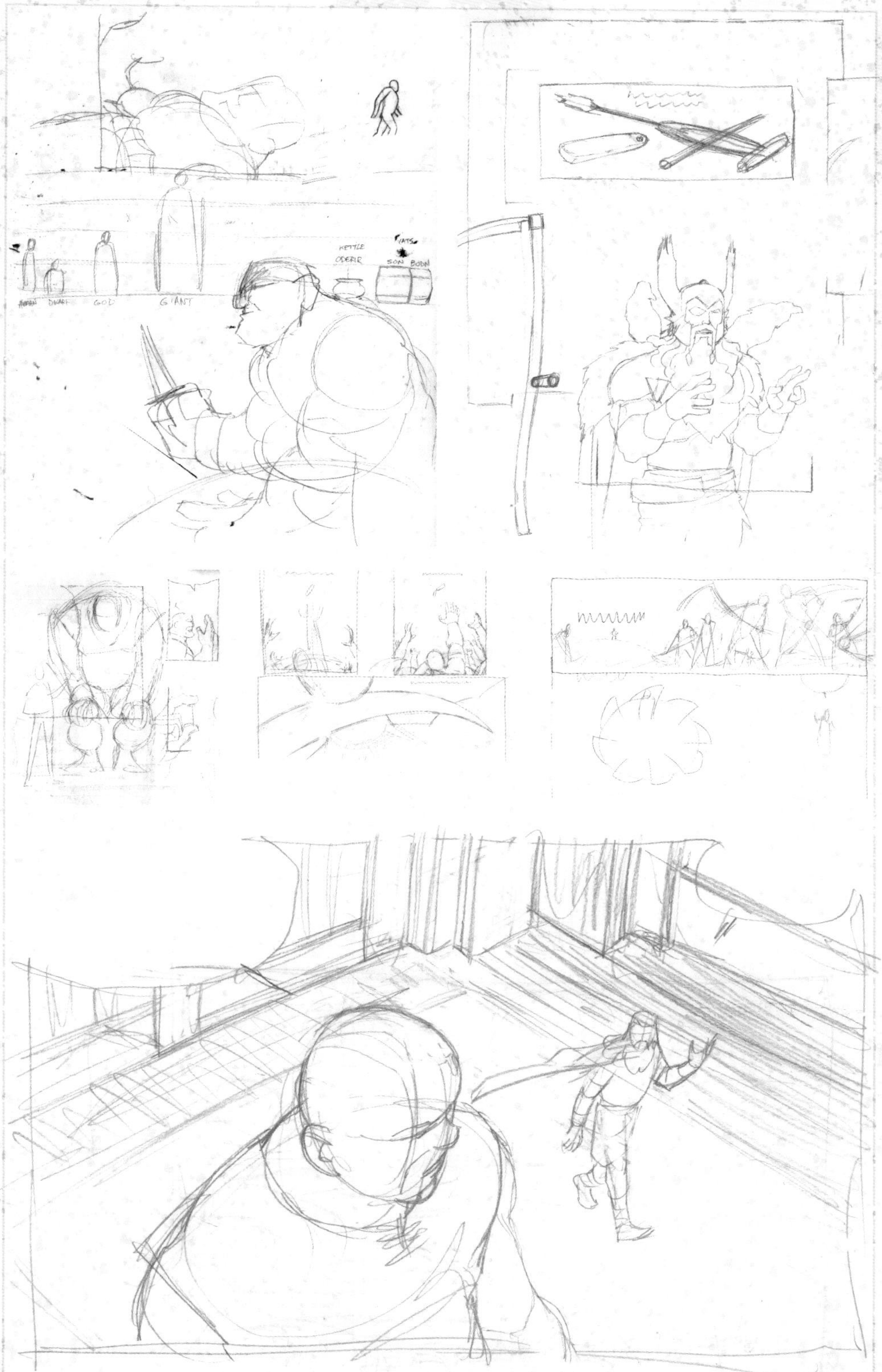
DWARF
GOD
GIANT
KETTLE
ODERIR
VATS
SON
BODN

SKETCHES

Here is preliminary work done to figure out the relative sizes of the various characters and work out some scenes. I often worked out shots on separate sheets of paper before I did the unthinkable and redrew Craig's layouts. I also changed the look of the auger in the final art to a much simpler design.—MH

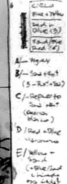

COLOR TESTS

I painted little color sketches for every scene, making sure that it all had a consistent look. I also wanted to make enough differences in the color choices from one scene to another so the pages didn't look too boring. One example: while Idunn is kidnapped by Thiazi, there's no blue skies, as I wanted to show that everything was dull in Asgard without her. —Gabriel Hernández Walta

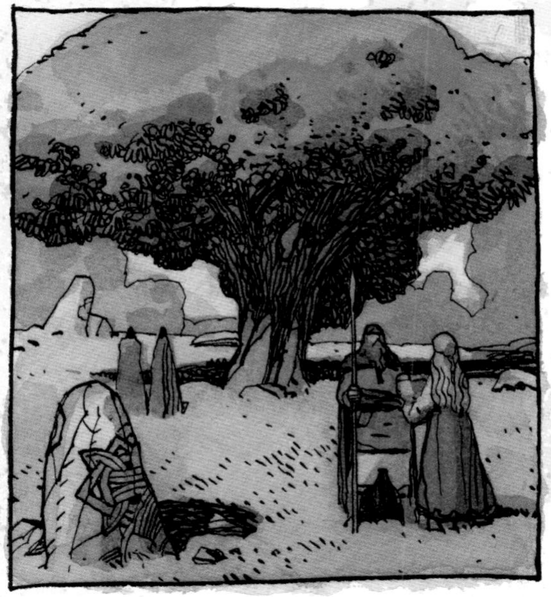

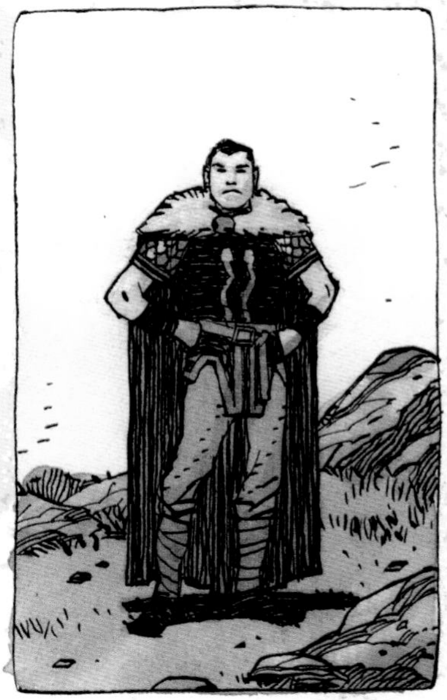

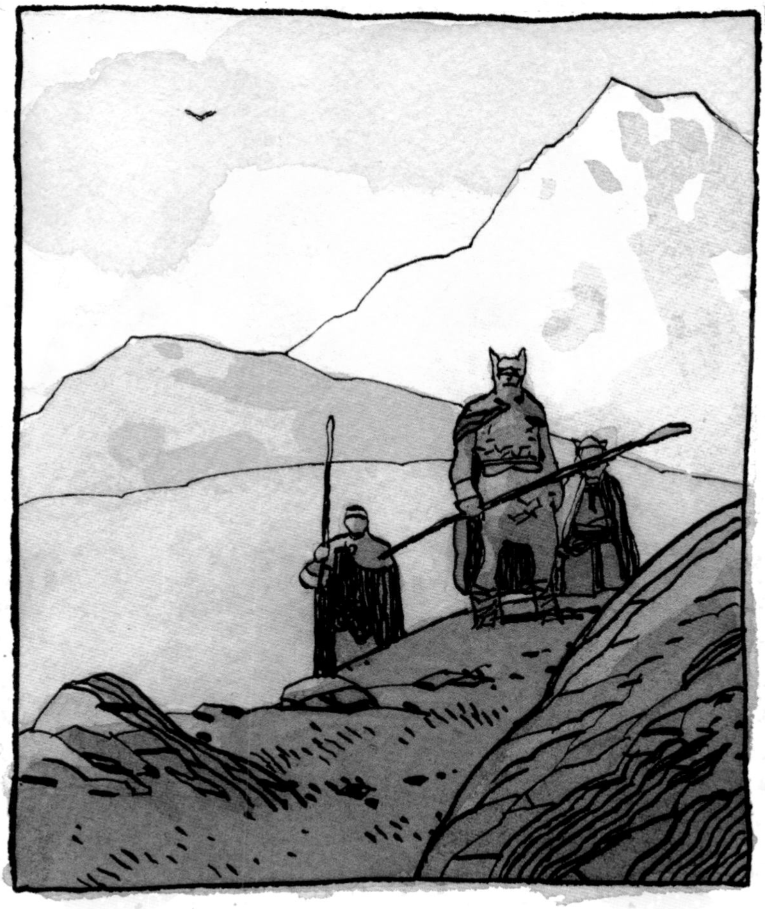

COLOR TESTS

After deciding the color palettes, I made some ink and watercolor samples to get the right "feeling" for the book. I wanted to make justice to Craig's compositions and also to show my admiration for the work of Ivan Bilibin, whose Russian fairy tale illustrations had a huge impact on me when I was a teenager.—GHW

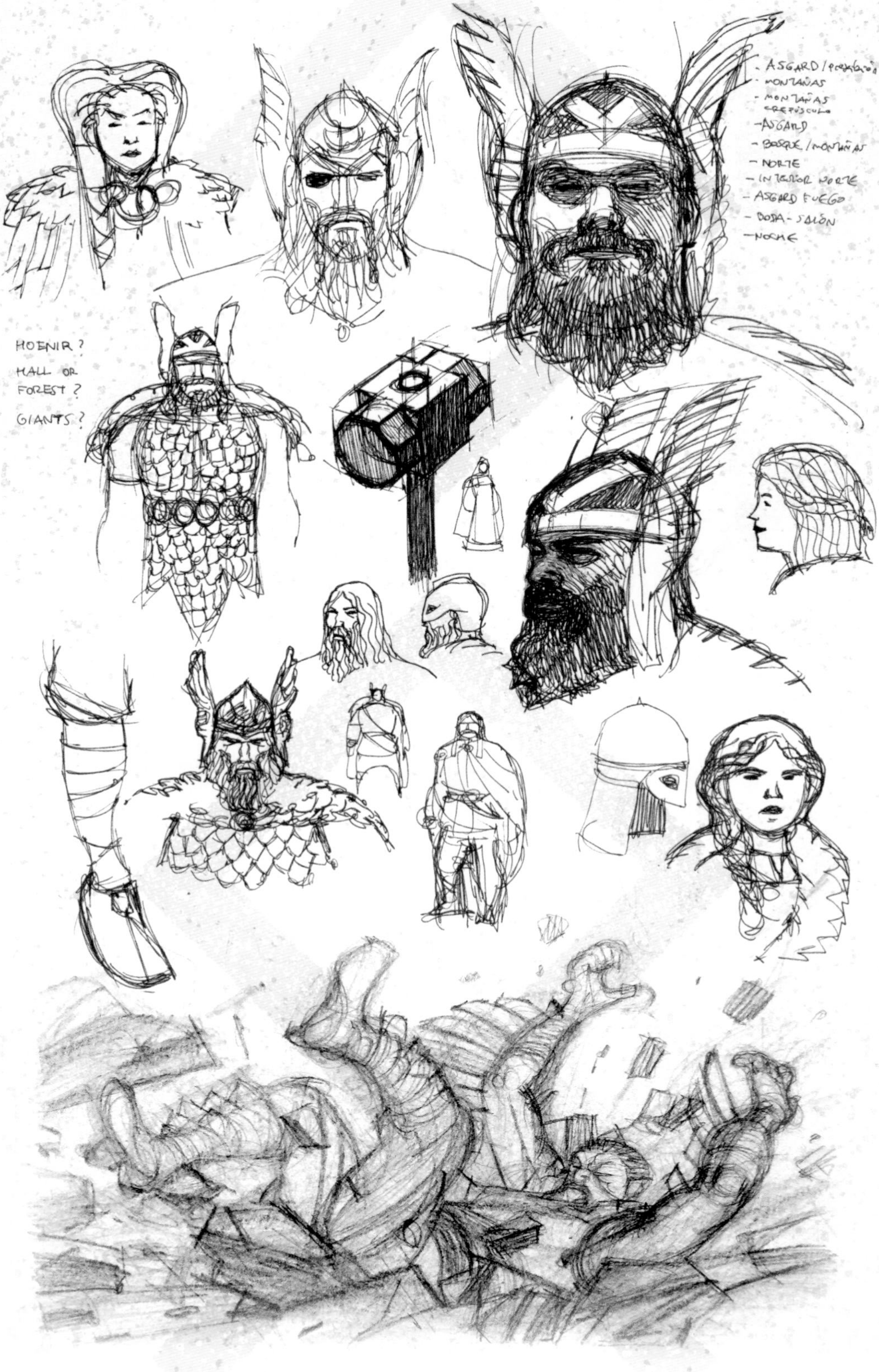
- ASGARD
- MONTAÑAS
- MONTAÑAS CREPÚSCULO
- ASGARD
- BOSQUE / MONTAÑAS
- NORTE
- INTERIOR NORTE
- ASGARD FUEGO
- BODA - SALÓN
- NOCHE
HOENIR ?
HALL OR FOREST ?
GIANTS ?

CHARACTER SKETCHES

I first studied the designs that the other artists of the project had done of the Aesir gods. I wanted them to be clearly recognizable, but I also had to find my own way of drawing them. After that it was easier to design new characters, like Thiazi, and to make them look similar to the ones already designed.—GH

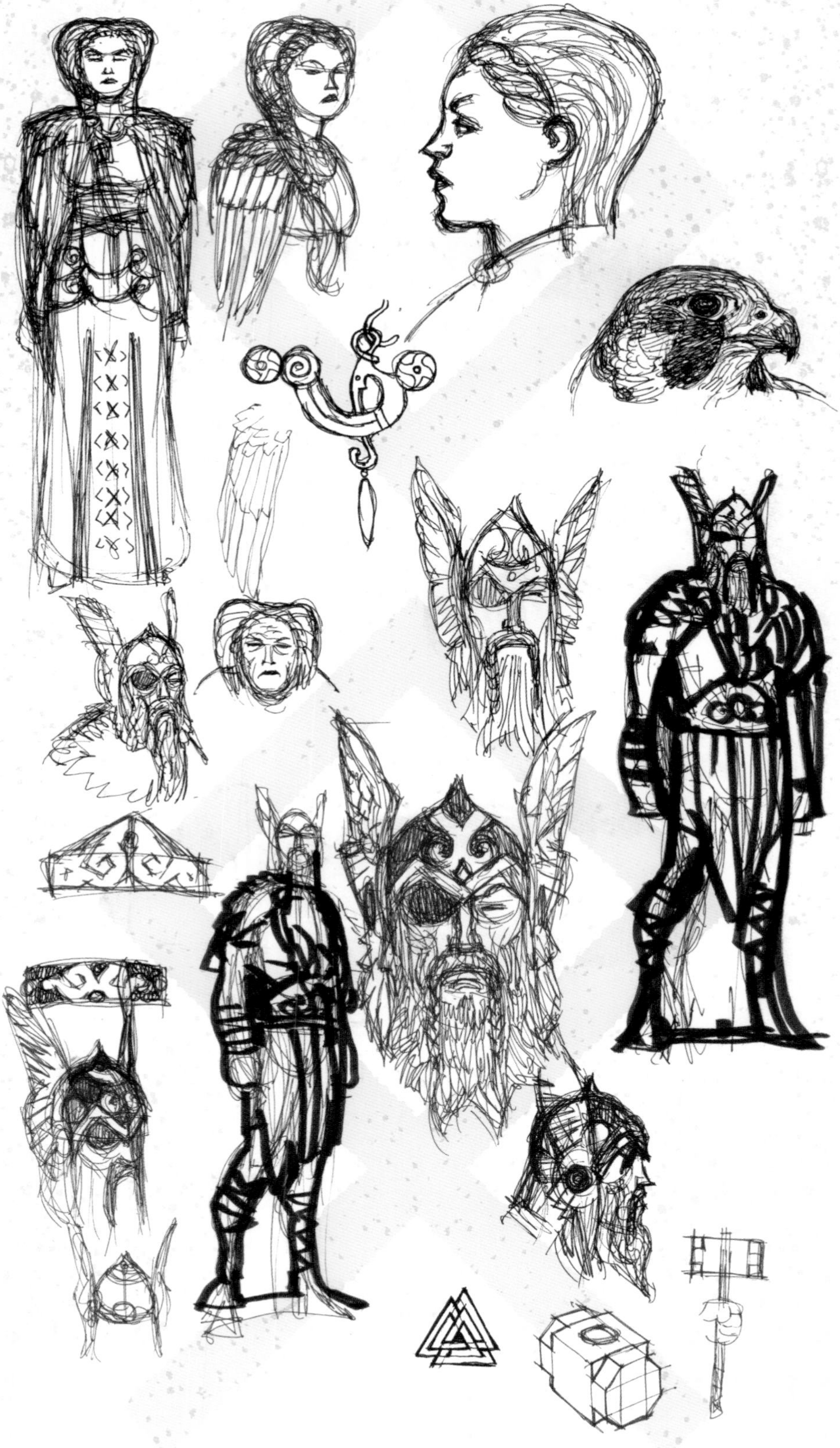

CHARACTER SKETCHES

I enjoyed drawing Freya and Odin a lot, though in most of the panels of this story they looked very old. (They really needed those apples, after all!)—GHW

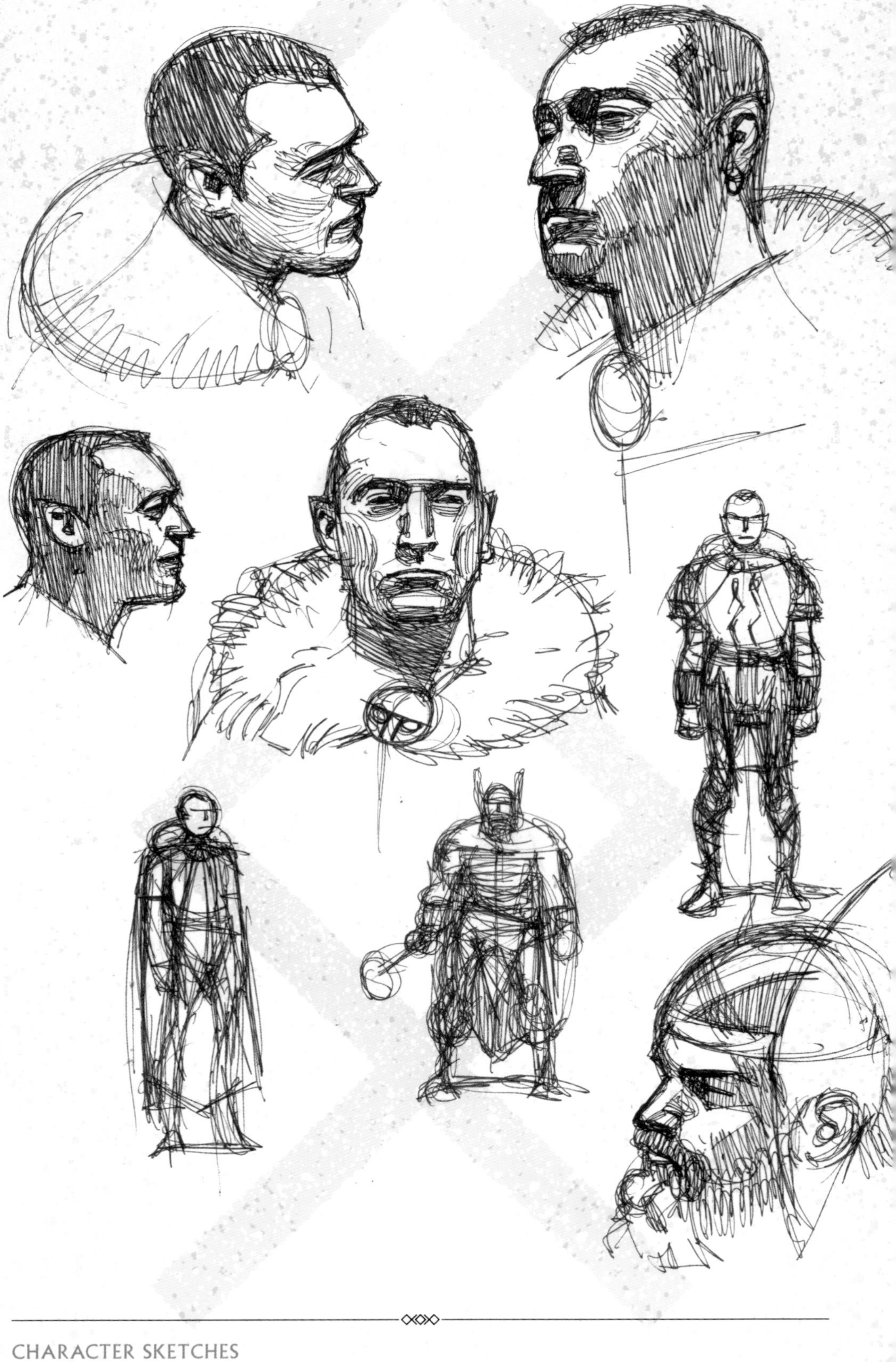

CHARACTER SKETCHES

Loki was so fun to draw! He is like a very histrionic actor, making his body language as important as his facial expressions. Also, he already was my favorite character when I first read these Norse gods stories in an old mythology book that my father gave me many years ago.—GHW

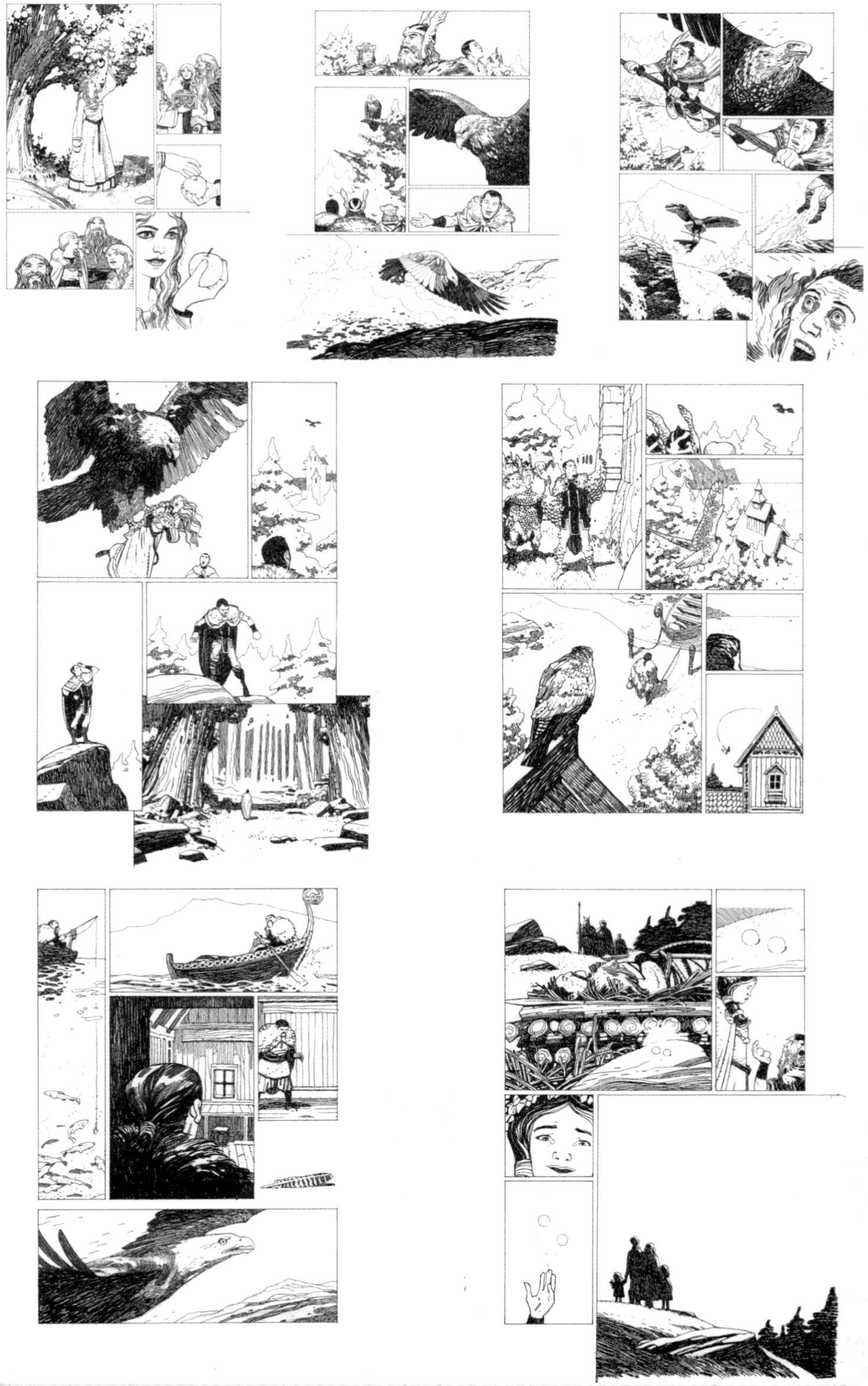

INKED PAGES

I've always liked to get an "engraved" look to my inked pages, with no real solid blacks. I thought that this inking style totally suited this particular kind of story, though I didn't want to lose the look of a pure comic-book drawing style. Of course, the dynamic layouts of Craig helped a lot to keep the story moving, instead of having a series of still illustrations.—GHW

MORE TITLES FROM

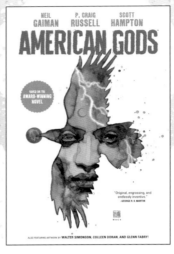

NEIL GAIMAN LIBRARY VOLUME 1
Collects *A Study in Emerald, Murder Mysteries, How to Talk to Girls at Parties,* and *Forbidden Bride*
Neil Gaiman and various artists
$49.99 | ISBN 978-1-50671-593-3

NEIL GAIMAN LIBRARY VOLUME 2
Collects *The Facts in the Departure of Miss Finch, Likely Stories, Harlequin Valentine,* and *Troll Bridge*
Neil Gaiman and various artists
$49.99 | ISBN 978-1-50671-594-0

AMERICAN GODS: SHADOWS
Neil Gaiman, P. Craig Russell, Scott Hampton, and others
$29.99 | ISBN 978-1-50670-386-2

AMERICAN GODS: MY AINSEL
Neil Gaiman, P. Craig Russell, Scott Hampton, and others
$29.99 | ISBN 978-1-50670-730-3

AMERICAN GODS: THE MOMENT OF THE STORM
Neil Gaiman, P. Craig Russell, Scott Hampton, and others
$29.99 | ISBN 978-1-50670-731-0

LIKELY STORIES
Neil Gaiman and Mark Buckingham
$17.99 | ISBN 978-1-50670-530-9

ONLY THE END OF THE WORLD AGAIN
Neil Gaiman, P. Craig Russell, and Troy Nixey
$19.99 | ISBN 978-1-50670-612-2

MURDER MYSTERIES 2nd Edition
Neil Gaiman, P. Craig Russell, and Lovern Kinderski
$19.99 | ISBN 978-1-61655-330-2

THE FACTS IN THE CASE OF THE DEPARTURE OF MISS FINCH 2nd Edition
Neil Gaiman and Michael Zulli
$13.99 | 978-1-61655-949-6

NEIL GAIMAN'S HOW TO TALK TO GIRLS AT PARTIES
Neil Gaiman, Fábio Moon, and Gabriel Bá
$17.99 | ISBN 978-1-61655-955-7

THE PROBLEM OF SUSAN AND OTHER STORIES
Neil Gaiman, P. Craig Russell, Paul Chadwick, and others
$17.99 | ISBN 978-1-50670-511-8

NEIL GAIMAN'S TROLL BRIDGE
Neil Gaiman and Colleen Doran
$14.99 | ISBN 978-1-50670-008-3

SIGNAL TO NOISE
Neil Gaiman and Dave McKean
$24.99 | ISBN 978-1-59307-752-5

CREATURES OF THE NIGHT 2nd Edition
Neil Gaiman and Michael Zulli
$12.99 | ISBN 978-1-50670-025-0

FORBIDDEN BRIDES OF THE FACELESS SLAVES IN THE SECRET HOUSE OF THE NIGHT OF DREAD DESIRE
Neil Gaiman and Shane Oakley
$17.99 | ISBN 978-1-50670-140-0

HARLEQUIN VALENTINE 2nd Edition
Neil Gaiman and John Bolton
$12.99 | ISBN 978-1-50670-087-8

NEIL GAIMAN'S A STUDY IN EMERALD
Neil Gaiman and Rafael Albuquerque
$17.99 | ISBN 978-1-50670-393-0

SNOW, GLASS, APPLES
Neil Gaiman and Colleen Doran
$17.99 | ISBN 978-1-50670-979-6

NORSE MYTHOLOGY VOLUME 1
Neil Gaiman, P. Craig Russell, Mike Mignola and various artists
$29.99 | ISBN 978-1-50671-874-3

AVAILABLE AT YOUR LOCAL COMICS SHOP OR BOOKSTORE
To find a comics shop in your area, visit comicshoplocator.com. For more information, visit DarkHorse.com